KU-012-162

A Sense of Belonging

By Pamela Hill

Published by Juliana Publishing

Book cover design and print by
Hillside Printing Services

ACC. No: 02688518

Published by Juliana Publishing

Copyright © Pamela Hill 2008

All the characters in this book are
fictitious and any resemblance to actual
persons living or dead is purely coincidental

Juliana Publishing
Highview Lodge
Oulder Hill Drive
Rochdale
OL11 5LB


Printed and bound in Great Britain by Hillside
Printing Services, Rochdale Tel: 01706 711872
www.hillsidegroup.co.uk

IBSN 978-0-9559047-0-7

Mattie Henshaw sighed despondently. She wiped the beads of sweat from her saturated brow with the sleeve of her ragged cardigan and though exhausted she continued to scrub the kitchen floor vigorously to remove every last speck of dirt before her foster-mother returned home, otherwise she would be on the receiving end of yet another heavy beating.

That loathsome Hilda Parkes had no compassion, Mattie reflected, as she repositioned her bucket and mop to attack the remaining section of the floor that led into the larder, that area being the most difficult to clean, where it seemed, an army of feet marched over it each day, not that she was ever the recipient of more than the occasional morsel of food from its shelves.

The worn and discoloured linoleum that had once covered the complete floor had seen better days and Mattie suspected it had been down for many a year, long before that unforgettable day, six months ago, when she was brought to the foster-home following her mother's untimely death.

Jean Henshaw had stepped into the path of a bus, consequentially leaving Mattie and her two brothers Seth and Jack with no surviving parent.

Caringly, the Social Worker had promised to do her best to place them in the same foster-home but regrettably that hadn't been possible, she explained when Mattie, the eldest at the age of fourteen, was acquainted with her foster-parents, Hilda and Albert Parkes, the latter being, to all self-acclaimed intents and purposes, a caring man with a mission in life to help the less fortunate.

That day, Hilda had served them buttered currant teacakes and tea in a china cup but once the Social Worker had left, there were to be no further treats, in fact there would be little food of any kind to fill her hungry belly. Contrary to the care and support Mattie had anticipated, she was shunned after being advised of the daily duties she must perform on her return from school, in addition to the mountain of chores demanded of her at the weekend.

Mattie stopped scrubbing and pricked up her ears when she heard the front door close, praying it was Hilda who had come home to the empty house and not Albert but regrettably, her prayers had not been answered on that occasion when she recognised the heavy footsteps of Albert who approached the door and walked in.

She kept her head down and continued to dry the floor with the blackened cloth as he moved towards her. 'You'll make some feller a good wife one day,' he stated sarcastically but she neither acknowledged him nor did she allow herself to make eye contact with him. 'Where's Mrs. Parkes?'

'She's gone shopping but she won't be long,' she mumbled in reply without lifting her head.

'Is that so?' he replied in a sing-song voice as he gently stroked the nape of her neck, then he laughed mockingly and walked from the kitchen, closing the door behind him.

She wiped the remaining section of the floor and emptied her bucket of filthy water down the sink.

2

After washing her cloth, she swilled the black grit from around the sink before returning the bucket to the outside washhouse. She felt sickly and lethargic and lingered a moment to take in some air. Was her nausea caused by her hunger she wondered, or was it caused by the thought of her being alone with her foster-father? Those questions were soon forgotten when she returned to the kitchen to find Hilda, who had arrived during her absence, emptying her bags of shopping.

Purposely, she neglected to acknowledge Mattie's presence and only when she offered to help put the groceries away did Hilda speak. 'Drag that big sack of potatoes into the washhouse and shove it behind the open sack!' she commanded imperiously.

There wasn't a 'please' or 'thank you' but Mattie expected no such politeness from that ill-mannered vulgar woman who was scarcely heard to utter little more than the occasional grunt to her husband.

She continued to pay no attention to Mattie as she generously dusted the seasoned haddock with flour and proceeded to fry it. The appetizing smell soon filled the kitchen but Mattie was aware there would be none for her. It was Saturday and that was *boiled egg* night for her.

Only on *corned-beef hash* nights did the three of them regularly share, as opposed to enjoy, the same food, when Mattie was allowed two tablespoonfuls with two slices of dry bread.

Though it usually smelled greasy and tasted very salty, not once did she complain or she would have been ordered to bed with nothing.

When she sat down at the table, Mattie's thoughts turned to her mother who had been an imaginative cook despite their limited means. Not once had they suffered the pangs of an empty belly when she was alive, in fact theirs had been a joyful family home, filled with happiness and laughter. She transferred her thoughts to her two brothers, who had also been taken into care by Social Services and although she had neither seen nor heard news of them during her six months in care, she hadn't dared to ask of their welfare when visited by her Social Worker.

There had been but one visit during that time and Mattie had been harshly forewarned to speak only when spoken to and affirm she was being very well cared for if asked. Hilda had delivered a spectacular performance at that meeting. She had monopolised the entire conversation, while incredulously, Mattie had listened as Hilda paid homage to her charming disposition while expressing the pleasure they each derived from her presence in their home.

The only question directed at Mattie was whether she liked her new school and as that was a welcome escape, she merely answered her in the affirmative without further amplification of her reply....

When she had finished her egg, Mattie jumped up from the table and collected the dirty dishes.

The same agenda applied nightly. As she washed the dishes, Albert would get changed to go out and Hilda would take her chair by the kitchen fire with half a dozen bottles of beer. When she had finished them she would fall asleep, thus allowing Mattie to slip quietly to her room after stoking up the fire.

That evening was no exception as Hilda flopped down in her armchair, flicked the top off the first of her six customary bottles, took a long swig, belched and banged down the bottle on the hearth.

By the time Mattie had washed the dishes, Hilda was snorting like a pig. She had pulled up her thick grey serge skirt well past her knees, revealing huge mottled legs and healing sores caused by her sitting too close to the burning embers.

It was time for Mattie to slip away. The need for sleep beckoned her to her bed as she tiptoed silently to her room.

After changing into her white calico pyjamas, she knelt by her bed, her hands clasped tightly together and whispered reverently, 'Please Lord God, spare me tonight. I've been a good girl.'

Her limp body ached from head to toe. Saturday was a gruelling day and after stripping each of their beds, she had done the washing, rinsing and finally the ironing after she had dried the bedding outside on the line. On her hands and knees, she had given the kitchen floor its weekly scrub and had scraped and cleaned the cooker thoroughly.

She clambered into bed and pulled up the covers around her neck, tucking them in securely under her shoulders. Sleep was imminent when she closed her weary eyes and within seconds, she was in the park with her two brothers, laughing as they chased each other around the grassy slopes. She had a ball in her hand and Seth was trying to take it from her. When she rolled on the grass, he leapt on her, still trying to open her hand but he smelled strange. It wasn't

Seth's normal sweet breath she could smell. It was a vile, repulsive yet familiar odour that she couldn't place. Still in a deep sleep, she attempted to heave him away but he was strong and he held on to her.

'*Stop it*!' she cried out aloud. '*Get off me, you're hurting me. What are you doing Seth*?'

'Who's Seth?' he asked her with a raucous laugh and she awoke with a start to find Albert in her bed.

He reeked of whisky and Mattie pummelled him with her fists as tears began to flow from her eyes.

'Don't fight me,' he panted hotly. 'You know you always lose.'

Once again, she was reliving her worst nightmare but lacked the strength to oppose his advances. She had tried and had failed countless times previously so no matter how vehemently she tried to resist, she knew he would violate her.

When his hand travelled up her thigh, she caught her breath and closed her eyes while attempting to rid all thoughts from her mind of what was about to happen. If she did nothing more to oppose him, her suffering would soon end and afterwards, he would leave her room and she would cry herself to sleep....

With tears still flowing from her eyes, under her breath, she sang; 'All things bright and beautiful; all creatures great and small. All things wise and wonderful; the Lord God made them all....'

'*Right....that's quite enough noise*! *Pay attention children*,' Miss Davies called out to the chattering class. 'The weekend's over now so are you ready to give me your undivided attention? Well...are you?'

There was a disinterested response of conformity before she said, 'Please take out your history books and turn to page forty-two and we'll run over what we discussed last Friday. *Mathilda Henshaw....stop yawning and sit up straight this minute*!'

The other children sniggered, causing the colour to flush in her cheeks. Mattie detested her outdated first name and likewise, she detested Miss Davies, who persistently addressed her by her full name.

As her teacher continued to speak about William the Conqueror, Mattie's thoughts were again being channelled to another matter. She had to get away from that foster-home and from that evil family but where would she go when she had no one in whom she could confide and who would believe her if she did? At best, she would end up in reform school if she were ever to disclose their secret and at worst, she could be locked away for a lengthy time, Albert had threatened her. As the abuse had continued for six months, she would be asked why she had failed to report it sooner and how could she answer such a question? She knew it was wrong but she could do nothing about it....She was trapped.

Abruptly, her thoughts were interrupted by Miss Davies who shouted, '*I won't repeat myself again Mathilda. Answer the question now*!'

Oblivious of the question posed, Mattie appeared anxious and afraid of further reprimand she replied, 'Please miss, I'm really sorry. I couldn't understand what you were saying so I don't know the answer.'

'Good gracious me Mathilda Henshaw, I simply can't imagine what's going to become of you girl!

You have extreme academic ability, yet you choose to daydream throughout my lessons of late. If you persist in being inattentive I shall have to speak to your foster-mother about your behaviour.'

'*Please don't, Miss Davies. I'm really very sorry. I promise it won't ever happen again*,' she cried.

'*Be quiet*! I've never known such insolence. This is your final warning. Next time, you'll be severely reprimanded. Do you understand *that*?'

Contritely, she uttered, 'Yes Miss Davies.'

During the rest of the history lesson, she listened attentively, raising her hand every time a question was asked. Still covered in bruises from a previous beating, she wanted no repetition of the one a few nights ago, when she had inadvertently allowed the kitchen fire to burn too low. Hilda had a very heavy hand and when she delivered a blow, the evidence remained for many weeks. She was relentless in her punishment even for a minor matter.

When the dinner bell ended the morning session and the history mistress had taken her leave, Sadie Williams, one of the more outspoken pupils in the class, announced with a derisive guffaw to anyone who happened to be listening, 'Enjoy your sausage and mash with the yucky onion sauce.'

Sadie Williams was notorious for her disparaging remarks to her classmates in the belief that *she* was superior to them because her father was a factory-owner. She wanted for nothing and no doubt when she was collected by car each day, she would enjoy an individually prepared gourmet luncheon, Mattie envisaged. Still, the sausage and mash with yucky

8

onion sauce would taste like nectar compared to the slop Hilda dished up and she looked forward to her school dinner as it was the only time she received a decent-sized plateful of food.

At most, for breakfast, she would be given half a slice of toast with a scraping of jam.

The evening meals were horrendous and the best night by far was *boiled egg* night, though often the egg could be sloppy or hard as a rock.

The soup, or rather the broth, as her foster-mother referred to it, tasted like dishwater and Mattie was gratefully relieved when Albert requested a second helping since that meant there'd be insufficient for her. On such occasions, she would be given a small piece of cheese or perhaps a few sardines together with two thick slices of bread and margarine. Water was provided with meals though a cup of weak tea wasn't uncommon at breakfast-time.

'Breakfast is the most important meal of the day. Don't you ever forget that Mattie Henshaw,' Hilda constantly reiterated.

She was under no illusion that Hilda would have pocketed her school dinner money had there been a means of so doing but it was too great a distance for her to walk home for lunch, much to the chagrin of Hilda and the delight of Mattie who was spared the suffering of any additional culinary disasters.

Sadie Williams' mother, Sally, was on the Board of Governors at Statham Cross Secondary School and displayed a keen interest in both the running of the school and the welfare of the scholars.

9

Though situated in a Manchester suburb that was structurally degenerating with age, it was an above-average school with a reputation for discipline and a highly respectable standard of education.

Sally and her husband Charles were disappointed when, three years earlier, their daughter Sadie was unsuccessful in her Eleven-Plus examination for the local Grammar School but it was expected, Charles said. Sadie's intoxicating social activities had taken precedence over her schoolwork. He made no secret of the fact that he blamed Sally for allowing Sadie far too much freedom instead of providing her with the encouragement needed for development of her scholastic potential and a heated exchange of words had followed.

'I agree it's a shame but it's hardly the end of the world,' Sally said. 'I never paid too much attention at school either but I did alright for myself didn't I? I'm quite sure you'll be able to find Sadie an office job at the factory. Besides, she'll earn more money working for you. I've no doubt she'll be married in a few years' time so I don't see that it matters. I'm already introducing her to the right people.'

Irately Charles yelled, '*Good God woman*! She's eleven, that's all. Are you completely mad? You're heading for trouble if you ask me.'

Arrogantly she replied, 'Well I wasn't asking you Charles and it does no harm at all to plant the seeds early.'

'Is that right?' he retorted. 'Then answer me this. What if some young lothario happened to plant *his* seeds early, if you get my drift?'

'There's no need for any vulgarity Charles,' she reprimanded him. 'Nothing like that will happen to our daughter. She knows right from wrong and....'

'Ugh!' he interrupted with irony. 'She might well *know* right from wrong! My prime concern is that she'll remember to *practise* what she knows.'

'I'll make sure she does,' she replied snootily but despite Sally's assurance, little was done to repress Sadie's euphoria derived from the good life.

Lethargic and nauseous again Mattie dawdled on her way home from school with but one thought on her mind. There had to be some way of ending the suffering caused by her abusers....but what?

'*What time do you call this girl?*' Hilda bellowed when she arrived home late and without awaiting a reply she cracked her across the head.

'*Ouch,*' Mattie yelped in obvious discomfort.

'*Well, I'm waiting. Answer me girl. Where have you been till now?*'

'I had to stay behind while my teacher went over some schoolwork with me,' she lied, stepping back to avoid another crack.

Threateningly she yelled, '*Well don't do it again!* Get them potatoes peeled now and then there's half a cabbage to chop as well. If Mr. Parkes has to wait for his tea, he'll give you a clip round the ear.'

Mattie didn't answer, nor was she concerned by the threat of a crack from her foster-father. He was capable of a lot worse than giving her a short sharp clout and since he hadn't come to her bedroom the previous night, he was due again tonight. He rarely

11

went more than a couple of days without putting in an appearance.

As she peeled the potatoes, her thoughts remained on him, an ugly man with two long protruding front teeth who put Mattie in mind of a rabbit. His right eye that turned outwards, protruded to the extremity of its socket when he was angry and he was bald.

She shuddered at the thought of his facial features and his foul breath when he attempted to kiss her. She couldn't tolerate another night of his abuse and she wouldn't. She would threaten to tell Hilda. She would do whatever was necessary to stop him but she would *not* suffer that ordeal ever again.

After tea, when she had finished her chores, she went up to her room to give further consideration to her plan. Later, she heard the front door close when Albert went out and she hoped that by then, Hilda would be dead to the world in front of the fire.

She ensured everything was quiet before she crept downstairs, her having planned that if Hilda should awake, she would relate she had been coughing and had needed some water but fortunately, Hilda was sleeping soundly when she peered round the door.

Without a sound, she opened the cupboard where the housekeeping money was kept in a jar and when she emptied out the contents, with quivering hands, she counted out seven pounds in notes and twelve-shillings and sixpence in change. By the time Hilda awoke to discover her loss, it would be far too late to find her, so in the belief she might just as well be hung for a sheep as a goat, Mattie stuffed all of the money into her skirt pocket and replaced the lid on

12

the jar before returning it to its rightful place in the cupboard.

She had abandoned the idea of enlightening Hilda about her husband's evil deeds, as it would merely be her word against his. Her revised plan was to run away though she had given little thought to where she would go but none of that mattered. Her prime objective was to escape and the matter of her final destination would be determined later.

Once in her room, she collected her possessions and threw them on a bed-sheet, gathering it up and loosely knotting it before placing the bundle behind her door in readiness for her getaway.

She hadn't bargained on Albert's early return and was shocked to hear the front door being locked. If he were to remove the key, then her plans would be scuttled and furthermore, she would be exposed as a thief.

She prayed he would go straight to his room and waited apprehensively for him to pass her door, but instead he stopped. In horror, she could only watch as the door-knob turned and he elbowed his way in.

'What have we here?' he enquired as the bundle prevented the door from fully opening.

'Just some old things I'm throwing out,' she lied.

He took hold of her by the shoulders. 'I'm happy you're still awake Mattie. You've been waiting for me haven't you?' he asked with a sickening smile, his good eye lecherously scouring her body.

His words and actions angered her. As if it were not bad enough to be subjected to his contemptible vile sexual demands several times weekly, he had to declare his belief in her willing complicity and so when he pulled her towards him, she glanced round the room for some object with which to strike him.

Her tennis racquet was the sole accessible object and quick as a flash, she grabbed the handle. In the same continuous movement she swung the head at him before he had a chance to retaliate. He turned a little as he caught a glimpse of what was to happen, resulting in the solid wooden edge slicing his head above his brow as it landed right on target. He gave a shrill cry and lurched towards her. Her adrenaline pumping, she replied by swinging back her arm and thrusting it forward at speed again, striking him for a second time in the same place. His bulbous right eye suddenly appeared more pronounced and blood gushed from the deep head wound as first he halted then staggered prior to his falling motionless at her feet.

Mattie was terrified to hear Hilda's voice as she hurried up the stairs to investigate. '*For the love of God*! *What's going on up here*?' she was yelling.

For some moments, after she thrust open the door, she gaped in disbelief at the limp, prostrate body of her husband.

'*You've killed him you wicked child. I could see you were trouble the very first time I clapped eyes on you*! *Oh no. You're going nowhere*!' she yelled and blocked Mattie's path as she tried to rush past with her bundle through the open doorway.

Through fear, Mattie discovered an inner strength and manhandled the big woman out of her way but Hilda grabbed her by the hair and dragged her back.

'*Get off me you evil bitch*,' Mattie screamed and the next second, she felt a hard slap across her face that knocked her sideways.

With nothing to lose, she retaliated and during the ensuing scuffle, they wrestled their way towards the landing at the top of the stairs.

As Mattie attempted to further her escape, Hilda lunged forward towards her and fell heavily down the stairs, hauling Mattie down with her.

Hilda let out a scream and then there was silence when she landed face-down at the foot of the stairs.

Mattie scrambled around the floor, gathering up her belongings that were scattered around the hall, thankful that the key had been left in the door thus enabling her to achieve her long-awaited escape to freedom.

Her footsteps echoed loudly as she ran down the street and twice she stopped and turned in the belief she was being followed but the street was strangely deserted.

She was filled with horror as she brought to mind the mayhem she had left behind. She had killed her foster-father, albeit unintentionally and she would undoubtedly be blamed for killing his wife too.

Why had he chosen to come back early tonight of all nights, she asked herself.

If she stayed in these parts, she would be arrested for murder yet if she succeeded in getting away, she would never see her two brothers again. It was all too much to bear....

Mattie repositioned her knotted bundle across her shoulders. Her back was aching and her right ankle that she had twisted badly during the earlier scuffle was beginning to swell and throb but she continued to hurry down the street.

The church bells chimed ten o'clock and though it was an exceptionally cold night, she was so fraught with fear she didn't feel the cold, despite her being only scantily clad.

She wiped the tears from her eyes as she relived the past thirty-minutes. What would become of her now? Because of her, two people were dead but it *wasn't* because of her, she told herself. *She* was the victim.....*she* was the person who had been wronged but other people wouldn't see it that way. *She* knew she wasn't an evil girl. She had been forced to take such action because of a situation in which she had found herself, a situation she couldn't tolerate any longer. Albert Parkes had been a despicable man.

She quickened her pace as she passed by the old graveyard beyond the church, a dark and eerie place at night and she trembled at the thoughts of Albert Parkes' being laid to rest in such a grave when his body was ultimately discovered.

The painful ankle was becoming unbearable and the more she walked, the more agonizing it became. She had developed a pronounced limp and she was sure she couldn't walk much further.

Diagonally across the road was a side entrance to the Railway Station. Furtively, she headed towards it, her head held low in order to avoid recognition by anyone who might know her.

The money she had stolen from the Parkes' house would be more than enough to buy a train-ticket to

London where nobody would ever find her and in a few hours' time she would be well on her way.

She reached down into her pocket to find the five-pound-note and breathed a huge sigh of relief that she hadn't lost it during the earlier struggle.

'Where to?' the ticket clerk asked as she hovered by his window.

'Do you have a train to London tonight and how much will it cost please?'

'One-way or return?'

'One-way please.'

'How old are you miss?' he asked, eyeing her up and down.

'Er....sixteen,' she stuttered.

'Well, you don't look anything like sixteen to me. Do your parents know you're off to London?'

'*I'm sixteen....and I can do as I please!*'

Passengers from a train that had just arrived were walking towards the exit when a teenage girl poked her mother repeatedly to attract her attention.

'Mum, that girl over there....it's Mattie Henshaw,' she told her excitably. 'She's in our class at school, you know which one I mean, the one in foster-care who dresses like a tramp and look at that bundle on her back. I'll bet anything she's run away from her foster-home.'

With a dismissive chortle, Sally Williams replied, 'Sadie, you have *such* a vivid imagination. Having said that, I must admit it's rather a strange place for a young girl to be alone at this time of night. You'd better wait here for me and I'll wander over and try to eavesdrop on the conversation. I wouldn't want to do anything to alarm her, nor would I want her to come to any harm.'

As she approached the ticket office she overheard the clerk say, 'Take a taxi at Victoria for Piccadilly. The London train leaves there at midnight and you should arrive at London Euston around six o'clock tomorrow morning. That will be eighteen shillings and sixpence for a single adult fare.'

Mattie was about to hand the five-pound note to him when Sally Williams interrupted, 'Excuse me. I believe you're a friend of my daughter's at school. You're Mattie aren't you?'

Mattie was horrified and quickly looked round for a means of escape but Sally read her body language and took hold of her. 'I don't know what's going on but believe me when I tell you that it isn't safe for a fourteen-year-old girl to be travelling to London at this late hour. Why not come home with us where we can discuss everything? I'm sure that whatever your concerns might be, they can be resolved,' she said reassuringly.

'She told me that she was sixteen,' the ticket clerk interrupted. 'I knew she was lying!'

'Well, I'm pretty sure she had good cause,' Sally advised him. 'Come along with me Mattie. Things aren't ever as bad as they seem on the surface and I won't let anything happen to you. I promise.'

'*It's too late. Let go of me. I must get away from here,*' she cried.

'Be that as it may, you're not going anywhere at this unearthly hour. We'll go back to our house and we'll talk about it. How does that sound?'

Mattie knew she would have to submit. She had discovered the identity of her captor after spotting Sadie Williams skulking in the background. Of all the people in the world to recognise her why did it have to be that stuck-up cow? Yes, why indeed?

Though obliged to nod her head in agreement, she was devastated as Sally led her to her car. She had come within a hair's breadth of making her escape but nothing could save her now.

Sadie chatted excitedly to her during the journey home. 'It's so unbelievable! You were going all the way to London on your own. You are so brave,' she said admiringly in the hope that Mattie would spill the beans and also in the knowledge that she would be regarded as the most popular girl in the class if she could relate the entire story to all her classmates the next day. 'Why were you running away?'

Demonstratively she replied, 'Leave me alone and stop asking questions. I don't want to talk about it.'

'Yes, let it drop Sadie,' Sally intervened. 'Mattie has made it perfectly clear that she doesn't wish to discuss the matter so respect her privacy, please.'

When they arrived at the house, Sally asked, 'Are you hungry dear? Would you like me to make you a couple of ham sandwiches on nice crusty bread and a hot milky drink?'

Mattie was ravenous and the offer of sandwiches and a hot drink brought a faint smile to her lips. 'I would like something to eat please. You wouldn't believe how hungry I am. Thank you.'

'Come along then. I might even be able to rustle up slice of cake for you too.'

Earlier, Sally had studied the frail-looking child who appeared all skin and bone and was reminded of Sadie's report some months ago of a child who had lost both her parents. Her initial enquiries then had revealed that the child had been placed with a caring foster-family but the manner in which Mattie was clothed clearly established that there had been neither care nor concern for the poor mite and Sally was determined to ascertain what had caused her to abscond though she felt it might be better to wait a while before questioning her.

'Would you go to your room Sadie,' her mother requested. As she was about to protest Sally added, '*Now* please. I'd like to speak to Mattie alone for a few minutes.'

Sadie left the room without a word, disappointed that she would be unable to hold the attention of her classmates with the revelations she had expected to enjoy.

'Come through to the kitchen Mattie and let's see what we can find for you. You'll stay here tonight with us and we'll discuss your concerns tomorrow by which time everything will appear much better. I suppose I ought to contact your foster-parents to let them know you're safe. I'm sure they must be very worried about you.'

'*No, you mustn't....you can't*,' she cried with fear in her eyes.

'Alright, but you have to promise you won't try to run away again. If you remain here, I can help with whatever is troubling you but if you run away, then I can't. You're only fourteen and wherever you go, somebody will find you and bring you back. When you feel up to it, we'll discuss everything and I'm sure that Social Services will do all they can to help with the problem too, whatever it might be.'

'I want nothing to do with them. It was *them* who stuck me in that place,' she said, bursting into tears.

'Mattie, I am a mother and I believe I know most things about teenage girls. I have one myself,' she reminded her as she placed the plate of sandwiches on the table. 'Nothing you say will disturb me and I'm probably the best person who could have found you tonight because I *will* sort it out, whatever your problem might be.'

With tears streaming down her face she said, 'Do you really think so?'

'I'm certain I will,' she replied caringly. 'Now try to enjoy your supper and dry your eyes.'

Mattie blew her nose and attacked her sandwiches like a ravaging lion attacking its prey and when she had eaten them, she licked the tip of her finger and used it to pick up every crumb on the plate.

Sally watched as she raced through her food and wondered what secret Mattie might be concealing. Beneath her dark dishevelled hair, hid a beautifully structured face with large expressive eyes that were filled with misery and Sally's heart went out to her.

She polished off the thick slice of cake with equal speed and sighed. 'That was very nice, thank you. Mum used to make cake like that before....'

Sensitively, Sally interrupted, 'I heard about your mother and I'm very sorry. I can't begin to imagine what it must be like at your age to be left without a mother. You must miss her very much. I understand that you have brothers and sisters too.'

'I have two younger brothers and no sisters but I don't know where they are as I haven't had news of them since we were taken into care. Seth's twelve and Jack will be ten now.'

'What....you've had no contact with them at all?' she asked in disbelief.

'No, I've never seen them or heard from them for six months.'

'Didn't you mention that to your Social Worker? Surely she visited you regularly?'

'She only came once and I was told by my foster-mother not to speak unless spoken to. She asked me about my school, that's all and then she left.'

'If that's true, then it's a shocking state of affairs. This is nineteen-sixty-six. It's not the Middle Ages. There ought to have been regular contact with your brothers and that's a matter I shall most definitely do something about. You *will* see your two brothers again and very soon. I can assure you of that.'

With misty eyes she asked, 'Do you mean that?'

'I certainly do. I'll call Social Services first thing in the morning to find out where they are.'

'*No*!' Mattie screeched. '*Please, you mustn't call Social Services. They'll call the police.*'

She smiled. 'Nonsense, what could you possibly have done that would be bad enough for the police to be called?'

Mattie took a deep breath. 'I....I've killed both my foster-parents. You will help me to get away from here won't you?' she asked with beseeching eyes.

After showing Mattie to her room and reassuring her that she had no cause for concern, Sally settled down in the lounge with her thoughts.

When Charles returned from his Masonic meeting half an hour later, he was very distressed by Sally's disclosure. 'Good God, if that's true, then we have a murderer in our midst!' he exclaimed. 'The child wouldn't dream of making any such claim without foundation. What were you thinking about to bring her into our home and what about Sadie? Did you even once consider *her* safety and well-being?'

'I've taken care of that. I've locked her bedroom door as a precautionary measure. Sadie won't leave her room any morning until I've called her a dozen times. She's quite safe but I don't know what to do about Mattie. I really ought to call somebody. The poor child looked so neglected. She was dressed in rags when we found her and she was ravenous.'

'Was that all the girl said to you about her foster-parents? Didn't she give any indication of what had happened to bring any of this about?'

'No and I didn't think it was my place to question her further. I needed her confidence but it's obvious that something terrible has happened.'

'Surely there's an emergency number we can call at Social Services? The police are bound to have a number.'

'She didn't want me to call Social Services and I promised I wouldn't.'

'For heaven's sake Sally, the girl told you she'd killed two people. You can't sweep that under the carpet. Somebody needs to get round there to find out what's going on. She could simply be attention seeking but it needs to be resolved and it isn't *our* problem. Please phone the police now and ask them to find the number for Social Services or I'll do it. We have to get to the bottom of this.'

'I can't remember Mattie's surname and I've no idea where she lives so I'll have to wake Sadie.'

'You'll do no such thing! You must allow Social Services to resolve it. Had they been dutiful in the first instance, this problem might never have arisen. Only one visit in six months! It's scandalous if it's true.'

The night duty officer at Social Services proved to be very obliging and was able to identify Mattie from the sketchy information available.

Sally informed him that it was imperative for the Social Worker to be contacted immediately as there was a potential problem to investigate that couldn't wait until morning. Mattie was there with her, she explained and she gave him her name and address.

A policewoman, accompanied by a Social Worker arrived within the hour. She confirmed that Albert Parkes was indeed dead and that his wife was in a stable condition in hospital where she had provided a statement that Mattie had tried to kill her too.

At first, Sally was too distressed to answer when questioned about her knowledge of the incident.

Her husband brought her a drink and she slowly began to describe how she and her daughter Sadie had prevented Mattie from boarding a train. Mattie had said very little, she advised the policewoman, though she *had* disclosed that she had killed both of her foster-parents and that was why *she* had called Social Services after putting her to bed. It was all so unbelievable, she remarked. Mattie looked so feeble that she couldn't believe her capable of performing such an act.

Charles intervened, choosing his words carefully. 'According to what the child told my wife, there's been no input, worthy of mention that is, by Social Services. She claimed to have had one visit during her time at that foster-home and she further claimed she had never once seen her brothers. Would that be correct?'

The Social Worker twitched and stated nervously, 'I'm Mattie's Social Worker and I visited her about three months ago. Her foster-parents informed me that everything was alright and Mattie gave me no reason to believe otherwise.'

'Did you speak to her alone?' Charles enquired.

'Well er....no. According to my notes, I asked her about her school and she said she was happy there. Apart from that, I didn't record anything more that Mattie said. I wasn't there very long.'

'Typical!' Charles grunted. 'So why didn't Mattie ever see her siblings?'

'That was because her foster-parents informed me that she didn't want to unsettle them and I accepted what they said. Some foster-children find it difficult in new surroundings and prefer it that way.'

''*Her foster-parents said*'' he repeated furiously. 'And what did *Mattie* say? Don't bother to answer that. You obviously didn't think to ask *her* what *she* wanted. I find it beyond belief that when the child had lost *both* her parents, you simply banged her up in a foster-home and took little or no further interest in her welfare and needs. She's heard nothing....not one word about her brothers for the last six months. It's an absolute disgrace and you haven't heard the last of this....'

'This isn't resolving anything,' the policewoman interrupted. 'I need to see Mattie right away.'

'Can't it wait until morning?' Sally asked. 'She's exhausted. She'll be fast asleep by now.'

'No, I'm sorry. I really have to see her now.'

'I mean to be present during any questioning. The child's under age,' Charles told her. 'I shall also see that Mattie gets proper representation.'

'That's why I'm here,' the Social Worker advised him.

'Ugh!' Charles exclaimed sharply. 'I said *proper* representation and that's what I meant.'

Mattie was fast asleep and for the first time since she'd entered the house, she looked peaceful.

Sally felt so much compassion for her and bitterly regretted the need to disturb her. 'Mattie,' she said quietly, shaking her gently. 'I'm sorry but you have to wake up.'

She blinked before opening her eyes fully, unable at first to recognise where she was until she focused her eyes on Sally and then the full realisation of the night's terror returned to her mind and she sat bolt upright in bed.

Taking hold of Mattie's hand, Sally said quietly, 'You need to come downstairs. It's important that you do as I say. There's been a fresh development that has brought this unfortunate matter to a head. I promise that you're not going back to that dreadful place but in order to protect you, I've had to report what you'd told me to the authorities. If you can be open and honest about what happened earlier, then I'm sure it will help you. My husband will arrange the best possible representation for you so you have nothing at all to worry about.'

Mattie burst into tears. 'You promised not to tell Social Services or the police and you also promised you'd let me see both my brothers. *'You're nothing but a liar like the rest of them*!'

'No Mattie, listen to me. I am trying to do what's best for you. You must believe that and soon you'll realise this *is* for the best. You can't spend your life hiding from the authorities. You're only fourteen. You were right about your foster-father, he *is* dead but your foster-mother's in hospital and *she* will get better. Please tell me what happened earlier tonight. I really do want to help you.'

'I can't tell you....I can't tell anyone. It's just too awful. That's why I had to get away from there and when that revolting man tried to stop me, I lashed out at him with my tennis racquet and he fell to the floor. I didn't mean to kill him....honestly I didn't. It was an accident. I was only trying to stop him. I couldn't bear it anymore,' she wept openly.

Sally had her suspicions but she didn't wish to air those thoughts, nor did she want to put words into Mattie's mouth. If she were right, the pitiable child should be excused for whatever she had done. Her foster-parents had been in a position of trust and it would appear they had abused that trust should her thoughts prove to be accurate.

Her teachers likewise had much to answer for she felt. The mere sight of the child should have alerted them to the fact she was neither loved nor cared for. Everyone responsible for her welfare had failed this sorry creature.

Ashen-faced, Mattie asked, 'What will happen to me now?'

'There are people downstairs who need to talk to you, concerned people who will try to help you and you must tell them exactly what happened tonight. There's no cause to be concerned. My husband will be present and he won't allow them to ask anything they shouldn't. Trust me, please.'

'You said that earlier and I believed you.'

'And I'm repeating what I said. This really is the right thing to do.'

In silence, Mattie dressed into her day clothes and accompanied Sally downstairs.

As the bedraggled girl entered the room, Charles stood up. When he walked towards her Mattie froze on the spot and looked anxious.

Quick to observe his presence made her nervous, Charles stepped back. 'Please, sit over there Mattie. No one will hurt you anymore,' he said gently.

Sally sat down by her side and held her trembling hand.

The Social Worker talked to her first and Mattie recognised her from her previous visit to the foster-home. She explained that the policewoman needed to ask her some questions and Mattie barely nodded her head as she stared ahead restlessly.

'In your own words, will you explain to me what happened tonight,' the policewoman asked.

Without pausing for thought, Mattie replied, 'I hit him and knocked him down.'

'Who did you knock down?'

'Mr. Parkes.'

'And did something in particular cause you to do that?'

She hesitated before replying, 'I....I just had to get away from there. I couldn't stand it any longer. I'd had enough of.....' Her voice trailed into silence.

'Enough of what Mattie?'

'You know....' she stated uncomfortably, catching Charles' gaze.

'No, I don't know. Why don't you tell me about it please?' she asked sympathetically.

'Because I....I don't ever want to talk about it.'

'You have to Mattie. Please try.'

'I've told you. I hit him and he fell down.'

'Yes, but *why* did you hit Mr. Parkes?'

'*Because he wouldn't stop*,' Mattie cried out. '*He wouldn't stop....*'

She rubbed her tearful eyes with the back of her hand and Sally comforted the child as she sobbed. 'It's alright dear,' she said. 'You're doing fine.'

'What wouldn't he stop?' the policewoman asked slowly and clearly. 'You have to tell me Mattie.'

'*Touching me....climbing into my bed and doing horrible disgusting things to me. I hate him and I'm glad he's dead. I hate him, I hate him,*' she yelled.

'*That's enough*!' Charles interrupted, raising his hand. 'I'm quite sure we all have a clear picture of what's been taking place and as Mattie has nobody else to rely on, I shall assume the role of temporary guardian until one can be appointed. May I take it you won't be contesting that?' he stated, glowering at the Social Worker, who failed to respond.

'How would you like to stay here with us Mattie? You'll be safe here,' Sally said caringly.

She wiped her hand across her tear-stained face. 'If you're sure it's alright, yes I would please.'

Charles stood up. 'Right, that's settled then. Any additional questions can wait until another day. It's well past midnight and we're all exhausted. Here is my card. Be good enough to keep me informed of any developments and meanwhile, I'll arrange legal representation for Mattie. I'm off to bed now.'

When the Social Worker and policewoman stood up to leave, Sally escorted them to the door saying, 'I can't even begin to imagine what that poor child has suffered.'

'I'll be in touch soon,' the police officer replied.

Avoiding Sally's eye, the Social Worker scurried after her without uttering another word.

There had been very serious shortcomings in the control and supervision of this child and the Social Worker was aware there would have to be a full and detailed investigation of all the relevant factors that had gone unchecked, thereby causing a vulnerable young person to take her foster-father's life.

When Sally went back to the sitting room, Mattie was staring into space with tearful eyes.

She took Mattie in her arms. 'The worst is over. You were very brave and you told the truth which is always the best policy. It will be so much easier for you to tell your story again next time. Just try to remember that nobody is judging you. You only did what you had to do so try to put it out of your mind for the time being. You shouldn't have been placed in such a situation.'

Despite Sally's words of comfort, she continued to stare ahead in silence.

'Listen, I have an idea. How would you like to go shopping in the morning for some new clothes? All teenage girls love new clothes. Do you think you'd like that?'

'Yes I would Mrs. Williams. I'd give anything to get out of these rags. Er....can I ask you something please?'

'Of course dear....what is it?'

'Will you promise me you won't tell Sadie what happened to me? I feel so ashamed and I don't want anyone at school to know about it.'

'I promise. I won't mention one word. If she asks, I'll simply say you were running away because you weren't happy there. That's near enough to the truth and it's all anyone else needs to know. Come along, let's get you back to bed now. It'll be time to get up again soon.'

'I'm really sorry I called you a liar. I don't know what came over me. I know you were only trying to help and I should never have said such a thing.'

'Don't worry about it. In your position, I'm sure I'd have said the same thing. It's already forgotten.

I'll give you a call at breakfast time,' she answered with a warm smile.

Mattie paused before she rushed towards her. She clasped her arms around Sally's neck and gave her a kiss on the cheek. 'Thank you for everything.'

Sally hugged her warmly. 'You're very welcome my dear and everything *will* turn out right....you'll see.'

Sadie arrived for breakfast before Mattie the next morning, her avid enthusiasm for an update of the previous night's events clearly visible on her face.

'What happened last night? Have you managed to find out anything more?' she questioned artfully in an attempt to elicit as much information as possible.

'Well, your suspicions were one hundred per cent accurate Sadie. Mattie *was* unhappy at that foster-home and she was running away, just like you said. It was lucky you spotted her.'

Sadie felt triumphant. 'I told you I was right,' she gloated. 'So *why* was she unhappy there?'

'Well, I would imagine if you're living in foster-care, isolated from your family, it must be difficult so I've told Mattie she can stay with us for a day or two until things are sorted out.'

'*Stay here*! But she *stinks* and have you seen the state of her clothes?'

'*How dare you say that Sadie*! Can't you display one spark of common decency? The poor child has lost both her parents and has nothing to her name. In such circumstances I'd have thought *you* would have been more than happy to show some concern and provide Mattie with a few of *your* clothes. You have more than sufficient for your needs! I feel so disappointed in you at times.'

Sadie lowered her head in shame. Her mother was right. Perhaps she wasn't a bad girl. Mattie hadn't had the opportunities that she'd had and there was no doubt she was one of the most gifted girls in her class at school. It might work to her advantage she thought, were she to befriend her. She might assist with the some of the homework that Sadie found to be such a laborious toil.

'I'm keeping her off school today and I'm taking her shopping for some decent clothes. I shall speak to the headmistress shortly and I don't want you to mention a word to anyone. Mattie doesn't need the contempt of her classmates. She's a vulnerable girl who deserves more than a little consideration after everything she's been through.'

'I'm sorry....I can't imagine what it must feel like to lose both parents. I'll see what I can find for her to wear to go out with you. You can't take her out looking like she did when she arrived. I don't know about shoes though. Shall I wake her and ask what size she takes?'

'No, leave her please. I'll attend to that later and remember, not one word at school. I mean it Sadie, not even a breath!'

By the time Mattie awoke, Sadie had already left.

'Good morning,' Sally said cheerfully when she appeared. 'Did you sleep well?'

'Eventually, thank you. At first, everything kept going round and round in my head. Er, would it be alright if I had a bath please?'

'I was just about to suggest that. Would you like me to wash your hair for you?'

'If you show me where everything is, I'm sure I can manage.'

'By the way, Sadie has found you some clothes so help yourself to whatever you like. She's left them in the room next to yours. If you can find any shoes that fit, choose the ones you like best.'

'I'm very grateful Mrs. Williams. Thank you.'

'Not at all....come on, sit yourself down and enjoy your breakfast.'

'Will I have to talk to the police again?'

'I'm sure you will but we'll take things a day at a time. So, are you looking forward to choosing some nice new clothes?'

'Yes, very much,' she replied with a forced smile, while secretly she was petrified of what might lay ahead.

When Mattie reappeared dressed to go out, Sally couldn't believe the transformation. Apart from her hair which was still somewhat unkempt, she looked clean and tidy and she had managed to find a decent pair of shoes that were a considerable improvement on the old and tattered ones she had been wearing when she arrived.

'You look lovely!' Sally exclaimed. 'Do you feel any better after your bath?'

'I suppose...' she replied. 'Everything still keeps going round in my head though and I'm concerned about what could happen to me. I'm terrified at the thoughts of having to face Mrs. Parkes again. She never liked me from the minute I arrived there.'

'Like I said, try to put it to the back of your mind Mattie. There'll be a lot of very red faces at Social Services and I'm sure that everything possible will be done to bring this matter to a speedy conclusion. You should not have been placed in that situation. None of it is your fault. You were let down by the system so try to remember that.'

She didn't mention that Charles had called earlier to inform her that he had arranged for Mattie to see Meredith Spencer later that afternoon.

Meredith Spencer was Charles' cousin and had an excellent reputation as a most competent solicitor, specialising in Family Law that encompassed child cruelty, custody battles and associated matters.

Charles had called her for advice but after hearing the details, she had volunteered to handle the case personally and having numerous connections within the Social Services network, she was feared for her determination in leaving no stone unturned during an investigation.

'Are you ready to make a move?' Sally asked and without awaiting a reply she picked up her car keys and Mattie followed her to her car.

By lunchtime, they had purchased a wide-ranging selection of clothes and accessories.

'Shall we visit a hairdresser before we go home? Your hair could do with a trim or maybe a restyle. What do you say?' Sally questioned.

'I'd like that. My mum used to trim my hair once a month but it hasn't been done since she....'

'Then we'll find somewhere,' Sally cut in hastily to avert Mattie's distress at speaking the words that revived such painful memories.

As Mattie waited for a stylist, they chatted about Statham Cross School. 'I'm a member of the Board of Governors. Academically, it's a well run school,' Sally told her, though she felt that there were other issues she needed to raise at the next meeting. She had been shocked earlier, when Mattie was trying on clothes, to spot several bruises on her arms and legs and those couldn't have gone unnoticed by her teacher during physical education lessons and she would most certainly be bringing *that* to Meredith's attention later. 'Are you happy at your school?' she enquired.

'Yes and the schoolwork is easy most of the time but I'm always being told off by my history teacher for not paying attention in class.'

Sally confessed, 'Well, if it's any consolation at all, I never liked history either.'

'It's not that I don't like it. It's interesting really but because it's the last lesson before lunch, I'm too tired to concentrate and for a couple of weeks, I've felt sickly. I would have been happier if I'd gone to Grammar School though. I passed the Eleven-Plus exam but mum couldn't afford to buy the uniform. Besides, as she explained, if she did it for me, she would have had to do it for Seth and Jack too. I was disappointed but I had to abide by her decision. As it turned out, Seth didn't pass and Jack hasn't taken his yet. He's only ten but he wants to join the Navy he says when he leaves school.'

'Will you come in now please?' the stylist called. 'What are you having done today?'

'What do you think?' Sally said. 'Would you like your hair to be cut and styled or do you prefer just a trim? It's up to you what you choose.'

'Is it alright if I leave it to you to decide?' Mattie asked the stylist. 'I don't really know what I want. I've never been to a hairdresser before.'

'Well, yes....if that's alright with your mum.'

Sally didn't correct her. 'You do what you think will suit her face. I'm sure it will turn out lovely.'

When she returned an hour later, Sally looked up from her magazine and hardly recognised her with the feather cut that framed her pretty face.

'Do you like it?' Mattie asked eagerly.

'Yes, it looks lovely! That style really suits your face. Sadie will have the shock of her life when she sees you later.'

Meredith arrived shortly after lunch while Mattie was in her room upstairs.

After exchanging pleasantries, Sally provided her with a résumé of what had transpired over the past few hours.

'I'll need to discuss everything with her first and then she will have to be medically examined. It's a necessity,' Meredith advised. 'I've arranged that for tomorrow morning with a female doctor who's very experienced in such cases and she'll put her at her ease. How is she today?'

'She's doing extremely well when one considers what she's been through. I haven't questioned her further and she hasn't mentioned anything more to me but I took her out shopping this morning and I was appalled to see that she's covered in bruises. I didn't say anything but the poor child is black and blue. She must have taken some severe beatings.'

'Let me make a note of that. Have you mentioned our meeting to her?'

'No, I thought it best to wait until you were here. Should I leave the room while you talk to her?'

'Let's see what Mattie wants. Would you call her please?'

Sally went upstairs and explained to Mattie that a relative of theirs, a solicitor, had turned up to talk to her. 'She's a really nice lady and there's nothing to be afraid of. Come on down and I'll introduce you.'

Mattie had barely entered the sitting room when Meredith stood up and smiled.

'Hi, I'm Meredith,' she said. 'I understand you've been having a very hard time in your foster-home!

Please, sit next to me and you can tell me all about it and then I'll explain to you what happens next.'

Mattie took her place and felt very much at ease with the friendly lady with the nice name.

'I love you hairstyle,' she told Mattie. 'You have such beautiful thick hair. You're very lucky. I can't do anything with mine.'

'The stylist told me I had thick hair when she was cutting it,' she replied with a relaxed smile.

'Right, I think you know why I'm here Mattie but I'll explain again. I'm here to represent you and my job is to ensure that you are treated fairly and also to ensure that you don't say anything you shouldn't when questioned. You have to answer the questions truthfully but often, the truth can be expressed in a different way so I want to explain how you should tell your story to anybody who might ask you. Do you understand what I'm saying?'

'I....I think so,' she replied hesitantly.

'Good! Well, first of all, I need to ask you some questions and you may take as long as you need to answer. I understand that you might have to recall certain incidents so you don't need to hurry. I'll be making notes as you're telling me but that's for my benefit so that I don't have to remember everything later. Would you like it better if Mrs. Williams left us alone? Some children prefer it that way but she's happy to stay if that's what you want.'

'I think I'd like her to stay then.'

'Excellent. So may I begin Mattie by asking when you moved in with your foster-family?'

'About six months ago. It was last November.'

'Right, in your own words, I need you to tell me how things have been during your time there. That means I need to know about good things as well as bad things, for instance, if things were good at first, I'd like you to explain to me when and why things went wrong. I need to know all about the bad things and when they started. Please remember I'm used to hearing quite unsavoury accounts, so you don't need to hold anything back. I won't interrupt so you tell me when you're done and I won't be offended or disturbed by what you tell me. Just tell it like it's a story and then we can discuss everything in more detail afterwards. Are you happy to do that for me?'

'Yes,' she replied quietly.

'Whenever you're ready then.'

She paused for several seconds before she began. For her age, she spoke eloquently, describing how her mother was killed in a road traffic accident and that she and her two brothers were taken into care and placed with different foster-families. She spoke from the heart with particular emphasis on several aspects of her narrative such as the first time Albert Parkes came to her room and forced himself on her. She described her shame and subsequent fear when he threatened what would happen if ever she were to reveal to anyone what had taken place.

From time to time, her eyes met Meredith's and each time, Meredith smiled and nodded as a gesture of reassurance.

She told of Hilda Parkes' cruel beatings for trivial misdemeanours, illustrating her story by examples. She provided details of her daily chores, the meals

40

she ate, the hunger pangs she suffered, the fatigue she experienced, her distress at not knowing of the whereabouts of her brothers and the repeated visits to her bedroom by Albert Parkes. She expressed her feelings of anger and loathing and when she could tolerate it no longer, she explained how she devised her plan to escape. In detail, she spoke of the ugly confrontation with Albert Parkes that night and the ensuing occurrence with her foster-mother.

'That was an *accident*,' she emphasised. 'She *fell* down the stairs.'

Finally, she described how she ran away and was found by Mrs. Williams who brought her home.

During her emotional account, Sally was close to tears as she listened attentively to the young girl's suffering.

'Well done,' Meredith said. 'I know that couldn't have been easy but you have given me what I need to proceed. I have one question for you. When you grabbed your tennis racquet, was it your intention to kill Albert Parkes?'

'*No*!' she answered defensively. 'I wanted to stop him doing those horrible things to me. I wanted to get away. If he had come home at the normal time, I would have been gone. Everything happened in a matter of seconds.'

'Was your foster-father touching or holding you at the precise moment you hit him?'

'I told you, he was holding my shoulders and so I stepped back to grab my racquet and I swung round with it in my hand. I intended to hit him but I didn't intend to kill him, honestly. I was concerned about

41

getting away and I didn't want anything to stop me from leaving....that's the truth.'

'In that case try to remember when asked that you swung your tennis racquet at Mr. Parkes to protect yourself and knock him away from you because he was touching you inappropriately. That word means improperly. That's very important. It's called self-defence and it means that you were trying to defend yourself.'

'Well, I was. That's exactly what I was doing.'

'Then remember to stand by that explanation. I've arranged a meeting tomorrow morning with a lady doctor but it's nothing at all to worry about. She'll need to ask you a few questions and she might want to examine you. She's a very nice lady and like me, she's had a lot of experience in dealing with similar situations with other young girls.'

When Mattie appeared surprised, she said, 'Yes, this kind of abuse is not uncommon. You're not the first and sadly you won't be the last. Terrible things take place from time to time and you don't have to feel ashamed or embarrassed. The investigation will soon be over and then you can start to get your life back. You're a strong-minded girl Mattie and I'm surprised at how well you've done today. I shall be present during any further questioning, so finally, is there anything you'd like to ask me?'

'I'd like to see my brothers. Would you be able to arrange that please?'

'I'm already working on it Mattie. I hope to have some news soon so if there's nothing else, I'll be on my way.'

As a casual aside to Sally, she remarked, 'I have a meeting with Social Services at three o'clock. That should be quite interesting!' Sally merely raised her eyebrows by way of response.

'Thank you very much Meredith,' Mattie said.

'No, thank *you*,' she responded cordially. 'I think you're a very brave girl.'

Mattie beamed. 'It's been very nice to meet you,' she said before hurrying upstairs to hang up the rest of her new clothes.

'What a remarkable child,' Meredith commented. 'Still, I suppose it's to be expected. She's suffered so much that she takes everything in her stride. It's so pitiful and I pray that her life takes a turn for the better now.'

Sally couldn't help but agree with her and replied, 'I intend to make sure it does. She has a delightful surprise in store tonight.'

'Is Charles collecting the boys?'

'Yes, they'll be here by six-thirty in time for their tea. I feel quite emotional about their reunion. It's been lovely to see you again. Don't let's leave it so long next time.'

She laughed. 'We always seem to say that don't we? Still, I'm certain we'll be seeing quite a bit of each other over the next few weeks.'

'What do you think will happen to Mattie?'

'Nothing whatsoever! It was a provoked attack by a terrified child. There'll have to be an investigation of course but no charge will be brought against her. Social Services and Hilda Parkes have much more to fear than Mattie but at this stage, I don't want to say anything further to her. What I'm telling you is strictly off the record. Officially, I'm in no position to guarantee the outcome so tell her not to worry if you feel she's acting out of character or displaying signs of being pre-occupied with painful memories and I hope to be in touch soon. Don't forget to give my love to Charles.'

Sally arranged place settings for six on the dining room table and went back to the kitchen to finalise the preparations for their evening meal. After much deliberation about what to prepare, she decided that simplicity was the safest option and she chose fried chicken and chips followed by a home-made apple pie with ice-cream. Charles would have to sacrifice his roast beef and three vegetables in favour of the menu she was sure would please all the children.

Sadie arrived home around four o'clock and ran cheerily into the kitchen. 'That smells good! What are you making?'

'I'm doing fried chicken for a change.'

'Mm! Sounds delicious. I'll look forward to that. How's Mattie today? Do you know anything more about what happened?'

'I know nothing more than I did the last time you asked,' she answered truthfully. 'Don't go pestering her. She still doesn't want to discuss it. You didn't say anything at school did you?'

'No, I said I wouldn't....where is she anyway?'

'Upstairs in her room. Try to be kind to her Sadie and be thankful that you have your parents to care for you. Poor Mattie has no one to care for her.'

'I know.... Did she get any new clothes?'

'Go and see for yourself.'

'I might as well get my homework done too. I'll do it with Mattie and then she can catch up on some of the work she's missed today.'

'Good idea! We're eating at six-thirty.'

'Why six-thirty?'

'*Questions questions*! Because *that's* the time it'll be ready,' she replied with an exasperated sigh.

Sadie ran upstairs and knocked on Mattie's door before barging into her room. She stopped abruptly and stared at her wide-eyed. 'Wow! I can't believe my eyes. You look amazing and your hair is great. Stand up and give us a twirl.'

She jumped off her bed and spun round with both arms outstretched. 'Your mum's been great Sadie. She's bought me loads of clothes. I can't remember the last time anybody was so kind to me,' she said with a beaming smile.

'Well, I would have walked past you in the street, I'm telling you. You don't half look different.'

'I feel different. I'm really glad you saw me last night. I can't imagine what would have happened to me had I got on that train. I have so many things to thank you and your parents for.'

'In that case, you can help me do my homework. There's French and maths and I'm useless at both! We learned some new equations today and I can't make head nor tail of them. They made no sense at all to me when the teacher was explaining them.'

'Right, get your books out and we'll have a go at them together. I'm not bad at maths.'

Sadie sighed. '*You're* brilliant in every subject. I wish I were half as clever as you.'

'Well you've only yourself to blame. You're on a different planet all the time. Are those the maths?'

'Yes, they're called simpleterraneous equations or something that sounds like that.'

'*Simultaneous*, you numbskull!' Mattie chuckled. We've done equations before and they're easy. *I'll* explain them to you and maybe you'll remember in future.'

'I very much doubt it but you can try.'

It was peculiar, Sadie thought, how she suddenly felt bonded to Mattie. She looked so different in her new clothes and she had a lovely face that she'd not noticed before. Come to think of it, she'd not seen her laugh before either but then she'd probably not had much cause during her last six months in care. She was glad her mother had invited her to stay for a few days as she could really get to know her now and she'd feel like the cat that got the cream when she accompanied her new friend into school in front of all the gawping kids who would be gobsmacked when they clapped eyes on the new Mattie.

'Right, I understand them now thanks,' she said, returning her book to her satchel half-an-hour later. 'You explained them a lot better than Miss Stevens did. Shall we have a bash at the French homework now and then it'll all be done?'

'What is it tonight?'

She scowled. 'We've a full page of vocabulary to learn and I'm never sure which noun is masculine and which is feminine.'

'Some are simple to remember,' she said opening the book. 'Look at these for example....that end in 'ion' like *la natation*. They're *always* feminine....at least, I've never come across one that wasn't.'

'I didn't know that,' Sadie admitted.

'You do now and it's something you won't ever forget. I use what's called, 'association of ideas' if I struggle to remember vocabulary.'

'What does that mean?'

'Well, if I can't remember the translation, I think of an English word that looks or sounds something like the French word. Let me find you an example. Right....look at the word for *hat*. That's *le chapeau* and it's pronounced *sha-poh*. Well, a hat looks a bit like an upside-down po, so if I can't remember the French word for hat, I think of a po, so I'm halfway to remembering the word....do you see?'

'I haven't a clue what you're blathering on about. What's a *po*?'

Mattie giggled. 'Of course! *You* won't have a po 'cos *you* have a toilet indoors. A po is a guzunder!'

'I still don't understand. What's a guzunder?'

'It *guzunder* the bed,' she chuckled. 'The correct name is a chamber pot and ordinary everyday folk like me have to use one if we need to get up during the night to go to the toilet.'

'I *still* don't understand what you mean. Why do you not use the toilet like everyone else?'

'Because *we* don't have an inside toilet! *We* have a pot called a po under the bed!'

'*You are joking*! Everybody has an inside toilet. Tell me you're joking Mattie.'

'Welcome to the real world Sadie and believe me, more people have a po than a toilet and while we're on the subject of French words, chamber pot means bedroom pot and *la chambre* is the French word for bedroom so that's another word you've learned. To remember its gender, think of a lovely lady floating around the bedroom in her lacy long nightdress and you'll remember it's a feminine word. That's what I meant by 'association of ideas'.'

'I don't believe a word you're saying about a po.'

'Alright, just suit yourself what you believe,' she replied petulantly before slamming the French book closed. 'I'm going to give you a quick test now, so tell me the French word for 'the hat'.'

'*Le chapeau*. Yes....*le chapeau*.'

'And what's the word for 'the bedroom'?'

'Er...*la chambre*!'

'Excellent! So, once you've mastered the skill of 'association of ideas', it doesn't matter how daft it is as long as you remember the word.'

'Smarty-pants!'

'Does it work?'

'Yes it works! I'll try to learn the rest now but I'll never forget *le chapeau* or *la chambre* again!'

They were singing and dancing round the room to pop music when Sally later knocked and entered.

'Mattie's such a scream. She's had me in stitches with some of the things she says,' Sadie told her.

'Good! I'm delighted to know the two of you are getting along well. It's nearly six o'clock so wash your hands please and I'll call you as soon as your dinner's ready.'

When Charles arrived with the boys, he showed them into the lounge where Sally greeted them.

'Are you excited to be seeing Mattie again?'

'Aye, not half!' Seth replied on behalf of both of them and with cheeky grin. 'We didn't have a clue where Mattie were and Jack's never shut up talking about her since we found out earlier. Is she alright?'

'Yes she's fine, though I think she might be quite emotional when she sees you. We haven't told her you were coming.'

'What's '*motional*' mean?' Jack asked.

''*E*motional'. That means upset but in a nice way. She'll be very pleased to see you, so much so that she might cry,' she explained.

'Just like a girl,' he scoffed with a broad smile on his lips. 'They're always crying.'

Sally laughed. 'I'm sure you're right Jack. I hear the two of you are together in your foster-home. Do you like it there?'

'Yes, it's great and there's one other lad there too but he'll be leaving soon. He's going back home to his mum who's been ill. We'll miss him when he's gone,' Seth said.

Sally and Charles exchanged darting glances and Charles nodded his head. 'I see we're on the same wave length,' he acknowledged. 'I'll give Meredith a quick call.'

'Come through to the dining room boys and wait in there for Mattie. I think it's better that she meets you alone on this occasion.'

They followed in silence, each in deep thought as Sally left the room and went upstairs for her.

'Right, are you both ready for something to eat?' she asked the girls.

'I'm absolutely ravenous!' Sadie said and Mattie nodded in accord.

'Mattie, would you come downstairs first please? Some people are here who would like a quick word with you.'

Though apprehensive, she said nothing in Sadie's presence and silently followed Sally.

'They're in there,' she stated, opening the dining room door that she swiftly closed as Mattie entered.

'*Seth....Jack, you're here*!' Sally heard her shriek but could only imagine the sentiment they shared as she left them to enjoy their special moment.

'*I can't believe it*!' she screeched, running swiftly towards them. '*You really are here*!' Taking them in her arms she sobbed. Their presence completely overwhelmed her and she was unable to contain her tears as she held them tight.

'Are you alright?' Seth asked with deep concern.

'Oh yes....I'm just so happy to see you. I had no idea where you were or if you were being properly cared for and I've been so worried about you. Have you both been together?'

'Yes, and there's no need to worry about us. It's great where we are. That man who brought us here said you'd run away from your place. Wasn't it up to much there?' Seth questioned.

'It was horrible but none of that matters anymore. You're here now and you're both well and that's all that matters to me. I'm *so* thrilled to see you both and just look at you Jack. Haven't you grown?'

'I've joined the school football team,' he told her proudly. 'Every Saturday morning, we play against other schools and you'll never guess....I scored my first goal last week.'

'Good for you Jack! So what about you Seth? Do you play football too?'

'No, I'm not very keen on sport. I enjoy reading and I want to be a librarian when I leave school.'

'You'll need qualifications for that.'

'I know. I've talked to my teacher and he reckons I can go to night-school to get whatever I need.'

'I'm really proud of both of you and I know mum would have been proud too.'

Sally tapped on the door and walked in. 'I guess that was some surprise wasn't it Mattie?'

'You're the best person in the world,' she said as she ran to give her a hug. 'Thank you so much.'

'It's my pleasure and now, if everyone's hungry, we'll have our dinner.'

'*I'm starving*,' Jack announced. '*Is it ready*?'

'Er....just remember your manners Jack!' Mattie scolded and Sally laughed.

'You sit down with your brothers Mattie and I'll call the others.'

Within minutes, the four ravenous children were tucking into their chicken and chips and the earlier poignant atmosphere had changed to an ambience of calm and contentment. Sally watched the foster-children with tears in her eyes as they sucked their sticky fingers and Jack looked up and grinned at her across the table, while Seth remained silent and in deep thought. Mattie....she looked radiantly happy.

Charles leaned towards Sadie, "There but for the grace of God go I". Make sure you remember that!' and turning his attention to Sally he said, 'I spoke to Meredith.'

She smiled and nodded her head and then asked Sadie, 'Did you finish all your homework?'

'Yes mum and Mattie was such a big help. She's taught me how to remember French vocabulary and we had a right laugh doing that!'

'Well, I'm delighted that you enjoyed doing your homework for a change. I too could have benefited from a little help Mattie when I was trying to learn French vocabulary. I was pretty useless at French.'

'Mattie's help wouldn't have meant much to you mum unless you'd have known what a po was!' she giggled.

'A what?' her mother asked.

'A po!'

Mattie was embarrassed and kept her head down.

'*I know what a po is*!' Jack cried. '*You pee in it.*'

'Just keep quiet Jack!' Mattie stated ashamedly.

Charles howled with laughter. 'When I was a lad, we called it a guzunder!' he informed everyone.

'You mean po *is* a real word?' questioned Sadie in disbelief.

'Of course it is,' he replied. 'Many houses today still don't have an inside toilet so it's a necessity.'

'And I thought you were kidding,' she told Mattie who was sitting red-faced but within seconds they were all laughing.

It had been an edifying discussion, Charles stated and added that if everybody had finished discussing chamber pots, he'd love to have some apple pie and ice-cream.

When the two boys were dressed to leave, Sally assured them that it was the first of many reunions they would be having with their sister. 'It's been a pleasure to meet such well-behaved boys,' she told them. 'You must come here again very soon.'

They thanked her politely for their enjoyable meal and hugged Mattie before leaving.

'See you soon,' Seth called as the car was driven away at speed.

Mattie sighed heavily. 'I still can't believe what's just happened. It's like a dream come true and when I think I almost ran away….'

'Well, thankfully we found you in time and things should start to improve for you soon Mattie,' Sally sighed optimistically. 'Your troubles are over now.'


'Would you like a magazine?' Meredith asked as they waited to be called into the surgery.

'No thanks. I'm too tense. I'm dreading this and I can't wait to get out of here,' Mattie said, cracking her finger joints and twitching nervously.

'We shouldn't be long and it's nothing to worry about,' Meredith reassured her. 'I'll be by your side during the questioning and then I'll wait for you out here. The examination will only take a few minutes. When answering the questions, you have to be very specific about your foster-father's abuse, so tell Dr. McAndrew everything. That's important and don't forget you've done nothing to feel ashamed about. Social Services and the foster-family are to blame.'

53

'Well I *do* feel ashamed *and* I feel sick,' she said.

'You can come in now,' the nurse informed her. 'What beautiful hair you have,' she added as Mattie walked towards her.

Mattie attempted to smile as she walked into the surgery with trepidation, where she was greeted by a chubby and cheerful Scottish doctor who instantly made her feel at ease.

'Come along in dear. I'm Dr. McAndrew. Please sit yourself down and you've no cause to be afraid of me. I promise I don't bite,' she chortled. 'A wee birdie told me you'd met up with your two brothers again yesterday. I'm sure that must have been quite a surprise.'

'Yes it was,' Mattie replied.

'And were they well?'

'Yes thank you. They were very well.'

'I'm delighted to hear that. Right dear, you know why you're here. I have to ask some questions and I shall be writing down what you tell me so it might take me a wee while. It's important that you try to remember everything. Now I'm pretty sure there'll be things you won't like to say to me, certain words for instance but that's to be expected and nothing at all for you to worry about. I'm here to help should you get into difficulty. Alright my dear?'

Mattie nodded her head and the questions began, continuing for some twenty minutes, during which time, Dr. McAndrew repeatedly reassured her that she was responding well.

During the ensuing medical examination, Mattie wept incessantly.

'Right, that's fine my dear,' she advised her. 'I've finished now. You slip your clothes back on and I'll go talk to Meredith until you're ready.'

Meredith was waiting in the reception area when Dr. McAndrew sat down beside her and expelled a huge sigh. 'This is one of the worst cases I've come across. There's no doubt that she's been beaten and abused for a considerable time. That's evident from the degrees of bruising and scarring about her body and she's terribly undernourished. Furthermore, the medical examination revealed that she's about eight weeks pregnant. Would you like me to tell her and advise her of her options?'

Meredith was distressed. 'I suppose we should be informing Social Services first but I'm inclined to say yes, tell her now. She's a determined child and she'll handle it, I'm certain. She has to be told and the sooner she's told, then the sooner she'll come to terms with it. It's her body and it's her baby. That makes it her decision.'

'I also believe that's the best course of action, to get it all over and done with today and it might be better if you were there when I tell her. She knows and trusts you Meredith.'

'Come and sit down Mattie,' Dr. McAndrew said kindly, directing her to a chair next to Meredith.

Mattie looked anxious and Meredith took hold of her hand. 'Is there something wrong?' she asked.

'There's nothing physically wrong with you but my examination has revealed that you're pregnant.'

To that, Mattie said nothing. She neither replied nor did she make eye contact with Dr. McAndrew.

'Do you understand what I'm saying Mattie?' Dr. McAndrew asked with sensitivity.

She nodded her head. 'I'm having that repulsive man's baby. That's what you're saying to me. Well I don't want it....*I don't want it*!' she screamed. '*I don't want it*! *Do you understand*?'

'I understand perfectly and there are options open to you....choices, my dear.'

'*Listen to me*! *I don't want it and I'm not having it*,' she yelled at the top of her voice.

'If that's what you decide, we can take care of it,' Dr. McAndrew told her.

'*I've already decided*,' she screamed hysterically before bursting into tears. '*Why won't you listen*?'

Meredith put her arm around her and said calmly, 'Don't upset yourself Mattie. Everything is going to be alright. You'll see. You don't have to go through with it. It's a straightforward procedure and then it will all be over.'

'It will *never* be over,' she wept bitterly. 'I want my mum to come back. I want everything to be as it was before she died. Nothing will ever be the same again and what will people say? They'll be pointing at me and sniggering. That's what everybody does when a girl gets pregnant. I'm not sinful but people will think I am.'

'Nobody apart from the authorities has to know,' Dr. McAndrew reassured her, 'I do believe though that Mrs. Williams might have had her suspicions when you were sickly and she was most concerned about you. She's your friend and she'll give you her full support. I want to leave matters as they are for a couple of days and then I'll see you again to make absolutely sure you haven't had a change of heart. You might feel differently in a day or two.'

'I'll *never* change my mind. I *hate* that man. I'm *glad* he's dead!' she said with hatred in her eyes.

'I do understand and I really am so sorry.'

Meredith took Mattie's hand in hers. 'We'll be on our way, if there's nothing else you need,' she told Dr. McAndrew.

'Right Meredith and I'll see you again in a couple of days Mattie. Try not to worry and have plenty of rest. We *will* sort everything out, I promise you my dear. Goodbye!'

'Should I tell Mrs. Williams everything?' Mattie asked as they made their way home.

'In your shoes, I know that *I* would but it's your decision. She's been very supportive and you need loyal friends at a time like this. Your secret would be safe with her. She'd never tell Sadie.'

Mattie stared out of the car window in silence for the rest of their journey.

Meredith walked her to the door and when Mattie went inside, she left.

'Are you alright?' Sally enquired.

Mattie nodded. 'Is anyone else here?'

'No, just the two of us. Is something wrong?'

She threw her arms around Sally's neck. 'It was really horrible and there's something I have to tell you. I'm having a baby.'

Close to tears she said, 'My poor darling. Try not to worry. We'll help you all we can. It's not the end of the world, believe me.'

'I'm getting rid of it. I've already told the doctor. I'd rather *die* than have *his* baby,' she said bitterly.

'I understand how must you feel and I'll support you every step of the way, whatever you do.'

'Promise you won't tell Mr. Williams or Sadie,' she begged. 'I couldn't bear it.'

'My lips are sealed on the subject. I'll never tell a living soul, I swear.'


Over the following weeks, Mattie remained quiet and downcast and Sally was becoming concerned. The investigation by the police and Social Services was drawing to a close and although Mattie wasn't being charged with any criminal offence, that news hadn't provided the fillip that Sally had anticipated.

Regular visits from her two brothers now scarcely brought a smile to her face. She appeared lethargic and depressed and as the school's summer holidays approached, Sally became more concerned. Sadie's perpetual questioning didn't help matters either.

The onset of Mattie's melancholy coincided with the termination of her pregnancy, following which she refused to see a doctor or counsellor and spent most of her time in her room doing her homework when she arrived home from school each day.

Sally suggested that she might like to accompany them on a family holiday but that invitation brought no positive response either.

The turning point eventually came when a letter from Social Services arrived, notifying Mattie that she been allocated a place at the Grammar School, starting in September.

For the first time in weeks, Mattie seemed happy and more talkative and when a second letter arrived a couple of days later, informing her that she would be joining her two brothers in their foster-home, she was ecstatic. Her life was returning to some kind of normality, not that she didn't greatly appreciate the kindness of Mr. and Mrs. Williams who had helped her through this very difficult time, she told them. She likewise expressed her gratitude to Sadie, who had become a close and very special friend.

When the time came for her to leave, she was sad.

Sally told her, 'Sadie is going to miss you, in fact we'll all miss you and we'll always be very grateful to *you* for all your help with Sadie's schoolwork. I hope you'll come and see us from time to time.'

'Oh I will….you'll be sick of the sight of me,' she laughed. 'I intend to visit Sadie whenever possible and I've no doubt she'll be phoning me every night about her schoolwork. I'll always be thankful that you brought me here that night. You've been like a mother to me and I won't forget everything you and Mr. Williams have done for me.'

'It's been our pleasure. Take care of your brothers Mattie,' she called out as the two girls climbed into Charles' car.

'Your foster-home's not very far from here is it?' Sadie asked.

'It's about half a mile away. I'll have to find out if I'm allowed visitors and if not, I'll have to come to your house. I'm definitely not going to lose my best friend.'

'Me neither,' Sadie echoed with a smile.

3

Mattie soon readjusted to the regime of Grammar School and as a new pupil, most girls wanted to be her friend but she was happy to retain Sadie's and only Sadie's friendship.

She was delighted with her new foster-home too and found Richard and Olive Schofield, her foster-parents, to be special people who went out of their way to be caring but Mattie remained vigilant when alone with her foster-father and was careful to keep her distance. She had developed a condition called androphobia....a morbid fear of men, following her experiences with Albert Parkes and sought to be in the company of women whenever possible.

Her new Social Worker visited regularly and gave careful consideration, as opposed to lip service, to all her needs. For the first time since her mother's death she had spending money of her own and was allowed a reasonable amount of freedom to pursue her leisure interests.

Initially, it felt strange not to have any household duties. Other than keeping her own bedroom clean, nothing else was required of her and for that, Mattie was thankful since she found her schoolwork quite challenging, her having enrolled at the school three years after the other girls in her class.

Her teachers were delighted with her progress and her overall knowledge soon began to surpass that of all the other girls in her year. She had an insatiable appetite for knowledge, her foster-parents were told when they attended the parents' evening.

Mattie devoted her efforts to her weaker subjects, namely chemistry and geography in which she had fallen behind at Statham Cross School. Her dogged determination to succeed in every subject provided the impetus to push herself at every opportunity and her relentless example of fortitude was used by her teachers to encourage a similar enthusiasm in lesser determined girls.

When the time arrived to take her GCE 'O' level examinations, she was entered for ten subjects and attained a distinction in all but one.

During morning assembly, Mattie's headmistress commended her for her resolve and described her as an admirable example to others in foster-care.

In the sixth form, she was voted head-girl and she was proud of and humbled by the appointment, she declared during her maiden speech.

She was offered places at Oxford and Cambridge and when her 'A' level results were published, she enrolled at Cambridge to read Law.

It had been her resolve, from the age of fourteen to follow in Meredith's footsteps. Meredith was her idol as well as her mentor. In seeking justice for the mistakes committed by Social Services, she had left no stone unturned and important lessons had been learned, they admitted repentantly while accepting responsibility for their omissions and inadequacies. Nevertheless, Mattie firmly believed the same thing could happen again to another vulnerable child.

Had it not been for the welcome support of Sally and Meredith, Mattie doubted that she would ever have recovered from her harrowing experiences and if perhaps, at some time in the future, she could be of assistance to others in untenable situations, then her mission in life would be complete, she believed.

Following Mattie's graduation from University in nineteen-seventy-five, Sally organised a celebration party to pay homage to Mattie's accomplishments.

When Meredith appeared, laden with flowers, she was quick to congratulate her. 'I was sure you'd do well. Sally told me that you got a *first* in both your degrees. That's better than I did!' she confessed.

'It wasn't expected I assure you,' Mattie laughed. 'I found it very difficult at times.'

'What utter nonsense, so have you accepted a job anywhere yet?'

'I'm still considering my options. I've been head-hunted by several large companies up and down the country but I think I'd prefer to work in these parts. I don't want to lose contact again with Jack or Seth. I know Jack's away for a lot of the time but he does come home on leave periodically and Seth's here. I might take some time out to collect my thoughts on the matter. There are many wonderful opportunities but I don't want to rush into anything I might regret later. I want it to be the right decision.'

'You should come and work with me,' she stated excitedly. 'Why don't you give that some thought? We get on well together.'

'Work with *you*? You must be joking. You're my idol! I'd never stop feeling inferior.'

'You were only a child then but you're a woman now Mattie. You might not have realised but there are only fourteen years between us. I'm not exactly old enough to be your mother. I would have had to be very enterprising at the age of fourteen for that!'

Meredith had scarcely uttered the words when she realised her mistake and glancing round to be sure nobody was in earshot, she spluttered, 'I'm so sorry Mattie. That was a most insensitive and dim-witted remark to make. I didn't think. Forgive me please.'

'Don't apologise. It's water under the bridge now. Something bad happened and I dealt with it. I don't regret my decision and I never will.'

'I don't know what to say Mattie....I....'

'Then say nothing,' she interrupted and changing the subject she asked, 'What do you think I ought to change my name to? I've always detested the name Mattie! Can you imagine a plaque on my door that says, 'Mattie Henshaw'? 'Cristobel O'Hara' sounds quite professional don't you think?'

'*Cristobel O'Hara,*' she screeched with laughter. '*You can't be serious.*'

'Of course I'm not....I'm joking but I have to lose 'Mattie Henshaw'.'

'Right, I'll give it some thought then. What about 'Prunella Pinkerton' or 'Desdemona Doolittle'?'

Their hysteria was suddenly interrupted by Sadie who threw her arms around Mattie's neck. 'It's so good to see you, clever-clogs. How's tricks?'

'Can't grumble,' she responded with a broad grin. 'It's good to see you again too.'

'Come over here and I'll introduce you to Keith, my boyfriend. He's just talking to dad.'

'Is Keith your latest beau?'

'For the time being he is. You know me!'

'Indeed I do!'

'So, what about you Mattie? Have you some dark secret you're withholding from me? Do you have a gorgeous hunk in your life at the moment?'

Mattie felt the colour rise in her cheeks. 'No, I'm not looking.'

'*You* don't need to look. I bet guys are queuing up to date *you*! You look stunning tonight.'

Mattie was relieved when Sally wandered across. 'Charles and I are very proud of your achievements. We have *two* solicitors in the family now,' she told her. 'We still think of you as family you know.'

'Thank you Mrs. Williams. I still think of you as family too.'

'Then drop the 'Mrs. Williams' please. You make me feel ancient. Can I get you a drink?'

'That would be lovely. I'll have whatever you are having.'

When Sally returned with her drink, she enquired about her future plans.

'I haven't made any yet. I'm taking some time out to consider my options. It's refreshing not to have my head in a book. Meredith's just suggested that I go and work for her.'

'*With* me, not *for* me,' she corrected her. 'I have a huge workload and I simply can't cope on my own. To avoid my having to turn clients away, I've been seriously considering taking on another solicitor for some time. I wish you'd give it serious thought.'

'Alright, I'll think about it and I'll let you know.'

'I believe you're staying at your foster-home with the Schofield family again?'

'Olive was adamant when she knew I was coming back here. They don't take foster-children anymore. When Jack joined the Navy, they felt they had done their bit for society. Seth still boards there and they offered me a room until I sort myself out which I'll have to do quite soon. My grant is almost exhausted and I don't want to get into any debt. Sally invited me to stay here with them but she's done so much for me over the years that I couldn't take any more from her. Someday, perhaps I'll find a way to repay her for all her help.'

'She doesn't want repayment. Your achievements are repayment enough. She couldn't be more proud if you were her own daughter and don't forget how *you* helped Sadie. She'd never have ended up with any 'O' level passes, let alone *eight*, had it not been for you. She became dedicated to her studies after you went to University. It gave her an interest away from the frenetic social life to which she'd become addicted. She's still talking about going to Teacher Training College and I believe she will. She's been making enquiries you know.'

'Yes....she told me and I advised her to go for it. She'd make a good teacher. I know she's not very happy working for her dad. The work doesn't seem to stretch her enough. Besides, she's been out with every bloke at the factory now,' she laughed.

'And *Sadie* will never settle for a factory worker!' Meredith quipped.

'Who won't settle for a factory worker?' someone interrupted and they turned to find Sadie listening to their conversation disapprovingly.

'Er....we were talking *about* you, not *to* you. Butt out!' Meredith said light-heartedly. 'It's very rude to eavesdrop on other people's conversations!'

'I wasn't eavesdropping! I came to ask if you're ready for something to eat. Mum wants to serve the buffet when everyone's here. Do you have any idea what time Olive and Richard will arrive?'

'They should be here now. They were picking up Seth from night-school on their way here. It's such a shame Jack couldn't make it. It's ages since I've seen him. The last time we heard from him, he was in Singapore. He's certainly seeing the world.'

'How old is he now?'

'He was nineteen last April. Doesn't time fly? It seems no time at all since we were children. Seth's twenty-one now and I'm not saying,' she laughed.

'You don't need. You're nearly twenty-four, the same as I am. I often think back to that night. Why *were* you running away? You never did tell me.'

'It was a culmination of things....it was nothing in particular but I'm pleased I did because that's how I came to meet *you*, properly I mean. I'll let you into a little secret now. I despised you when I first went to that school. I thought you were a conceited cow,' she howled. 'That was before I knew you properly,' she added by way of apology.

Sadie joined in the laughter and admitted, 'I was! You taught me a lot about life. I could easily have become a right obnoxious bitch! Well come on, I'm waiting. You're supposed to tell me I didn't!'

'Give me a chance....I'm still thinking about it.'

'What a cheek!' she said and Meredith laughed.

Their chatter was halted by the arrival of Richard and Olive who hurriedly approached Mattie. Olive hugged her lovingly and smiled. 'It's just a token to acknowledge our pleasure,' she said, handing her a beautifully wrapped gift. 'Richard and I are so very proud of your achievements.'

'Thank you,' she beamed. 'Is Seth not with you?'

'Yes, he'll only be a minute or two. He's having a cigarette outside.'

'I'll slip out and find him. I *do* wish he wouldn't smoke! Excuse me,' she remarked irritably and she walked towards the door. '*Seth*,' she called out and as he acknowledged her, another figure appeared in the background at the end of the drive. As he drew closer, Mattie screeched with joy. '*Jack? Oh Jack. Why didn't you tell me you were coming?*'

He grinned at her. 'What, and spoil your surprise? Congratulations! I knew you'd pass all your exams with flying colours. When we were kids, you were always the brainy one!'

'I needed to be to keep tabs on you two,' she said as she clung to him. 'When are you going back?'

'Charming! I've only just arrived and you want to know when I'm leaving!'

'Stop it! You know very well what I mean. I want to know how long I have you for John Henshaw.'

'Sunday name!' Seth smirked.

'I'm here for five days, *Mathilda*.'

Mattie scowled at him. 'Alright, you win. I won't say that again. Anyway....I'm seriously considering changing my name from Mattie.'

'What on earth for?' asked Jack.

'Because I don't like it. It's old-fashioned and I'd prefer something er....more modern and attractive.'

'But it were grandma's name,' he responded in a tone of disappointment.

'Precisely....and Grandpa's name was Eli. Would *you* like to be lumbered with that?'

Seth laughed mockingly. 'You'd not pull so many birds with a name like Eli. They'd run a mile. She does have a point Jack and it is *her* name so if she wants to change it, then it's *her* decision. Don't you agree *Eli*?'

'I guess so. What did you have in mind?'

'Meredith suggested Prunella Pinkerton.'

Jack was horrified. 'You can't be serious!'

'Well....it's a bloody sight better than being called *Eli 'Enshaw*!' Seth commented scornfully and in a broad Lancashire dialect.

When the jocularity had subsided, Jack remarked, 'We'll always love you, no matter what you decide to call yourself....and we'll always remember how you cared for us when we were little after dad died. You were only seven and you missed most of *your* childhood. You are deserving of everything you've achieved and me and Seth are really proud of you.'

'Come on, don't be maudlin! This is supposed to be a party. I did what I had to do and nothing more. You were good kids so I guess we've all turned out well considering....'

Seth butted in, 'Where's your next trip to Jack?'

'I don't know yet, probably Hong Kong. I won't find out for a few days. The Far East is fascinating so I hope it is there. It's poles apart from the west in every conceivable way. I've been giving quite a lot of thought to signing-up for twenty-two years.'

'Be careful,' Mattie advised him. 'Consider what you'll be sacrificing. If you decide to get married, it can be disastrous for your wife and family who are left behind. Many such marriages end in divorce.'

'I'm not planning on getting wed for a long while. I'll still only be in my early forties when I come out so there'll be time enough then to get wed.'

'That's if there's anybody left,' she pointed out.

'Well, there'll be them divorcees you mentioned! Don't you go worrying your pretty little head about me,' he smirked. 'Anyway, isn't it about time *you* were tying the knot?'

'No, I'm a career girl. I'll *never* get married.'

'Of course you will. You haven't come across the right guy yet but you will eventually.'

When Sally summoned her, Mattie lost no time in making her escape.

'Come and look at the buffet. I hope there's going to be enough food,' Sally said and as Mattie hurried away towards the dining room, she was angry at her ill-conceived instigation of that unpleasant topic of conversation with her brothers.

'Now be honest Mattie. Do you reckon there'll be enough food here? I can do some more sandwiches if you think we need them.'

'You're joking. There's enough food here to feed an army! Have you made all this yourself? It looks fantastic.'

'Sadie's helped quite a lot. I have to admit, she's becoming quite domesticated though I would never have believed it possible when she was growing up. She idolises you and I have such a lot to thank you for. She's serious about going to Teacher Training College too. She made reference to you one day as 'Phoenix' and said you were amazing. I didn't want to show my ignorance by asking her what it meant but I'm quite sure you will know.'

Mattie explained. 'In legend, Phoenix was a bird who died in fire and a new and better Phoenix arose from the ashes and lived again. I suppose it's a fair simile except it was *you* who delivered me from the ashes. I would never have achieved a thing without your support. I owe my life to you and Charles and one day, I hope to repay your generosity.'

'You already have Mattie....tenfold! Shall we call everyone in?'

It was a lovely party and Mattie was surrounded by all her friends and family. She felt sorry when it had to end. 'You did so well,' she told Sadie. 'The food was delicious. I couldn't have organised and produced a spread like that for so many and I think Keith is a charming young man. He never took his eyes off you all night,' she whispered.

'Yes....I quite like him. He's different from other guys but if I go away to college, I'll probably lose him. Three years is a long time for him to wait.'

'You'll be home regularly. It'll soon pass.'

'Are we ready to make tracks?' Olive interrupted. 'We don't want to overstay our welcome.'

As Sally escorted them to the door, Mattie smiled. 'It's been such a delightful party and thank you so much for arranging it.'

Charles smiled at her. 'We're very proud of your success and I ought to add that I wouldn't refuse a little 'pro bono' help if I'm ever in need.'

'I'll be practising Family Law, Charles so I doubt you two lovebirds will ever need me,' she laughed.

'If Sally and Sadie keep spending all my money quicker than I earn it, I'll need you very soon,' he jested. 'You take care Mattie.'

He stepped aside as the women hugged and when he closed the door, Sadie commented, 'Why do you never give Mattie a hug dad? She's just like a sister to me.'

For once, he was lost for words and Sally jumped to his rescue. 'Let's get these dishes cleared away and get to bed. I'm shattered!'

'Me too,' Sadie answered and her former question was eradicated from her mind as she followed Sally to the kitchen. 'It was a great party mum and Keith was very pleased to have been invited.'

As she closed her eyes, Keith was in her thoughts, Keith, who was so kind and dependable but would he wait three years for her she wondered. Then she sighed heavily before she tumbled into a deep, dark and welcome abyss.

Mattie too fell into a deep sleep the moment her head touched the pillow but hers was intermittently disturbed by the sound of coughing in the adjacent room, Seth's room. It was a rasping retching cough that troubled her as it continued well into the night. There would be an occasional period of quiet before it started again but each time, the duration appeared more prolonged.

She slipped on her robe and went to Seth's room where she found him sitting on the edge of his bed. 'Whatever's the matter?' she questioned anxiously. 'You've been coughing on and off all night.'

'It's a virus that's all. It'll clear up soon,' he told her before taking another sip of his water.

'You should see the doctor Seth. It sounds worse than a virus to me.'

'I've already been. He gave me some antibiotics to clear it up.'

'When was that?'

'Oh....four or five weeks ago.'

'Why on earth haven't you been back? Surely he told you to if it didn't go away?'

'I thought it'd get better on its own.'

'Well, you're going back tomorrow. If I've asked you once, I bet I've asked you fifty times to pack in smoking and you were smoking again tonight.'

'I'll be fine. Don't keep mithering me. If he gives me some more antibiotics it'll clear up in no time.'

'You promise you'll go in the morning? There's a Saturday surgery.'

'Alright, I promise. Go back to bed. I'm sorry if I've disturbed you Mattie. I'll be alright now.'

Three hours after Seth left for the surgery the next morning he hadn't returned and she was becoming increasingly worried.

Mattie rushed towards him the second he opened the door. 'Where have you been till now? I've been frantic. What did he say? Are you alright?'

'Yes, I'm fine. The doctor sent me for a chest X-ray as a precautionary measure but he didn't believe it were anything for me to worry about. I should get the result in about a week.'

Four days later, on the Wednesday, Seth received a letter and handed it to Mattie. 'That's strange, the doctor wants to see me. Why couldn't he have just said in the letter that I were clear? Maybe he wants to change my medication,' he remarked, dismissing any thought that it might be bad news.

Mattie was troubled, though said nothing in reply to alarm him. 'Get your coat. We'll go now.'

'No, I don't need my big sister to hold my hand. I'm capable of going on my own,' he complained.

'*I said I'm coming with you and that's final!*'

'Alright but you know we'll be waiting for ages. Still, it'll be company for me I suppose.'

The deep furrow lines in her brow did nothing to hide Mattie's anxiety when the doctor invited them to sit down.

'Right young man,' he stated, removing the report from the pouch. 'You need to have some tests to get the bottom of this.'

'Right,' Seth answered, standing up to remove his jacket.

'No, I won't be doing them here. I need to admit you to hospital right away. I'm afraid your X-rays show a shadow on your lung. It may be nothing of concern but we need to have it checked out and so the sooner you get there, the sooner they can start. They'll probably keep you in for three or four days while they run the tests.'

Seth looked shocked and Mattie was in tears. Her father died from lung cancer in his early thirties and

73

she remembered how much he had suffered during the last few months of his life. Surely it couldn't be that Seth was suffering from the same disease....or could it? She was dry in the mouth merely thinking of the possibility.

'Do you have transport?' the doctor enquired.

'Er....no,' Mattie replied, still feeling dazed.

'Then ask my receptionist to call you a taxi. Like I said, the sooner you get there, the sooner they can settle you in for your tests. I'm sending you to the Royal. Take this letter with you and they'll tell you where to go. Good luck lad. Let's hope you're soon on the road to recovery.'

'Thanks doctor,' he said, closing the door behind him. 'I don't believe this,' he told Mattie.

'Neither do I but it's probably nothing much,' she stated reassuringly although she was disturbed by a nagging unease at what it *might* be and prayed she was wrong. Several days' wait for test results was going to be a long and worrying time.

Following Seth's admission, three junior doctors who appeared no older than Seth visited in turn to record details of his symptoms, the time of onset of his incapacitating illness and the treatment he had so far received. Each enquired about family medical history and when Seth was asked about the cause of his father's death, he replied that he didn't know.

'I'm not aware either,' Mattie prevaricated when the third young doctor turned to her for a response. 'We were young children when dad died so I never knew the cause of his death so I'm sorry that I can't help you either.'

When he left, Seth complained, 'Why doesn't the first one take everything down in triplicate and give a copy to the other two? I'm sick of answering the same questions over and over again.'

'Shut up Seth! They are junior doctors who have to learn what questions to ask and how to diagnose. One might pick up on something that the other two have missed. It's for your benefit too.'

'Well, I'm fed up already and I want to go home. Fancy having to waste time in a dump like this!'

'Folk would die if there weren't dumps like this,' she replied caustically. 'You're in here to get better, not to pass judgement on the décor. For once, try to act your age instead of your shoe size! Shall I see if I can get a cup of tea? I know I could do with one!'

'Aye, I could murder a cup of tea but don't worry if you can't get one.'

As Mattie was about to leave the ward, the ward Sister was entering with a well-dressed doctor who inclined is head at her and smiled before allowing her to pass first through the doorway.

'Thanks,' she mumbled, barely catching his eye, though conscious that his eyes were following her as she hurried away.

When she returned, carrying two steaming mugs of freshly-brewed tea, Seth was propped up in bed. 'Boy, am I ready for a drink!' he remarked. 'Would you believe I've just had to go through everything again with another doctor? He were older though. He were the Cardio-Thoracic Consultant, whatever that means. He'd not been here more than a second when them others turned up like three bad pennies and he kept asking them questions as well as asking me other things but I couldn't tell him anything that I hadn't already told the others. He said somebody would be along shortly to start the tests. Why don't you get off home now and come again tomorrow? I feel alright now. It's only when I'm lying down that I cough because I'm a bit breathless.'

'I suppose I could come tonight with Jack if he's nothing planned. He'll be shocked when I tell him you're in hospital.'

'That's up to you. You don't have to traipse back here if you don't want.'

'*Of course I want to come back*!' she snapped at him irritably. 'I don't like travelling on my own at night, so if Jack can't make it, I'll ring the hospital for an update and I'll be back tomorrow. You look a bit better now Seth.'

'Then stop worrying about me and don't you go upsetting our Jack either. He's only here for a few more days so let him enjoy his leave.'

On her way out, Mattie approached a nurse in the corridor and enquired if she could speak to the ward Sister.

She escorted her to Sister Flanagan's office where she tapped on the door and showed Mattie in.

'I'm sorry to disturb you but I need to inform you of a material fact I withheld from the doctors who attended a patient, Seth Henshaw. It's regarding the cause of his late father's death and Mr. Henshaw is unaware of that cause.'

'I understand, though it might be better were you to speak with the Consultant, Mr. Wyndham if he's still around. I'll check if he's in his office. I won't keep you a moment.'

Seconds later, she returned and escorted Mattie to the doctor who had held the door for her earlier.

He arose from his seat and smiled broadly. 'Hello again, I'm Mark Wyndham. Please take a seat,' he said cheerily. 'How may I help you?'

'I'll leave you to it,' Sister Flanagan announced.

'*No, there's no need to go!*' Mattie protested with desperation in her voice. '*Please stay. I'll only be a moment.*'

'As you wish,' she replied.

Mattie quickly explained the purpose of her visit and stood up to leave. 'Is it likely that Mr. Henshaw has the same disease?' she questioned, at the same time taking hold of the door handle.

'I couldn't possibly speculate at this point in time I'm afraid. Needless to say, where there's a family history, it racks up the odds slightly but the X-rays prove nothing and without any test results, I'm not able to express an opinion. Why don't you pop in to see me tomorrow? I might know something by then and in the meantime, try not to worry. It can be one of any number of things.'

She faked a smile and thanked him but before he could answer, she was gone.

'How very strange!' Sister Flanagan commented. 'What did you make of that? Does that young lady know something about you I don't?'

'I've never met her in my life before....honestly,' he insisted as she laughed. 'Do I have an enormous pair of horns sticking out of my head?'

She ruffled his dark curly hair. 'Not that I can see. Are you certain you two don't know each other?'

'Like I told you, I've never seen her before today but I'll admit that I wouldn't mind seeing her again. She's beautiful.'

'Well, I wouldn't say she shares your enthusiasm for another meeting. How bad is that for your ego?' she grinned as she punched his arm.

'It's her loss. Listen, you're a staunch gambling woman. How about a small wager? I bet you I can persuade her to see me again.'

She laughed raucously. 'What, you mean outside this hospital? You're definitely on! You haven't got a cat in hell's chance and anyway, she could have a husband for all you know.'

'She wasn't wearing a ring,' he pointed out.

'My my....you're very observant. She was only in the room for about thirty seconds. So how much do you want to bet....a tenner?'

'Can you afford to lose a tenner?'

'What's more to the point, can *you*?'

'Listen, the tenner I win from you will finance the night out,' he replied with an optimistic smile.

'In your dreams, Mr. Wyndham, in your dreams,' she repeated pompously as she left the room.

'You'll see,' he called after her.

Jack was distressed to learn of Seth's admission to hospital. 'Were he right bad?' he quizzed Mattie.

'He's had a cough for a week or two and when it didn't clear up with the antibiotics, his doctor said he wanted some tests carried out, that's all.'

Olive was worried. 'I've heard him coughing over the past few weeks but I didn't think anything of it. It didn't occur to me that it might be serious.'

'I'll drive you up to the hospital tonight,' Richard volunteered. 'That way, each of us can spend a bit of time with him. He'll be glad of the company I'm sure. It's a long day in a hospital bed.'

'Well, I'm definitely coming,' Jack echoed. 'Will we get to know anything tonight Mattie?'

'Probably not. The waiting is the worst part and the test results could take days but thankfully, Seth doesn't appear too bothered.'


'Have I kissed goodbye to that tenner yet?' Sister Flanagan taunted when Mr. Wyndham appeared on the ward.

'No, not yet but you will,' he replied confidently. 'Incidentally, do you happen to have the admission sheet for Mr. Henshaw?'

'And why would the likes of Mr. Mark Wyndham be wanting to see that?'

'You just keep your sweet Irish nose right out of my business,' he replied with a twinkle in his eye.

'Her name's Mattie....Mattie Henshaw and she's his sister.'

He laughed and winked at her. 'Is nothing sacred around here Sister? I don't suppose you managed to find out whether or not she was married.'

'I could make a calculated guess if you'd like to waste another tenner! Do you want to take me on?'

'I need facts not fantasy. Either you know or you don't know!'

'Huh....and you're supposed to be the bright one! Well let me just say, unless she's married to a chap who's also called Henshaw, then she's single!'

'Oh....right,' he replied feeling foolish.

'You know you're not allowed to date a patient's relative don't you? Conflict of interest and all that!'

'Mr. Henshaw won't be my patient forever. I am merely making tentative enquiries at this stage. Do we have any tests results yet?'

'No, it'll most likely be morning before we know anything. They were only referred a short time ago. Mr. Henshaw's become very restless over the past hour or so. Do you want to take another look at him while you're here?'

'Yes, I think I'd better,' he replied.

Approaching the bed, he could see that Seth was in obvious discomfort.

'How are you feeling?' he enquired.

'I....I can't get my breath,' he wheezed. 'My chest feels very tight.'

'Alright, don't try to speak. I can give you some oxygen to assist your breathing. Raise his back-rest please, Sister. That should help a little and I'd like thirty-minute observations on this patient,' he said.

'Hopefully, the antibiotic injection should start to take effect soon but be sure to call me if there's any deterioration in his condition. Someone will be here shortly to check on you Mr. Henshaw and you must try not to worry. You're in very good hands.'

'Is it serious doctor?' Seth asked apprehensively.

'Without any test results, I can't say one way or the other. Stay calm. It'll help your breathing.'

He closed his eyes and attempted to breathe more slowly. The oxygen mask allowed him to relax and he didn't open his eyes when Sister Flanagan told him she would check on him again soon.

As he lay there, he wondered what would happen about the job that he was supposed to start in three weeks' time. He had studied conscientiously for his qualifications and had beaten five other candidates who had also been short listed for that job. He *had* to recover in time for that....He simply had to....

At each of the thirty-minute observations he was asleep and his breathing was no longer laboured but when Mattie arrived with the others at visiting time, she was shocked to see an oxygen mask on his face.

When she stroked his hand, his eyelids flickered before he awoke fully, and he tightened his fingers around hers and smiled when he noticed her look of concern. 'It's alright,' he said, removing his mask. 'Don't worry Mattie. I were a bit breathless earlier but I'm feeling much better now. This is just to help me breathe easier.'

'Have you had anything to eat?'

'No, I must have been asleep when they brought the food trolley round but I'm not bothered. I don't suppose I've missed much. I'm not very hungry.'

'Have they told you what's wrong yet?'

'They didn't know anything when I asked earlier. That Consultant came to see me again and he said he'd be back later but I think I've been asleep since then. Right, enough about me. How are you lot?'

'We were worried when we heard,' Jack replied.

'Shall I try to get you a cup of tea?' Mattie asked.

'Please, I'm gagging for a drink. My mouth's like the bottom of a parrot's cage and these beds are that hard they give you backache. Could you help me to sit up please?'

Richard pushed past to the top of the bed. 'How's that?' he said when he'd plumped up Seth's pillow.

'Much better thanks. What time is it?'

'Ten past seven. You talk to the others and I'll get you a drink. Don't go away!' she grinned.

Seth scowled. 'I wish!'

'*Miss Henshaw*!' Sister Flanagan called as Mattie passed her door. 'Do you have a moment please?'

'Of course....I was hoping to see you before I left for an update.'

'We've no news yet but your brother seems more settled than earlier. I wanted to know whether you had a phone number where we could contact you if we needed to get in touch. There wasn't one listed on Mr. Henshaw's admission sheet.'

'I can give you this number but I'm in temporary accommodation presently. You can reach me there anytime,' she said, handing her the slip of paper on which she'd written Olive's number. 'It's alright to leave a message with either Mr. or Mrs. Schofield if I'm unavailable and I'll call you as soon as I get the message.'

The Sister made a note of what she'd been told.

'Could I order a cup of tea and maybe something to eat for my brother please? He was sleeping when they brought the meals round.'

'I'll attend to it. I'm sure someone can rustle up a couple of sandwiches. I'll have a tray sent through.'

'Thank you. It'll be such a relief to know the test results when they're available. The waiting is very stressful.'

'I know but try to keep an open mind. We should know something soon.'

Seth's eyes glowed when the pretty young nurse arrived shortly afterwards with his sandwiches and tea. 'Have I ever told you that you're my favourite nurse?' he asked with a smile. 'The quickest way to a man's heart is through his stomach you know.'

The nurse blushed and forced a smile when Seth's visitors laughed and she beat a hasty retreat.

'I hope she's not giving you your next injection,' Jack commented with a broad grin. 'Ouch!....I must admit though, she's a bit of a corker!'

'Her name's Stephanie. We had quite a long talk earlier. She's a *nice* girl Jack. She's definitely not *your* type.'

'What the hell is *that* supposed to mean Seth, not *my* type?'

'You know exactly what I mean, *Eli,*' he stressed before taking a huge bite of his sandwich.

'I thought you weren't hungry,' Mattie remarked as Seth's cheeks bulged like two overripe apples.

Seth gulped and cleared his throat before saying, 'To be honest, I were absolutely starving and these sandwiches are *very* tasty. I feel much better now.'

'Well, I'm delighted to see there's nothing wrong with your appetite. That's always a good sign and hopefully, you'll have your test results back soon. We should leave you to rest now and I'll come back tomorrow afternoon.'

Richard shook Seth's hand and left the ward with Olive who wished him well.

'I'll be coming tomorrow as well,' Jack told him. 'I'll fetch you something too. Would you like some fruit or something to drink?'

'Just fetch whatever you think. It's been great to see you all and thanks for coming.'

Mattie turned one last time at the end of the ward and waved to Seth who smiled affectionately at her and returned her gesture. She blew him a kiss and he gazed at her with pride. Her mother would have been very proud too, he thought as she disappeared from view.

'Upon my soul, Mr. Wyndham, you're certainly up with the lark today,' Sister Flanagan commented glibly. 'What's wrong? Couldn't you sleep?'

With an expressionless face, he answered, 'I just happened to be passing and I thought I'd pop in.'

'Oh, did you now? In that case, I'm sure you'll be delighted to know he had a comfortable night.'

'To whom are you referring?' he asked naively.

'It's no use trying to pull the wool over my eyes. You know perfectly well who I'm referring to. His sister was here again last night. I talked to her for a few minutes before I went off duty.'

'Oh really? Is she coming again today?'

'How would I know? I'm not her keeper. Anyway I'm not here this afternoon. Sister Lloyd and I have changed duties so you'll have to talk to *her*.'

He shuffled his feet restlessly. 'You disapprove of my interest in Miss Henshaw don't you?'

'It isn't my place to approve *or* disapprove and no matter what I said, you'd take no notice of me,' she replied judgementally.

As he walked to the door, like a scolded dog with his tail between his legs, she called out, 'Hang on a second....I've got something here for you,' and with a wry smile, she handed him a slip of paper.

'What's this?' he asked, taking it from her hand.

'I dunno! It looks like a phone number to me.'

His face glowed. 'Sister Flanagan, you are such a treasure! Did Miss Henshaw give it to you for *me*?'

'Don't you go counting your chickens....she gave it me for the records when I asked for it and you'd better not go telling anybody you got it from me do you hear or I'll have your guts for garters.'

After he closed the door behind him, he beamed. He had a high opinion of Sister Flanagan. She was a first-rate 'salt of the earth' woman and everybody else thought highly of her. She had been a Sister on that particular ward for many a year and she was an invaluable asset to the hospital. Hidden beneath the bullet-proof exterior was an altruistic friend with a wicked sense of humour and a heart of gold.

She was a gambling woman too but she only bet on certainties and he hoped that her recent flurry of good fortune was drawing to a close since this was a wager Mark wanted to win. Mattie Henshaw was a delightful and charismatic creature and he wanted to know more about her.

Maybe he could learn something from her brother were he to orchestrate his questions suitably. It was certainly worth a try, he decided.

Later that morning he visited Seth alone. 'Do you feel any better today?' he enquired.

'I slept alright but I'm still having problems with my chest and I can't seem to get shut of this cough but the oxygen helped a lot. I'm no worse.'

'That's good. Are your family visiting later?'

'My brother and sister are coming this afternoon. My sister's rather concerned about the test results. She hasn't said anything but I can always tell when she's worrying about something.'

'I see! Is she so disposed?'

He looked confused and Mr. Wyndham rephrased his question. 'Does your sister have cause to worry about you? Have you had problems before?'

'No, I've never had any problems with my health. Mattie worries about all kinds of things. You could say she's had a difficult life. She had to look after me and my brother Jack when we were kids. First our father died and then our mother got killed in a road accident when Mattie were only fourteen.'

'And she took care of you single-handedly?'

'No, we were all taken into care then but we were separated. Me and my brother were placed together and Mattie got sent to another foster-home but hers were a terrible place that she won't even talk about. She's an amazing young woman, considering what she's been through and she's achieved such a lot as well. The night before I were admitted, we threw a party to celebrate her success. She's just qualified as a solicitor you see. She's very clever.'

'She's also very beautiful Mr. Henshaw.'

'Aye she is....with a personality to match.'

He took the bit between his teeth and remarked in a nonchalant manner, 'I guess you'll miss her then when she gets married.'

Seth laughed. 'I'll be old and past caring by then. She has no interest whatsoever in men.'

'I find *that* very hard to believe.'

'It's true Doctor. I wish she *would* find a nice guy and settle down. I'd be made up if she did!'

He decided that his questions should proceed no further and believing he may have overstepped the mark already, he didn't wish to raise suspicion by questioning him further but he had found the earlier temptation to continue irresistible particularly when Seth had been so forthcoming with information and he had certainly learned a great deal more about the mysterious and delightful Mattie Henshaw.

He made to move away. 'That was very good Mr. Henshaw. That was a simple test of your ability to converse and your breathing appeared fine.'

'I wondered why you kept asking me questions.'

'It's all part and parcel of the diagnostics. You're certainly better than you were yesterday. I'll check on you again later, perhaps this afternoon and with any luck, we might have some news by then.'

'I hope so. Thanks doctor.'

Seth was reading the newspaper when Stephanie appeared at his side with a kidney bowl containing a fear-provoking hypodermic needle.

'It's time for your next antibiotic injection.'

Seth bowed his head. 'I'm sorry about yesterday, what I said. I didn't mean to embarrass you. It was a daft thing to say and I wanted to apologise.'

'It's alright....I'll get my own back in a minute!'

'It's only what I deserve. Were you annoyed with me?'

'Not at all,' she smiled. 'I would have preferred it had there not been so many visitors listening at the time you said it.'

'It wasn't a chat-up line....honest.'

'Now I'm disappointed. Lie still and relax then it won't hurt as much.'

Seth felt the needle as it penetrated his arm and he caught his breath.

'Sorry,' she said. 'I've finished now and it'll wear off in a minute. You look a bit brighter today.'

'I always feel bright when you're around. You're like a breath of fresh air on a winter's morn.'

Her smile broke into a laugh. 'Where on earth do you find all those expressions?'

'I must have read it in some book or other. I'm a librarian or at least I will be when I start a new job in three weeks' time. I like to read. I especially like old books. Someday, when I've some money put by I intend to own a collection of first editions.'

'That doesn't sound very exciting in fact it sounds positively boring.'

'Believe me, it's fascinating. I couldn't begin to explain the pleasure of being able to see, let alone touch a first edition of an important manuscript or journal with its dusty cover and aged brown curling pages. It's like returning to a former life, a journey back in time. It's hard to explain but I'm sure you'd understand if I took you to a museum.'

'I'd much rather you took me to a disco.'

'Oh no, a museum is so much more....er what did you say?'

'I'd rather you took me to a disco,' she giggled.

'Are you serious? Do you mean that?'

'*Yes*! We can go to a dusty old museum another time!'

'I'd love to take you to a disco er....Stephanie.'

'In that case, hurry up and get better. I won't hang about waiting forever.'


'I've brought you some chicken sandwiches and two Eccles cakes,' Mattie stated, placing the wicker basket on Seth's bed. 'Olive's made the sandwiches and Richard tried to smuggle two bottles of beer in the basket when my back was turned, so I removed them when I found them.'

'Aw Mattie! You're a spoilsport. How am I going to eat all that without a drink?'

'You have got a drink. Jack's brought you a bottle of Lucozade. That's *much* better for you.'

'Gee thanks a million Jack! Do you know, I were only thinking earlier how I could just murder a long cool refreshing glass of Lucozade. You must have read my mind!'

'Shut up complaining. You're obviously feeling a lot better. You know that you're not allowed beer in hospital. What do you think Sister would say if she caught you drinking alcohol on her ward?'

'From where I'm sitting, all sisters are alike!' he replied cantankerously.

'You eat your sandwiches! There's best butter on them. Have you received any test results yet?'

'No, but the Consultant's coming to see me again later. He's been once and he thought I seemed a bit better.'

Jack leaned over the bed. 'Have you been chatting up that pretty young nurse again?'

'I have and what's more I'm taking her out when I get out of this blasted dump,' Seth declared before taking another huge bite of his sandwich.

'Yeah....right! She'd have to be crackers to go out with you when I'm about,' he sniggered. 'I'll show you a good chat-up line if she comes on the ward.'

He had barely uttered the words when Stephanie was there at the bedside saying, 'The Consultant's making his rounds and he'll be here in a minute so I want to straighten up your bed Seth.'

'You can straighten up *my* bed any time you like,' Jack smirked.

'Thank you. I'll bear that in mind,' she answered caustically. 'If or when I tire of Seth, I'll be sure to look you up but please don't hang about *too* long. Meanwhile, you might just find someone who isn't as particular as I am.'

Seth laughed aloud and Jack looked downcast as Stephanie beat a hasty retreat. Angrily, Mattie said, 'Never before have I witnessed such reprehensible behaviour. You should be ashamed of yourself!'

Seth howled with laughter. 'That's a chat-up line? You're losing your grip mate, so if you don't mind, I'd rather stick to my own, though I must say yours were a damn sight more palatable than your lousy bottle of Lucozade and it made me *feel* a lot better too. That's the best laugh I've had for a long time.'

'Just stop it, the pair of you!' Mattie interrupted. 'You're worse than a couple of kids.'

'Hey up! The Consultant's here,' Seth announced with a look of concern.

'Good afternoon to you Mr. Henshaw,' he stated and smiled warmly at Mattie. 'Miss Henshaw,' he added in acknowledgement of her presence.

She glanced at him briefly and directed her eyes towards Seth.

'Right, I have been looking at the test results that have come back and apart from a minor pulmonary infection, nothing else has been revealed, which is good news. There has been an interesting disclosure however and I feel duty-bound to confess that three junior doctors and I failed to thoroughly investigate a relevant feature of your lifestyle relating to your employment field Mr. Henshaw. You're a librarian I'm told. Would that be correct?'

'Not yet though I hope to be in three weeks' time, God willing.'

'But you handle many books, some of which are very old I understand?'

'Well....er....yes I do. I work at an old bookstore at the moment. I've worked there for a few months now but I don't understand what that has to do with anything.'

'Luckily, nurse Jackson here was quick to put two and two together and it's possible you are suffering from a form of asthma. A simple allergy test would confirm this and so I've arranged for it to be carried out immediately. As the breathlessness is of recent origin and taking into account what nurse Jackson has revealed, I would suggest that dusty old books are the most probable cause. If that proves to be the case, you should be able to work as a librarian in a modern-day library without the problem recurring but you would need to avoid all contact with old or dusty books. Do you have any questions?'

'How sure *are* you?' Mattie asked.

'Let's say I'm quite confident. I merely wanted to ease your concerns and I should be able to tell you a lot more tomorrow.'

'Thank you very much,' she replied.

'My pleasure. Go easy on the Lucosade,' he said and Seth laughed.

When Mr. Wyndham moved out of audible range, Seth breathed a huge sigh of relief and said, 'What fantastic news. Shall I tell you something? I could have kissed that doctor when he told me!'

Though Mattie decided to add no comment of her own, her thoughts were in line with Seth's remark and her relief was beyond description.

4

Mattie was about to serve Jack's breakfast when the phone rang. 'Answer that will you,' she called to him. 'My hands are full of grease.'

Jack raced to the phone. '*It's for you Mattie*,' he yelled from the hall.

'Go and get your breakfast. It's on the table,' she said, wiping her hands on her apron before picking up the receiver. 'Hello....can I help you?'

'Miss Henshaw?'

'Speaking....who's that please?'

'Mark Wyndham.'

'Sorry....who did you say?'

'Mark Wyndham, Cardio-Thoracic Consultant at the Royal. I'm treating your brother.'

Mattie's heart was racing. '*Is something wrong? Has something happened to Seth*?' she shrieked.

'Your brother's absolutely fine. I'm just calling to say that he has asthma. It's been confirmed today.'

'Oh that's wonderful news. I'm so pleased,' she replied with relief in her voice.

He laughed. 'Yes well, I suppose that depends on how you look at it.'

'What? Oh yes of course but I'm sure you know what I mean. I'm so relieved that it's nothing more serious and I can't thank you enough for letting me know. It really is such a load off my mind. For the past few days I've been so worried.'

'Then I'm pleased to be the bearer of good news by providing a diagnosis at last.'

'I can hardly believe it. Does Seth know?'

'Yes and he wanted you to know right away. It's a manageable condition that shouldn't give him any further trouble as long as he avoids contact with old or dusty books. Are you planning to visit him later today?'

'Yes, hopefully around three o'clock.'

'Maybe I'll see you then.'

'Thank you so much for calling, Mr. er....'

'Mark,' he interrupted.

'Thank you,' she repeated and hung up hastily.

'Are you alright? You've got a face like a turkey-cock. Were that the hospital?' Jack asked.

'Yes and Seth has asthma. It's such a load off my mind to know it's nothing more serious.'

He sighed and enveloped her in his arms. 'You're such a worrier Mattie. I do wish you'd make time to put yourself first for once. You can't play the role of mum forever you know. *You're* entitled to a life.'

'You two boys are my life,' she replied tenderly. 'I love you both so much.'

'We know that and we love you too but we're not boys now....we're men. We can fend for ourselves. *You* don't have *any* social life. Why don't you have a night out once in a while and enjoy yourself? So many times I've heard Sadie inviting you to parties but you always make an excuse not to go.'

'It's not what I do Jack. I'm different from other women. I never socialise because I don't like being in the company of people I don't know. I'd feel out of place and I'd hate it.'

'I don't understand you Mattie. Didn't you have parties and social evenings at University?'

'Yes, there were plenty but I didn't go to them. I devoted my time to my studies.'

'You're missing out on so much. I'm going back to sea in a couple of days but next time I'm home, me and Seth will take you out. We'll have a slap up meal somewhere nice.'

'Thank you Jack. I'll look forward to that. That's something I *would* enjoy,' she replied softly.

Seth appeared greatly improved when Mattie and Jack visited him later.

'You gave us all such a scare but you look grand now,' Jack remarked, giving him a brotherly hug.

'Aye, I reckon it might have been that Lucozade that did the trick,' he answered with a mischievous grin. 'I'll feel better again once I'm out of this place though. If I just need to rest, I can do that at home.'

'You'll come home when you're discharged and not a moment before so don't go asking to leave. A few more days could make such a difference. Just remember what you felt like when you couldn't get your breath properly. I don't want any repetition of that,' Mattie told him.

'Has your lovely nurse called to see you today?' Jack enquired.

'Yes....three times!'

Jack laughed. 'She'll have made an effigy of me, full of pins by now I wouldn't mind betting.'

'No, we had a laugh about it earlier. She thought she might have gone too far but I told her you have a keen sense of humour. Once I'd explained to her how it came about, she saw the funny side of it and she hasn't taken offence.'

'I have,' he replied petulantly before expelling an uncontrollable guffaw. 'Actually, you've done well there Seth. She's a lovely girl with a personality to match and she can certainly stand her corner.'

'Well, if ever you want coaching in chat-up lines, you only have to ask. I don't mind giving you a few pointers, little brother.'

Jack grabbed the spare pillow that was resting on top of the bed and used it to strike Seth playfully.

Seth retaliated by grabbing the one from beneath his head and walloping Jack around the head.

Their tomfoolery was abruptly curtailed by Mark Wyndham's untimely arrival at their side when he casually remarked, 'You appear to be much better today Mr. Henshaw. Do these scoundrels generally behave in this manner?' he questioned Mattie.

Mattie felt the colour rising in her cheeks as she answered, 'Believe me, you don't want to know.'

'Oh indeed I do. If this is typical of your brother's normal behaviour, I see no reason why he shouldn't go home later. He's obviously well on the way to a full recovery.'

'Gee, thanks Guv!' Seth exclaimed.

'I'll need to run through your notes quickly and if everything is satisfactory, I'll sign you out later this afternoon. Will you be staying a while longer Miss Henshaw?'

'If Seth's coming home, then I'd like to wait for him if that's alright.'

'No problem. There'll be a prescription to collect from Sister's office. Once discharge is authorised, it will be ready for you.'

'Thank you so much for everything you've done Mr. Wyndham,' she said.

'Not at all....that's why I'm here,' he replied with a smile. 'Your brother will be invited back in about six weeks' time for me to review his progress and it is important that he attends.'

'I'll make sure he does. Thank you again.'

Seth and Jack looked embarrassed while awaiting a reprimand and she spared no time in her delivery. 'I can't believe you behaved in such a childish way! As for you Jack, only this morning you were telling me that you were *men* and not *boys* anymore. I'm at a loss to know *what* Mr. Wyndham thought to catch you acting the goat like that.'

'We were just having a laugh Mattie. Anyway, he weren't looking at *us*. He scarcely took his eyes off *you* while he were here, in fact I reckon the old boy fancies you!' Jack advised her mischievously.

'Don't be ridiculous and he's not an old boy!' she snapped. 'He's hardly a day over thirty.'

Jack decided to capitalise on the situation. 'What do you say Seth to having a top-notch doctor in the family. Imagine, a doctor *and* lawyer in the family.'

'That sounds fine to me! Only yesterday, he were quizzing *me* about her, asking all sorts of questions. You're right Jack. I think he's smitten.'

'*Stop it*! *Stop it I tell you*,' she cried.

'Hey....come on now Mattie. We're only fooling around,' Jack apologised. 'Lighten up....please....we didn't mean to upset you.'

There was an uncomfortable silence before Seth spoke again. 'I were a bit worried that I wouldn't be better in time to start my new job. I'm grateful that you made me go to the doctor Mattie. Me and Jack are very fortunate to have you for a sister. You've always looked out for us, isn't that right Jack?'

'Yes it is and I've told Mattie that we'll take her out for a nice meal when I'm next on leave.'

Mattie stood up. 'I'm just having a walk round to stretch my legs. Do either of you want anything?'

'No thanks,' they replied in unison.

As soon as she disappeared from view Seth said, 'I'm worried about Mattie. She's acted very strange since mum died. I haven't a clue what's wrong with her and if I say anything, she bites my head off.'

'Mattie were very close to mum. Don't forget, we were only little when our dad died and I can't really remember him if I'm honest but I do remember that Mattie took care of us all the time. She used to do everything for us, like washing us and putting us to bed every night. I can still remember all the stories she told us at bedtime. It were just like having two mums. *We* never suffered like *she* did. She weren't like a normal kid when you think back. She didn't do things other kids did. I can see her now, standing by the ironing board. She could hardly reach it and yet never once did she complain about anything.'

'You're right, she didn't and she used to laugh a lot in them days too,' Seth said. 'She were a happy-go-lucky young lass. Haven't you noticed how she never laughs anymore? She's always has a strange and serious air about her these days and behaves a bit funny sometimes.'

'How do you mean...funny?'

'I don't know. I can't put my finger on it. It's as if there might something wrong with her, like in her head. Her eyes are always darting about as if she's looking for something or somebody. I can't explain it Jack and then there's this thing she has about not socialising. She won't do things that other girls do. It's not normal. She should go out and enjoy herself at her age. I just wish she'd talk to us about it.'

'Leave her be Seth! We've no right to interfere in her life. We don't like Mattie telling us what to do. Happen she'll grow out of it eventually, whatever it is that's wrong with her. When she starts work, that might alter her.'

'Aye, you might be right. Anyway, time will tell.'

Mattie wandered through the hospital grounds in a virtual trance before taking refuge in a shady spot by a small fountain.

The flowerbeds were bursting with thousands of blooms and she inhaled deeply to enjoy the fragrant perfume.

She studied a Red Admiral butterfly, flitting from one flower then to another and it revived childhood memories of Jack who had once cried bitterly when one such butterfly had settled on his sleeve, while Seth had laughed mockingly at his brother's fear.

She had cupped it in her hands to show Jack that the delicate and harmless creature was beautiful and she had explained in depth how God had painted it with bright colours so that everybody would love it. Jack had smiled at her through his tears and he was never afraid of butterflies thereafter. Yes, those had been much happier days....

'A penny for your thoughts,' somebody said and Mattie glanced up into the eyes of Mark Wyndham.

She appeared anxious and he took a step back.

'I apologise if I startled you. It's extremely hot in my room and I needed to catch a breath of air. This is such a delightful spot in the shade and I regularly amble down here for a ten-minute respite when I'm able. I find it very relaxing. It's a place where I can lose myself in thought for a while. Is that what you were doing?'

'Something like that,' she said, avoiding his eye.

'I believe that congratulations are in order. Your brother mentioned that you'd recently qualified in Law. Do you mind if I sit down?'

She looked around and shuffled to the end of the garden seat without a word passing her lips.

'Thank you. I've been on my feet all day and it's very tiring when it's a hot day like today....so have you started work now?'

'No, I'm still deciding what to do. I've had quite a few offers but I haven't accepted anything yet.'

'When I qualified, I would have given an arm to take time out but we were all steered into hospitals immediately and the hours we worked!' he sighed. 'Still, one adapts.'

'I guess so,' she replied. 'Er....would you excuse me please? I should make my way back now. I've enjoyed talking to you.'

'I'll walk with you, that is if you don't mind. Tell me....what does your other brother do?'

'Jack's in the Royal Navy. He joined up when he was seventeen. He always wanted to be a sailor.'

'Oddly, my mind was set on being a doctor. Did you always want to read Law?'

'No, I only decided a few years ago.'

'So what made you choose Law?'

'Er....I have to go. I must get back to Seth. He'll be wondering where I am,' she gabbled and hurried away before he could speak another word.

Mattie ran blindly down the central corridor and when she arrived at the corner to make her turn, she collided with a woman and almost knocked her to the floor.

'*I am so sorry,*' she cried. 'Are you alright? Have you hurt yourself? It was all my fault. I should have been looking where I was going.'

'Don't worry my dear, there's no harm done. I'm fine....Mattie? It is Mattie isn't it?'

'Yes....er....Dr. McAndrew?'

'Well, fancy my bumping into you, literally,' she laughed. 'My, how you've altered! You were just a wee scrawny lassie last time I saw you but look at you now. You're an exquisite young lady. Tell me, what brings you here my dear?'

'My brother was admitted a few days ago but he's coming home later today.'

'Fully recovered I hope?'

'He's doing nicely. It was a respiratory problem that turned out to be asthma. I was worried it might have been something much more serious.'

'Well, I'm delighted to hear it wasn't. Listen, I'm between patients and I have a fifteen minute break so I was just away to the cafeteria. Come and have a cup of coffee with me and we can catch up on all the news. It's not the best of coffee but it wets the back of the throat,' she chuckled. 'Do you still hear from Meredith at all?'

'Very much so. She's one of my dearest friends. She wants me to go and work with her.'

'Does she dear....doing what?'

'Family Law....I've just qualified.'

'That's wonderful news! I'm delighted my dear.'

'Thank you. So you're working here now?'

'Heavens no! I do cover for someone two days a week and that's too much, believe me. It's not what you'd call the Ritz is it dear?' she laughed.

When they reached the cafeteria, Mark Wyndham was leaving with a cup of coffee in his hand and he held the door as they entered. 'Miss Henshaw,' he acknowledged with a pleasant smile.

Dr. McAndrew appeared surprised that he knew her. 'How's your fine young son?' she asked him.

'Still keeping me on my toes Doctor as always,' he replied before closing the door behind them.

Addressing Mattie she revealed, 'Mr. Wyndham has the most loveable wee child I've ever seen *and* he has inherited his father's good looks.'

They chose a table near the window overlooking the rose gardens. 'So tell me....how have you been Mattie?' she questioned caringly.

'Extremely busy,' she laughed. 'It feels strange to wake up in the morning and not be surrounded by piles of books.'

'Ah, I remember it well, but I meant, how do you *feel*? Have you been able to put everything behind you and move on with your life?'

'No, I'm still extremely distrustful of men. I tend to panic if I'm alone with a man so I do my best to avoid such situations but it isn't always possible.'

'Did you ever talk to anyone about it?'

'No, I couldn't bring myself to do that, in fact this is the first time I've admitted to anyone that there's still a problem.'

'Mattie, in your line of work you'll come across all kinds of people and half of them will be men but that doesn't mean they're child molesters. Just try to reach beyond that. I could put you in touch with a therapist who might help.'

'Thank you but I'd rather not. I vowed when the investigation was over that I would never discuss it again with a living soul. My recollections are much too painful. I don't want to keep reaping it up and I most certainly don't want to answer questions like, 'how did it make you feel?' posed by some faceless individual who has never suffered such indignity. I want to live my life one day at a time and someday, I might be able to eradicate some of the memories. I know that I won't ever trust a man again. The abuse I suffered never leaves my mind and the images are as clear to me now as the reality was then. I believe however, that I've become a more dynamic person in other ways and I can use that to advantage in my line of work.'

'Did you ever tell your brothers?'

'No, apart from the authorities, no one knows and I intend to keep it that way.'

'If ever you change your mind about counselling, please call me. Will you promise me that Mattie?'

'Thank you, I promise and now, if you'll excuse me, I need to get back to Seth. If I don't hurry, he'll be arranging a search party for me.'

'It's been lovely to see you again dear.'

'You too, and thank you for making time to talk to me.'

'Anytime, my dear....anytime at all and I do mean that,' she replied with a warm smile.

'Take good care of yourself Jack,' Mattie said as he threw down his bags on the pavement to give her a brotherly hug. 'I miss you so much when you're not here. I wish you could have stayed longer.'

'I'll be home again before long and I'll bring you something back from Hong Kong next time. Take proper care of yourself Seth and look after Mattie. She's all we've got now.'

'Don't worry about us! We'll be fine. Enjoy your trip,' he said, shaking Jack's hand vigorously.

As Mattie began to clear away the breakfast pots she ran the back of her hand across her tear-stained face before Seth could see she'd been crying but he was well aware of her distress each time Jack left. He sat down with his newspaper, leaving her to her thoughts.

As predicted, she recovered from her melancholy within minutes. 'Are you going out with Stephanie tonight?' she asked.

'Aye, we're off to the pictures. It's some mushy film she wants to see....girl stuff!' he grunted.

Mattie laughed. 'I suppose *you'd* have preferred a western to a 'chick-flick'.'

'Listen, I'd prefer anything to them 'weepies',' he replied sullenly.

'You have to realise Seth that girls are emotional. They like romantic films with happy endings where girl meets boy and they fall madly in love.'

'Not every girl falls in love. You don't for one! I wish you could fall in love and be happy.'

'I *am* happy Seth. Now I've made up my mind to work with Meredith, my entire life will change and I'm looking forward to providing a useful service to deserving people.'

He decided to change the subject. 'When you start work you'll need a car you know.'

'I'm aware of that and I've been making enquiries about driving lessons. Less than a mile away there's a new instructor who has recently opened a Driving School. Her name's Elizabeth Bass. The sign above the entrance reads 'Pass with Bass',' she grinned. 'I suppose it's quite a captivating name that would-be drivers will remember.'

'You're not seriously considering learning with a *woman* are you?'

'Don't be such a chauvinist Seth! Women make *much* better drivers. All men think about is speed. Women are much more careful.'

'Frustrating you mean! They just mosey along at twenty miles an hour in the middle of the road with no consideration whatsoever for other road users.'

'Be quiet Seth! You're just a bigot. *You* haven't learned to drive yet so what would *you* know?'

'I know that I'd never trust a woman to teach me, that's for sure!' he replied superciliously.

105

'Right, when I've passed, remember what you've just said when it's pouring down and you want me to drive you somewhere. You can walk!'

He muttered something inaudible and buried his head in his newspaper without further comment.

After giving him time to settle down, Mattie said, 'I was thinking of looking for a place to rent nearer to town. I can't stay here forever, taking advantage of Olive's hospitality. What would you think about sharing with me? It would be somewhere to bring Stephanie instead of roaming the streets every night and it would be easier for you to get to work if you were near the centre. We could share the expenses and I'd feel happier if someone else were there.'

He pondered for a moment before saying, 'I can't think of a reason why not.'

'Well, mull it over for a bit and we can talk about it later. There are a few things to consider. I'll need to get a deposit together for one.'

'I've got a bit put by. I've been saving three quid a week from my pay at the bookstore. I reckon I've got at least fifty quid saved up now,' he announced proudly.

'Fifty pounds? That's excellent Seth but I'm not taking *your* money. If we need to use more of yours towards the deposit, I'll pay back my share when I start work.'

'That's settled then. I'll look in the paper tonight and see what's available.'

Mattie threw herself down into the armchair and mumbled, 'I'm exhausted. I'm not opening another

106

box today. Everything else can wait. Rome wasn't built in a day as the saying goes.'

'We've all day tomorrow as well to get straight,' Seth reminded her. 'It's going to look smart when we've done but I were convinced that sofa weren't going to go through that doorway!'

'It's lovely isn't it? It was so thoughtful of Sally to give it to us, though why on earth she decided to replace her three-piece-suite is a mystery. It's just like new and it fits in here perfectly. It matches the carpet and curtains too.'

He smirked and awaited Mattie's outburst. 'Aye, that's what I call a damn good courting couch!'

'*Seth Henshaw*! *You're disgusting*!' she yelled at him, but when she saw he was grinning from ear to ear she laughed too. 'You just remember to behave yourself! There'll be none of your hanky-panky in this flat! Don't you just love it? A place we can call our own at last.'

'How do you fancy a cup of tea?'

'Thanks Seth, I'd love one, that's if you can find the kettle. The tea and sugar are in a cardboard box by the cooker and the milk's in the fridge.'

By the time Seth returned with the drinks, Mattie was sleeping soundly. She looked content and so he left her to recover from their arduous day.


It was late September and Mattie's third week at the office with Meredith. She was representing the father, Andrew Sutton, at a child custody hearing in Court the next day and Mattie had assisted her with some of the preparatory work.

Uncorroborated allegations of his cruelty to their two sons had been reported by his estranged wife at the point when Andrew Sutton applied to the Court for equal custody rights following their decision to live apart but an investigation undertaken by Mattie had revealed that Mrs. Sutton was planning to take the boys out of the country to join her new partner in Spain, though apparently that important fact had not been disclosed to the Court.

This was to be Mattie's first day in Court, her role being to keep focus on proceedings and produce the appropriate documents required by Meredith.

She catalogued the legal precedents meticulously and checked that all documents were present before bundling them together in chronological order.

Someday soon, she would present her first case in Court and she eagerly awaited that day's arrival.

'Do you think Mr. Sutton will get joint custody?' she asked Meredith on their way to Court.

She shrugged her shoulders. 'It's difficult to say. I can't predict the outcome. We've a strong case but at the end of the day, it's the Judge's decision. I'm not familiar with the one who's sitting today but as he's male, it might just give us the advantage.'

'Did you speak to Mr. Sutton last night?'

'Yes, we had a quick word about procedure and he was apprehensive about the outcome. Today's a very important day for him. He could lose both his boys and any appeal would be complex if they were out of the country. Still, we have to remain positive. Let's just keep our fingers crossed that the Judge is sympathetic to our case.'

The proceedings lasted almost an hour and when Meredith had earlier informed the Judge that it had come to her notice that the boys would be leaving the country, should sole custody be awarded to their mother, the Judge looked over his spectacles at her solicitor and questioned why this fact had not been reported sooner if indeed it were true.

When he raised his eyebrows and acted confused and restless, Mrs. Sutton became hysterical and had to be restrained by the usher.

'That should help us a lot,' Meredith whispered to Mattie with an optimistic smile.

In his summing up, the Judge made reference to a previous adjournment for the purpose of obtaining evidence to corroborate Mrs. Sutton's allegations of cruelty to the children and he concluded that in the absence of any such medical or other substantiating evidence having been provided, he could not accept that any acts of cruelty had occurred and it was his belief he added, that Mrs. Sutton had fabricated the verbal accusation against her husband to strengthen her custody application and damage his character.

'*I don't want him to have joint custody…. do you hear me?*' Mrs. Sutton screeched at the Judge and the usher had to move forward for a second time to suppress any further outburst.

'Loud and clear,' the Judge answered caustically. 'Having considered all the evidence before me from this and the foregoing hearings, my decision is that I award *sole* custody….to Andrew Sutton.'

Mrs. Sutton had to be escorted from the Court by her solicitor and the usher.

'That was fantastic,' Mattie chuckled as they left the building. 'I was holding my breath until he got to the end.'

'Well it was the right decision,' Meredith replied. 'The mother came across as a callous bitch....thank heavens!'

'And did you see Mr. Sutton? The poor chap was nearly in tears. Do you think she'll appeal?'

'If we can agree a mutually satisfactory provision for access, then she'll probably accept the decision. I'll be speaking to her solicitor about that later. The mere fact that she's leaving the country leaves little time for anything else and she won't like the idea of trailing back and forth from Spain. So tell me then, what's *your* verdict on your first case?'

'I enjoyed it if that's the right word.'

'Good....I'm pleased to hear it. There'll be plenty more to get your teeth into.'

'I've been meaning to ask, can you spare me for a couple of hours on Friday morning? Seth has to go back to hospital for his six-week check-up and I'd like to go with him.'

'You don't have to ask me. Take the morning off. Don't bother to come in first.'

'Thanks! Are you still OK for Saturday night?'

'I wouldn't miss it for anything. I'm dying to see your flat. Have you finished everything now?'

'More or less. Sally and Charles are both coming and Sadie is bringing Keith....her latest boyfriend. Seth's girlfriend Stephanie will be there as well, oh and Olive and Richard will be there too,' she added as an afterthought.

'Do you want me to bring anything?'

'No, the food's already organised. I'm doing a hot and cold buffet because there isn't enough room for everyone to sit at the table but there'll be plenty of food. Sadie volunteered to help prepare everything. I'll tell you what you *can* bring. You can bring your *boyfriend*,' she told her with an impish smile.

'And I'll tell *you* what....I'll bring mine if *yours* is going to be there,' she replied. 'Touché!'

'Er....excuse me! I've good reason for not having a boyfriend. What's yours?'

'I don't have *time* for a boyfriend.'

'What a load of rubbish! You should *make* time. You've heard the song, 'Nobody loves a fairy when she's forty'.'

'*I'm not forty*!' she protested. '*I'm thirty-seven*!'

'Actually, you're almost thirty-eight and that's a mere two years off forty, *that's all*,' she responded argumentatively. 'And you *still* haven't managed to find anyone suitable!'

'Well *you've* obviously not heard the expression, 'Life begins at forty' and for your information, not that I have to justify myself to you, I've had *plenty* of offers, so shut up because I don't want to listen to your derisive comments, thank you very much.'

Aware she had touched a nerve, Mattie attempted to apologise. 'I'm not trying to incite an argument. I am just saying that you can't be too choosy at your age. You have to *seize* your opportunities.'

'*My age*?....*My age*?' she cried heatedly. 'Then I suppose I ought to *seize* the next unattached bloke who happens to walk through the door.'

111

Mattie cocked her head to one side. 'Listen, I can hear somebody walking up the stairs....now's your chance!' she smirked.

There was a gentle knock on the door and Mattie laughed when Meredith gave her a threatening stare before calling out, 'Come in.'

Mattie exploded into a fit of hysterics as the door appeared to be thrust open by an enormous bouquet of flowers that totally screened the head and torso of the bearer, leaving nothing but his lower legs and highly polished shoes visible.

Meredith's face was crimson with embarrassment when the caller revealed himself and overzealously, she gushed, 'Why, Mr. Sutton....how wonderful to see you!'

With a beaming smile he declared, 'These are for you Miss Spencer....for everything you achieved.'

'They're beautiful! Thank you so much but there was really no need,' she replied, walking round her desk to relieve him of his gift.

'It's simply a small token of my appreciation for your hard work on my behalf. I think I'm going to enjoy a full night's sleep tonight. I can't remember the last time that happened.'

She smiled courteously. 'We were both delighted with the outcome too....It was a victory for common sense. Unfortunately in such cases, common sense doesn't always prevail. There's still much prejudice against fathers being awarded custody but it was an excellent result in your case.'

A couple of times when Meredith turned her head in Mattie's direction, she could see her listening to the enforced and uncomfortable exchange and that caused her further embarrassment.

In an attempt to bring her humiliation to a speedy conclusion she asked, 'Would you like some coffee before you leave?' and she was mortified when he said, 'Yes, that would be nice thank you. I thought I could smell freshly brewed coffee when I walked in your office.'

She turned to Mattie to ask if she would attend to it as Mattie anticipated her question.

'I'll see to it. White with sugar?' she enquired.

'Yes, thank you,' he replied.

Mattie hurried away but was mindful to leave the door ajar to eavesdrop on the ensuing conversation. She listened as Mr. Sutton coughed nervously and cleared his throat. 'I was wondering if I might take you to dinner Miss Spencer. It would give me very great pleasure to thank you properly for all you've done for me.'

Meredith was flabbergasted and following what seemed like an eternity before she could think of a suitable reply, she spluttered, 'Mr. Sutton....what a kind thought but I'm afraid that won't be possible. You are my client and as such, I'm not permitted to meet you socially. In this profession, we are bound by a strict regulatory code of conduct and it would be unethical for me to accept but I thank you most sincerely for your thoughtful invitation....'

'One lump or two?' Mattie hurriedly interjected, plonking his mug of coffee on the desk in front of him before he could make an excuse to leave.

'Er....one will be fine,' he replied distantly.

'Listen, I've just had a thought,' Mattie told him. 'I'm having my house-warming party on Saturday. I've recently moved to a flat with my brother Seth. Meredith will be there, so if you came as *my* guest, nobody would be breaking any rules as you're not my client. We could make it a *double* celebration. *Please* say you can come. That wouldn't breach any regulations would it Meredith?'

Meredith gave her a watery smile. 'Er....well, yes, er....I suppose technically it would be alright. Yes, of course....I mean....er....what a good idea Mattie.'

'Good, that's settled. I'll write the address down. The others will be there at seven-thirty. Don't have anything to eat beforehand because there'll be loads of food. I take it you'll be there then Mr. Sutton?'

'The name's Andrew and I'm delighted to accept. I'll look forward to it. Thank you er...'

'Mattie,' she replied.

As soon as he'd finished his coffee he stood up to leave. 'Shall I collect you on Saturday and then you could leave your car at home?' he asked Meredith.

'It's better that you don't but thanks for the offer. I'll see you at the flat,' she replied demonstratively, thus leaving no scope for further discussion.

'Oh yes, of course....I understand.'

'Thank you once again for the lovely flowers.'

'Seven-thirty on Saturday....Until then....' he said and with a wave of the hand he was gone.

Meredith waited until Andrew was out of audible range before glaring at Mattie. 'I can't believe you did that!' she chastised her furiously. 'Did I *ask* you to interfere in my life?'

'Did I ask *you* to interfere in *mine* ten years ago?' she asked with an expression of innocence.

'That was totally different as well you know. You needed my help then,' she replied defensively.

'And you need mine now. You need a guy and so I capitalised on the opportunity. I make no apology for that. You criticize me for avoiding men but you avoid men too. What's wrong with Andrew?'

'I never said there was anything wrong with him. I simply don't want to get involved with him!'

'Involved? Who mentioned getting involved? He made a kindly gesture! He invited you to dinner to thank you and you snubbed him, plain and simple! I'm not asking you to marry him or have his baby! It was one evening out he requested and you had to humiliate him. You can be so standoffish Meredith and it isn't an endearing quality, believe me. You'll end up on the shelf if you're not careful.'

'Well! That's really rich coming from you of all people. The kettle calling the pot black! You run a mile if you see a guy....I'm sorry Mattie. I shouldn't have said that. Forgive me please.'

She allowed the remark to pass unchecked. 'Just try to enjoy the evening. He seems a decent enough guy who's probably lonely and remember, there'll be plenty of people there so you can introduce him to someone else if you want to escape.'

'Promise me you won't *ever* do anything like that again.'

'I will *not* make any such promise!'

'You can be so exasperating,' she sighed. 'I don't know what I shall wear to the party now.'

Mattie scoffed, 'Now *Andrew* is coming, you are trying to make an impression. That's promising!'

'Shut up and find something to do,' she snarled in an attempt to appear annoyed but the twinkle in her eye said otherwise.

Mattie and Seth arrived fifteen minutes early for Seth's ten o'clock appointment to find the waiting room packed to the door. 'Look at all these people! We're going to be here for hours at this rate,' Seth grumbled. 'I told you not to bother coming.'

'What time's *your* appointment supposed to be?' the woman next to him enquired but before he had time to reply she told him she had been waiting for over an hour.

'We all have!' a bloke yelled out across the room. 'It's ridiculous! I don't know why they bother with appointments. They're always running late.'

'He'll have buggered off through another door for his coffee-break,' a different bloke piped up. 'He'll have made sure he weren't late for that!'

Everyone tittered and the room returned to a quiet normality for several minutes until the next patient arrived when the grumbles recommenced.

Suddenly the Consulting Room door opened and a woman walked out.

'About bloody time too!' an obese loud-mouthed man bellowed at the top of his voice to the woman who quickened her pace and rushed past everyone.

'Shut your gob,' his wife grunted, elbowing him hard in the ribs. 'Everybody's looking at you. Don't you care what folk think?'

'I don't give a bugger,' the man complained loud enough for everyone to hear. 'I've got piles and this chair's as hard as a bloody brick.'

Mattie lowered her head and attempted to stifle a giggle and Seth merely sighed. At that moment the nurse called out, 'Seth Henshaw.'

Everybody looked round and when Seth stood up, there was a communal gasp of disbelief.

Mattie, who hadn't intended joining her brother, shot after him like a conjoined twin and before the door closed she heard the obese man yell, 'Did yer see that? Did yer? They've just bloody-well walked in and gone straight in. Bugger me!'

'Good morning,' Mark Wyndham said, beaming broadly at Mattie as he made a hand gesture for her to take a seat. 'How have you been?'

'Very well thank you but then *I* haven't been ill,' she replied pointedly.

'No, of course not,' he replied with a short burst of laughter in the realisation she had read him like a book. 'It's good to see you again.'

Mattie inclined her head and smiled.

'So, Mr. Henshaw, have you had any recurrence of the asthma symptoms since I last saw you?'

'No, I've been alright and I haven't had to use my inhaler once.'

'Excellent! Do you remember to have it with you wherever you go?'

'Yes, it's here in my pocket now.'

Mark stood up. 'Would you sit on the bed please and open your shirt. I want to listen to your chest. Right, would you take a deep breath please....now out....and again. Fine....out,' he said, removing his stethoscope. 'Would you blow into this now? Take a deep breath, hold it and when I tell you to breathe out, continue breathing out until you have expelled all the air from your lungs. Well done,' he informed him as he read the result. 'You can sit down now.'

Mark returned to his desk. 'Everything seems to be normal and your chest sounds perfectly clear, so unless you suffer a further setback, there's no need for you to see me again.'

'Are there likely to be further problems?' Mattie asked.

'Well, it's a condition that can be triggered again by any allergic reaction. We've already established an allergy to dust. There is no evidence to suggest anything else but there could be. As long as he has his inhaler, he should be alright. If you're worried about anything, please call my secretary and I'll be happy to get back to you.'

'Thank you very much Mr. Wyndham.'

'My pleasure,' he replied looking deeply into her eyes. 'Good luck Mr. Henshaw.'

'Thanks. Oh, I almost forgot. We've changed our address. Do you need it for the records?'

'Yes, I'd better make a note,' he replied, looking directly at Mattie. 'I'll take your phone number too if I may,' he added and she detected a softer tone in his voice.

He stood up and shook Seth's hand and when he stretched out his hand towards Mattie, she replied likewise, while conscious that he lingered for some time before releasing his hold. Their eyes met one more time before she turned to leave the room and she made haste through the door ahead of Seth.

In silence, she hurried through the waiting room oblivious of the mutterings directed at them by the frustrated onlookers.

Mark Wyndham was in her thoughts and she was unable to comprehend his body language. Had she misread what she had seen she wondered, yet from their very first meeting she had seen something in him that stirred her within....his dark brown intense eyes that stared deeply into hers and that smile....a smile that spoke a thousand words. She was being ridiculous, she chastised herself. He was a married man with a family. What did *she* know about body language? She knew nothing at all about men.

'Get your skates on, there's a bus coming,' Seth said. He grabbed her hand as they ran towards the bus stop. 'Just made it!' he panted. 'I'll be thankful when you've passed your driving test.'

'I can't imagine why. You'll still be using the bus remember?'

Seth laughed and squeezed her hand. 'Thanks for coming with me Mattie. Mr. Wyndham's a nice guy isn't he?'

'Yes, he *is* a nice guy,' she replied and inwardly she sighed, 'He's a very very nice guy.'

At the end of a lengthy and exasperating morning surgery Mark felt weary.

His son Adam had disturbed his sleep for most of the night complaining of severe stomach pains that had continued intermittently until the early hours.

119

As a precautionary measure, he had brought him into work and Nurse Jackson had accompanied him to the Casualty Department to have him examined. Grumbling appendicitis was diagnosed by the duty doctor who had arranged immediate surgery for the child and throughout the morning, Mark had rushed back and forth to the children's ward to monitor his son's progress resulting in extremely long delays at his morning surgery.

The few short minutes spent in Mattie's presence had been the highlight of Mark's morning. Had he merely imagined some slight response when he had stared deeply into her eyes? She was unlike anyone he had known before....a mystical magical creature with the face of an angel and yet each time they had met, Mark had witnessed an aura of desperation or tristesse in her expressive eyes.

By the fountain, six weeks ago, he had wanted to learn more about Mattie but their moments together had been curtailed by her premature departure. He had watched her from his window as she wandered towards the fountain and had made it his business to follow her. He had relived those special moments a hundred times since.....

His thoughts were interrupted by nurse Jackson as she knocked on his door. 'Adam's awake and he's asking for you but don't worry, he's fine.'

He sighed audibly before saying, 'I can't believe I never thought of appendicitis. Not once did it enter my mind. I just thought it was a tummy upset.'

'Stop punishing yourself and go to him. It's over with now and it won't ever trouble him again,' she replied with a comforting smile. 'Everybody knows you're a terrific father Mark and anyone could have made such a simple error.'

Mark spent the next hour with Adam, relieved to learn there were no complications.

Adam was comforted by his father's presence and drifted in and out of sleep for the period of his visit. He would remain on the children's ward for three to four days, Mark was informed.

As he was leaving the ward, Dr. McAndrew was heading towards him en route to the cafeteria. 'Tell me, how's your wee boy?' she enquired caringly. 'I heard he'd been admitted.'

'He's doing well thanks and I feel so much better now I've spoken to him.'

'I'll slip in later to see him. He's such an adorable child and he'll be charging around before you know it. Children are so resilient. They soon bounce back. Have you had lunch? I know it's late but I'm away to grab a sandwich.'

'I haven't even had time for a drink today. Would you mind if I joined you?'

'I'd be glad of the company. It's been chaotic this morning....a typical Friday,' she grumbled.

'Tell me about it! I've had earache from most of my surgery patients this morning as I was running over an hour late. As it happens, I'm delighted I've caught up with you as I've been meaning to talk to you about something. What can you tell me about Mattie Henshaw?'

Mattie Henshaw?' she echoed and looked at Mark questioningly. 'Why do you ask?'

121

Mark smiled bashfully. 'Well....let's just say that I'm interested in her.'

'Correct me if I'm mistaken but I was under the impression that you already knew her.'

'I was treating her brother and our paths crossed a time or two. I'm aware that she's recently qualified as a solicitor but that's about all I know. I've tried talking to her but she shies away from me. I'd like to get to know her better but I'm afraid to scare her away.'

'She's not for you Mark. Just put her right out of your mind. You'll be wasting your time. Mattie's a career girl.'

'But career girls are allowed a life away from the workplace aren't they? I happen to like her.'

'Listen, I know what I'm talking about. You must trust me and heed my warning. I don't want you to get hurt. God knows you've had enough tragedy in your life already.'

He looked puzzled. 'I don't understand you. Why on earth would I get hurt?'

'I can't say anything more. I've already said too much. Please believe me Mark....Mattie Henshaw's definitely not for you.'

5

Sadie could barely contain her excitement as she and Mattie prepared the buffet food for the house-warming party. I simply couldn't believe it when I was accepted at Manchester. I'd almost given up on the idea of Teacher Training and Keith was over the moon when I told him.'

'It's going well between the two of you isn't it?'

'Yes, he's a super guy. He's very considerate and his parents are great too. His mum owns a boutique and she dresses exquisitely. His father's a physicist but I don't really know what he does. I didn't want to show my ignorance when it was mentioned but I know it pays well. They're not without money.'

'Neither are *your* parents!' Mattie reminded her. 'You're very fortunate Sadie. I'd give my right arm to have parents even if they were as poor as crows.'

'You have Seth and Jack and you have *me*.'

'You know what I mean. I don't feel like I *belong* anywhere. It'll not be too long before Stephanie and Seth get married so then he'll move out of here and Jack's talked about signing on for twenty-two years in the Navy so I'll be left on my own.'

Sadie gave her a hug. 'You'll meet somebody too Mattie. It just hasn't happened yet. You need to get out a bit and spread your wings a little. Don't you ever meet anyone in the workplace?'

'I meet lots of people but let's just say I'm not the marrying kind.'

'Well I certainly don't want to stay single. I want to get married and have a family of my own.'

123

Sadie wrapped the sandwiches in foil and placed them in the fridge. 'Right, what's next?'

Mattie checked her list. 'If you start the salad, I'll finish off the trifles and then I think we're done.'

'How are you doing with your driving lessons?'

'It's all coming together now. I've applied for my test this week. With a bit of luck, I'll be driving in another month.'

'Driving what? You don't have a car!'

'Seth and I are looking out for an old run-around. As long as it's reliable, we don't care what it looks like.'

'I'll ask dad if he'll make some enquiries at work. Remind me tonight.'

Seth arrived with an assortment of drinks as Sadie was about to leave. 'Thanks for your help,' he said, kissing her cheek.

'See you later,' she said as Charles could be heard sounding his horn.

When Andrew Sutton arrived with a large parcel and two bottles of Champagne, Seth lost no time in relieving him of the bottles. 'We don't want to drop them!' he said. 'I'm Seth, Mattie's brother.'

'Andrew Sutton....I'm an acquaintance of Mattie and Miss Spencer. Pleased to meet you.'

'She's called Meredith,' Mattie reminded him as she wandered over to greet him. 'She'll be back in a minute. She's just darted into the bathroom to make herself beautiful for you!'

He laughed and handed her the parcel. 'This is for you and your brother. If it isn't to your taste, please feel free to exchange it. You'll find a leaflet inside with others to choose from. It doesn't take a lot of brainpower to guess it's a picture. I thought it might fill a blank wall.'

'Oh Andrew! We didn't want you to bring a gift did we Seth?'

'Of course we did,' Seth contradicted, winking at Andrew. 'You told me earlier that you'd show him the door if he turned up empty-handed.'

'*I never did*! I said no such thing Andrew.'

'I believe you,' he laughed. 'Besides, I owe you and Meredith much more than a picture.'

'Wait till he gets the bill,' Meredith interrupted as an audible aside to Mattie. 'Hi Andrew!'

He turned to address her and for a moment he was speechless but his eyes revealed his thoughts. 'You look amazing Meredith.'

'Thank you very much. Let me get you a drink.' Whisking him away, she asked, 'What do you think of the flat?'

'I haven't seen it yet. I've only just arrived.'

'I'll take you round later then. Right, what would you like to drink?'

'I'll have a beer if there's one going please.'

Excitedly, Mattie ripped the wrapping paper from the picture. 'Oh look Seth!' she exclaimed. 'Isn't it lovely?

He nodded. 'I like that. I much prefer modern art to traditional. It'll look great on that bare wall.'

Mattie went to find Andrew to thank him for his gift. 'It's perfect and just what we needed in here. Everyone,' she called out, 'This is Andrew!'

Following a welcoming response, Seth turned up the music and one or two started to dance.

'You've made it very cosy here,' Sally remarked. 'Have you both settled in now?'

'Yes and we love everything about it. It feels like home and doesn't the suite look lovely?'

'Surprisingly so. It matches the décor perfectly.'

Stephanie wandered across to talk to them. 'Great party!' she told Mattie. 'Do you need any help with the food yet?'

'Just wait while I check....*Is anyone hungry*?' she yelled above the noise of the music.

'*Starving*!' a few of the guests called back to her.

As they arranged the food on the table, Stephanie made reference to Seth's final check-up with Mark Wyndham the previous day. 'I hear it went well.'

'It did and we were in and out in no time.'

'You were lucky! Mark was running over an hour late. It was bedlam. He was in such a state about his little boy.'

'Why, what do you mean?'

She explained what had happened and Mattie was concerned. 'Is the child alright now?'

'He's coming along nicely but it was a worrying time for Mark. If anything had happened to Adam, he would have gone crazy I'm sure, in fact I don't know how he kept it together when his wife died.'

'He's a widower?'

'Well and truly! According to rumour....and it *is* only rumour, his wife committed suicide,' she told Mattie. 'She died soon after Adam was born.'

'The poor man,' she said. 'How tragic!'

'Enough about Mark! Will you shout to everyone that the food's ready. We're here to enjoy ourselves and I, for one, have been looking forward to this all week.'

For the remainder of the evening, Mark's tragedy lingered in Mattie's thoughts. She knew how much it hurt to lose someone close and the indeterminable sadness it caused to those left behind.

'Help yourselves to food and drink. There's a lot left,' Seth announced as the party continued.

'That reminds me, there are a couple of bottles of Champagne in the fridge,' Andrew told Charles. 'If you'd like to fetch them, I'll ask Mattie to find the glasses and perhaps you'd like to propose the toast to their new home.'

'I'd be delighted,' he replied.

When the guests raised their glasses and wished them happiness in their new home, Mattie thanked them and said, 'There are two celebrations tonight. Andrew is over the moon to have received an Order granting him sole custody of his two children, so I would like to say very well done to Andrew.'

'To Andrew,' everyone called.

His cheeks reddened and he replied, 'Thanks but it was because of Meredith's endeavours. She must take all the credit. I did absolutely nothing.'

'*You* will be paying the bill,' she quipped. 'And I can assure you, *that* won't be *nothing*!'

Everyone laughed at her quick-witted remark and she took hold of his hand. 'Don't worry,' she said. 'You won't need to re-mortgage your house.'

'I was beginning to wonder,' he grinned.

'Will there be any more toasts to propose?' Sadie interrupted. 'I could get used to this. I'm partial to a drop of Champagne.'

Keith took her by the arm and led her towards the hall. 'There could be Sadie.'

'There could be what?'

Keith slipped his hand in his pocket and removed a small box and when he opened it, she stared wide-eyed at the beautiful diamond ring on a cushion of blue velvet. 'I was going to do this when we were alone,' he said softly. 'Will you marry me Sadie? I love you very much and I want to spend the rest of my life with you.'

'Yes, of course I'll marry you Keith,' she cried. 'I love you too.'

She clasped her arms around his neck and kissed him tenderly. 'I'm so very happy,' she whispered. 'In fact, I think this is the happiest day of my life.'

'Mine too darling. I was terrified you'd say it was too soon.'

'Why on earth would I have said that?'

'I thought you might have preferred to wait until you'd finished your studies.'

'Definitely not. I'll be home every night so it's no different than going to work.'

'Well I think it is. You'll have to keep on top of your study work.'

'That won't be every night. We'll have plenty of time together. I wonder what mum and dad will say when we tell them.'

'They already know and they're delighted. I felt I ought to mention it to them first and do it right.'

'We'd better get back before all the Champagne's gone. Three toasts at one party....that's something of a record don't you think?'

'I imagine there'll be more than three toasts at our wedding,' he said, giving her a peck on the lips.

Hand in hand, they returned to the others. '*May I have everyone's attention please*,' Keith bellowed at the top of his voice. Everyone listened in silence as he continued, with a broad grin stretching from ear to ear, 'I'm the luckiest guy alive. Sadie has just agreed to marry me and I'd like to propose a toast to my beautiful bride to be.'

'Could we change that?' Charles interrupted. '*I'd* like to propose a toast to both Sadie *and* Keith and I'd also like to take this opportunity of welcoming Keith as a new member of our family. I hope they'll be as happy together as Sally and I have been.'

'What an action-packed party this has turned out to be,' Mattie said joyfully as she admired Sadie's engagement ring. 'I'm really thrilled for you both. Do you intend to wait until you've finished college or are you planning to have an early wedding?'

'I don't fancy waiting three years but we haven't discussed it yet. That was the last thing I expected tonight. Keith was so nervous when he asked me,' she giggled. 'It'll be your turn soon Mattie and I'll be equally happy for you when that happens.'

Mattie smiled but said nothing in reply, unable to reveal that each time she looked at a man, she saw the face of Albert Parkes and was reminded of the revulsion that was forever in her thoughts. Would those memories *ever* be obliterated from her mind?

'We've heard from our Jack today. Instead of the usual postcard, he's sent us a long letter from Hong Kong. He thinks he might be home for Christmas. I do hope he is. It would be lovely for the three of us to be together.'

Seth studied the contents, slowly digesting all the information. 'It sounds like he's having a good time in Hong Kong. He made the right decision when he joined the Navy but I miss him.'

'Me too but it's wonderful for Jack. He's seeing such amazing things yet who'd have thought, when we were little, that one of us would be travelling the world? I'd give anything to visit far away places,' she sighed pensively.

'You must be joking!' he scorned. '*You* won't go *anywhere*!'

'I'd go with you or our Jack,' she snapped at him argumentatively. 'Alright, I admit I wouldn't go on my own but I'd feel safe anywhere with you.'

Sitting bolt upright in his chair, he stated, 'Right, let's put that to the test! There's a trip to the West End of London in November. The nurses who work with Steph have organised a weekend excursion to the Theatre Royal. Michael Crawford's appearing in 'Billy'. The coach leaves on the Friday evening about seven o'clock and arrives back home Sunday around six. It includes two nights' accommodation. The show's on the Saturday and there'll be time for the women to go shopping in the afternoon so do I put your name down? Are you going to join us and have a bit of social life for once?'

'Er....I don't know,' she replied nervously.

'*See what I mean*!' he castigated her. 'You won't do *anything*! That's the reason I never bothered to mention it in the first place.'

Defensively she protested, 'Well I wouldn't know anybody would I?'

'What's that got to do with anything? You know me and you know Steph! You don't have to know *everybody*. There's over fifty folk going.'

'And who would I share a room with? I wouldn't fancy being alone in a strange hotel and I wouldn't want to share with someone I didn't know.'

'You're just looking for excuses. You could share a twin room with Steph.'

'Yeah right,' she sneered. 'You'd love that and so would Stephanie....not that I'm interfering in your love-life.'

'I haven't a clue what that's supposed to mean,' he spluttered and blushed.

'Oh grow up Seth! I'm not your mum. You're old enough to make your own decisions. I'm not going to spoil your weekend away with Stephanie. I can just imagine what *she'd* say if you told her she had to share a room with me rather than you.'

'So that's the only reason you won't come then? What about Meredith? Why not ask her?'

'Because she spends her weekends with Andrew and the children.'

'Who else do you know?'

'Look, I'm not just asking *anyone* because I need a babysitter. I can't help the way I am so let it drop! You're beginning to get on my nerves now. I'm not coming and that's final.'

There was no further mention of the weekend in London until the following Saturday when Mattie joined Stephanie and her friend on a shopping spree to the City.

It was the first time Mattie had met Lucille, a fun girl and very much an extrovert who enjoyed life to the full. During the fifteen minute train journey, she had Mattie in stitches with her humorous anecdotal stories of incidents at the Royal where she worked with Stephanie but she was on a different ward.

She told of a process whereby new recruits were 'initiated' in the presence of their colleagues. 'You might think it a cruel practice but the victim shortly becomes the perpetrator as fresh members of staff join the service. The doctors participate too, as each one falls victim to an initiation ceremony soon after his or her arrival. It's just harmless fun and nobody takes offence or gets hurt,' she explained.

'It isn't uncommon to send a young male student nurse to the dispensary for a pair of fallopian tubes. The dispensary staff participate too and we wait on the ward until he returns carrying a pair of coloured drinking straws, one red, one yellow in his gloved hand, after being warned he mustn't bend them or allow them to become contaminated. Sometimes it goes on for days with some students performing the most ludicrous acts imaginable before they realise what's happening, much to the amusement of every other nurse. It's amazing how gullible some of the students can be. One lad even came close to tasting the contents of a bedpan to check if the patient had sugar!' Lucille laughed heartily as she recalled that incident and Mattie could hardly believe it, though Lucille assured her it was true.

'One incident backfired on the perpetrator though when a pimply-faced male student was sent to ask Matron if she had a brain cell. A second nurse was meant to stop him before he knocked on Matron's door but she'd been called to an emergency, so the unsuspecting clown barged in when summoned and asked her the question,' she shrieked.

'Matron bellowed, *'You evidently haven't so tell me now who's sent you here!'* and the scarlet-faced student, still unaware of his faux-pas, stuttered and told her that another nurse needed one right away. *'Is that so? Well young man, she'll need several by the time I've finished with her,'* she hollered before frog-marching him back to the ward to identify the culprit.'

Mattie screeched with laughter. 'I wouldn't have wanted to be in that nurse's shoes. I bet *she* was in trouble with Matron.'

'It was me and I certainly was!' she confessed. 'I had to empty bedpans for a week but it was worth it for the laugh everyone had. Matron's still there but she's retiring at the end of the year. I get along with her alright now. It must have been a couple of years later before she disclosed, confidentially, that when *she* was a young nurse, she was worse than anyone for playing tricks on new recruits. She was forever in trouble for *her* antics which goes to show we're all as bad as each other. It still happens every time someone new turns up.'

'You enjoy your work don't you?'

'I do, most of the time and we have an excellent social club as well. There's always something new being organised. Steph tells me that you're joining us on the London weekend trip next month.'

'Is that right?' she replied wide-eyed, slanting her gaze in Stephanie's direction. 'How strange, I don't seem to recall my agreeing to that.'

Stephanie was noticeably embarrassed. 'Seth told me what you'd said and so I offered to share a room with you. Please come with us Mattie. I don't want you to miss such a good weekend away. We'll have a brilliant time.'

'*I'm* not sharing with anybody,' Lucille informed her. 'You're welcome to share a twin room with me if you like.'

'Right, that's two offers you've had so there'll be no more excuses. You're coming,' Stephanie stated.

Mattie was given no option other than to concede defeat. 'Alright then, I'll come as long as you don't go off with anyone and leave me on my own.'

'I won't,' Lucille promised.

For the rest of the day, Mattie thought of nothing else. She had never been to London and she eagerly awaited the trip.

Charles phoned Mattie the next week with good news. 'I think I might have found you a small car. It's three years old with very low mileage and it's only had one owner. It belongs to one of the lads in the office who's ordered a new one. I've had a look at it and apart from a very small bump at the back, it's in good condition. When I told him you were a new driver who needed a reliable car he assured me it was sound, so if you'd like to have a look at it, he said he'd bring it round and I'll come with him.'

She was overjoyed. 'Oh, that's great Charles. I'm taking my test next Friday and fingers crossed, I'll pass. My driving instructor says I shouldn't have a problem.'

'Right, I'll call you again when I've made proper arrangements. Any night after seven?'

'That's perfect. I'm in all week. Thanks Charles.'

When he arrived the next evening with the young man named Alec, Mattie was thrilled with the car.

'I bought it new and it's been regularly serviced. It runs very well and it's reliable,' Alec assured her with a sincere smile.

When the selling-price was under discussion, she looked to Charles who intervened and negotiated a lower price that Mattie was happy to pay.

'Let me take you out on Saturday and I'll knock another tenner off,' he propositioned her.

'I'm more than happy with the price as it is,' she replied good-humouredly.

Alec grinned. 'You drive a very hard bargain. Go on then, twenty quid off. That's my final offer!'

Charles fidgeted uncomfortably but Mattie was in total control of the situation. 'I'll be out in my new car on Saturday night but thanks for the offer,' she replied with a light-hearted smile.

Alec looked downhearted as Mattie counted out the money. 'You can be stakeholder, Charles and if it's convenient Alec, you can leave the car at work and I'll pick it up on Friday around noon. I'll need the particulars for my Insurance Company now and then I think that's everything.'

Charles gave her an apologetic glance as they left and phoned her later to express his sincere regret. 'I didn't anticipate that happening and I'm very sorry if Alec offended you. He's a pleasant enough young chap who really didn't mean any harm.'

'Think nothing of it. I've had plenty of practice at saying no and it didn't bother me in the slightest. I was worried I might have offended him. Did I?'

'I doubt it but I think his pride might have been a little dented,' he laughed. 'He's quite a ladies' man and rarely receives a refusal but he'll soon get over it. I'm quite sure of that.'

'No harm done then. Thanks for all your help.'

'Anytime,' he replied.

Following a wobbly start to her driving test when she stalled the engine, she managed to settle down and soon began to feel at ease with her driving.

Mattie had requested a female examiner but when she arrived at the test centre, she was informed that the female examiner had been replaced by a male as she'd had to go home because she was unwell.

Mattie was given the option to go ahead with the male or reschedule her test date and so, after careful consideration, she chose the male, rather than wait what might be many weeks for a new test date.

She felt ill-at-ease sitting alongside an unfamiliar male and for several minutes was unable to relax or concentrate fully on her driving. Had she refused to take her driving test that day, then questions would have been asked of her and she would have found those questions very difficult to answer, particularly if posed by Seth.

At the end of her test, she smiled with relief when the examiner handed her the pass certificate and her instructor, who eagerly awaited her return, revealed equal sentiments of delight with the result.

When she took Mattie to the factory to collect her car, Charles accompanied Alec to the car park so he could explain all she needed to know.

'Are you sure you won't change your mind about tomorrow?' he asked optimistically.

Once again, Charles was tense but Alec laughed heartily when she replied, 'Thanks for the offer but I don't want to be another notch on your bedpost. I hope you like your new car.'

'It's your loss!' he stated.

'I know....it's disappointing but I imagine I'll get over it in time. Nice doing business with you.'

When Alec returned indoors, Charles smiled and said, 'You handled that very well. I was very proud of you Mattie.'

'One must move on Charles. It's a painfully slow process but I'm getting there by degrees. I'm sure I would have been tongue-tied had I been alone but your being here helped. Thanks for everything.'

'Are you sure you feel confident to drive home? I could follow on behind if you like.'

'I passed, so the examiner must have thought me capable. I'll drive round the factory yard to get used to the car and I'll be fine. It's not far to drive home. By the way, don't forget to tell Sally and Sadie that I passed first time.'

'They won't let me forget. I'll see you soon.'

As Mattie packed her overnight bag and knelt on the lid to fasten the zip, she was very excited about the forthcoming trip to London. Michael Crawford had long been one of her favourite entertainers.

Stephanie had provided her with a brief account of the storyline of 'Billy' while informing her that the reviews of the show had been excellent.

The white blouse she had recently bought added the finishing touch to the elegant navy trouser suit she had chosen to wear for the journey.

When the taxi driver sounded his horn, she rushed to the window and acknowledged him. 'You'd best hurry up....the taxi's here Seth,' she called to him.

Carrying his raincoat across his arm, he hurriedly appeared with his bag. 'I'm ready now,' he panted. 'Sorry for keeping you waiting. I could have done with an earlier finish today.'

'Are you sure you've got everything?'

He checked his inside pocket. 'Yes, everything's here. Give me your bag and let's be on our way.'

Lucille and Stephanie were already seated on the coach when they arrived.

'*Here Mattie*,' Lucille called to her and waved to attract her attention.

'Are we the last ones to arrive?' she asked as she hastily took her place beside Lucille.

'No, there's half a dozen missing yet. Would you prefer a window seat?'

'No, I'll have it coming back. Stay where you are. I can see everything from here thanks.'

After loading their bags in the hold, Seth climbed on the coach and sat down next to Stephanie. 'That were a rush,' he panted. 'I got home late and hardly had time to get myself washed and changed.'

'Pity you did. I could have given you a bed-bath when we arrived,' she whispered in his ear.

'Just behave,' he laughed.

'Where's the fun in that?'

Seth took hold of her hand. 'I can't tell you how much I've been looking forward to this break. Did your mum have anything untoward to say?'

Stephanie smiled. 'She threatened me not to bring any trouble home.'

'We won't,' Seth promised as he patted his breast pocket. 'Trust me!'

Lucille stood up and looked around. 'Apart from that double seat across from you, the coach seems to be full now. We should be on our way soon.'

'Sorry guys!' somebody called out apologetically. 'I'll remember to get a nine till five job if I'm ever here again.'

Mattie leaned into the aisle to catch a glimpse of the latecomer and her heart missed a beat as Mark Wyndham approached the empty seat beside hers.

When he turned to ask if the seat had been taken, his eyes expressed both surprise and pleasure at her presence. 'Hello!' he greeted her warmly and with a broad smile. 'I didn't know you'd be here.'

Returning his smile, she answered, 'I'm here with Lucille and Stephanie.'

After removing his jacket, he sat down alongside. He seemed different she thought, eyeing him from head to toe. Wearing casual jeans and a blue open-necked shirt below a light tan sweater, he appeared much less intimidating than when formally dressed at the hospital.

'Are you a fan of Michael Crawford?' she asked.

He grinned. 'I must admit that I am. He's terrific and so versatile. He epitomises the word stupidity. Did you ever watch, 'Some mothers do 'ave 'em'?'

'I've never missed a single episode,' she giggled. 'Aren't we sad?'

'I wouldn't say that. After a hard day's work, it's good to kick off my shoes and relax. A good laugh is better than any tonic, they say.'

'*Who* says? I haven't heard that one before.'

'I've no idea. It was probably Michael Crawford,' he smirked. 'So are you planning to go shopping in the West End?'

'I intend to go shopping in *every* end if I've time. It's my first trip to London.'

'You'll be impressed then, I can promise you that. A weekend isn't very long but you will experience a cultural difference from that found in the north of England. I'll guarantee you won't be disappointed. It's a truly amazing city. I've been many times and there's always something new to see or do.'

Mattie felt a dig in the ribs. 'Are you with me or with him?' Lucille questioned tetchily.

'Sorry,' she whispered. 'I was rather surprised to see him, that's all. I didn't know *he* would be here.'

'So how do you two know each other?'

'I met him at the hospital. 'He treated Seth when he had an asthma attack.'

140

Lucille grunted, 'You must have created quite an impression. Mark isn't generally *that* familiar with patients' relatives. Come to think of it, he's not *that* familiar with staff either. I've been after him for a year or more but he's never even given me a second look. Maybe you could help me out this weekend, that is if you're not after him yourself.'

'*Lucille*! I am most definitely not *after him*. I was grateful when he helped Seth and he was very kind. Mr. Wyndham's not even a friend. He's merely an acquaintance. You're welcome to him, that's if he wants you. I haven't the slightest interest in him.'

'Alright, don't get your knickers in a twist. I only asked. Like I said, I'll need your help. *Will* you help me?' she asked, fluttering her eyelashes.

'I'll do what I can but we probably won't see that much of him.'

'Try to find out the name of the hotel he's staying in. We're not all in the same one.'

Mattie continued to peer out of the window at the ever changing scenery that fascinated her when she felt another dig in the ribs.

'*Well go on then, ask him*,' Lucille shrieked.

'What now?'

'*Yes*! I'll look away. Catch his attention and bring it up in the conversation in a casual....er....discreet kind of way. Don't make it obvious. Just try to be subtle.'

As she turned towards Mark he looked at her and smiled. Though barely able to contain her laughter, with a serious expression she said, 'Lucille wants to know which hotel you're staying in.'

He threw back his head, expelling a throaty laugh only too aware of Lucille's efforts to snare him and Mattie's unfortunate remark had served to provoke the spontaneous eruption of laughter for which he was immediately embarrassed and remorseful.

Lucille was horrified and turned her head towards the window. 'Just you wait till we're alone. I'll kill you....I will, I'll kill you,' she snarled through her teeth.

Mattie and Mark exchanged glances and laughed silently together....and there it was again....she saw it clearly....that intense look in his eyes as his face took on a more serious expression. When she could hold his gaze no longer, she turned her head away but Mark had recognised it too in Mattie's eyes.

Following his conversation with Dr. McAndrew, he had tried hard to cast her from his mind yet she was there again at the very forefront of his thoughts and she was within arm's length of him. Why was it her presence disturbed him so much? Why did she excite and arouse him with little more than a casual glance or a shake of her beautiful hair?

He maintained a close watch until Lucille closed her eyes and stretched out his hand towards Mattie, gently tapping her arm.

When she turned towards him, he mouthed, 'Do you have a pen?' and reinforced his question with a hand gesture depicting a writing hand.

Mattie opened her bag and passed him her Parker fountain-pen, given to her by Olive and Richard at her celebration party.

'Paper?' he mouthed.

She handed him a small notepad and watched as he scribbled a note. He tore off the sheet on which he had written, 'I'm sorry for laughing. She's a man eater! Nice pen! Was it a gift?'

Mattie nodded when she had read the note and he passed her another. 'You can't beat having a stylish pen. You can always judge a person by the pen they use.'

She stretched out her hand for the pen and wrote below his remark, 'Is that also a dictum of Michael Crawford?'

He smiled as he wrote his reply. 'No that was me. Promise me something....PLEASE. Don't leave me alone with Lucille, not for one solitary second. She scares me to death.'

She passed him her reply. 'OK I promise.'

He wrote his final note and returned the notepad to her. 'Thanks Mattie!' it said.

Mattie was filled with mixed emotions. Mark had never addressed her by her Christian name before. It had always been 'Miss Henshaw' until now. For the first time in her life, she liked her name and in her imagination, she could hear Mark's gentle voice saying it and it pleased her very much. She wished *she* could be the same as other women....like Sadie who had recently become engaged to be married to Keith....or like Stephanie who gazed affectionately at Seth and who couldn't wait to spend the weekend away with the very man she worshipped....but *she* was different. *She* would never experience true love or the warmth of a man's body when he held her in his arms....Yes, *she* was different....

She wiped away a single tear that trickled down her cheek before she closed her eyes and fell asleep.

When she awoke some time later, the City lights of London were emblazoned on the skyline.

'You're good company!' Lucille remarked.

Mattie glanced at her apologetically. 'I'm sorry. I must have dropped off.'

'Ugh! That's an understatement. You've been fast asleep for ages....anyway, it doesn't matter. I dozed off too. I feel peckish now. How about you?'

'I could manage a hot drink. A nice milky coffee would go down a treat.'

'We'll find somewhere when we get off. I need a pee! I'm bursting!'

'Isn't there a toilet on the coach?'

'Maybe.' She leapt to her feet and looked round. 'I think there's one at the back. Let me pass and I'll have a look.'

When Mattie moved into the aisle, she was inches away from Mark and she smiled. Somehow, he had managed to curl his long legs round the double seat and he was sound asleep. Several passengers were moving about, preparing to leave the coach but he didn't stir. 'Mark,' she said softly and when he still didn't respond, hesitantly she stretched out her arm and found the courage to prod him. '*Mark*,' she said louder. He opened his eyes and looked at her. 'It's time to wake up. We're almost there.'

'What....oh....thanks. Did you say we'd arrived?'

'Almost. Come on, wake up Mark,' she repeated. 'Everybody's making a move now, so you'll be left behind if you don't hurry.'

144

When the driver released the door it was bitterly cold outside and the wintry night wind was quick to infiltrate the coach causing Mattie to shiver.

'The Trafalgar,' the driver shouted out. 'Please be sure to collect all your belongings before you leave the coach. Remember to check under your seat too.'

Lucille returned quickly to her seat and with her arms wrapped around her body she shuddered. 'It's freezing outside,' she grumbled. 'I wish I'd brought my coat on the bus now instead of packing it in my bag. I didn't think it'd be this cold.'

'We'll be inside in a few minutes,' Mattie said.

When Mark remained seated, Lucille asked, 'Are you not getting off here?'

'Yes but there's no hurry. My bag's in the hold. I've nothing on the coach but my jacket.' Rubbing his hands together he remarked, 'It's a trifle nippy!'

'It's bloody freezing,' she corrected him. 'Now if you were a *gentleman* Mark, you'd offer to lend me your thick sweater.'

'Yes and if you were a *lady* Lucille, you wouldn't presume to ask!' he replied with an artificial smile and Mattie laughed.

'Charming! Did you hear that?'

As Lucille slowly edged her way down the aisle, Mark reminded Mattie of her promise.

'Don't worry, I haven't forgotten.'

'When they had checked in and as Stephanie and Seth were about to go to their room, Mattie asked, 'Are you joining us on the City trip tomorrow?'

'If you don't see us at breakfast, then we won't be coming. We'll catch up with you whenever....'

'*Have a good night*!' Lucille called after them in a sing-song voice, grinning from ear to ear.

Mattie was furious. 'Just keep quiet Lucille.'

'Oh for heaven's sake, why don't you lighten up? I'm just having fun!'

'Goodnight ladies,' Mark said. 'I'll see you in the morning.'

'Goodnight,' they replied together.

'Not bad....not bad at all,' Lucille remarked as she wandered around the bedroom. 'This is *much* better than I expected. We were in a right dump last time! Which bed do you want?'

'I don't mind. They're both the same.'

'Take that one then,' she said, throwing her travel bag on her bed. 'Right lady, I've got a bone to pick with you! What were you doing, dropping me in the mire like that with Mark? That was about as subtle as a train wreck.'

Mattie reacted defensively. 'I could see no point in beating about the bush Lucille. You wanted me to ask didn't you? Besides, I didn't want him to get the wrong idea about *me*. It was *you* who wanted to know and I intended to make that perfectly clear.'

'I can't argue with that! You made it clear alright! That was apparent from Mark's hysterical outburst. I've never felt so humiliated in all my life.'

'I'm pretty sure you have but anyway I'm sorry. I was just having fun,' she responded deprecatingly, echoing the expression that Lucille had used earlier with regard to Seth and Stephanie.

Lucille heaved a sigh. 'I was never in the running with Mark. God knows I've tried hard enough.'

146

Mattie flashed her a cursory glance. 'Then maybe you're trying *too* hard,' she suggested.

'No, I don't think it's that. As far as I'm aware he hasn't dated anyone at work and there are plenty of girls to choose from. My belief is that he won't mix business with pleasure.'

'Maybe Mark's not ready for another relationship yet. He recently lost his wife didn't he?'

'That was ages ago. I thought he'd come to terms with that now. He was distraught when it happened and he took a lengthy period of time off work. We didn't find out very much. There was a great deal of speculation regarding his wife's death and all kinds of rumours were floating around the hospital but he never spoke about it when he returned to work and nobody liked to mention it.'

Mattie finished all her unpacking and stuffed her holdall in the bottom of her wardrobe. 'Are we too late for cup of coffee? I'm parched.'

Lucille looked at her watch. 'It's only ten-thirty. Maybe they'll serve coffee at the bar but I'd prefer something stronger. Shall we go down and see?'

Mattie nodded. 'We need to find out where we go for breakfast and what time it's served.'

En route to the bar, they called at reception where they were told that breakfast was available between seven and ten o'clock. The receptionist pointed out the restaurant, at the same time advising them that eight-thirty was their busiest time.

'Nine o'clock will be early enough,' Lucille said. 'We'll be finished in plenty of time for the coach at ten o'clock.'

Mattie recognised a few of the members of their party and Lucille wandered over to join them.

One young man jumped up and pulled two extra chairs towards their table.

'This is Mattie,' Lucille said. 'She's the sister of Seth who's going out with Steph on surgical.'

'What would you like to drink?' asked the young man who had brought them their chairs, posing his question at Mattie.

'Thank you. I'd like a cup of coffee please if they serve it here.'

'How about you?' he asked Lucille.

'I could murder a gin and tonic please.'

Addressing Mattie, 'I'm Tom,' he told her with a broad smile. 'I won't be long.'

'What does he do?' Mattie enquired of Lucille as he walked across to the bar.

'Tom's a junior doctor and it's his first year at the hospital. He's twenty-five and available. I could put in a good word for you if you were interested.'

Mattie's cheeks flushed. 'I'm not the *slightest* bit interested, thank you very much,' she said heatedly. 'I was merely trying to making polite conversation if you must know.'

'Alright, keep your shirt on. I thought you....'

'I *said* I'm not interested....right?' she interrupted dogmatically. 'Don't you dare say a word! I mean it! I'm getting sick and tired of other people telling me how to lead my life.'

'Listen, I'm sorry Mattie. I didn't mean to upset you. I was just trying to make conversation too. Is there something wrong?'

148

'No, I'm tired I guess. I shouldn't have snapped at you like that. I'm sorry too....I overreacted.'

Tom returned with Lucille's drink and sat down. 'They'll be here with yours shortly. They'd just run out of coffee so they're making a fresh pot.'

'Lovely. Thanks Tom.'

'So Mattie, what do you do?'

'I'm a solicitor.'

'What....like property transactions....that kind of thing?'

'No, I practise Family Law.'

'Ugh, that's sounds boring. Now if you had said Criminal Law, I would have thought that might be interesting but Family Law....'

'You'd be surprised. It covers a very wide field.'

'Such as?'

'Hey! I'm taking the weekend off remember? It's not *that* enthralling that I want to spend my leisure time discussing it. Suffice to say, I enjoy my work and it pays the weekly shopping bill.'

'And some!' he laughed aloud. 'I've yet to meet a solicitor who wasn't wealthy.'

'You've met a lot then?' she quipped.

He pondered momentarily before answering her. 'Now I come to think of it, I can't bring anybody to mind. I know,' he laughed, 'That Perry Mason chap but he was more into mysteries.'

'Pity he's not here then. He might have been able to throw some light on what happened to the coffee you ordered.'

Tom looked round the room but there was no sign of the waiter. 'I'm sorry. I'll chase it up at the bar.'

Without delay, he returned with a tray and as he placed it in front of her he said, 'If you want a job doing, do it yourself. Let me pour. Cream madam?'

'Yes, thanks. This is very nice and well worth the wait,' she said as she took a sip.

'You're welcome,' he replied, shuffling his chair closer to hers.

'Is there room for one more here?' someone said and Mattie recognised Mark's voice.

Everyone moved round to make enough room for another chair.

'I thought you'd gone to bed Mattie.'

'I wanted a coffee first.'

He raised his eyebrows. 'It keeps you awake you know. Caffeine is a stimulant.'

'I'll risk it. It's delicious.'

Tom interrupted, 'So tell me, how long have you been practising law?'

'Only for a few months, though it seems so much longer.'

'Does Family Law involve Court work too or is it merely pen-pushing?'

'Not at all. There's oodles of Court work. That's what makes it so interesting.'

'If I ever need a Family Lawyer, I'll know where to come now,' he said, taking hold of her hand.

She withdrew her hand with the speed of a bullet, causing Tom to spill half of his beer down the front of his shirt. 'I am *so* sorry,' Mattie cried, appearing flustered. 'You startled me.'

'Don't worry. There's no harm done. As a matter of fact, you startled me too.'

150

Mattie's involuntary reaction didn't go unnoticed by Mark who recalled their first meeting when she had insisted on Sister Flanagan's attendance during their brief discussion about Seth's medical history. 'Are you alright?' he asked her with concern.

'Yes, it was just a stupid accident. I'm overtired I expect. It's been a very demanding week.'

Mark cast his eyes around the others who were all involved in conversation before he leaned forward. 'If ever you feel in need of anyone to talk to about *anything* Mattie, I'm an excellent listener. That's all I wanted to say.'

'I don't know what you mean.'

'I believe you do. Sometimes it can be difficult if not impossible to find a suitable person in whom to confide. I know that as well as anybody. The offer's there....that's all I want to say. The rest is up to you. May I get you another drink....a proper drink?'

'No thanks. If I can manage to drag Lucille away, I'm going up to my room. Will you be going on the City trip tomorrow?'

'Will you?'

'Yes, it leaves at ten.'

'Then I'll be there. Please remember what I said,' he advocated gently. 'Goodnight.'

'Goodnight and thank you Mark. Thanks for the coffee Tom and it was nice talking to you....really. I'd like to apologise again for my silly accident. I'll see you around.'

'I hope so,' he replied.

Unable to fall asleep, Mattie stared at the ceiling, repeatedly counting the pattern repeats in the white embossed paper while sleep persistently continued to be an unattainable yearning.

She remembered Mark's words of concern but of all the people in the world, he was the one in whom she couldn't confide, despite his having both seen and sought some explanation for her earlier shock-reaction to Tom's sociable gesture. Mark must have believed her mad to behave as she did but *was* she indeed mad she asked herself. Could Albert Parkes have driven her to the very brink of insanity by his vile deeds? Still to this day she had nightmares and only too often would she awake cold and clammy, expecting to find that evil man in her bed. Perhaps Dr. McAndrew had been right to advocate therapy but how could she ever describe and convey those heinous experiences to a total stranger? She wanted all such memories obliterated from her thoughts yet psychotherapy would only serve to reinstate to the very forefront of her mind, every monstrous detail of what men do to women in the name of love.

She wept silently for some time before eventually falling into a deep and gratifying sleep.

'You're quiet,' Lucille observed as Mattie studied the breakfast menu.

'I didn't sleep much. Maybe it was because I was in a strange bed.'

'Well, I slept very well. I went out like a light and woke up ravenous. I'm having a full English,' she announced, closing her menu. 'I'm that hungry, I'm sure I could eat a cow on a doormat!'

Mattie laughed. 'I haven't heard that one before. I'm just having toast and marmalade.'

'Huh! I'm not surprised you're like a bean-pole if that's all you have for breakfast.'

Angrily, she replied, 'I eat what I want to eat and I am *not* like a bean-pole.'

'I was paying you a compliment, so don't act so snotty! You have a terrific figure, whereas....look at me....I'm like the proverbial Michelin man! I have more spare tyres than a heavy-goods vehicle and I can't imagine why when I'm rushed off my feet all day at the hospital.'

When the waitress appeared and placed Lucille's huge breakfast in front of her, Mattie said, 'That's why!'

'That's why what?'

'That's why you're overweight. There's got to be over a thousand calories on that plate and I expect you'll be having toast and marmalade too.'

'I'm on my holidays,' she said defensively. 'I've paid for a full breakfast so I'm having one.'

'Suit yourself but don't complain when you can't fasten your zip tonight! I'll be able to fasten mine.'

'May I join you?' Mark asked.

'Please,' Lucille spluttered through her mouthful of food before gulping it down. 'Sorry about that,' she added, clearing her throat.

'Good morning Mattie. Did you sleep well?'

'Yes I did Mark, thank you.'

Lucille gaped at her in disbelief. 'You said to me that you'd hardly slept a wink!'

Mattie was embarrassed. 'Pardon me Lucille but I believe I said that it took me some time to drop off because I was in a strange bed,' she corrected her.

Mark laughed. 'I'm sorry I asked. I wasn't trying to provoke an argument between the two of you.'

'Just ignore her,' Lucille stated. 'She's probably annoyed because I wouldn't let her dip her toast in my egg! What are you having?'

'Just something light. Besides, there isn't enough time now to wait for a cooked breakfast. I'm on the last minute because I've been talking to Adam.'

'Has he fully recovered now?' Mattie enquired.

'Er, yes thanks,' he replied, surprised to hear she was aware of his son's recent illness. 'How did *you* know about Adam?'

'Girl talk!' Lucille interrupted before Mattie had chance to respond. 'Mattie knows every little detail about you Mark. She makes it her business to find out, don't you? I'm just nipping to the loo....'

Mattie cast a disapproving look in her direction as she scurried away and Mark laughed. 'Now can you see why I don't want to be alone with her? Lucille suffers from verbal diarrhoea and you can't predict what she'll say next. Her nickname at work is 'rent-a-gob'. I suppose her heart's in the right place but I have to admit she's far too much for me to handle.'

'Well, for the record, I didn't ask anything. It was Stephanie who told me about your son's operation. It was the same day that Seth had his check-up and she was very surprised to learn that *we* hadn't been delayed at your surgery when everyone else had, by more than an hour.'

'Ah....I've been well and truly exposed now!' he revealed with a broad grin.

'Why, what do you mean?'

'I'd seen your brother's name on the surgery list so I made a point of seeing him on time,' he stated. 'I thought, or I should say hoped, that you might be with him and I wanted to create a good impression by not keeping you waiting.'

'You did, but you created mayhem in the waiting room as well. World War Three almost broke out as Seth's name was called because we'd arrived only moments before. I hadn't intended coming in but I needed to escape from the other patients who were revolting because we'd jumped the queue.'

'I found them rather revolting too,' he sniggered. 'I'm glad you *did* come in as it was the highlight of my day,' he added softly.

She lowered her head to avoid eye contact. It was a complimentary remark and Mattie was becoming concerned. The last thing she wanted was to cause Mark any pain and she couldn't go on believing she was imagining things. He wasn't simply patronising her. He wasn't that kind of man. He was telling her that he enjoyed her company, in a round about way and waiting for her like response.

Fortunately, Lucille saved the moment when she reappeared in her usual buoyant fashion and asked whether there was any coffee left in the pot.

'Hurry up then. It's almost ten,' Mark replied.

If there had ever been any doubt in Mattie's mind, it was laid to rest when he leaned towards her and whispered, 'Right, cards on the table! I won't give up Mattie. I'll never give up and believe me, I can be *very* persistent.'

She stared at him blankly and in silence.

Nothing further was said and she made a point of choosing a window seat on the City trip in the hope that her obvious act of rejection might curb Mark's enthusiasm to pursue her.

During the oratory, the passengers were directed to look to their right at the statue of Eros and when she looked across, Mark was watching her with an expression that acknowledged his awareness of her actions. He winked at her and his smile broke into a laugh when she flashed him a disparaging glance.

When the three hour trip was drawing to a close, Lucille was again thinking about food. 'We've time for a quick sandwich before we go shopping,' she told Mattie.

'Alright but make sure it's very quick. I'm dying to look round all the shops. Don't forget, I haven't been here before.'

'Are you coming with us for a sandwich Mark?' Lucille asked.

Mattie nodded to confirm her consent when Mark raised his eyebrows to seek her approval.

In the café, their conversation evolved around the City trip and when Mark had learned earlier that it was Mattie's first visit he wasn't surprised that she had been overwhelmed by the splendid architecture. She was predominantly impressed by the Palace of Westminster, describing it as the most phenomenal exhibit of craftsmanship and creativity imaginable.

'I would have enjoyed seeing more of the sights and I'll definitely come here again. I love looking at beautiful things,' she told Mark as they prepared to leave.

'So do I,' Mark responded softly and with hidden meaning that only Mattie recognised. 'Enjoy your shopping and I'll see you later.'

She was fascinated by the London Underground system and during the return journey, she admitted to Lucille that she would never have found her way around London without her help.

'You would,' Lucille replied. 'Once you've done it, it's easy and it's the quickest way to travel.'

'Weren't the Christmas decorations wonderful in the stores? I've never seen *anything* quite as mind-boggling and I most certainly wasn't expecting that in November.'

'They're different every year. Each store chooses a theme and I suppose they try to outdo each other.'

'Well, they're certainly innovative. How on earth do they conjure up their themes? That's what I want to know. Where do they get such ideas from?'

'Search me! The United States I would imagine. I believe their stores are incredible at Christmas. Are you happy with what you've bought today?'

'Yes I am. I've enjoyed our shopping very much. I'm pleased you twisted my arm to join you for the weekend. I wouldn't have missed it for anything.'

'Do you mind if I ask you something Mattie?'

'What's that?'

'Don't get angry....what's with you and Mark?'

Her cheeks flushed with discomfiture, she paused before stuttering, 'Nothing....nothing at all.'

'It doesn't look like *nothing* to me. He can't take his eyes off you,' she persisted, labouring the point.

'Well I definitely haven't encouraged him.'

'Listen, I gave up on him ages ago. I just thought I'd give it one last shot, being as we were together for the weekend but I simply don't exist in his eyes. If you're happy about it, go for it. He's one special guy. There aren't many like him around.'

'Yes he is but truly, I'm not interested,' she said. When Lucille cackled disbelievingly, she repeated, '*I'm not*!'

'That's madness. I've seen every female at work chase after Mark Wyndham and he's avoided every one like the plague but he definitely fancies you.'

'Then he'll have to get over it,' she snapped.

The reference to madness cut Mattie to the quick. *She* believed she could be mad and now Lucille was confirming that belief. Was that how other people saw her she wondered. Was that why Meredith had offered her the job....to keep a watchful eye on her? What would Tom make of her behaviour last night? Mark hadn't failed to notice and had offered to be a willing listener if she felt like talking. The palms of her hands were sweating and as a rush of adrenaline pumped through her body, she started to panic. She felt claustrophobic and in need of some air.

As the train pulled into a station, it slowed down and stopped. She was on the verge of grabbing her shopping bags and jumping off when unexpectedly, Seth stepped on with Stephanie. '*Seth*,' she called to him and as he turned to face her, she felt the fear drain from her body.

'Are you alright?' he asked. 'You're very pale.'

'Am I? Well, I feel alright. Perhaps I'm overtired. We've been in every shop in London I think.'

'We have too,' Stephanie said, grinning from ear to ear. 'It's been such a lovely day and you'll never guess what Seth's bought me.'

'Then tell me, what?' Mattie asked impatiently as Lucille listened attentively.

She stretched out her hand. 'How about that?'

'Oh that's so beautiful,' she gasped, admiring the sparkling diamond engagement ring. She clung to them both and Seth grinned proudly. 'I'm so happy for you, for both of you. This is a weekend you will never forget.'

'For more reasons than one,' Lucille piped up.

'Shut up!' Mattie scolded as Seth and Stephanie screeched with laughter at Lucille's predicted reply to Mattie's foregoing remark.

'Help me out here Mattie. Which of these dresses should I wear tonight?' Lucille asked.

She studied them both critically. 'I'd say the blue one. It's lovely.'

'You're right and it's more comfortable than the other. Have you decided what you're wearing?'

'The proverbial little black dress. I don't possess much evening wear since I never go anywhere.'

Lucille decided to bite her tongue for were she to make a confrontational remark now, she could ruin the entire evening but she couldn't understand why a beautiful and talented young woman like Mattie could be so reclusive and withdrawn.

Stephanie, when asked, had been unable to satisfy Lucille's morbid curiosity though she had learned from Stephanie that Seth too was deeply concerned by his sister's unstable and unsocial behaviour. He had however abandoned all attempts to explore the matter further when Mattie had made it crystal clear that it was not a subject for discussion.

'Wow! That's fabulous,' Lucille announced when Mattie reappeared in the bedroom. 'I couldn't wear anything so short with my 'prop forward' legs.'

Lucille's opinion was important to her. 'Do you think it's *too* short?' she asked. 'Be honest.'

'Of course not! It covers your knickers....barely. I'm joking,' she said when Mattie looked shocked. 'It's perfect and you look gorgeous.'

Mattie brushed her hair and checked her make-up. 'Right, I'm ready. Are you going out like that?' she enquired with a grin, making reference to Lucille's bathrobe and shower-cap.

'Just give me a minute. If I'd have put my clothes on before I did my slap, it would have been daubed all down the front of my frock!'

When she was dressed, Mattie smiled. 'You look lovely. That style's really flattering and the colour emphasises your blue eyes....yes, it's very nice.'

'Thank you,' she said as she walked across to the window. 'Hey, the coach is already here and I can see a few getting on so we'd better be quick.'

'One thing first....Will you promise me there'll be no wisecracks about Mark tonight? It makes me ill-at-ease and I'm sure it embarrasses him too.'

'Alright, I won't say a word but you're making a big mistake if you ask me.'

'Well I wasn't asking you, so let's leave it at that shall we?'

160

As they stepped into the lift, Lucille said chirpily, 'I've been looking forward to this show so much. I do hope we've got good seats.'

'Me too and I'm sure they will be.'

There was no sign of Mark on the coach as Mattie walked ahead down the aisle and opted for the first pair of available seats. Seth and Stephanie, who had waited for them, took the seats alongside theirs and Mattie breathed a sigh of relief.

It was not until they arrived at the theatre that she discovered Mark had been sitting at the back of the coach, hidden from view.

He made no attempt to join them in the foyer and when they were directed to their seats in the stalls, he was sitting behind them on the next row.

At one point, she turned and caught his eye before quickly turning away and then the lights dimmed as and the music commenced.

When Michael Crawford first appeared, there was tumultuous applause, overpowering the music.

Following an excellent first half, when the lights were turned up, members of the audience started to make their way to the bar.

Mattie was waiting patiently in the lengthy queue as Mark approached and offered to buy her a drink.

'It's alright, I'll get these. What would you like?' she asked.

'Thank you. I'd like a dry white wine with a dash of soda please. Are you enjoying the show?'

'Very much. As it's my first West End show, I'm impressed with everything. How about you?'

'It's excellent. He's very talented isn't he?'

'Next!' the barman called and Mattie pushed her way through the crowd of inconsiderate people who were standing in groups and blocking the bar area. Lucille was nowhere to be seen when Mattie turned round with two of the three drinks.

'Let me take those,' Mark offered, removing the drinks from her hand. 'Follow me, there's plenty of room over here.'

Mattie collected the third drink and accompanied him to the far side of the bar.

'You look lovely tonight,' he said, looking deeply into her eyes.

'Thank you,' she replied graciously. 'Trendy suit. Very stylish indeed!' she added, feeling obliged to return an equally complimentary remark, though it was well deserved. 'Debonair' was the appropriate word that sprang to mind though she didn't say it.

'Have you eaten?'

'Not since lunchtime. We didn't even have time for a quick snack. Lucille insisted on staying down town until the shops were ready for closing, not that I'm complaining. I enjoyed every moment and the shops were fantastic.'

'I'm pleased to hear you made good use of your time. I fell asleep for two hours and then I went for a brisk walk for another couple of hours so I didn't eat either and I'm ravenous! Maybe the three of us could eat together after the show?'

'I've been up and down everywhere looking for the pair of you,' Lucille interrupted breathlessly. 'I thought you'd gone back in. Is that mine?' she said to Mark who was holding two glasses.

He handed her the glass. 'I was trying to arrange somewhere for us to eat later. Are you hungry?'

'Daft question! I'm always hungry. Why don't we invite Steph and Seth too? It'll be an opportunity to toast their good news.'

'What good news? Have I missed something?' he asked Lucille.

'Haven't you heard? Stephanie and Seth, Mattie's brother, got engaged today.'

'Oh right, that's *very* good news. To be honest, I didn't know your brother was here Mattie. I haven't seen him about.'

'Ah well, that's because they've been having their money's worth out of the bedroom,' Lucille replied dryly before Mattie had chance to stop her.

'Lucky old Seth!' Mark exclaimed with a guttural laugh, avoiding eye contact with Mattie who glared furiously at Lucille.

'Everybody's going back in,' Mattie announced brusquely before striding out to return to her seat.

Lucille shot after her. 'Hey what's up with you?'

'You know very well what's wrong. You have a one-track mind! Do you ever think of anything else apart from sex?'

When they took their seats and the lights dimmed, she uttered with a sigh, 'That's all I seem to be able to do these days....think about it.'

'Why am I not surprised when you chuck yourself at everything in trousers? You....You're nothing but an embarrassment Lucille.'

'And you're normal I suppose?'

'Shut up and watch the show,' Mattie snarled.

163

Their disagreement was hurriedly forgotten when the show recommenced and at the end, there was a standing ovation for the cast.

Back in the foyer, Mark waited for the others.

Stephanie and Seth were the first to arrive and he was quick to congratulate them as he shook Seth's hand warmly and kissed Stephanie's cheek. 'We're going for something to eat. Has Mattie told you?'

'No, we haven't found her yet. We were going to look for a restaurant after the show.'

'I know a good place within walking distance of the hotel. I'll just have a quick word with the coach driver. Keep everyone together till I get back.'

When he returned he advised them that the driver would drop them close by the restaurant and so they hurriedly made their way to the coach.

It was a superb venue, catering for all tastes and one that Mark had used several times previously, he made known as they waited for their table for five to be prepared.

They were spoiled for choice from the extensive menu and opted to rely on Mark's recommendation. Stephanie and Mattie chose the braised duck breast with a black cherry sauce, the men went for rib-eye steaks and Lucille, who couldn't make up her mind, eventually decided on the home-made beefsteak pie in red wine sauce.

'Are we having a starter?' Lucille asked.

'Believe me, you don't need one. The portions are huge and I mean *huge*,' Mark informed her.

'*Look at the size of that steak,*' Seth roared when the waiter served him. 'It's hanging off the plate.'

164

'I did warn you,' Mark said.

Everyone commented positively about the quality of the food and when the wine waiter arrived with a bottle of Champagne provided by Mark, they raised their glasses to the happy couple's engagement.

Mark had made it his business to sit beside Mattie and at the end of the evening, he leaned towards her and said quietly, 'As I've been given my marching orders, I thought it would be nice to part company on a high note. I've enjoyed our time together and I hope I haven't offended you in any way.'

'Of course you haven't Mark,' she said and came close to touching his hand but lost her nerve at the moment of contact. 'You're a very special man.'

'I'd better return this,' he said, reaching into his pocket. 'It was to have been my excuse to call you once we were home.'

He handed her the pen he had borrowed earlier.

She smiled at him. 'I didn't realise you still had it. Thank you Mark, especially so for suggesting this restaurant. It's been a perfect evening.'

'For me too,' he replied warmly.

6

Mark adhered to his promise and made no further contact with Mattie though she was rarely out of his thoughts.

Mattie threw herself into her work and tried to put all thoughts of Mark to the back of her mind.

When Lucille attempted once again to voice her concerns with Stephanie, she wasn't forthcoming.

'It's her life,' she told Lucille. 'She has to sort it out for herself. Just let her get on with it in her own way. It's none of our business.'

Emphatically she stated, 'But *Mark* really fancied her….he *did*,' she added, driving the point home.

'Well *she* obviously didn't fancy *Mark* so just let it drop.'

Undeterred, she persisted and covering her mouth with her hand, she appeared shocked.

'What now?' she asked with an infuriated sigh.

'I've just had the most horrible thought.'

'*What*?'

'I shouldn't say….no I won't say….I'd better not.'

'Give it up Lucille! You know perfectly well that you're going to tell me so get on with it without all the unnecessary melodrama.'

She hesitated, took a deep breath and waited for Stephanie's undivided attention before announcing, 'I bet she's a lesbian. It would explain everything.'

'Don't talk so wet!'

'I'm telling you. Why else would she behave like that with men? Has she *ever* had a boyfriend?'

'I don't know. I haven't known her very long.'

'My God and I shared a room with her!'

'Now you're just being ridiculous. She knows *you* aren't a lesbian in fact *everybody* knows *you* aren't a lesbian the way you conduct yourself.'

'But *she* could be.'

'What if she were? It still isn't our business and don't you go spreading malicious gossip about her. She's a nice girl and she's going to be my sister-in-law soon so keep it shut. I'm warning you.'

'Alright, you've made your point. I won't repeat it to anyone else....but you will tell me if you hear anything won't you?'

'*Shut up!*'


It was early in December and Mattie was making her Christmas preparations. There were several lists scattered across the table when Seth arrived home from work and he smiled as he read some of them.

It would be their first Christmas together in their flat, Jack would be home in ten days' time and Seth knew that Mattie wanted everything to be perfect.

Stephanie was coming for Christmas dinner and Mattie had also invited her widowed mother when she realised she would be alone on Christmas Day. Secretly, Seth was dreading the arrival of his future mother-in-law for a complete day.

Meredith was spending Christmas with Andrew and his two boys. Their relationship had flourished since discovering they had much in common at the housewarming party there a few weeks ago.

An amicable agreement had been reached about parental access and Andrew's two children would be flying to Spain for a fortnight in the New Year to stay with their mother.

'Oh hello, I didn't hear you come in,' Mattie said when Seth was seen to be scrutinising the papers on the table. 'Are you ready for your tea?'

'I'm starving! Listen, correct me if I'm wrong but I seem to be missing something here. I've just been reading the shopping list. Are there a hundred more invited that you haven't bothered to mention?'

'I don't want to run out of food over Christmas.'

'Run out of food? You have to be joking! This lot will last till *next* Christmas and I don't know where you think you're going to store it all.'

'You don't need to know. Come and get your tea and another letter's arrived from our Jack.'

Seth opened the letter and started to read it. 'Oh, Jack's got three weeks' leave. That's brilliant,' he commented. 'And he wants me to arrange that meal he mentioned last time he were here. He says if it's left until he gets home, everywhere will be full. Do you have anywhere in particular in mind?'

'I don't know anywhere. Where do you normally take Stephanie?'

'Believe me, you wouldn't be seen dead in any of them crummy places. We have cheapies 'cos we're saving up. We'll pick somewhere that's a bit posher for us three.'

'They'll be expensive at Christmas you know.'

'So what? We're allowed a treat once in a while aren't we? That were a terrific restaurant where we ate in London. What a great place that were though I couldn't lay claim to being overly enamoured by the Champagne when I first tried it. All the bubbles went right up my nose and I thought I were going to start sneezing. I got used it though when I'd had a few glasses and it were very kind of Mr. Wyndham to buy it us,' he said, shovelling a pile of food into his mouth. 'This fish tastes good. What is it?'

'It's haddock and Mr. Wyndham is called Mark,' she reminded him.

'I can't bring myself to call him Mark, not when he were that Consultant in hospital. Somehow, it's disrespectful but I noticed *you* were getting on with him very well. Have you heard anything more from him since we got back from London?'

'No of course I haven't,' she replied curtly to end the discussion right there.

In the sudden realisation that he'd said the wrong thing he changed topic. 'Shall I get that tree up this weekend? I were thinking it'd look well over there in that corner by the fire.'

'Yes it would and I'd like that....thanks Seth.'

It was Saturday, the twentieth of December. Jack would be arriving the next day and Mattie was very excited about having her complete family there as she made up the camp bed she had borrowed from Sally. There wasn't much room to move about with two beds in Seth's room but he had assured her that Jack would be accustomed to overcrowded sleeping areas on a ship.

She smiled and reflected on bygone times when she removed Jack's scruffy Teddy from a cardboard box on top of her wardrobe. She beat it against her body to remove any dust particles and placed it in the centre of Jack's pillow. As a child, everywhere he went, Teddy had to go too.

She returned to the living room to open the cards and other mail that had just been delivered.

There was a card from Meredith and Andrew and one from Sadie and Keith. She didn't recognise the writing on the final envelope and when she opened it, before reading the words, she glanced inside and her heart pounded. It was signed by Mark.

Inside there was a separate note that said, 'I know I promised but it's just a card to let you know I still think of you often. I'm a much better surgeon than I am a poet! Have a great Christmas Mattie, with my deepest affection, Mark.'

She turned to the front and read the greeting, 'To a special friend at Christmastime.'

The words inside brought tears to her eyes. It was an open card and Mark had written his own words.

'At Christmastime we think of friends
and special times we've shared;
Recalling happy moments
and emotions that are stirred.
This Christmas greeting just for you
is simply sent to say,
You're in my thoughts where you'll remain
for ever and a day.
Mark'

Mattie blinked the moisture from her eyes before placing the card in its envelope and then she hid it at the back of her writing case. Were she to display it with the others she and Seth had already received,

170

she ran the risk of Stephanie's disclosure to Lucille who would undoubtedly broadcast the information to any willing listener at the hospital. In any case, it was a message from Mark to her, a confidential and intimate exposé of his feelings for her.

She felt distressed that she couldn't openly return his feelings, especially since she could give him no explanation for her actions though secretly, *he* was rarely out of *her* thoughts.

The arrival of Jack the next day and the advent of Christmas took control of her emotions.

They listened with incredulity to his captivating revelations of the Far East. Hong Kong sounded to be a magical place and Jack related how, during his shore leave, he had visited many places of interest. He had toured the Home Territories with a dozen of his shipmates and had seen thousands of ducks, he laughed. He had learned about the political history and finally he had been invited aboard a sampan on which a Chinese family of twelve were living.

'What's a sampan?' Mattie asked.

'It's a small Chinese skiff....a little boat of simple construction with a roof made from mats. There are scores of them and people live in them on the water around the harbour, often because they don't have anywhere else to live. There are thousands of poor people,' he told her sadly. 'The shopping malls are to die for though. They are reputed to be the biggest in the world and everything is so cheap, compared to England that is. You'd love it there Mattie. I've brought you something back that I know you'll like but I'm afraid you can't have it yet.'

When he saw the look of disappointment on her face, he laughed. 'It's your Christmas present but if you like, you can have it now.'

'No, I'd rather wait until Christmas Day.'

'You'll be sorry if you do.'

'Go on then,' she said. 'You've twisted my arm.'

He vanished and returned carrying a large floppy parcel that he dropped in her lap. 'Happy Christmas Mattie.'

'It will be now I have my family here,' she said, frantically tearing at the wrapping paper while Seth took note.

'Jack! It's beautiful!' she cried out, unfolding the large decorative tablecloth. 'It's a Christmassy one! I've never seen anything like it before. Look Seth, look the appliquéd Christmas decorations. There's Father Christmas with his sack and just look at the reindeer....oh and there's a snowman and over here are sprigs of holly. Those are red poinsettia leaves. It's fantastic and you are too Jack for buying it for me. Fancy your choosing something like that.'

'It weren't difficult, believe me. No matter where you go, the shop windows are full of them in every colour, shape and size. There's a dozen napkins too and they've all got them point whatsit leaves on as well. I picked a large tablecloth because you can let it dangle down if it's too big. It's better than being too little. Anyway, when you're married with a pile of kids, you'll probably have a bigger table than the one here,' he teased with a satirical smile but Mattie refused to rise to the bait as she folded it carefully and put it away in the drawer.

172

'It's perfect and Sadie will be pea-green when she sees it. She's collected loads of stuff for her bottom drawer already but she hasn't got anything like this. I'm warning both of you now, don't spill anything on it on Christmas day or I'll choke you!'

'Oh Gawd!' Seth grumbled. 'It looks as if you've just spoiled our Christmas Jack. I'm bound to spill something now she's said that.'

'Then you'd better make sure that you *don't* Seth Henshaw,' Mattie replied firmly.

'Yes Seth, don't be so gormless!' Jack echoed.

'Huh....you're a fine one to talk! You've got egg yolk all down the front of your shirt.'

'Maybe I have but I didn't get it on the tablecloth did I?' he said, shoving his face up close to Seth's.

'Shut up,' Mattie laughed. 'You're worse than a couple of kids. It's just like the old times don't you think? I'm so pleased that you're home Jack. We're going to have such a lovely Christmas.'


It was the hospital Christmas party on the twenty-second of December. There had been a greater than normal demand for tickets and sixty staff members had put their names on the list. As the coach could take only fifty-three, volunteers had been sought to make their own transport arrangements.

'I'll be taking my car so if you like, I'll pick you up and take you,' Mark told Stephanie.

She was grateful for the offer and thanked him. 'I arranged with Lucille for her to stay at my place so there'll be two of us to collect if that's alright. You don't mind taking Lucille as well do you?'

'If I must,' Mark scowled, already regretting he'd volunteered and knowing he would be badgered by Lucille all evening.

The venue, a flamboyant restaurant in Chinatown, had been booked for almost a year. Their Christmas parties had been held there before and everyone had enjoyed the atmosphere and the vast choice of food on offer.

When they arrived, Lucille made a point of sitting beside Mark, much to his displeasure.

'Have you heard anything from Mattie since we were in London?' she asked him.

'No I haven't. Is she well?'

'She seems alright but I've only seen her a couple of times. I nearly wet myself last week when Tom asked if the Ice Queen would be here tonight.'

'Why did he refer to her as the Ice Queen?'

'I'd have thought that was obvious. Because she's icy cold. She doesn't like *men*, if you know what I mean,' she replied quietly.

Mark looked bewildered. 'No, I don't know what you mean Lucille....enlighten me.'

She glanced around to make sure nobody was in earshot before whispering, 'I think she's a lesbian.'

Mark was horrified. That thought had never once crossed his mind, so had he misinterpreted the look in Mattie's eyes and could that have been the secret she had withheld from him? Would Dr. McAndrew have known about that when she told him to forget about her? Many more questions invaded his mind to disturb him as he reflected on Lucille's words.

'Excuse me,' he said, throwing his napkin down.

'If you're off to the bar, I wouldn't say no to a gin and tonic please,' she called after him.

Her audacious request was to fall on deaf ears but much as Mark despised her, if it were true, should he not be thanking her for preventing his making an even bigger fool of himself?

He ordered a whisky on the rocks and knocked it back in one. 'Put another in there please,' he said to the barman. 'Make it a double.'

He hovered by the bar for several minutes before returning to the table.

'Are you alright?' Lucille enquired.

'I'm perfectly alright,' he snarled deprecatingly. 'Why wouldn't I be?'

'I'm sorry Mark. I just thought that you ought to know what people are thinking.'

'*What people are thinking*? Who else is there who believes this nonsensical notion of yours?'

She paused to consider her reply. 'I mentioned it to Steph....but she didn't believe it.'

'So nobody believes it! It's merely something *you* concocted that's nothing but a figment of your own perverted imagination....right?'

'Well er....I suppose....yes but it *did* appear to be the most likely explanation for....'

'You should keep your silly thoughts to yourself Lucille. It's called defamation of character and you could be in a lot of trouble were you to repeat such an allegation. For my part, I don't believe one word of it and I don't want to discuss it anymore.'

'Sorry,' she mumbled contritely. 'I think I'll get myself a drink. Would you like something?'

'No thanks. I've already had more than enough. I'll stick with the water,' he replied curtly.

Lucille barely spoke again during the meal, which provided some satisfaction for Mark. While he had to acknowledge she was good at her job, away from the ward, he found her completely irresponsible and irksome. Even if her suspicions *were* proved to be true, he would have preferred to hear the revelation from someone else's lips.

At the end of the meal, a colleague, Chris Sykes, invited Mark to join him at the bar and Mark seized the opportunity to escape Lucille's childish prattle.

'Thanks for that. Here, allow me get them,' Mark said. 'I'm relieved you dragged me away.'

'From the delectable Lucille?' he sniggered.

'I'm not joking Chris when I tell you *that* was the least enjoyable meal of my entire life. Lucille's an absolute bloody nightmare!'

Chris grinned. 'Well if it's any consolation, I got lumbered with the silly bitch last year. That's why I came over, to rescue you.'

'Thanks again....I owe you.'

'I'll make sure you don't forget. She'll be all over somebody else now you've given her the elbow and it might be me. Let's stick together until it's time to leave. There's safety in numbers.'

'Suits me,' he replied. 'Listen, would you excuse me? I'll be back in a minute.'

'You'd better!' Chris warned him.

Mark had seen Dr. McAndrew who was heading towards the ladies' room and was anxious to talk to her when she came out.

When she reappeared, he took her arm and led her to the reception area where there was a comfortable settee. 'Dr. McAndrew....Helen. Please help me. I'll go crazy if I don't talk to somebody. Please give me two minutes of your time,' he pleaded.

'My poor boy! It's obvious you paid no regard to my warning. This is about Mattie I take it?'

He nodded and stared at her with troubled eyes.

'Tell me what's happened now but I'm promising nothing in return. If I can help you then I will but I won't betray a trust....not even for you.'

Mark explained about the London City weekend, his feelings for Mattie and his belief she had shown some feelings for him too.

'Did she *say* she had feelings for you Mark?'

'Not in so many words....I kind of sensed it, and then later, she made it absolutely clear there was to be no further contact when we came home.'

'Did you do anything to upset her?'

'Like what? I wouldn't do anything to hurt her.'

'Not intentionally I know but was there anything at all that springs to mind?'

'No....not with me that is. She was talking to Tom in the bar. They were having a discussion about her job or something. There were plenty of other people around too and then she reacted very strangely.'

'Tell me what you saw Mark.'

'As I said they were just talking and he took hold of her hand, that's all.'

'And what did Mattie do when that happened?'

'She snatched her hand away and then she said it was because he'd startled her. She was embarrassed because she'd spilled his drink and she became a bit edgy afterwards. I offered to talk to her about it but she said there was nothing wrong. That was about it. When we were all out together, we enjoyed each other's company and I believed I was making some progress. She was both responsive and attentive.'

'How did Mattie react when you were alone?'

'I don't recall being alone with her. Other people were always present. Please Helen, can't you help me to understand her?'

She thought long and hard before answering him. Mattie was displaying the same symptoms she had witnessed when, as a girl, she would be fearful if a male advanced towards her or addressed her during the investigation. 'This is so difficult for me Mark,' she sighed. 'I want to help but I'm afraid I can't.'

'Do you mean can't or won't?'

'Alright, I won't. You're trying to put me on the spot and you're out of order.'

'I'm not at all. Come on Helen....please. I'm not asking for breach of doctor-patient confidentiality. You're a gynaecologist....you're not professionally involved with her. You're merely her friend.'

Helen stood up to leave and he grabbed her arm.

'Just answer me one question then and I swear I won't bother you ever again and I'll never disclose you told me.' With searching eyes, he asked, 'Is she a lesbian?'

'No Mark, definitely not,' she told him before she walked away.

For several minutes after she left, Mark remained seated with his head in his hands, oblivious of staff and colleagues who peered at him questioningly as they passed by.

Those four words had been a great relief to hear though he was still no wiser in his understanding of Mattie. Helen had been frank with him a few weeks earlier when telling him to dismiss Mattie from his thoughts but yet on this occasion she had told him nothing....or had she?

He tried to remember their conversation. Though Helen, a skilful interrogator, had refused to divulge anything, she had asked him questions so could he deduce anything from her questions? She had asked about Mattie's reaction when Tom took hold of her hand. She had questioned him about her demeanour when alone with him. He recalled his first meeting with her when she had begged for Sister Flanagan's presence and then there were those remarks Lucille had made about the Ice Queen, so-named because she was cold and didn't like men.

Mark was horrified when he recalled his ultimate remark to Helen that she was simply Mattie's friend and not professionally involved with her and all at once, the pieces began to fall in place. Helen was a gynaecologist and Mattie was terrified of men. 'My God!' he cried out. 'What happened to you Mattie?' and his eyes were filled with tears.

'I'd just about given up on you,' Chris said when Mark returned.

'Sorry, I got tied up. You know how it is.'

'Was she a fit piece?'

'What? Oh no, it was work related,' he smiled.

'In that case, I won't quiz you about it. What are you having?'

'I'll have scotch on the rocks!'

'Hey, aren't you driving?'

'No, I'm well over the limit already. I'll get a taxi home and collect my car tomorrow morning. I'm on late start so I'll have plenty of time. Best make it a double.'

'Are you alright mate? You look rather tense.'

'I'm fine. I'm trying to forget that I had to sit next to Lucille throughout dinner.'

He gave a throaty laugh. 'I'd better order a bottle then. It took me a week to get over it last year.'

At the end of the night, Stephanie wandered over to the bar. 'People are starting to make their way to the coach Mark. Are you ready for leaving now?'

Red-eyed, he turned towards her. 'Have a d-drink Steph,' he said, slurring his words. 'What d-do you want?'

'*Mark....you're drunk*!'

'No I'm not,' he replied argumentatively. 'I'm a b-bit merry,' he added and almost fell off his stool.

When Lucille approached, he drawled, 'Lu-cille, c-come on and have a d-drink with me. Where have you b-been all night? It's been a very g-good night hasn't it?'

'Come on Mark,' Stephanie stated, taking control of the situation. 'You've had more than enough to drink. You're going straight home to bed.'

'How about one f-for the road f-first?'

'I said *no*. Come on, try to stand up straight.'

'P-party-pooper. I was just enjoying m-myself.'

She glared angrily at Chris. 'Stop laughing!' she demanded. 'You're just encouraging him. This isn't funny and *you* ought to know better. Pull yourself together and give me a hand....he can hardly stand up, let alone walk and you Lucille, go and ask the barman to phone a taxi. Don't stand there looking useless. Do something helpful for once!'

When Lucille scurried away, Stephanie and Chris supported Mark who clumsily lumbered his way to the outside door for some air.

Initially, Mark remembered nothing the next day when he awoke on the settee. A half-empty glass of whisky stood on the small table by his side.

His head throbbed and he screwed up his eyes in pain. Little by little, he began to recall the events of the previous evening up to the point where he had spoken to Helen McAndrew.

Trying to stand, he staggered, before fumbling his way to the lavatory where he vomited profusely.

He had walked in the bedroom when he looked at his watch, shocked to discover he was an hour late for work already. Moreover, it would take at least fifteen minutes to drive to the hospital....but where was his car? He couldn't possibly have driven a car in such a state....

He stripped off and warily climbed in the shower, standing motionless for some minutes as the warm water soothed and refreshed him.

An hour later, he tried to act normal as he walked into his surgery where he was met by his secretary, Jill, who laughed and remarked, 'I wasn't expecting to see *you* today. How do you feel?'

'Don't ask,' he said. 'Did I make a complete fool of myself last night?'

'I wouldn't worry if I were you. Everybody had a skinful and so nobody's going to judge you. It was a good night wasn't it?'

'If you say so,' he replied awkwardly. 'Right I'm off to the ward to check on my patients. Has anyone missed me?'

'Only me. Chris came looking for you earlier but I told him you'd just slipped out for something.'

'Thanks, you're a life-saver. Incidentally, do you happen to know what I did with my car last night? I've had to come by taxi as I can't remember.'

Jill laughed. 'You left it at the restaurant. No way could you have driven a car, the drunken state you were in. You really don't recall how bad you were do you?'

'No and I'd prefer not be reminded, thanks!'

7

Mattie took a step back to admire the dining table she had painstakingly prepared and it looked very Christmassy, like her mother's table always looked, she recalled with emotion.

She realised how her mother must have scrimped and saved to provide their Christmas feast with four mouths to feed. She would roast a large capon and the appetizing aroma of home-made sage and onion stuffing would fill the house.

Only when they had finished their meal were they permitted to open their presents and they would sit round the open log fire, warm as toast, as they each took turns at opening the two gifts they received.

One particular Christmas came to mind....the one when Mattie received a doll's pram and she recalled how she could barely wait to go outside to proudly parade it around the neighbourhood.

She learned some years later that her mother had bought it from the local second-hand shop for a few shillings and had lovingly renovated it little by little when the three of them were asleep, polishing and buffing the rusted chrome until it shone like new.

Her mother's skills as a seamstress had proved to be invaluable and provided additional income from dressmaking and alterations that she carried out in the evenings and at weekends for her endless range of customers.

Her mother used to have a huge 'rag-bag' that she continually topped up with remnants and scraps of left-over fabrics from dresses and curtains she made for her customers and in her spare time, she would painstakingly stitch together equal-sized squares of material, of different colours and patterns, to make patchwork quilts and pillow shams for each of their beds. She had made one such quilt and pillow sham for the doll's pram too and it had been so beautiful, Mattie brought to mind.

Seth, an avid reader, always got two books and he would read both of them from cover to cover before the day's end and that Christmas was no exception.

That was the same year Jack received his Teddy and it remained his favourite possession throughout his childhood.

Only last week, it had evoked nostalgic memories for him when he found it on his pillow and he threw his arms around his sister and sighed, before saying in a broken voice, 'Those were good times Mattie.'

'They were,' she agreed sorrowfully. 'They were the best.'

Mattie was abruptly returned to the present when Seth and Jack returned from the pub.

'Are we allowed in now?' Seth asked, referring to their earlier enforced eviction because they were, as she had complained, under the feet.

'Yes, everything's under control,' she told them. 'What time will Stephanie and her mother be here?'

'Anytime now,' Seth stated, looking at his watch. 'There's a right good smell. Is everything ready?'

'Yes, more or less. I've lifted the turkey out of the oven and the vegetables won't take long.'

'Do you realise this is the first time since we were kids, that the three of us will be sitting down at the table together for our Christmas dinner?' Jack said. 'It feels great to be a family again.'

Argumentatively Seth butted in, 'What are you on about Jack? Are you going a bit simple? We used to have Christmas dinner together in the foster-home with Olive and Richard when Mattie were there.'

'Yes but I meant as a *family*....in our own place. It feels different somehow....'

'*I* know what you mean Jack,' Mattie interrupted sensitively. 'I was thinking exactly the same only a few minutes ago. It *does* feel different somehow.'

Jack heaved a sigh. 'I wish mum could have been here too!'

'So do I!' Mattie concurred sadly.

'I wish you'd both stop being bloody mawkish!' Seth complained. 'It's Christmas Day....a day when we're supposed to be enjoying ourselves.'

Jack was livid. '*What the hell's up with you*?' he retorted. '*You're the only bugger pulling his dial*!'

'*It's you*! You're forever reaping up the past and I can't stand your sickening sentimentality. We have to move forward. We can't keep living in the past. Mum's gone and so has dad so learn to live with it. They're not coming back....ever....so let it be!'

'He can be a right insufferable git at times,' Jack grumbled to Mattie. 'I'm convinced it's because of all them damned books he reads.'

'Listen, in his own way, I'm sure that Seth is just as sentimental as we are. People show their feelings in different ways. Don't argue please. Let's make it a good Christmas....right Seth?'

'Aye Mattie. Whatever you say,' he replied.

Seth remained quiet and in deep thought. He was anxious about Mattie's future and Jack's perpetual references to the past only served as a reminder and he wanted her to forget whatever she had suffered at her original foster-home. She hadn't absconded without good cause and had related it was a horrible place. He suspected that her carers had given her a hard time and more than a few good hidings. There had been noticeable weight loss as well as bruising to her legs the evening he and Jack had first visited the Williams' house for tea but he had never raised it with her nor had he brought the matter to Jack's attention.

With her brothers around her, nobody would ever think there was anything odd about her. Mattie was sweet-natured and loving as their mother had been but if he should fly the nest, like Jack, what would happen then? Could Mattie survive alone? He had plans of his own to make but how could he begin to think of his future as things stood?

Periodically, Stephanie badgered him about fixing a date for their wedding. They had saved a modest amount of money towards a house deposit and she couldn't understand why he was holding back. At one point she had questioned his commitment and suggested he might be having second thoughts but he had reassured her of his undying love, his prime objective, Seth explained, being to provide her with the best, which meant they would have to save a lot more money. It wasn't just a question of finding a house they could afford, he added. They'd have to furnish it too. At the time, she had accepted Seth's reasoning but the pressure was on again and it was now wearing Seth down. He didn't want to lose her by procrastinating further but neither did he want to leave Mattie alone when he felt she might fall apart were he to move out.

Furthermore, Seth was dreading the arrival of his fiancée's mother who went to extraordinary lengths to badger him about the wedding, while reminding him that she was growing older. She wanted to be a grandmother while she was still of an age to enjoy her grandchildren....'*Grandchildren*' she had stated in the *plural*, and Seth recalled how he had almost choked on his pot of tea when she had uttered those words.

'*They're here*!' Mattie called excitedly.

Seth invited them in and introduced Mrs. Jackson to Mattie and Jack who expressed their pleasure at meeting her and wished her a Merry Christmas.

'May I take your coat, Mrs. Jackson,' Mattie said, stepping forward.

'Do call me Ethel. After all, we'll be family soon won't we Seth?' she said with a beaming smile.

'Here, I'll hang it up,' Seth volunteered without answering her question and he cursed as he left the room. 'She's hardly got in through the bloody door and she's started already!'

When Stephanie followed and gave Seth a warm hug, his tension drained from his body.

'Merry Christmas sweetheart. You look lovely,' he said with an adoring smile. He kissed her on the lips gently before they returned to the others where Ethel Jackson began yet again.

'It was so kind of you to invite me here Mattie,' Ethel said. 'This is such a nice place. You've made it so comfortable and homely. I was only saying to Stephanie earlier that the two of them should try to choose warm colours for their house.'

Mattie looked surprised. 'Have you found a house then?'

'No,' Seth interjected hastily. 'We're still looking round. All the ones we like are out of our reach, so we might have to save up for a while yet.'

'You have to creep before you walk Seth,' Ethel advised him. 'I can still remember our first house. It was a two-up two-down with an outside toilet and it was a very cold house and so we....'

'I want better than that for Steph,' he cut her short brusquely. 'I'm not prepared to settle....'

Before he had had time to finish his sentence, and with intent to prevent the imminent argument that was looming in the background, Mattie jumped up. 'Would you help me in the kitchen Ethel?'

'What? Oh yes of course my dear.'

As Mattie whisked her away, she turned to Seth and mouthed, 'Stop it now!'

'What would you like me to do?' Ethel asked.

'I've never carved a turkey. Will you do it please? There's a sharp knife on the plate.'

Ethel laughed. 'I remember the first time I tried to carve a turkey. 'I'd overcooked it and it was like a pile of sawdust but I've improved a bit since then. Shall I carve light and dark meat?'

'Yes please and do plenty. I have two very greedy brothers.'

188

'I remember my husband's hearty appetite. He'd always scrape his plate clean, God rest his soul.'

'What happened to Stephanie's father?'

'Steve? He was killed in the Korean War. It was nineteen-fifty-four. He'd only served six months.'

'How tragic! I'm sorry Ethel. I hadn't heard about that. So he was just a young man when he died?'

'Only thirty-one. He was in the Infantry Brigade. Apparently, they were waiting for back-up when a plane bombed the building where they were seeking refuge. There were fifteen of them and they were all killed....blown to bits and only weeks before he was due to come home.'

'That's so awful! How do you come to terms with something like that?'

'You just have to get on with the rest of your life. I was eight months pregnant with Stephanie and my shock at receiving the telegram sent me into labour right away. She arrived the next day and after that, I devoted my entire life to her care. I knew scores of women who lost sons or loved-ones in World War Two and the Korean War. You just have to pick up the pieces and keep going. Life is full of tragedy. It certainly was during those war years. I saw many a tear and I shed plenty myself in the early days but then I told myself for Stephanie's sake, I had to put the past behind me. Let's face it, you only live once don't you? You can't dwell on the past forever.'

Mattie gave careful thought to those wise words. Mark was suddenly at the forefront of her thoughts. He had suffered heartbreak and had moved on and Ethel had suffered heartbreak and had also moved

189

on so why couldn't *she* put the past behind her and move on too?

It was at that moment she made her decision. She had allowed Albert Parkes to rule her whole life, to dominate her future like he had dominated her past and it must stop. She vowed there and then that she would go to whatever lengths necessary, yes....even therapy if it meant she could live like other women. She would attend to it in the New Year. It would be her New Year's Resolution, to rid the past from her mind.

'You're so right Ethel. You *do* only live once and you *do* have to move on,' she replied.

As they tucked into their Christmas dinner, Mattie looked round the table and smiled, feeling a weight had been lifted from her shoulders, and when Seth proposed a toast to Christmas Day, she added, 'And a Happy New Year to everyone too.'

After dinner, Jack disappeared and returned with a heap of presents. 'Don't forget you've had yours,' he reminded Mattie. 'This one's for you and Seth,' he told Stephanie. 'It's for your new home.'

She opened it carefully and gasped when she saw the identical tablecloth to Mattie's. 'Oh, thank you so much Jack,' she cried. 'It's gorgeous.'

'I bought one for Sadie too,' he told Mattie. 'I'm hoping to see her before I go back to Hong Kong.'

'You will. She's coming to our New Year's Eve party next week.

They continued to exchange Christmas presents and when everyone had finished opening them all, Jack pulled another from his pocket. 'This one's for our wonderful sister for everything she's ever done for us. We love you Mattie and thanks for making our Christmas Day so special.'

Mattie burst into tears when she opened the small box containing a solid gold bangle. 'Oh Seth, Jack! It's beautiful but you shouldn't have, really. It's far too expensive a gift.'

Seth grinned. 'Well look at the inscription inside then. It says, 'Made in Hong Kong'. Jack got it out of a large fortune-cookie didn't you Jack?'

'Sure did,' he replied winking at Seth.

She held it up to read the dedication, 'To Mattie with our love, Seth and Jack'.

She clasped it around her wrist. 'I'll never take it off, ever,' she said with a loving smile. 'Thank you both so much.'

'Thank you for being our big sister Mattie,' Seth answered warmly.


It was New Year's Eve and Mattie had spent most of the day preparing the party food. Sadie and Keith were invited and Mattie had felt obligated to invite Lucille too after being pestered by Stephanie.

Meredith had called to say that Andrew's children could spend the night with his parents which meant that they too could come to the party.

Mattie had baked individual turkey and vegetable pies, using the left-over turkey that she had frozen on Boxing Day. When the outside temperature had suddenly dropped to below freezing point, she felt a hot supper would be preferable to a cold buffet. She had also cooked a large pan of mushy peas, making it an easy supper to serve as everything just needed reheating. A dozen or so mince pies left over from Christmas and the half Christmas cake kept hidden away from Jack and Seth would suffice as dessert.

'Come here Mattie. Stop slaving in the kitchen,' Jack called out. 'I'm only here a few more days.'

'We've got a full house tonight and they all need feeding. I know for a fact that you'll be on the front row when the food's dished up.'

'Maybe I will but I don't eat as much as Seth,' he protested. 'He's a right glutton.'

'Well, I'm warning the pair of you now....guests first. You're only allowed to get your supper when the others have been and not before.'

'Aw!' Jack exclaimed. 'That's not fair. So what if there's nowt left?'

'Then you'll have to go without. Anyway, there'll be plenty of food so stop being so soft.'

'They smell good them pies, Mattie. I guess you don't have any spare ones for now.'

'You guess right Jack and there's only one each tonight so *don't* take two.'

The two brothers exchanged glances and laughed. 'She's a bit of a nag isn't she?' Jack whispered.

'I heard that Jack Henshaw,' Mattie called from the kitchen. 'Have you tidied that room up yet?'

'We have,' Seth shouted back to her, at the same time hurrying to shift the untidy pile of newspapers scattered all over the sofa. 'Shift them pots Jack or we'll get even more earache.'

Mattie overheard them and smiled to herself. She still had the upper hand with her two brothers and though she dreaded the day when Jack went back to sea, she was deliriously happy when they were all together, albeit for a short period of time.

Tonight, she would have all her friends there too and she wanted to make it a party to remember.

'Mattie's fixed you up with a blind date tonight,' Seth told Jack. 'She's called Lucille and you won't need a chat up line for her. As soon as she sees you, she'll be all over you like a rash. She works at the hospital with Steph. She's a nurse too.'

'She'd better not be ugly,' he snorted.

'I wouldn't exactly describe her as ugly....what do you say?' he called to Mattie.

She laughed to herself and decided to play along. 'I don't know. I certainly wouldn't describe her as pretty. Her facial moles spoil her but beauty is only skin deep Jack. If she had a bit of dentistry on her teeth she'd look better but I've seen worse....at least I think I have.'

'I'm going out,' Jack snarled petulantly. 'I'm not being lumbered with the likes of that. I can have my pick of girls when we're in dock. Save my pie. I'll have it later when everybody's gone home.'

'What am I going to tell Lucille now?' Seth asked faking concern. 'She's been really looking forward to tonight. Don't spoil her evening Jack. She hasn't managed to find herself a boyfriend for ages. How long has it been now do you reckon Mattie?'

'I'd say the best part of a year, mind you it's not for the want of trying. She's not choosy Jack so you don't need to feel she wouldn't fancy you because she would.'

'Aye!' Seth confirmed. 'She fancies owt in pants. You never know, she might be able to teach you a trick or too.'

Jack looked bewildered and still failed to realise it was a wind-up but his brother was having a whale of a time. 'Didn't she tell you Mattie that she won the world's ugliest baby competition?'

Mattie couldn't contain her amusement a moment longer and giggled. 'Jack, you are so gullible,' she said, throwing her arms around his neck.

'Aye, you are,' Seth agreed. 'Who's ever heard of an ugliest baby competition? But all the rest is true though,' he stated straight-faced. 'So you'd better watch yourself tonight!'

Alright, so you've both had your bit of fun at my expense,' he uttered with embarrassment.

'You might just like her,' Mattie said by way of apology. 'We're joking....she's a very nice girl.'

Seth laughed. 'Aye, if you threw a sack over her head. Still, there's no need to worry about her when you've got a hot tasty turkey pie to look forward to. You know Mattie's food will be good and you can always knock back a few bottles of ale early on to cloud your vision before you escort Lucille to your bedroom to show her your Teddy,' he howled.

Jack picked up the newspaper and ignored Seth's remarks. He could be really infuriating at times, he grumbled to himself, though it was very comforting to see Mattie with a smiling face for a change. She had worked very hard to organise the party and he certainly wouldn't do anything to spoil her evening no matter what Lucille proved to be like.

As things turned out, he found Lucille to be a fun girl and enjoyed her presence immensely. The party was a tremendous success with plenty of food and drink and at midnight, they drank a toast to the New Year, nineteen-seventy-six when Mattie made her New Year's Resolution to completely obliterate her former painful memories from her mind.

The evening out Jack had promised Mattie was on the following Tuesday at a recently opened Carvery Restaurant in the country, a venue recommended by some of Seth's work colleagues and Mattie eagerly awaited the day's arrival.

Seth had persuaded Mattie to invite Stephanie too though she would have preferred just the company of her brothers on their special family treat but she nevertheless agreed to Stephanie's inclusion.

The roaring log fire in the lounge was welcoming and Mattie was equally enthralled by the splendidly decorated Christmas tree that almost reached to the ceiling. 'It puts ours to shame,' she told Stephanie.

She sighed. 'I can't wait to see *our* first Christmas tree but Seth is so painstakingly cautious, I wonder if we'll ever get married. The more we save up, the more house prices go up. At this rate, we'll still be saving for a house when we're on the pension. It's just a vicious circle.'

'Seth was always very cautious as a child,' Mattie commented. 'He didn't run around playing football like other kids. His head was always in a book but he loves you Stephanie and he would never let you down. He's well worth waiting for and I know he'll be a good husband.'

'I know, that's why I don't want to keep putting it off. It takes ages to organise a wedding and I'll be twenty-two next month. I want to start planning for a family before I'm too old. Most of my friends got married years ago.'

Mattie smiled. 'You're hardly Methuselah! I'll try to hurry Seth along. When Jack goes back, I'll ask him to have a proper look in the paper. What type of house are you looking for?'

'We want a three-bedroom semi if we can find a decent one in our price range. Then, when we start a family, we'll have enough rooms without having all the upheaval and expense of moving again.'

'That sounds sensible to me. I'll have a word with him. I promise.'

Jack and Seth returned with the drinks. 'This is a smart place,' Jack remarked. 'The food looks great. We went for a quick shufti. There's a huge joint of beef, a large roast ham, a turkey and something else that might be lamb. Apparently, the chef carves the meat and then you help yourself to everything else, according to a bloke who works at the library with Seth. When we get our table, they serve the starters and sweets there.'

'I fancy the ham,' Stephanie said, licking her lips. 'What about you Mattie?'

'I might have the beef if it's well cooked.'

Seth interrupted, 'You don't just have to pick one. You can have a bit of everything if you want. I'll be having plenty of each.'

'That's because you're a right gluttonous pig like you've always been,' Jack remarked.

196

'*Pack it in*!' Mattie stated firmly. 'When you start acting the goat, you always end up arguing.'

'That were delicious,' Jack announced, smacking his lips at the end of the meal.

'You're right, it were,' Seth concurred. 'In fact, I could eat that again!'

'See what I mean?' Jack said and then he laughed when he saw Seth winking at Mattie.

Mattie took Jack's hand in hers. 'Thank you Jack, it's been lovely. Everything was delicious. I'm only sorry you're going back so soon.'

'I'm not sorry,' Seth scorned. 'You can't swing a cat round in our bedroom and he snores!'

Jack glared at him. '*I do not*!'

'We're off again,' Mattie said. 'Get the bill paid Jack before there's a fight in here. It's been a lovely evening and I don't want it spoiling now.'

Jack beckoned the waiter and gave him the cash and a tip. 'Are you ready to make tracks then? We could call in The Barn Owl for one quick pint and I could say cheerio to my mates till I'm back again, if that's alright with you Mattie.'

'It's fine by me,' she replied.

They took a taxi to The Barn Owl but the moment they walked in, Mattie felt out of place in the rowdy pub. It was a disreputable-looking dive and she felt intimidated by the locals but Jack assured her it was a safe enough place where the lads congregated to have a few pints and a laugh.

Mattie cast her eyes round the dingy smoky room, concerned about Seth who had gone to the bar with

Jack. Most of the customers were smoking and the ashtray on the table was overflowing with cigarette ends. She could see several others in the same filthy state on other tables around the room.

The staff were rushing back and forth between the customers, collecting the dirty glasses and serving drinks as more people arrived for last orders.

'What an obnoxious place this is,' Mattie said to Stephanie who nodded in agreement.

'It is! I definitely won't be having my hen-party here.'

'Well, you can count *me* out if you do. It's filthy everywhere,' she demonstrated by running her hand across the dirty wet table. 'If I had a cloth, I'd clean it myself and look at the state of the paintwork. It's supposed to be white and it's absolutely caked with nicotine stains.'

'There's a woman over there emptying ash-trays. Maybe she'll get round to this one before long.'

'I would imagine her bag will be full before she reaches this side of the room,' Mattie answered. 'I can't believe Jack suggested coming to a place like this. I can't wait to get out of here. I'm really sorry Stephanie.'

'Hey, don't you go apologising for Jack. It wasn't your idea. When I can catch Seth's eye, I'll call him over and tell him we don't want to stay long.'

A middle-aged chap walked towards their table. 'Can I share your ashtray love?' he asked.

Without waiting for any reply, he stubbed out his cigarette and the smoke wafted up Mattie's nostrils causing her to cough. 'Sorry love,' he said. 'There's no empty ashtrays anywhere. Can I get you young ladies a drink?'

'We're with somebody thanks,' Stephanie said to him with an indifferent smile.

As he walked away, Seth returned with the drinks and when he placed them on the table, at the same time obscuring Mattie's view, the cleaner stretched out her hand to pick up the ashtray.

Mattie saw her fumble for the ashtray and leaned forward to push it nearer to the edge and when the cleaner took hold of it, Seth moved aside to take his seat. Their faces were very close as their eyes met, and there was instant recognition by both parties.

Mattie felt a sudden rush of adrenaline throughout her body....the woman was Hilda Parkes.

Hilda glared menacingly at her before she yelled, '*Mattie Henshaw, you filthy murderous whore*! *You should have got life for what you did*!'

Mattie glanced around helplessly, aware that the outburst had silenced everyone in the room and the next moment, she felt two hands gripping her throat when the overweight Hilda hurled herself forward. Jack was at the scene in seconds, grappling with her but was powerless to heave her away and with both hands clasped securely around Mattie's neck, Hilda continued to hurl abuse while shaking her like a rag doll and Jack feared for her life.

During his effort to restrain her, the assailant fell to the floor, dragging Mattie down with her.

'*Get the boot in Jack*!' Seth bellowed as he tried unsuccessfully to elbow his way into the melee and Jack responded by forcefully kicking her in the ribs.

199

It was a powerful blow, causing Hilda to release her hold, at which point two onlookers rushed forward to pull Mattie to safety.

Hilda screamed out and then there was silence as her head flopped sideways.

The dumbfounded audience remained motionless until someone shouted, '*Send for the police and an ambulance quick. I think she's dead.*'

'I've sent for the police,' the Landlord announced as he gazed at the prostrate woman. 'I think it's too late for an ambulance. Right, will everybody move over there out of the way please.'

'Excuse me, I'm a nurse,' Stephanie interrupted, kneeling down to check her pulse. 'She's alive,' she informed the Landlord. 'Send for an ambulance and tell them to hurry. Her pulse is very weak.'

Mattie had been helped to a chair and Jack was by her side, kneeling down with his arms around her. 'You're going to be just fine Mattie. Don't worry, it's all over with now. Just try to remain calm,' he said quietly.

'What happened? What was all that about?' one of the onlookers asked Jack.

'I've no idea,' he said. 'Please, just leave us alone mate. Give her some space.'

Seth leaned over, his face close to Mattie's. 'Are you alright?' he whispered.

She nodded once and continued to stare ahead in silence until the police arrived.

'Right, move back please....go on....right back as far as you can,' one of the male officers instructed the crowd. Will you lock all the doors Landlord and don't let anyone enter or leave the building until the ambulance crew arrives.'

A policewoman was attempting to talk to Mattie but she remained unresponsive and stared blankly ahead without movement apart from an occasional blink of the eyes. Not once did she cast her eyes in the direction of Hilda Parkes.

Stephanie was holding her hand. 'She's in shock. I'm a nurse,' she informed the officer.

'Did you see what happened?'

'Everybody saw what happened. It was horrible. That woman there attacked her,' she said, pointing to Hilda Parkes. 'She was choking her and I'm sure she'd have killed her if two men hadn't managed to pull her away. She went absolutely crazy!'

'And do you know what might have provoked the alleged attack?'

'Nothing....there was no provocation whatsoever. We were sitting at our table waiting for our drinks to be brought from the bar. She was walking round the room emptying ashtrays and when she reached our table she suddenly began to hurl abuse at Mattie and then for no apparent reason, she attacked her. It all happened very quickly....'

'Can you remember what she said to your friend before the alleged attack took place?'

Stephanie distinctly recalled every word spoken by the obnoxious woman but she decided to reveal nothing further to the policewoman at that point in time. 'No, not really,' she replied. 'As I said, it all happened so quickly. Mattie didn't even have time to respond before she was attacked and dragged to the floor. It was a terrifying experience and I'm just relieved Mattie wasn't killed. She could have been.'

There was a loud knock and the Landlord hurried to the door to admit the ambulance crew.

As one member of the team attended to Mattie's needs, the other members assisted Hilda Parkes for several minutes before heaving her onto a stretcher to be taken to the waiting ambulance.

Mattie remained seated, covered by a thick grey blanket. She was trembling and tears had started to flow from her eyes.

'Will you be admitting her too?' the policewoman asked one of the crew members.

'I think we'd better have her checked over. 'She's not communicating with us so we're not sure about any injuries she might have.'

'Well, I'm telling you now, she's not going in the same ambulance as that fat cow!' Jack informed the policewoman. 'Me and Seth will take her there in a taxi. That maniac's nearly killed her once tonight so I'm damned sure she's not getting a second chance. I'm not letting her out of my sight.'

'Who are you?' the policewoman asked.

'Jack Henshaw, her brother and he's her brother too,' he replied, nodding in Seth's direction.

'Well, I'll need to question you both.'

'That can wait. There's plenty of other folk here who can tell you how she attacked my sister.'

'*Aye....that young lass did nowt wrong*!' one chap shouted out and moved forward. I were just moving away from their table after stubbing out my fag end in their ashtray when that big woman started calling the lass names. I turned round and gawped when I heard her. The young lass looked shocked and then *she* went for her....that woman. She were throttling the lass, and for the minute, everybody stood there stunned. We all saw what happened didn't we?' he asked in general terms.

There was muted response of concurrence by the other customers.

'We'll need to obtain eyewitness statements from anyone who saw anything,' a second police officer called out above the mutterings.

'That will be everybody here then,' another chap shouted. 'Everyone in the pub saw and heard what happened, like *he* just said.'

'And who might you be sir?' the officer enquired superciliously, taking his pencil and notebook from his pocket. He licked the tip of his pencil and eyed him up and down impatiently, awaiting his reply.

'*Hark at him!*' the man said, causing tumultuous laughter. 'Let me see....I *might* be Father Christmas but then again....I might not! If you asked us proper questions, we'd answer 'em proper, right lads?'

The officer's cheeks turned red and he cleared his throat. 'I'd like anybody who witnessed anything to move across here and the rest of you can stay where you are for the time being,' he said authoritatively.

Everyone wandered across, attempting to squeeze into the smaller area, causing even more laughter as they elbowed and shoved each other aside jocularly.

'I'm getting Mattie away from here. It's just like a bloody pantomime,' Jack snorted contemptuously at the policewoman. 'You'll find our particulars at the hospital. Come on Mattie....we're taking you to hospital and we won't let you out of our sight.'

Seth walked out ahead and whistled for a taxi that hastily took them to the Casualty Department.

Jack and Seth remained in the waiting room with Stephanie until called in to see the doctor following Mattie's examination.

'I'd like to keep Miss Henshaw here overnight,' he informed them. 'She's obviously in shock but I can give her medication for that. Maybe tomorrow she'll be more communicative. She has contusions around her neck, a swelling on the back of her head and her reflexes are poor but I can find nothing else wrong with her. However, I need to be certain there are no other significant injuries before we discharge her.'

'Can we stay with her for a while?' Seth asked.

'Perhaps for a few minutes but no longer. It's late so we don't want to disturb other patients.'

'We'll be quiet,' Jack said. 'Incidentally, I believe that woman who attacked Mattie were brought here too. I don't want her anywhere near my sister.'

'What's she called?' he asked looking at his list.

'I haven't a clue. She's a big scruffy woman with grey hair and looks sixtyish I'd say. Somebody said she were unconscious when they brought her here. It were about ten minutes before my sister arrived.'

'Yes, she is here. I'll make sure they're kept apart though she's still unconscious.'

'Good!' Jack grunted. 'I hope she stays that way.'

Jack and Seth were led to the ward when Mattie had been put to bed.

'Only five minutes,' the ward clerk advised them.

'Can you hear me Mattie?' Seth asked when they were alone but she made no attempt to either look at him or acknowledge his presence in any way.

'Don't worry. You're alright now,' Jack told her as he stroked her hand. 'I'm really sorry I took you to that place tonight and I'll never forgive myself.'

She tightened her grip around his hand and spoke tearfully. 'Get Meredith.' Addressing Seth and with beseeching eyes she reiterated, 'Get Meredith and she'll explain everything. I'm sorry. I should have told you myself a long time ago.'

She closed her eyes and tears ran down her face.

Seth dried her wet face with his handkerchief. He kissed her and said softly, 'We'll see you tomorrow Mattie. We love you very much. Try to rest now.'

When they left the ward, Stephanie was restlessly awaiting an update.

'She's still quiet but she seems alright,' Seth told her. 'We're coming back again tomorrow.'

'Did she not say anything about that woman?'

The brothers exchanged fleeting glances and Seth replied, 'No, she didn't say a word.'

When they arrived home it was turned midnight, and when they sat down in the living room, without Mattie's presence, there was an eerie atmosphere.

They started to discuss the earlier events and Seth asked Jack to repeat what *he* believed the cleaning woman had said to Mattie.

'I heard her distinctly. She screamed out that she were a murderer and a whore. Perhaps she mistook her for somebody else.'

'No, she yelled, 'Mattie Henshaw' first. It's been going round in my head ever since.'

'Aye, you're right, she did. I remember that now. She must be crackers then. There can't be any other explanation.'

'I'm not sure. I think there's something about our Mattie's past we haven't been told about. I spend a lot more time with her than you do and I've been a bit worried about her for a while. That's why I keep delaying the wedding because I don't want to leave her on her own. She acts very strange at times and what were all that about Meredith? What's *she* got to do with anything?'

'Well, if you don't ask, you'll never know. Give her a call and tell her what's happened.'

'Have you seen the time? It's well past midnight. She'll be asleep now.'

'Then wake her up dammit! If *you* don't *I* will. I want to know what's wrong. I'm supposed to leave in a few days but how can I go back to Hong Kong with all this lot going on?'

'Aye, you're right and I don't expect we're going to get much sleep anyway.'

Seth dialled her number but it continued to ring. 'She's not answering. She must be asleep,' he said.

'Just let it keep ringing. If she's in, she'll answer it eventually.'

After several more rings, she answered in a sleepy voice.

'Hi Meredith, it's Seth. 'I'm sorry to disturb you at such an unearthly hour but something terrible has happened tonight and Mattie's in hospital.'

At the mere mention of Mattie's name, she awoke fully. 'What do you mean? Why is she in hospital? What's happened?' she questioned frantically.

Seth explained the sequence of the night's events and Meredith was shaken by the news. 'Did Mattie say anything to you?'

'Yes, just as we were ready to leave. She hadn't spoken at all before that and then she turned to me and said I had to speak to you....that you'd explain everything that *she* should have told us a long time ago. That were all she said. I didn't know what she were talking about.'

'I'll just slip something on and come over. I'll be as quick as I can....about twenty minutes.'

'Can't you tell me now?'

'No, I promise I'll explain everything when I get there. Try not to worry. It isn't at all like it seems. Mattie's a sweet person. Don't ever doubt that and I'll see you shortly.'

'She's coming round,' Seth told Jack. 'She says it isn't true and that she'll explain everything. I'll put the kettle on. I think we're in for a long night.'

'Have we nothing stronger?'

'You get what you want. I want a pot of tea.'

Meredith was distraught when she arrived. 'This is terrible,' she commented as Seth took her coat. 'I didn't want to be the one to tell you but Mattie was adamant that you hadn't to be told. You were only young children at the time.'

'At the time of what?' Jack asked.

As she sat down beside him she said, 'First of all, tell me again what that woman said tonight.'

'She bellowed, 'Mattie Henshaw, you're a filthy murderous whore and you should have got life for what you did.' Them were her exact words and then she attacked her and tried to strangle her.'

Seth and Jack stared intently as they awaited her explanation.

'Alright, I'm going to tell you both everything. It isn't a nice story, in fact it's a tragic story and when you've listened to what I have to say, maybe you'll understand Mattie a little better and perhaps you'll also understand her reasons for not telling you what happened to her. I first knew Mattie when she was fourteen years old. She was my client. I was called on to represent her when she killed her foster-father who had been sexually abusing her since her arrival at that disgraceful foster-home.'

Seth gasped incredulously with a stream of tears flowing from his eyes and Jack was filled with rage as he too listened disbelievingly with clenched fists.

She continued, 'It wasn't murder. She killed him accidentally. It was the night she had decided to run away, while he was at the pub but he returned early and went straight to her room. She panicked when he took hold of her and she reached for something with which to fight him off so she could make her escape. She hit him across the head with her tennis racquet but he staggered towards her so she hit him a second time and he dropped dead at her feet. She never intended to kill him and had he not returned when he did, she would have run away and stayed away. Are you alright? Do you want me to go on?'

Seth nodded his head.

'The woman who attacked her in the pub was her foster-mother then....an evil woman who repeatedly beat Mattie. She had an appalling six months there. She was responsible for all the strenuous household tasks while her foster-mother drank herself stupid every night, thus allowing her husband to perform his evil deeds undetected. She was undernourished, dirty and dressed in rags when she was found at the railway station by Sally Williams who, thankfully, took her home. Charles telephoned me when Mattie confessed and I offered to represent her and....'

'I can't believe I'm hearing this,' Jack interrupted angrily. 'Where the hell were Social Services while all this lot were going on?'

'Where indeed! There had only been one visit by the Social Worker during that period. Hilda Parkes, the foster-mother, had ordered Mattie to keep quiet at that visit and it was *she* who informed the Social Worker that Mattie wanted no contact with either of you as she didn't want to unsettle you. You see, she was doubtless afraid you might see the bruises and start to ask questions. She knew nothing about her husband's sexual abuse and Mattie had nobody she could tell about it. Furthermore, Albert Parkes, her abuser, had warned her that should anyone find out, she would be sent to a much worse place than theirs so when she couldn't tolerate the abuse any longer, she devised a plan to escape.'

'Lucky for him that he's dead, so what happened to that fat cow? Did she get sent down?'

'*Oh yes*! She got four years for child cruelty and neglect and Mattie was very cooperative during the investigation. I believe that she was so relieved to escape from the foster-home that it helped her come to terms with most of what had happened to her. It provided her with an aim in life to help others and as the years went by, she achieved her aim through dogged determination. The only issue she couldn't conquer however was her fear of men but I imagine you've noticed that and questioned why she never associates with men?'

'I have,' Seth replied. 'That's why she won't go out anywhere isn't it? She snubbed that nice doctor when he were after her....said she weren't interested but I knew she were, deep down. It was obvious she liked him but I can understand now that her fear of men took over. I wish I'd known about this sooner. I feel guilty now for persistently nagging her for not socialising. I wouldn't have said a single word had I known. Can I ask you....that foster-father....did he damage our Mattie....inside like? You know what I mean,' he asked with a red face.

'No Seth but he did get her pregnant. She had to have a termination.'

'*My God,*' he cried. 'If he weren't already dead, I'd bloody-well kill him now with my bare hands. She were fourteen years old for Christ's sake. What kind of monster treats a child like that? I hope that bitch dies too. You should have kicked her harder Jack. You should have kicked her bloody head in.'

'Aye you're right there, I ought to have. Imagine our Mattie having to live with all that from the age of fourteen. Who else knows about this apart from us? Does Sadie know?'

'She only knows that Mattie wanted to run away because she detested her foster-home. Sally knows of course because she was the one who took her in. Charles is aware of the sexual abuse but was never informed she was pregnant. She wanted it that way. That was the worst part, when she learned she was pregnant and the termination couldn't come quickly enough and was done a day or two later. The Social Services Department was under a great amount of pressure to undertake a thorough investigation and to be honest they didn't attempt any cover-up. They accepted total responsibility for their shortcomings and though I'm not defending them, Social Services pulled strings to find a place for Mattie in Grammar School. They paid for everything she required such as her uniform, books and sports equipment. They were truly repentant for their shortcomings and did everything they could to right the wrongs they were responsible for. Your foster-parents didn't take girls but Social Services persuaded them to take Mattie so you could be together because she so desperately needed the security and support of her family.'

'Social Services didn't suffer like Mattie though, did they?' Jack asked angrily.

'Well, I gave them a very hard time. I threatened them with all kinds of action and then, one day out of the blue, their solicitor rang and made an offer of eight thousand pounds to be held in trust for Mattie until she was twenty-five years old.'

'Blood-money to cover a guilty conscience,' Seth retorted angrily. 'I sincerely hope you told them in no polite terms where they could stick it!'

'Actually I accepted their offer as it was the best I could hope to achieve. It was most unusual for the Social Services Department to make such an offer without a fight. I had to consider the alternative of going to Court and what that might do to Mattie. I wanted her to put it right to the back of her mind. I didn't want to prolong the agony for another couple of years and if I had, there was no guarantee she'd be awarded more so I concluded there was nothing positive to gain by going to Court. Social Services knew that they were to blame and it was time to let Mattie get on with her life.'

'What did Mattie say to the offer?' Seth sneered.

'Like you, she ridiculed it but I was acting in her best interests and Mattie was a child. Money wasn't the issue. It was retribution that Mattie was seeking. Someday, I'm sure she'll put the funds to good use. I doubt she'll use the money for her own needs but some deserving cause will benefit. I'm sure of that.'

'I can't believe we were never told about it,' Jack mumbled. 'All that time and she kept it to herself. You always thought there were something not quite right didn't you Seth?'

'I did but in my wildest dreams I never thought it would be anything as terrible as this. I'm sorry she didn't feel she could confide in us at the time.'

'You were twelve and Jack was only ten so it was hardly a suitable topic of conversation for children to be having and as time went by, Mattie decided it was in the past and there was never any reason why you should know. You could have done nothing to reverse the harm that had been done. It would have served no purpose whatsoever and Mattie wanted to protect you. Surely you can see that?'

'She must have been terrified last night when she came face to face with that bitch.'

'Yes and it were all my fault,' Jack said guiltily. 'If I hadn't suggested going to that pub, none of this would have happened. I feel like storming into that hospital and finishing off what I should have done last night.'

Meredith took hold of his hand. 'Just calm down Jack. Mattie doesn't need any more anguish. Let it take its course now. You mentioned that the police were called to the pub. What did you tell them?'

'Nothing much. I just told them about the attack and then we went straight to the hospital.'

'You mentioned that you'd kicked Hilda Parkes. Tell me, how did that come about?'

'She were choking our Mattie and I couldn't drag her off. She must weigh a good twenty stone. Seth shouted to me to get the boot in and I kicked her in the ribs so she'd let go and then two blokes pulled Mattie from under her when she released her hold.'

'Did many people witness what happened?'

'Everybody in the pub saw what happened.'

'Right then, listen very carefully. When you make your statement to the police, you must say you had done everything possible to secure Mattie's release before you resorted to physical force and when that failed you kicked her hard enough to cause her pain because you feared for Mattie's life. Tell them you were careful to kick her in the ribs where, you felt, it would do least damage. Do *not* deviate from that

213

or you could be charged with grievous bodily harm. You did what was necessary and no more. Stick to your guns and don't let the police put words in your mouth. Do you understand what I'm saying to you? Your concern was to save Mattie.'

'I wish I'd killed the ugly fat bitch!' he snarled.

'*Are you listening to me Jack*?' Meredith declared demonstratively. 'You must protect yourself. You acted in the heat of the moment. Your sister was in grave danger and you feared for her life. You have to remember that. You can't tell the police that you wish you had killed her. How hard did you kick her and how many times?'

'I can't recall. It all happened so quick. I think I kicked her once.'

'Right, then stick to what I've told you since you can't remember and if you feel you're getting out of your depth, tell them you want legal representation before you answer any further questions. You only did what you needed to do. That's the truth so don't deviate from that. I'm going home now and call me if you need anything at all. I'll call the ward Sister in a few hours and I'll try to see Mattie later and I suggest you try to get some sleep. Just remember, Mattie is going to need you, so don't say anything you shouldn't.'

'Thanks for everything,' Seth said with a watery smile as he accompanied her to the door.

The police turned up at the flat at nine o'clock the next morning to talk to Seth and Jack. They didn't recognise the policeman but the female officer was

214

the one who had spoken to Jack briefly the previous night at the pub.

'You work some long hours,' Jack commented as he invited them to sit down.

The policewoman smiled and explained that she had returned to duty on an early shift. 'I take it your sister remained in hospital last night?'

'Yes, we're going to see her later. Can I get you anything? Would you like a cup of tea?'

'No thanks. We're off to the hospital when we've asked you some questions so first of all, would you tell me in your own words what happened last night and especially how the argument started?'

'There weren't any argument,' Seth interrupted. 'That fat woman started yelling at our Mattie for no apparent reason and then she went for her. She were behaving like somebody not right in the head....like somebody demented.'

'Did you hear your sister saying anything at all to that....er....Mrs. Parkes before she yelled at her?'

'No, we were walking back from the bar but my girlfriend said Mattie never spoke a word.'

'We'll be speaking with your girlfriend later, Mr. Henshaw. What we need to know is what *you* saw and heard....not what anyone else told you.'

'We heard that big woman screaming abuse, like I said. Then suddenly, she flung herself at Mattie and they tumbled to the floor or that woman might have dragged Mattie down....I don't know.'

'What happened then?'

'Jack tried to heave her off. I couldn't get near to help him because everybody had crowded forward

215

but I could see that both her hands were still round Mattie's throat and she were throttling her.'

'Did you call out to Jack to do something?'

'Aye, I did because I thought that she were going to kill Mattie.'

'Can you remember what you shouted to Jack?' she asked and when he hesitated she said, 'Was it, 'Get the boot in Jack?' Is that what you shouted?'

'I might have said something like that. As I said, I thought that she were going to kill Mattie and Jack couldn't pull her off. She were a right big woman.'

Turning to Jack she asked, 'Were those the words your brother shouted?'

'I can't recall. All I remember is struggling on the floor and I weren't getting anywhere at all and she were lurching up and down with both hands round Mattie's throat so I jumped up and kicked her.'

'Exactly where on her body did you kick her Mr. Henshaw?'

'I kicked her in the ribs.'

'Are you absolutely sure about that?'

'I'm positive. I wanted her to stop and I thought if I gave her a sharp blow to the ribs it would hurt her enough to make her let go. I kicked her once, about half way down her ribcage. I'm not aggressive and I would never hurt a woman normally but she left me with no choice. There were nothing else I could do. I couldn't just stand there doing nothing could I?'

'What about all the other people who were there? Did nobody else come to your assistance?'

'No they just stood there. I suppose they were all gobsmacked just like we were. When I kicked her, she let go of Mattie and two blokes helped me then. They dragged Mattie out from under her.'

'Were you angry?'

'That's a damn fool question if ever I heard one! Of course I were! She were trying to kill my sister.'

'Weren't you so angry that you kicked her as hard as you could, several times?'

'That's a bloody lie! I kicked her once in the ribs and you'd have done exactly the same had it been a member of your family. I did nothing wrong....'

'I'd have done the same had I been able to get to her first,' Seth interrupted. 'He did what he had to do and no more and anybody who says otherwise is a liar. *She* started it, not us. Were we expected to do nothing? *Well....were we*?' Seth repeated when the policewoman failed to answer his question. 'What about her? Are you going to charge that bitch with assault? It were all her fault. She started it.'

'A police-officer will be speaking to Mrs. Parkes when she's well enough but at the moment, I'm just trying to establish the facts about what happened.'

'That's exactly what happened.'

'Would you give me your girlfriend's name and address please? I'll need to speak to her too.'

'Her name is Stephanie Jackson. If you're going to the hospital, you'll catch her there. She's a nurse and she went to that woman's assistance when she passed out and before you ask, I haven't a clue why she passed out. Jack didn't kick her hard enough to have knocked her out. I saw him.'

The two police officers stood up to leave. 'We'll be in touch,' the policewoman said.

Jack accompanied them to the door and appeared worried when he returned. 'Do you think we should have told them what Meredith said?' he asked Seth.

'We answered their questions didn't we? Nothing she said has any bearing on what occurred earlier in the pub. It wouldn't have changed what happened.'

'I know that but it would have explained why that woman attacked her,' Jack argued.

'Let them find out for themselves. I'm not saying anything I don't have to say. It's up to Mattie to tell them whatever she'd like them to know. We'd still have been no wiser had Meredith not turned up last night. I'm going to ring the hospital now to enquire about Mattie and I'll ask about visiting times.'

He was happy to hear she had spent a comfortable night and although the report from the ward Sister was mainly favourable, Mattie still hadn't spoken a word to anyone he was told. Visiting time was from two until four.

Seth received a call from Stephanie a few minutes later. 'I've just been to see Mattie,' she said.

'How's she doing? I've just spoken to somebody but they tell you nowt of any consequence.'

'She's still about the same. She didn't talk to me. She just stared into space when I tried to talk to her and she didn't touch her breakfast. I think she's still in shock. Are you coming in later?'

'Yes and the police are coming in too. They want to ask you what you know about last night.'

'Well, I don't know what I can tell them. I don't know any more than you do. I just saw the same as everyone else.'

218

'Then tell them that. They asked me if Mattie had said anything before the attack and I said that you'd told me she hadn't but they need to ask you. I told them you went to help that woman who were on the floor.'

'I can't tell them more than that. Listen, I have to go. We're not supposed to use this phone. Perhaps I'll see you later.'

Seth hung up and advised Jack that there seemed to be no noticeable change in Mattie's condition.

As Stephanie was returning to the ward, she came face to face with Lucille who was on her way back from a staff meeting.

'Hello,' Lucille said. 'What are you doing here?'

'I just slipped out to use the phone.'

'Naughty girl! You'll be in big trouble if someone catches you. How's Mattie doing?'

Although Stephanie hadn't intended mentioning the previous night's events, Lucille obviously knew something. 'She's still in shock,' she told her.

'In shock? What do you mean? Who's in shock?'

Stephanie chastised herself for opening her mouth but it was too late to retract what she'd said and so she felt obliged to provide an account of the attack, albeit very brief. That snippet of information failed to satisfy Lucille's curiosity however.

'Come on, out with it. Something else must have happened before that. She wouldn't just attack her for nothing. Who was she? Didn't she say anything to her first? You were there so you must know.'

Stephanie was left with no option but to disclose what Mattie's assailant had said.

'*You're joking*!' Lucille screeched with laughter. '*A murderer and a whore....Mattie?*'

'Just keep your voice down. Everybody will hear you,' Stephanie replied furiously.

'Do you think it's true?' she enquired wide-eyed.

'I don't know why I told you! You're impossible at times and keep away from Mattie. The last clown she needs at her bedside is you.'

Stephanie stormed away, infuriated with herself. Lucille wasn't fit to know anything, and she knew Lucille would reveal all to the next person she saw.

'Come in,' Mark called out and when he glanced up and saw it was Lucille, in an unreceptive tone he remarked, 'Oh, it's you!'

'There's no need to be like that. I've just come to tell you something.'

'Have you now? he replied impatiently, without raising his head from his paperwork again. 'Make it snappy then. I've a lot of work to do here.'

Attempting to sound distressed she stated, 'Mattie Henshaw was admitted last night.'

At the mention of Mattie's name, Mark looked up anxiously. 'Why....what's wrong with her?'

'Well, I've just seen Steph and apparently, Mattie was involved in a pub brawl last night and a woman tried to strangle her. She accused Mattie of being a murderer and a whore in front of everybody and the police had to be called. That woman's in here too. *She* was unconscious when they brought her in and she's still out for the count according to Steph.'

'Who's unconscious....Mattie?' he asked with an expression of horror across his face.

'No, not Mattie....the woman who tried to kill her. Mattie has contusions around her neck and she's in shock, in fact she hasn't spoken one word since she was admitted last night.'

'Where is Mattie?'

'Women's Medical. Are you going to see her?'

'I don't think so but I'll speak to her ward Sister later and thank you for letting me know Lucille.'

'You're welcome. I'll see you later,' she quipped with a flick of the hair.

Mark stared ahead vacantly for several minutes as he digested those two words....*murderer* and *whore*. Why would anyone utter such lies about Mattie he asked himself. Mattie was the sweetest creature he had ever known and it was inconceivable that those words could be true. Furthermore, why was Lucille the perpetual source of atrocious news and why did she seem to take great delight in it? Mark's stomach was churning and he felt sick while contemplating what to do next. Quickly arriving at the conclusion *he* was the wrong person to visit her, he thought of somebody else, somebody in whom she might place her trust.

Dr. McAndrew's receptionist appeared startled by his manner when he burst into the waiting room. 'Is she in?' he asked anxiously.

'She's with a patient but she should be free quite soon,' she advised him, looking at her watch.

'In that case, I'll wait,' he replied edgily.

He paced backwards and forwards until the door opened and when the patient left, without awaiting an introduction he barged in and slammed the door.

She looked up in surprise and raised her eyebrows at his demeanour.

'It's alright Helen, don't worry, I haven't come to ask for information. It took me quite some time but eventually I realised that Mattie was a patient and I apologise for badgering you before.'

'Please sit down Mark,' she said calmly. 'Tell me what's happened now.'

Mark related everything Lucille had told him and she listened carefully without interruption. '*I* can't turn up on the ward unannounced but I thought she might respond favourably if you were to visit her. She knows and trusts you Helen.'

'Do you trust me Mark?'

'I do and I knew after our last conversation why you couldn't divulge anything but actually you told me a lot in a round-about way. I was able to figure out that Mattie had suffered in the past, although I didn't want to believe it. I concluded that she must have been raped or sexually assaulted so I assumed that was the reason she had been taken into care.'

'Your assumptions aren't very far from the truth Mark and I think it's time you were told, in light of what's happened now. I *will* go and see Mattie and I'll report back to you. She might open up to me but first, I'll explain what happened to the unfortunate child. She's neither a murderess nor is she a whore. Mattie's a victim of tragic circumstances.'

Mark listened with incredulity as she related the facts. It was far worse than he could have imagined and he felt so much compassion and love for Mattie that he was barely able to contain his tears.

She stood up, walked towards him and placed her hand on his shoulder. 'Mattie's very resilient Mark. She's conquered everything apart from her fear of men. She needed help for that but she rejected that help. I've tried talking to her but she didn't want to resurrect the past. Go back to your room and I'll go and find Mattie and when I've talked to her, I'll be round to see you. She's stubborn, the same as you. She won't take my advice either. I warned you that you'd get hurt but you chose to ignore my warning. I don't know where you go from here Mark, I really don't.'

'I love her Helen,' he said with tearful eyes.

'I know you do so don't give up hope. None of us knows what the future holds.'


Seth and Jack complained impatiently outside the locked door to the ward. 'It's almost ten past,' Seth grumbled. 'It'll be time to go home before we get in at this rate. I hope Mattie's feeling better today. She frightened me last night. I wonder what she'll have to say to us now that we know everything.'

'I don't care as long as she says something. I just want her to start talking to us again. If she does, I'll never complain anymore that she's nagging!'

'Neither will I. Right, somebody's coming and I think they're going to unlock the door. Gawd, I feel lousy! I'm dreading this.'

'You and me both mate,' Jack replied.

They slowly inched forward with the crowd and approached the bed apprehensively. Mattie ignored them as they arrived at her bedside and Seth leaned over to kiss her, followed by Jack but there was no response whatsoever.

Seth sat down and took hold of her hand. 'Hello Mattie,' he said. 'Are you feeling any better today?'

He slanted his eyes in Jack's direction when she continued to stare ahead and Jack leaned across the bed and said, 'We spoke to Meredith last night and she told us everything and it's alright. You're going to be fine. You've nothing to worry about, nothing at all. We'll always be here to support you.'

'This is a complete waste of time,' Seth said. 'She doesn't even know we're here.'

A nurse approached and enquired whether Mattie had spoken to either of them.

'No, it's as if she's on another planet. She won't even look at us,' Seth answered.

'Are you related?'

'We're her brothers. There isn't anyone else. Our parents are both dead.'

'We'll need to request a psychiatric evaluation if she's the same tomorrow. She's had a nasty shock. Some patients snap out of it while others need help. I was hoping a visit from her relatives might do the trick. That usually works when they hear a familiar voice so keep talking to her. You aren't doing her any favours by sitting here twiddling your thumbs. I'll pop back and see you again later and hopefully, you'll have some better news for me.'

'Thanks,' Jack replied.

'I were going to bring you a bottle of Lucozade,' Seth said. 'Do you remember Jack bringing one for me when I were in here?'

'I do,' Jack laughed. 'And we had a pillow fight and Mr. Wyndham turned up and caught us. Do you remember Mattie?' He turned to face Seth. 'This is hopeless. She can't hear a word we're saying.'

Seth glared at him. 'We'll do what the nurse said! Mattie....pay attention....Jack has to go back to sea soon but he can't go anywhere if you won't talk to us. He has to know you're alright. Come on, talk to us please. We want to try and help you.'

Jack glanced around the ward, trying to think of something to say, when his eyes began to follow a plump middle-aged woman, wearing a hospital coat and who was walking down the ward. She smiled at him as she drew nearer. 'Hello, I'm Dr. McAndrew and you must be Mattie's two brothers.'

'We are. I'm Seth and this is my younger brother Jack. Are you the psychiatrist?'

'No, I'm a friend of Mattie's. I've known her for a very long time. I heard she was here so I've come to see if I can get her to have a wee word with me.'

'Do you know all about Mattie?' Jack asked.

'What do you mean?'

Jack felt tongue-tied. 'I meant do you know what happened when she was fourteen?'

'Do you?' she enquired, structuring her question simply though skilfully in order not to divulge any information.

'Yes, her friend Meredith told us everything last night.'

'Meredith Spencer?' she questioned in an attempt to gain their confidence.

'That's right. Do you know her?'

'Indeed I do. I know Meredith very well, so what did she tell you last night?'

Seth sighed. 'She told us all about Mattie's foster-father and the things he did to her.'

'I guess you were very upset weren't you?'

'We couldn't believe it when she told us. Did you know Mattie then?'

'Yes, I helped her through a difficult time in her life and that's why I'm here now. May I try?'

Seth moved aside and Dr. McAndrew looked her straight in the eyes. 'Right, come on Mattie. I know you can hear so you can stop your pretending with me. Your brothers are here and I'm not leaving till you talk to me. Come on dear, you know very well I'm your friend. Just say hello to me.'

'Go away and leave me alone,' she said, turning her head away.

'Good girl! At least that's a start. What's all this nonsense about? Fancy your not talking to Jack and Seth when they're worried to death about you. Say hello to them too.'

'I won't! I want everyone to leave me alone.'

'Why is that dear?'

'Because I'm a trouble maker. Everywhere I go, I cause trouble.'

Dr. McAndrew smiled. 'Get away with you. You didn't cause anything. Hilda Parkes was responsible for everything. Anyway, it's ended now. She won't be causing you any more trouble.'

Mattie turned to face her. 'Is she dead?'

'No, she isn't dead, more's the pity but she's been for a scan and she's had a serious stroke. She'd had

226

minor strokes previously and she'd been warned to take things easy. It probably happened when she hit the floor. She cracked her skull according to the X-ray. She won't be bothering you again. She'll spend the rest of her life in care.'

'Where I for one, hope she rots!' Jack interposed. 'Are you alright Mattie?'

'After a lifetime of surviving much worse, as you now know, I'll deal with it in my own time.'

Seth replied gently, 'We are both very sorry. That sounds so inadequate I know but I don't know how to put it into words....what I want to say.'

'I know,' she said, smiling faintly at her brothers.

Addressing Seth and Jack, Dr. McAndrew asked, 'Would you mind leaving us alone for a wee while? There's a drink dispenser at the bottom of the ward on your left. Just give us ten minutes please.'

'Do you want anything Mattie?' Jack asked.

'I wouldn't mind a cup of tea. I've had nothing at all since I came in last night.'

The nurse they had talked to earlier stopped them as they were leaving the ward and enquired, 'How's it going?'

'Great,' Jack smiled. 'She's talking to us now and she's thirsty.'

'Well done! I'll order her some tea and maybe a sandwich and some cake might just tempt her to eat a bit of something as well. I'll have it sent to her.'

'I wanted a quiet word with you,' Dr. McAndrew said. 'I saw Mark earlier. He knows you're here and he's so distressed about all your suffering.'

'*He knows*?' she asked with a dazed expression.

'He's known for a while....well not everything but he'd seen how you reacted to men and he'd sensed that something dreadful had occurred earlier in your life. He'd like to see you Mattie, just to talk to you. He loves you and he wants to help.'

'*No, I don't want to see him,*' she cried.

'Alright....I didn't promise him anything but he's a decent man and he'd never ever hurt you.'

'Don't you think I know that? I'd end up hurting *him* and I feel far too much for him to allow that to happen. Please, you have to tell him I don't want to see him. I'm no good for him and he must forget all about me.'

'If that's what you want, then that's what I'll tell him. Are you going to be alright now?'

'I suppose so. I just feel so ashamed when I think about everyone in the pub hearing what that woman called me.'

'Now you're being foolish. You've done nothing to feel ashamed about and I don't think for a minute that anybody believed a single word of it. You have recovered from worse than this Mattie and your two brothers will support you. They appear to be caring young men.'

'You're right. They're amazing and I don't know what I'd do without them.'

'You just concentrate on getting better, right? I'll try to pop in again before you leave and remember what I said about counselling. It really would help. Take care of yourself Mattie.'

8

'It feels great to be back home again,' Mattie said meaningfully as she flopped on the sofa. 'I'm sorry I spoiled the lovely evening.'

'Listen, that weren't you....that were all my fault. I can't believe I took you to a dive like that but let's try to put it behind us. That restaurant were terrific so it weren't all bad.'

Mattie wasn't paying attention to Jack. 'I suppose it was inevitable, that I'd bump into that obnoxious woman eventually. Still, from what Dr. McAndrew told me, I won't be bumping into her anymore. She came to see me again the next day and told me that the stroke had taken her speech and everything. In some respects, I feel pity for her. She's had a rotten life married to him and look at her now. She's like a vegetable.'

'I can't believe my ears,' Jack said angrily. 'After everything she's done, you feel *sorry* for her?'

'You wouldn't understand. Everyone's entitled to a decent life.'

Jack expelled an exasperated sigh. 'Including you Mattie! If you can't talk sense, don't talk at all. She did *nothing* to afford *you* a decent life, the way she had you slaving when you were there. She's an evil bitch who got her just desserts for what she did.'

Once again, Mattie wasn't listening. 'I've made a decision while I've been in hospital. I want to move away from here and make a fresh start somewhere else. I should have done that when I left University, when I had the opportunity. I'm just a liability here and I need to spend some time on my own and then maybe I can sort myself out once and for all.'

Seth looked dazed. 'What are you talking about? We don't want you to move away do we Jack?'

Before he could answer she continued, 'You have Stephanie and it's time you were married. You have your own lives to lead and you're hardly ever here Jack. You can still visit me wherever I am. We can gossip on the phone and keep in touch. I managed on my own at University and I was much younger then. It's something I must do. I can't go on living in the past, surrounded by painful memories.'

Nothing further was discussed and Seth believed that once Mattie had settled down again, she would forget about leaving but she had made up her mind.

When she returned to work, she advised Meredith of her plan. 'I haven't decided where to go yet but I have to move away and Seth's needs are important too. He's in danger of losing Stephanie if he keeps delaying the wedding and that's the very last thing I want on my mind. When Seth moved in with me, it was a short-term arrangement. I knew that at some point he'd want to get married and I was prepared to live alone when that happened but things haven't worked out like that. Seth feels he's responsible for me and I won't ruin his life. I've caused everybody enough heartache already.'

Although Meredith was somewhat dubious about Mattie's reasons for leaving, she gave her a vote of confidence. 'It'll do you good to spread your wings. You'll meet other people, though I don't know how I'm going to manage here without you,' she said.

'I don't know how I'll cope without you around,' Mattie sighed. 'I'll really miss you.'

'Don't bite my head off for asking but what about Mark?'

She avoided Meredith's gaze. 'What about Mark? I don't know what you mean.'

'I think you do Mattie. You have to confront your gremlins and running away won't help. It's good to have a change but it has to be for the right reasons.'

'Well, perhaps when I'm away from here, people won't keep reminding me about my gremlins.'

'But they'll still be there....they'll always be there unless you do something about them. You're such a strong person in every other way. Tackle your fears and resolve your issues....please, because wherever you go, there'll be men like Mark who will pursue you. You're a beautiful woman.'

'Could we end it there please?' she asked frostily. 'I'm trying to concentrate on my work.'

For the rest of the morning they kept their heads down and barely exchanged a word.

After lunch, Meredith decided to raise the matter again. 'When I was at University, I shared a room with girl named Samantha. She came from Devon and her parents ran a guest house on the outskirts of Torquay. I went to stay there with her once during the summer break. As I recall, the house had about fourteen bedrooms and there was a *huge* garden and conservatory. It was a beautiful country house yet we could meander to the beach in less than twenty minutes. Her mother explained to me that they had a regular clientele of holidaymakers each year and during the winter months, from January to March, they closed down to customers and took their own holidays, using the rest of that time for renovations, repairs and redecorating.'

'Is there a point to any of this?' Mattie interrupted impatiently.

Meredith ignored her petulance and carried on, 'I was told that when Sam's parents became too old to run the business, a substantial part of the house was converted into apartments. The family retained half of the first floor and sold off half of the remaining apartments, keeping the others to let as self-catering holiday apartments to their regulars. I haven't been in contact with Sam for a long time but if you were interested in Devon, I could call her and ask if there were any vacancies. I don't know what you have in mind but I can recommend the location. I certainly enjoyed my holiday there and it might be what you need to help you readjust after what's happened.'

She stopped writing and pricked up her ears. 'Do you think there'd be work available close by?' she questioned with interest.

'Yes, Torquay is only a couple of miles away.'

'Well, I don't suppose there's anything to lose by making enquiries. I'd quite like a place within easy reach of the sea. Thanks for that Meredith. Is Sam a solicitor too?'

'Yes, she qualified the year I did though she read Business Law. She works with the local authority's Legal Services Department. If you like, I'll call her tonight when she's home from work. We can have a chat and I'll make a few tentative enquiries.'

'Thanks, that's great. Incidentally, did Andrew's children arrive safely in Spain?'

'Yes, '*the wicked witch of the west*' came over for them. They've called to say they're having a whale of a time but Andrew's all of a lather, thinking she might not bring them back next week.'

'Of course she will. She'd lose all future access if she didn't.'

Meredith raised her eyebrows. 'Yes....but you try convincing Andrew of that!'

'It's going well between the two of you isn't it?'

'Very well. He's a caring, considerate guy who is also a fantastic father to his kids. They're two great boys. Andrew and I were talking about going away for the weekend before they come home. We don't get much time to ourselves so that would be good if it happened.'

'Then make it happen!' she told her.

Just after nine o'clock that night, Meredith called her. 'Guess what!' she squealed excitedly. 'I think you might be in luck with Sam. I've just spoken to her and she happened to mention that a few of the apartments *are* empty. I didn't reveal you might be interested in one because I'd discussed everything with Andrew first and suggested that the three of us go down for the weekend. When I told her, she was delighted to be seeing us, so you can weigh up the situation while you're there and if you don't fancy it, you can walk away without feeling obligated or embarrassed. Devon is a lovely county and I'm sure you'll like it there and Sam's very easy to get along with, so can you make it for the weekend?'

'Er....yes. With my social calendar, I'm available any weekend but it's hardly going to be a romantic interlude for you and Andrew with me around.'

'Excuse me....you won't be sharing our bedroom! We'll have lots of time together. Anyway, I'm very excited to be seeing Sam again. I haven't seen her for years.'

'Are her parents still alive?'

'I assume so....I didn't ask her. We didn't discuss anything in any detail. She had a headache and was about to go to bed but she was pleased that we were going to see her.'

'So when are we going?'

'If we leave early Saturday, we should be there by midday. I suggested Friday night to Sam but as she goes to bed around ten, I suppose she wouldn't like her parents to be disturbed if we were delayed. You know what traffic can be like on a Friday night and it always takes longer to drive in the dark.'

'Do you know, I'm really looking forward to the weekend! I've never been to Devon,' Mattie replied enthusiastically.

Andrew parked up in the courtyard outside Sam's house at eleven-thirty. 'Not bad that, not bad at all. Four-and-a-half hours precisely,' he boasted, proud of his achievement.

'What do you think of it Mattie?' Meredith asked as they stepped from the car.

Casting her eyes over the gargantuan building she stated, 'It's lovely. You certainly didn't exaggerate when you said it was an imposing residence.'

'Leave the bags for now Andrew. Let's go in and you can meet Sam. She's a great girl....she's so full of life and I know you'll just love her.'

Meredith ran ahead and pressed the doorbell. She waited for a while and when nobody answered, she pressed it again. Seconds later the door was opened by a thin-faced middle-aged woman with dark rings around her deep-set eyes and Meredith was startled by her pallid waxen complexion. She was wearing a headscarf, tied tightly around her head and knotted at the back. She smiled warmly at Meredith. 'That's Chemo!' she declared, pointing to the headscarf. 'It knocks hell out of you *and* ruins your hair too!' she laughed. 'It's so nice to see you again and you look amazing Meredith. Please come in.'

Meredith was distraught but was able to hide her sentiments without revealing that she had failed to recognise her friend. 'It's good to see you too Sam,' she managed to answer. 'I didn't know about....'

'Of course you didn't. How long has it been?'

She sighed. 'Too long Sam. Let's go inside where you can rest. I wouldn't have come had I known.'

Sam smiled. 'Why do you think I didn't tell you? I wanted you here, so I'm delighted. In the absence of any introductions by Meredith, I assume you are Mattie and you must be Andrew.' She shook their hands. 'I'm happy to make your acquaintance. Let's go through to the sitting room.'

As she led the way, Meredith glanced in Mattie's direction apologetically as they followed Sam into the sitting room.

'What a magnificent room,' Mattie remarked.

Sam smiled at her. 'Yes, isn't it? I spend most of my time here,' and she turned to Meredith saying, 'You can ask me whatever you want. I don't mind discussing it. I've had time to come to terms with it and I don't always look such a pitiful wreck.'

Though Meredith felt ill-at-ease, she believed she ought to say something. 'When was it diagnosed?'

'*Cancer*? You're permitted to speak the word. It would be er...two years ago. Yes that's right....two years.... though initially they used to refer to it as a brain tumour. Back then, everyone was alarmed by its proper name so they wrapped it up in acceptable dialogue to make it appear less life-threatening, but they shouldn't you know, because it gives you false hope. When your time is limited, you need to know to plan ahead....to do the things you've never done and that you always wanted to do. When I knew, I felt much better. I was able to get on with life and I've enjoyed the past two years tremendously. I'm never miserable and I'm overjoyed to see you and meet your friends so don't be gloomy. I'm not,' she said with a genuine warm smile.

'Do you have much pain?' Meredith asked.

'No, apart from the occasional headache I'm fine. It can be a bit rough for a couple of weeks after the Chemo but then I'm like the proverbial rubber ball. I bounce right back again. You'll hardly recognise me later. When I put my war-paint on, I'm a totally different person. Right, that's plenty about me! Tell me what *you've* been up to.'

'Nothing particularly exciting....just the same old hum-drum life, day in day out,' she advised Sam.

'Gee thanks,' Andrew stated, to peels of laughter. 'That's made *me* feel appreciated!'

'You know what I mean....at the office. Actually, Andrew is the highlight of my life,' she said, taking hold of his hand and smiling affectionately at him. 'He was a client. That's how we first met.'

'As a matter of fact, we were thrown together and not very diplomatically so by Mattie,' Andrew said. Turning to Sam, he explained, 'Mattie thought she ought to intervene to find a bloke for Meredith who apparently couldn't manage to find one for herself, and she was about as subtle as a train wreck.'

'*That's not true*!' Meredith shrieked. 'Mattie, tell Sam it's not true this minute.'

'Would I dare contradict Andrew to protect you? It's true!' she said and Sam howled with laughter.

'Just like the old days!' Sam made known. '*I* got all the blokes at Uni and *she* was pea-green.'

'*I was not*!' Meredith disputed. 'I simply chose to dedicate my time to my studies.'

'Whatever you say. So Mattie, how do *you* fit into this love triangle then?'

'I work with Meredith.'

'So you're a solicitor too?'

'I like to believe I am but Meredith's a hard act to follow. Highly respected, she's extremely busy and so I joined her when I qualified.'

Addressing Sam, Meredith said, 'I take it you've packed up work now?'

'I resigned five years ago. There's so many more pleasurable ways of filling one's days, speaking of which....' she said, turning her head to the door that was opening slowly. 'Come in darling. It's alright. Come here and meet my friends.'

Meredith stared at the door and Mattie gasped as the most delightful child she had ever seen entered the room and ran towards Sam.

'There's no need to be shy,' Sam told her. 'These people are my friends. Everyone, this is Akina, my daughter.'

'Well aren't you the dark horse?' Meredith stated. 'I didn't even know you were married.'

'That's hardly a prerequisite Meredith. In fact it's often an encumbrance,' she chuckled. 'I'm a single parent. Akina's father is Japanese. He was a tourist who stayed here for about four weeks over six years ago. Towards the end of his stay, we became close friends.'

'That's a bit of an understatement!' Meredith said matter-of-factly. 'I'd say *exceptionally* close!'

'Naturally, I didn't know I was pregnant when he was leaving and we didn't make any plans to keep in touch, so he never knew about Akina.'

Mattie beckoned her. 'Akina, come over here and let me see your pretty dress.'

The little girl walked slowly towards Mattie and sat down beside her.

'You have a lovely name. What does it mean?'

'Spring flower. Mummy chose it for me because I was born in April in the springtime. It's a Japanese name, like my daddy is Japanese.'

'Well, I think that's very appropriate Akina. You have beautiful shiny hair too and that's the prettiest dress I've ever seen.'

'Thank you very much. You have lovely hair but mine is a lot darker than yours and mine is straight. You have curls.'

'Yes I do. So tell me....how old are you?'

'I'll be six in April.'

'And do you like school?'

She grimaced and shot a sideways glance at Sam before replying, 'No, not really. I'd rather be home caring for mummy when she's sick.'

'Darling, would you ask nana if she would make some tea please? Don't try to lift the tray yourself. It will be far too heavy. Is tea alright for everyone?' Sam asked and when they nodded, the child left the room. 'Don't even ask Meredith! I've no idea,' she confessed, in anticipation of her next question.

'Sam, you're going to have to make arrangements just in case....what about your parents?'

'No way! They're far too old to bring up a child. Besides, they're likely to be long gone before she's out of her teens so what would happen to her then? Social Services foster-care? I don't think so!'

Mattie remained silent but was in total agreement.

'Don't you have any relatives?' Meredith asked.

'I do but nobody who's close and definitely none I would trust with my child. Anyway, I'm still here and I could be around for some time yet if the final session of Chemo is successful.'

'When will that be?'

Sam hesitated before answering. 'I've already had it, so now it's the waiting game.'

There was a rattling of crockery and Andrew said, 'Allow me.' He arose from his chair and hurried to the door to relieve Sam's mother of the tray that he placed on the table.

'This is my mum. Mum, you remember Meredith don't you?' Sam said.

'I would have recognised you anywhere my dear. You haven't changed at all,' she replied as she held her warmly. 'It's lovely to see you again.'

'You too,' Meredith replied with a smile. 'This is my friend Andrew and Mattie who works with me.'

'I'm very pleased to meet you,' she said, shaking their hands. 'I'm Emily....Emily Peters. Norman my husband will be here shortly. He's bad on his feet, arthritis you know,' she added, directing her remark at Meredith. 'There's nothing clever about growing old, as the saying goes.'

'I'll simply have to take your word for that,' Sam quipped and laughed brazenly.

'Did you enjoy a pleasant journey?' Emily asked without even raising an eyebrow at her daughter's flippant remark.

'It was lovely,' Mattie replied. 'I've never been to Devon before. The countryside is beautiful and the air smells so much fresher here too.'

Meredith walked across to the table and started to pour the tea.

'I can do that dear,' Emily said. 'You're a guest.'

'No, I insist. You sit down, please.'

'Thank you but I need to get something from the kitchen first.'

Emily returned with two large plates, overflowing with an assortment of sandwiches and cream cakes. 'Hand those round please darling,' she told Akina.

'Give everybody a plate first and then start with the sandwiches.'

Akina did as requested and took her place beside Mattie. 'Have you got a dog?' she asked her.

'No I haven't. Have you?'

'Yes and her name's Poppy. She's a teeny-weeny Yorkshire Terrier and she's very cute.'

Everyone was listening and howled with laughter when she said, '*Actually*, she's nana's dog.'

'I'll bet it's you who takes her for walks,' Mattie said with a smile.

Akina giggled. 'You're right. Do you want to see Poppy?' she asked, her appealing brown eyes wide open in anticipation of her reply.

'I'd love to see her.'

'Come on then,' she said excitedly, stretching out her small hand.

Mattie took hold and as Akina led her across the room she said, 'She's not allowed in here you see.'

Mattie looked over her shoulder at the others who were smiling and when she caught Sam's gaze, she recognised a desperate, heart-rending plea. At that moment, Mattie smiled lovingly at Akina with tears welling in her eyes, knowing that her own life had changed forever....


Once in the confines of their room, Andrew held Meredith in his arms as she sobbed uncontrollably. He held her tight, searching his soul for appropriate words of comfort but nothing remotely fitting came to mind. What words could he possibly speak that would lessen her pain and ease her distress?

She clung to him for some time before releasing her hold. 'I'll be alright now,' she told him. 'It was such a shock. I didn't even recognise Sam when she opened the door. I tried so hard to keep it together and then, when her daughter walked in, that's when I lost it. I came close to running from the room. It is *so* heartbreaking.'

'What can I say? Sam's your best friend and you had no prior knowledge of her illness. *I* was trying to choke back the tears and *I* don't even know her. I felt so much compassion for the child. As a father, I know how it feels when you think you're going to lose your child but at least I would have had access to mine had things turned out that way but Sam and Akina will lose each other forever.'

'What I find difficult to grasp is how they can be so matter-of-fact about everything. Did you notice, when Sam made such a frivolous reply to Emily's reference to old age, Emily didn't even flinch? Sam really shocked me when she made that remark.'

'That's because as a family, they are dealing with everything, drawing their strength from each other. Remember that with older people, there's a certain inevitability about death. They're programmed in a way to accept death, their having spent a lifetime of coming to terms with it. They begin by losing their friends, then their loved ones and they take it all in their stride. You should remember that Sam and her family have had a couple of years to adapt. You've only known for a few hours so you're bound to be upset but they've travelled way beyond that stage. What's important to them now is that they live each day to the full while they're still together. There'll be time enough for sadness and tears when Sam's gone. I think it's admirable that they behave as they do and we must play our part to appear joyful too, despite our inner thoughts.'

Meredith sighed. 'You're right but it's difficult to put on a brave face. I still remember our University days and what Sam was like then, when we were a pair of crazy teenagers without a care in the world.'

'But you've changed too. What's important is that she's delighted to see you again and you must try to understand that she doesn't see herself the way you see her. Look beyond the surface and see the person within. She's had two happy years since her illness was diagnosed so try to keep it together for the next forty-eight hours. You'll come to terms with it too as time passes and the next time we're here, you'll feel a whole lot better. Trust me.'

'You'll come again?' she asked tearfully.

'Of course we'll come again. We'll work through it together,' he said and kissed her. 'Come on, stop crying and wash your face. It'll make you feel a lot better. We can hang up our clothes later.'

As they were walking down the stairs, they could hear laughter in the kitchen. The door was open and they peered in to find Mattie playing at snakes and ladders with Akina.

'I'll play the winner,' Andrew volunteered when he realised Akina was well ahead.

'Then I hope you do better than me! I must have slithered down every blooming snake on the board,' Mattie complained as Akina giggled.

Meredith walked to the far end of the kitchen and began to dry the cups and saucers as Emily finished off wiping around the sink.

'I'm so thrilled you came,' she said to Meredith. 'Sam was pleased to be seeing you again after such a while and your friend Mattie is a delightful young woman. It's very difficult for me at my age, trying to keep Akina amused. At times, Sam needs to rest for quite long periods and the dear child wears me out. She's full of life and doesn't understand that I can't keep up with her. She can be such hard work.'

'At her age I can well imagine,' Meredith replied. 'Does she know er....everything?'

'Oh yes! Sam insisted she be told. She explained it to her about a year ago, when she felt Akina was of an age to understand. Norman and I were present and she chose her words very carefully. When she had finished, Akina asked if Sam would be able to watch over her from heaven and when Sam replied that she would *always* watch over her she just said, 'That's alright then', and she didn't shed one single tear. Isn't that amazing?'

'Are you sure she understood?'

'Yes, she understood alright and now they discuss it quite openly together. Because she was told at an early age, she accepted Sam's explanation. Only a few months ago, she asked who would care for her here after she'd gone away and Sam explained that someone would have to be chosen as her guardian. Akina than asked if that person would be a guardian angel as she'd learned about that at school and Sam told her *she* would be her guardian angel, whereas

244

her *guardian* would be somebody very special here on earth to care for her. When she questioned who that person would be, Sam said she hadn't decided yet and Akina asked if *she* could choose her special guardian. Sam promised her they would choose that person together, as it was a very important decision to make.'

'She's a truly amazing child,' Meredith sighed.

'She's one in a million.'

'And what about you Emily? Are you as resolute as you appear outwardly?'

'I have my moments of disquiet when I think of the child's future and I pray that she'll be happy but I'm fine about Sam. It's something her father and I have had to learn to live with, so we take life a day at a time. We behave as if everything were normal. We didn't expect Sam to be here now so every new day is a blessing for which we are thankful. We're fine Meredith.'

'*Yes*! Akina screeched. 'I've won you Mattie.'

'*Beaten*!' Mattie corrected her. 'You've certainly beaten me. Look Andrew, I'm still dithering about on the second line.'

With a twinkle in his eye he pulled up his chair. 'Right young lady,' he said. 'You'll definitely lose to me. I have two sons back home and I always beat them at snakes and ladders, so be forewarned. You are going to lose this game!'

'I bet I don't!' she grinned.

'We'll have to see about that.'

Everyone watched attentively as Andrew took the lead and soon, there was just one remaining snake to ward off before claiming victory over Akina who scrutinised the board competitively.

'Anything but a five,' he called out to the dice as he shook it vigorously before tipping it on the table. '*Oh no!*' he cried out as he threw a five and Akina squealed with joy as Andrew slithered back to the third row.

When she reached the end of the board after three more throws of the dice, he sat with his head in his hands, feigning despair at his defeat.

Everyone laughed when he asked, 'What about a game of golf Akina?' and more so at her reply, 'If you like but I'll probably win at golf too.'

No one had heard Sam come into the kitchen and when Meredith looked up she gasped, 'Wow, what a transformation. That's how you used to have your hair at University.'

'I did but can you remember the trouble I used to have with it then? It always curled the wrong way at one side. This is much easier. I just have to lift it off until the next time and it always stays the same. It's good isn't it? See I've got eyebrows now too!'

Andrew too looked stunned and Sam detected the look of disbelief in his eyes.

'It's all phoney Andrew. Females are compulsive tricksters. We have implanted boobs, artificial nails, false eyelashes, crowned teeth and many wear wigs. We squeeze into girdles to improve the figure, use lotions to hide the blemishes and wrinkles and shall I tell you the best part? Men don't have a clue until it's too late. I wouldn't mind betting that Meredith has had quite a few nips and tucks here and there!'

'*I have not,*' she protested.

'Indeed? So what's with the generous curvaceous boobs then? I recall you were as flat as a pancake at University and *I* haven't come across a bra to create a cleavage like yours.'

'I could kill you,' she said, looking horrified.

'You'll have to look sharp then. Don't forget, I'm already on the waiting list. I still insist you've had a boob job! Deny it!'

As Meredith lowered her head in shame, Andrew laughed audibly. 'Well, that's definitely a first. I've never known Meredith to be stuck for words before. Come on my love, spill the beans. You're amongst friends. Tell the truth and shame the devil. Did you have a boob job? I have to be perfectly honest when I say they don't wobble.'

'*Andrew!*' she screeched. 'Alright, if it makes you drop the subject, yes I have!'

Everyone laughed heartily and Emily interjected, 'You could have had half of mine. I've too much.'

'Lighten up,' Sam said. 'They look fantastic. You wouldn't have had them done had you not wanted people to notice.'

'I'm just thankful I waited till I'd left Uni. You'd have made sure *everyone* was told.'

'You're joking! They wouldn't have needed to be told.'

'And what are you grinning at?' Meredith asked Andrew crossly.

'I was just wondering what else I might discover about you....not that I'm complaining,' he said with an even wider grin that brought a smile to her face.

247

'Right, who wants a drink?' Sam asked, changing the subject. 'I could manage something.'

'Me too,' Mattie replied.

'Well, before I decide, what's the plan for later?' Andrew asked. 'Are we all going out for dinner? If we are, I can't drink and drive.'

'Oh have a drink. We can walk to the restaurant. There's a decent one a hundred yards up the road. I just feel like letting my hair down, or should I say, my wig!'

'Don't start that again,' Meredith threatened her. 'You might get me to reveal more secrets.'

'There's more?' Andrew laughed.

For the first time since their arrival, Meredith felt relaxed and at ease with the situation around her. It had felt good to exchange repartee with Sam and to laugh together about girly topics as they had done when they were young.

She slipped her hand in Andrew's, appreciative of his presence and as her eyes drifted towards Mattie and Akina, she realised that their visit would have a gratifying result. The bond between them was as if carved in stone and the expression of joy in Sam's eyes revealed that she knew it too. Sam and Akina had chosen their guardian.

'Do you like your room Mattie?' Sam asked.

'It's perfect. 'I have a lovely view of the sea from my window and I'd like to take a walk on the beach before we leave on Monday if I can find the time.'

Akina was bitterly disappointed. 'You're leaving on *Monday*? Mummy, please let Mattie stay longer. I don't want you to send her away.'

'I'm not sending her away darling. She has to go back with Meredith and Andrew. They have to go home too. They're only here for the weekend.'

'I'll come again....I promise. *Actually*!' she said, and everyone laughed. 'Actually, I was going to ask your mummy if she had any spare rooms and I was going to come back for a long time. That's why I'm here this weekend. I came to see if I liked it here.'

'And do you?' Akina asked eagerly.

'Yes, I like it here very much and I especially like you,' she said with a genuine smile.

'I pre....prepecially like you too,' she replied and everyone shrieked with laughter. 'Mummy, please can Mattie come back to stay? Please say she can.'

'Well, we have a spare room if she really wants to come back so we'll discuss it later.'

'You won't change your mind will you? Promise me Mattie,' she gabbled. 'Why don't we go now to the beach with Poppy? She hasn't had her walk yet and we can run along the sand in our bare feet.'

'Akina....Mattie's enjoying a nice quiet drink with friends so don't be a nuisance. If she wants to walk along the beach later, that's fine and if she doesn't, that's also fine. Right?'

'I'm sorry....I just wanted her to look at the sea.'

'And so she shall, when she's good and ready. Go and find granddad and wake him up now. He's fast asleep in the sitting room. Tell him another of your stories. He'll like that and we can enjoy our drinks.'

'Please don't forget our walk Mattie,' she said as she closed the door.

'She's like a breath of fresh air,' Mattie sighed.

249

'I think a force ten gale would be more accurate!' Sam said. 'She's so full of energy. So, enlighten me Mattie, I'm intrigued. Why do you want to move to Devon? Who's the guy you're running away from?'

'To be honest, it's my brother. We share a rented flat and he's supposed to be getting married shortly but he keeps delaying the wedding because he feels he can't leave me there alone. I've already told him I'm looking for somewhere else to live, so when I do move away, he'll have no excuse then.'

'So does he need an excuse? Is he uncertain of his feelings for his girl?'

'Not at all. My two brothers and I lost our parents when we were young. I'm the eldest. The three of us became very close as a family when we only had each other. When Jack, the youngest, joined up in the Royal Navy there was just Seth and I. Seth feels guilty about leaving me alone. That's why I need to move away. His fiancée, Stephanie, is a lovely girl isn't she Meredith?'

'She is and it's true what Mattie says. Stephanie *is* becoming impatient. They've been saving up for some time and she wants to get married but girls do don't they? They need commitment and a sense of security whereas blokes don't bother the same....'

'Is that right?' Andrew interrupted. 'Am I to take that as a proposal of marriage then Miss Spencer?' he asked guardedly and when Meredith appeared to be shocked and embarrassed by his interpretation of her remark, he howled with laughter. 'Alright, if it makes you happy, then I'll marry you,' he said. 'I assume you'll wait for my decree absolute.'

For the second time since their arrival, Meredith was stuck for words. 'I....I wasn't talking about us,' she stammered. 'I was simply generalising.'

'I see. So now you're withdrawing your proposal? Tell me Sam, can I sue for breach of promise? *You* heard Meredith proposition me.'

'Sorry Andrew, that went out years ago. Isn't life a bitch?'

Mattie was grinning from ear to ear and Andrew eagerly awaited Meredith's reply.

She faced him with tears welling in her eyes. 'Yes Andrew. Let's do it. Let's get married.'

He jumped up and swept her off her feet and the others applauded.

'This calls for a celebratory drink,' Emily stated. 'Andrew, there's a bottle of Champagne over there in the cooler. Would you see to it please and I'll get the glasses.'

He gazed fondly at Meredith. 'I've been planning how to ask you for weeks. I love you so much.'

She kissed him adoringly and smiled. 'I thought you might need a push but this wasn't planned.'

'Believe that and you'll believe anything. Like I said, women are fakes!' Sam said.

Meredith laughed. 'In some things perhaps but I love you very much. That's definitely true.'

As he went to open the Champagne, Sam asked, 'Is there nobody special in your life Mattie?'

'No,' she replied abruptly and as the Champagne cork exploded, Sam's attention was diverted to the chants of good wishes for Meredith and Andrew as they drank to the couple's future happiness.

When Mattie appeared in the hallway, Poppy was waiting by the door for her run along the beach and she wagged her tail impatiently as Akina took hold of her lead.

'Be careful Poppy doesn't pull you over,' Mattie cautioned as the dog flew through the open door.

'She'll settle down in a minute,' Akina said.

'Do you always take her to the beach?'

'No, sometimes we go up the lane into the fields. She likes running about in the long grass. Have you ever had a dog?'

'No, nor a cat. When I was young, we didn't have much money and like you, I just had a mummy and no daddy but I have two brothers as well and things were very different then.'

'You mean you were poor?'

'Yes....but lots of people were poor then.'

'Was it very bad?'

'No, we thought nothing about it. That was how it used to be and we accepted things as they were.'

'Did you have a bike?'

'No but I had a lovely doll's pram and it was the envy of every little girl around.'

'What does envy mean?'

'It means that they would have liked one too.'

'How old are you Mattie?'

'I'm twenty-four.'

'Mummy will be thirty-nine next....that's if she's still here,' she remarked impassively. 'If she's not, she'll have to have her party with the angels.'

Mattie wanted to gather up the child in her arms and hug her to her body but she resisted the urge.

She recalled her own feelings of when *her* mother died and secretly, she commended the child for her acceptance of what was to be.

'Do *you* like children....*really* like them I mean?'

'Very much. I would love to have a daughter just like you.'

Akina took hold of Mattie's hand. She squeezed it tightly and smiled.

Mattie was sufficiently astute to recognize what was taking place. At that tender age, the child was already laying the foundations for her future while Mattie was trying to answer her questions candidly but neither one revealed her innermost thoughts to the other as they continued to walk hand in hand.

'Look, there's the sea. Isn't that lovely? You can walk forever along the sand.'

'Yes, it is. Are you a good runner?' Mattie asked, removing her sandals, allowing the soft white sand to run between her toes.

Akina chuckled. 'You'll see....let's have a race,' she challenged as she unfastened the lead.

Poppy ran off ahead and the two of them chased after her, laughing until they were exhausted.

'Are you allowed ice-cream?' Mattie asked.

'I am sometimes.'

'Come on then. Let's try to find an ice-cream van. There must be one around here somewhere.'

'There's a shop. The vans come in the summer.'

Mattie swept the sand from her feet and stepped into her sandals. 'It'll have to be the shop then but choose a small ice-cream. I don't want to be in any trouble with mummy.'

'Don't worry....you won't be.'

They strolled back along the promenade, licking their ice-creams and each of them in deep thought. Poppy trotted alongside, exhausted by her long run along the beach.

'I'll save you a bit Poppy,' Akina promised. 'Do you like the beach Mattie?'

'It's beautiful and the sand is so soft.'

Nothing further was said for several minutes until Akina asked, 'Do you know what a guardian is?'

Mattie was shocked but controlled her emotion at the question. 'It's someone who takes responsibility for someone else,' she explained.

'I don't know that word 'repspontibility'....'

''*Responsibility*'. That means being there to take charge of or take care of something or someone.'

'Like mummy does?'

'Exactly....that's what a guardian does.'

'Will you be *my* guardian when mummy has to go away....please?' she asked with beseeching eyes.

'Darling, that's not my decision to make. It's for your mummy to say who'll be responsible for you.'

'*No....no it isn't Mattie. Mummy agreed we would choose together, honest,*' she cried.

'Well, let me say this to you. If your mummy asks me to, then I *will* give serious thought to taking care of you but you mustn't ask her when I'm around. If I'm there, she might feel that she *has* to say yes and that would be wrong. Let's just see what happens. As you know, I'm going home on Monday but I'll be back very soon, I promise.'

'You really *will* come back won't you?'

'I promise you. Now, what about Poppy? You've almost finished your ice-cream.'

'Poppy, I'm so sorry! Here girl,' she said and the small dog sat down obediently beside her to savour her long-awaited treat.

'I never intended to put you on the spot Andrew,' Meredith apologised when they went to their room.

He smiled and took her in his arms. 'I'm grateful you did. I'd been pussyfooting for weeks, trying to find the right time and place when we were alone. In my wildest dreams, I never expected it to crop up in front of an audience but I seized the opportunity when it presented itself. It felt right though it would have been very embarrassing had you refused me.'

'Not a chance. I think I knew right from the start. Do you think the boys will approve?'

'They'll be delighted. Ben thinks you're cool!'

'Does he now? And what does Alex think?'

Andrew's cheeks turned scarlet. 'Don't forget that Alex is older. He said one day, 'You ought to marry Meredith. She's fit.' Those were his exact words.'

She stared back open-mouthed. 'You're joking!'

'Believe me, I wish I were! I hadn't realised that he was growing up so quickly! I reckon it must be the fake boobs,' he smirked.

'Don't you dare start that again! I could have died when Sam opened her big mouth. Can you believe that she told everyone?'

'It broke the ice. Prior to that we were walking on egg-shells. She's a great character and I'm looking forward to this evening. Are we all going out?'

'I doubt Norman will come. He rarely leaves the house so he'll probably stay home with Akina. I'm pretty sure Sam will want to spend time talking to Mattie. The writing's on the wall there. Sam needs a guardian for Akina, and Mattie ticks all the right boxes. Haven't you noticed how Sam watches their every move when they're together?'

'I can't say as I have. Are you serious?'

'Deadly serious and I think Mattie knows it too.'

'Do you think Mattie would take on such a task? It's a huge responsibility to take on someone else's child.'

Meredith nodded. 'It is but then she's conquered almost insurmountable problems in the past. She's a very capable young woman.'

'Why....what do you mean?'

Meredith could have kicked herself for her faux-pas. Andrew knew nothing of Mattie's past and she couldn't reveal any information relating to a client. Hurriedly, she concocted an answer. 'The children were orphaned when they were very young. Prior to their mother dying, she had to take care of her two younger brothers. Mattie had a stressful childhood but she coped admirably....that's what I meant.'

'Right,' he replied, apparently satisfied with her explanation. 'What are you wearing tonight?'

'I haven't given it much thought yet. I'm taking a shower first and then I'll decide.'

'Wear something nice tonight being as it's a very special occasion....our engagement.'

'What do you mean? I always do wear something nice!' she exclaimed as she stepped in the shower.

Andrew sat on the bed, mulling over all that had transpired since leaving home earlier that morning. It had certainly been an eventful day, he concluded.

Emily decided against joining the young ones for dinner. 'You enjoy the evening with your friends,' she said to Sam. 'I'll be here to keep you company when they've gone home.'

Emily wouldn't budge when Sam persisted. 'My mind's made up. I can't recall when you last went out with people your own age. Have a lovely time,' she called after them.

Mattie found herself walking with Andrew while Sam and Meredith walked slowly behind them.

'Talk to me about Mattie,' Sam said. 'I'd like to know everything about her.'

'She's a good person Sam. That's all you need to know. I know why you're asking me and I wouldn't do anything to jeopardise Akina's future. She's the best person you would ever find if she's agreeable and Akina appears to have grown very attached to her too in the short time she's known her.'

'You always could read my mind Meredith. It's a very important decision to make and it must be the right one because I won't be around to pick up the pieces if anything goes wrong. Akina's little more than a baby and Mattie's very young.'

'In years maybe but not in life experience. She's twenty-four and old enough to be Akina's mother. Many young teenage girls have babies these days.'

'I know that but a new baby is a tiny human being who grows up to be a six year old one day at a time.

Akina's almost six now and she's quite a handful. Do you honestly believe Mattie would cope?'

'I know she would but aren't we putting the cart before the horse here? Mattie might not *want* to be Akina's guardian. Have you given much thought to that possibility?'

'Yes I have but I could hardly mention it before I considered her suitability. If Mattie *were* agreeable, would you be willing to prepare the paperwork? I'll need to revise my Will too.'

'You know I would and Andrew says he wants to come back again, so we can sort everything out the next time we're here.'

'Don't leave it too long then. Tempus fugit!' Sam replied dryly. 'So, are you still delighted about your engagement to Andrew now that you've had time to think about it?'

'*Ecstatic* is the word. He's a kind and considerate guy. He has two boys you know.'

'Has he? How old are they?'

'Eight and twelve, so *I'm* going to have my hands full too.'

She was stunned. 'You mean they live with *him*?'

'Yes....I told you he was my client. I obtained the Custody Order for him. His 'ex' lives in Spain and so rarely sees them. Having said that, they're over there with her now but they'll be home next week.'

'Fancy your being their wicked stepmother!' Sam laughed. 'I never had you down for parenthood.'

'Nor I you,' she replied flippantly. 'It's been quite an eventful day today hasn't it?'

'Hasn't it just and it isn't over yet!'

It turned out to be a delightful evening and earlier Sam had seized the opportunity to sit beside Mattie to learn more about her.

Mattie made no mention of her distressing time at her foster-home. She was intent on adhering to her New Year's Resolution to put the past behind her. Though excited about what might lay ahead, at the same time she was deeply disturbed about Sam who had very little time left to enjoy with Akina. Only a miracle could save Sam now, she contemplated.

When they were preparing to leave for home on Monday morning, Akina grasped Mattie's hand and stated, 'You'll come back here like you said won't you? I promise I'll always be a good girl.'

Mattie kissed her affectionately. 'I know you will. I'll be back very soon and I'll call you on the phone every week.'

Sam smiled at her through tearful eyes. 'I'm glad you came.'

'Me too and don't worry. Everything is going to work out right and I'll see you soon.'

As the car disappeared from view, Sam breathed a sigh of relief when Akina said excitedly, 'Mummy, don't you think Mattie's lovely?'

She wrapped her arms around Akina and for the first time for two years she felt as free as a bird. No longer did she have cause to feel anxious. She had crossed her penultimate hurdle and a huge burden had been lifted from her shoulders.

9

'You can be so infuriating Seth,' Mattie snapped. 'I've told you till I'm sick and tired of telling you, *I'll be fine.* Just stop worrying about *me* and get on with the planning of your wedding.'

'That's months away yet and how am I supposed to live here with all the expense it entails?'

'I'll give you the next two months' rent and when I start work, I'll send more. I don't understand why Stephanie can't move in with you. It's not as if you don't already sleep together! It beggars belief why you have to be so puritanical!'

'Because that's the way I am,' he replied crustily. 'I disapprove of couples living together and I won't be hypocritical to satisfy you,' he added, bearing an air of superiority.

'Lots of other couples do!' she argued.

'I'm *not* other couples and *you're* a fine one to be dishing out advice. *You* wouldn't live with a bloke even if you *were* married.'

'Then maybe when I leave here I'll change.'

'You've no intention of changing. You're simply running away. You'll lose Mark if you leave here.'

'*I'm not interested in Mark,*' Mattie yelled before disappearing into her bedroom.

Seth flopped down on the sofa and stared blankly ahead in silence. She was hell-bent on leaving and he'd done his damnedest to dissuade her but Mattie was old enough to make her own decisions. Perhaps it was a good thing for her to move away. After all, she was haunted by unhappy memories there and a complete change of environment might provide the cure. He hoped so....she had suffered long enough.

'I'm off out for a pint. Don't you go lifting heavy boxes while I'm away,' he called to her.

When Mattie heard the door close, she returned to the living room to call Sam. Emily took the call and they chatted for quite some time before she handed the receiver to Sam.

'How's tricks?' Sam asked.

'Alright....how about you?'

'I've felt good today. I walked down to the beach with Akina earlier. It's been weeks since I was able to do that. Do you want a word with her?'

'Yes but not just yet. It's you I wanted to talk to. Would you be able to put in a good word for me at Legal Services where you worked? I need to find a job as soon as possible when I arrive. I have to help Seth out with the rent here as he can't afford to run the flat on his own *and* pay the rent as well.'

'I'll give them a call on Monday and ask if there are any vacancies but I have a proposition for you first. We need somebody here to run the business. It's becoming too much for mum and when things begin to get worse for me, her time will be devoted to my care. How are your maths?'

'Pretty decent. I can't say I'm brilliant at calculus but I wouldn't imagine I'd need that at your place. I can do every day things like accounts and I know how to prepare a balance sheet. I doubt I'd have a problem with the work there.'

'That sounds fine to me Mattie. Mum wanted to advertise for somebody but I asked her to hang fire until I'd spoken to you. You can have the room you were in before, rent-free and you'd be paid a salary commensurate to your hours worked. It would give all of us time to get to know each other properly so what do you think?'

'I think that sounds brilliant.'

'Can I tell Akina? She'll be delighted. She hardly ever stops talking about you.'

Mattie laughed. 'Yes, you tell her, in fact I'll tell her myself if you like.'

'Let me please. It isn't easy to put into words but of late, I feel I'm losing her and it hurts so much.'

'Listen to me. You're not losing her at all. She's learning to readjust and it's her way of dealing with the future. Trust me, I know. I lost both my parents when I was young.'

'Maybe you're right. She was fine today when we went down to the beach. She was full of the joys of spring. Perhaps it's my imagination running wild. I don't want her to forget me Mattie.'

'Akina won't ever forget you. You're her mother. Nobody can replace a mother and if you're worried about me, I would never try to take your place.'

'You're a good person Mattie. I'm very lucky to have found you and mum's equally delighted. Fate brought us together. I'm totally convinced of that. Let me find Akina. I won't keep you a minute.'

When Akina picked up the receiver, excitedly she cried, 'Hi Mattie. What are you doing?'

'I'm sorting out my clothes. I've been busy since I came back. I believe you went down to the beach with your mummy today. Did Poppy go too?'

'Yes and she chased another dog into the sea,' she chuckled. 'When she ran out, she shook herself all over mummy and the water was icy cold.'

Mattie laughed. 'I bet your mummy enjoyed that.'

'She went mad. It was so funny....so do you know when you're coming back?'

'Very soon, I hope. I have a few things to sort out here but it shouldn't be too long now.'

'I can't wait to see you. Call me again soon.'

'Of course darling. Give my love to everyone.'

Meredith called Mattie later. 'I've got some good news. Andrew's mum says she'll have the boys for the weekend when you move down to Devon, so I feel happier now. I didn't fancy the thought of your driving such a long way on your own. Besides, you might not get everything in your car and so Andrew can put some in his and it gives me the opportunity to see Sam again.'

'That's great Meredith, thanks. I talked to Sam a little earlier and she said she felt better today. She'd strolled down to the beach and back with Akina so maybe the final Chemo session was successful after all. I certainly hope so.'

'I do too. I know she tries to put on a brave face but it must be difficult, living with what she knows, week in week out,' Meredith said sorrowfully.

'Are you not going to Andrew's tonight?'

'Yes, I'm leaving very soon. He took both boys to football today and then they went for a burger but they're home now. We're just having a quiet night in tonight and I think we're all going out for lunch tomorrow. By the way, did the police call you?'

'No! What about?'

'Isn't that typical? They rang me yesterday about something else and while we were talking they told me their investigation was over....the Hilda Parkes affair. Apparently, the others in the pub backed up Jack's account. They had taken about thirty witness statements and in the absence of any contradictory evidence from Hilda Parkes, they had arrived at the conclusion that it was justifiable action to prevent a more serious crime being committed. I asked them to let you know.'

'Well they didn't. Seth will be very relieved when he knows that it's over and I'll drop a line to Jack. I take it that Hilda Parkes is no better then?'

'No and never likely to be, I'm told. She's lost all ability to communicate and everything needs to be done for her. So, what have you been doing today?'

'Sorting through all my things. I can't believe just how much rubbish I've thrown away. I can't take it with me but I can't leave it here either. When Seth moves out he'll have more than enough stuff of his own to dispose of but I reckon I'm winning now.'

'Is he still badgering you....Seth I mean?'

Mattie laughed. 'Of course he is. He never stops talking about it. He thinks I'm crazy.'

Meredith didn't say anything but she had similar thoughts. Mattie remained adamant that she would take on the role as Akina's guardian if that's what Sam wanted and though she didn't doubt Mattie's determination or fortitude, she was concerned that subconsciously, Mattie might be trying to obliterate her fear of men from her thoughts by occupying her time wholeheartedly with Akina and she prayed she was wrong for both their sakes.

They left for Devon four weeks later and arrived to find Sam feeling a little better.

'I don't hold out any long-term hope,' she said to Meredith when they were alone. 'The prognosis is bad but I have peaks and troughs. Some days I feel wretched but for Akina's sake I attempt to put on a brave face. It's time to put my affairs in order now and I want all the necessary paperwork drawn up. I don't have to sign until I'm sure but I need it to be ready in case my health suddenly deteriorates.'

'When's your next check-up?'

'In about eight weeks. Right, that's enough about me! Have you fixed the date for your wedding yet?'

'No, Andrew's divorce isn't final. We've chosen an engagement ring though. Isn't that lovely?' she said, stretching out her hand.

Sam studied the ring. 'Yes, it is and I hope you'll be very happy. Andrew's a lucky guy. Listen, while we're alone, I'd like you to tell me a bit more about Mattie. Does *she* not have a boyfriend?'

'No, I don't think she's particularly interested in men,' she said guiltily. 'There was a doctor called Mark who was interested in her but she's not ready for that kind of commitment. She's a career girl.'

'That's disconcerting,' Sam replied. 'If that's the case, how on earth would she balance a demanding career and parenthood I wonder?'

'That's not for me to say. You'll have to work it out with Mattie. She would need to work in order to provide financially for Akina. Lots of parents work and manage to do both. Don't forget that Akina will be at school throughout the week as she is now and Mattie's not one to neglect her responsibilities. I'm quite sure you'll see things much more clearly over the next few months.'

'That's if I have a few months left!'

She ignored that remark. 'Where's Akina now?'

'I'll give you three guesses,' she answered and in unison they replied, 'With Mattie.'

'Don't rush things Sam,' she cautioned. 'Just let it take its course.'

'I will. I'm trying to be positive....really I am. It's just that now Mattie's here to stay, I don't want to feel rejected. It's so hard to let go. I realise I must loosen the reins little by little but it's not like giving away a kitten. She's my little girl and I love her.'

'Then love her enough to do what's best for *her*. No daughter could want for more than that. Enjoy watching them together and ultimately you will find peace with yourself.'

'You have some pretty clothes,' Akina remarked as she helped Mattie with her unpacking. 'Do you want me to put these jumpers in the drawers?'

'Yes please but only use the top two. I have lots of boxes to unpack as well and I need to find room for everything.'

'There's something wrapped in fancy paper here. It feels like a book. Shall I leave it by your bed?'

'Let me look,' she said and ripped off the paper to reveal a card and a book, obviously from Seth who must have packed it under her clothes and without her knowledge. It was the novel, 'Maggie Rowan'.

266

She smiled as she recalled her having mentioned to Seth some weeks ago that she would like to borrow it from the library. Mattie was very appreciative of his thoughtfulness. She put the card aside to open it later when she was alone.

'They're from my brother Seth,' she told Akina. 'He's a librarian. He works at a place that's called a library where you borrow books to read.'

'We've got one in our classroom at infant school. We can't take the books away but we can lend them to read in the classroom.'

'You can *borrow* them,' she corrected her. 'Your teacher *lends* books to the children and they *borrow* books from her. Can you see the difference now?'

'I think so but there are such a lot of new words to learn. Every day I learn new words but I'll never know them all like you do Mattie.'

She laughed. 'Of course you will. Think about all the words you know now, yet when you were born, you didn't know *any*.'

'Well, that's because I was only a baby then!' she remonstrated.

Mattie, amused at her response, was beginning to realise she had much to learn about young children but knew she would enjoy the challenge. Akina was very bright for her age with an inquisitive mind and a logical approach to matters that Mattie applauded.

'Right....I think I've moved quite enough things for now. Why don't you go downstairs and talk to Meredith and Andrew and I can get changed?'

'Do you need any help?'

'I think I can manage, thank you,' she smiled.

267

When Akina had left, Mattie removed Seth's card from its envelope. The front of the card said, 'Good luck in your new home', and when she turned to the centre, she smiled at the words Seth had penned....a blatantly obvious reference to Mark.

'Love cannot endure indifference. It needs to be wanted. Like a lamp, it needs to be fed out of the oil of another's heart, or its flame burns low. Henry Ward Beecher'.

Below those words he had also written, 'Be true to yourself Mattie, love Seth'.

Mattie suddenly felt very distant from Mark. She had long been aware of her feelings for him so *was* she indeed running away and *was* she using Seth's wedding as an excuse for her inability to be true to herself? Had Seth and Meredith been right from the start? Well time would tell, she concluded, placing Seth's card beside her book but Mark remained in her thoughts for the rest of the day.

Over the weeks Sam witnessed the strengthening of the bond between Mattie and Akina and Mattie made a point of involving Sam, whenever possible, in all the events they organised. As spring quickly headed towards summer, they arranged outings and often they would have picnics in the park or on the beach. Sam was happy to watch them play together and Akina's laughter was music to her ears.

It was May and Mattie had been living there for two months when the date arrived for Sam to return to hospital for her latest test results.

Sam appeared pensive and preoccupied during the journey and Mattie believed it better to leave her to her thoughts. With a low percentage possibility of a full recovery, it was the moment of truth, maybe the final curtain, Sam felt as she waited to be called.

She breathed heavily and her heart was pounding rapidly as she walked into Dr. Allen's surgery.

He looked up and smiled with sensitivity, his eyes speaking volumes before his lips spoke those words she was fearful of hearing. 'I'm afraid it's not good news Sam.'

Dr. Allen was most sympathetic in his delivery of the tests results and Sam sat quietly with her head in her hands for some time before she asked, 'Are we talking about weeks or months?'

'I don't wish to give you false hope Sam. You've always demanded the truth so at best, I'd say three months,' he replied caringly, awaiting her response.

She deliberated thoughtfully then asked, 'Do you think I could go into the hospice towards the end? I have a young daughter at home.'

'I'm quite sure that would be possible and I'll put you in touch with our representative who will make the necessary arrangements. She'll be happy to help with other matters such as nursing care at home. I can't express how very sorry I am,' he stated.

Mattie blew her nose and managed to restrain her inner emotions that were tearing her apart as she led Sam from the room.

'It's what I expected,' Sam said. 'Let me have a few minutes to collect my thoughts. We'll go for a cup of coffee. I can't face going home just yet.'

They sat by the window in the hospital cafeteria and Sam admired the border flowers in full bloom.

'It feels odd to think that I'm seeing these flowers for the last time. I probably won't see another rose bush growing and I definitely won't see snow again or another Christmas. More importantly, I won't be around for Akina. I won't see her growing up, her graduation or her wedding and I'll never know my grandchildren. Those are my deepest regrets.'

Mattie was distraught, despite her best efforts to remain calm and composed for Sam's benefit. 'Try to remain focused on what you still have. You are here now and you still have Akina. Please try to be positive and enjoy everything you can while you're still able. If there's anything special you want to do, anything at all, just say the word and I'll do my best to arrange it for you.'

'As a matter of fact, there is something. There's one thing I've always wanted to do. *I'm* not able to do it now but maybe you'll be able to do it for me. I've always wanted to take Akina to Disneyland. If you ever have the opportunity, will you take her?'

'I'll make it happen Sam. You can rely on me for that. Is there anything else?'

'There's one more thing but it's a very tall order. I don't want you to feel guilty if you can't manage to do it.'

'Tell me.'

'I'd like Akina to visit Japan. I'd always intended to take her to learn about the culture and the history when she was older. I don't know where her father is but that doesn't matter. I wouldn't try to find him if I knew. I just feel she should see the country and meet the people. It's hard to explain but with Japan

270

being an equal part of her heritage, she might have the need to experience a sense of belonging. I don't expect you to understand.'

'Believe me, I know all there is to know about a sense of belonging and I agree with everything you say. I think it's important too and I'll do my utmost to plan a visit when she's old enough to appreciate and gain culturally from that wonderful experience. Besides, I'd love to visit the Far East too. Are there any other things you want me to do?'

'Just make sure Akina's happy. That's all I would have tried to achieve. I'm saying these things now because I might not have the opportunity later on. I know you'll do your very best for her.'

Mattie smiled compassionately and stretched out her hand. Come on, let's make our way back. Your parents will be waiting for your news.'

'I'd like to tell them on my own Mattie but I think I'll leave it a bit longer before I tell Akina. Would you keep her occupied please when we get home?'

'Of course. I'll take her to the beach with Poppy.'

They drove back home in total silence and when Mattie went inside, she found Akina and suggested it was time for Poppy's walk. 'Come along, I'll race you to the beach,' she challenged her.

'You'll lose,' Akina chuckled, running off ahead.

'We'll be a couple of hours....is that alright?' she asked Sam.

Sam smiled. 'That'll be perfect.'

It was dusk when Mattie and Akina returned and Sam was waiting for her daughter with outstretched arms. 'Did you have a lovely time?' she asked.

'Yes and guess who won....again,' she announced proudly.

'I'm shattered. I don't know where Akina gets all her energy from. Poppy's exhausted too. How did it go with your parents?' Mattie said when Akina was out of audible range.

'As well as could be expected, to quote a familiar phrase. There were a few tears but then we've been there several times before. We're all fine now and Mum's making our tea. Are you hungry?'

'I'm starving.'

'I am too. There's nothing like bad news to give you a hearty appetite.'

Mattie sighed. 'There's no need to put on a brave face for me. Save it for Akina.'

Sam took her hand. 'Listen, for the past two years I've been walking a tightrope, never knowing if I'd fall off or make it to the end. That's exactly what it feels like when you're living on borrowed time but now it's different, because I know and it's a blessed relief. I don't expect you to understand but I feel a sense of relief that I won't hear more bad news. I'm thankful I don't have to report results to my parents anymore. I really am fine. I told you at the hospital that I'd be alright in a few minutes. We've decided to play party games after tea and there won't be any more tears! Why not call Meredith first and tell her the news?'

'No, I'll call her later. I'll mention the papers too and she can send everything down.'

When Mattie cast her eyes around the living room after tea and watched the others laughing joyfully at

Emily who acted out a charade, she applauded her amazing friends for the strength and courage each displayed. Each had the ability to move forward to make the most of Sam's remaining time and Mattie felt ashamed that she had not succeeded before now in putting her past to rest. She had undoubtedly lost Mark forever due to her stupidity and weakness and now, more than ever he was in her thoughts. For the first time since their initial brief encounter, she both wanted and needed him desperately.

When Mattie called her, Meredith was devastated and sobbed uncontrollably. 'Should I have a quick word with her now?' she asked.

'Call her tomorrow when you've had some time to calm down. Sam would like it to be a joyful time now and she'd like the papers sent for her signature please. She needs to get her affairs in order now.'

'I'll send them tomorrow. I still can't believe it.'

'I know, none of us can believe it. Why don't you give Andrew a call? He always knows what to say to you,' Mattie advocated warmly. 'I'll talk to you again tomorrow.'

'Come and sit beside me Mattie,' Sam said when the others had gone to bed. 'I'd like to know what Meredith said when you told her. I imagine she was very upset and shocked?'

'She was....she was distraught. She sends her love and best wishes and says you're in her thoughts.'

'That's kind. Meredith and I were inseparable at University. It's such a shame that we didn't remain close over the past few years but it happens doesn't it? She's the only real friend I've ever had. We had so much fun then. We used to do some crazy things together. Did you enjoy University Mattie?'

Mattie gave some thought to her answer. 'I don't think *enjoy* is the word I'd use. I didn't dislike it. I just concentrated on my work. Unlike you, I had no particular friends there.'

'What about boyfriends? Was there nobody who was special back then?'

'No, I wasn't interested. I kept myself to myself,' she replied, avoiding eye contact with Sam.

Sam inhaled deeply before the next question she knew would prove contentious. 'What about Mark, your doctor friend. Do you love him?'

She was shaken at the mention of Mark's name. How could Sam know anything about Mark, unless Meredith had told her and if she had, what else had she divulged to Sam she wondered.

Unconvincingly, she replied, 'Mark was someone I met when Seth was in hospital. He was little more than an acquaintance.'

'Mattie, this is *me* you're talking to. I might be ill but I'm certainly not brainless. I believe we're close enough now to talk about our innermost thoughts. You've heard all of mine. Tell me about Mark and why you felt the need to flee to the opposite end of the country to escape. What did he do to you?'

'Nothing at all. He's a wonderful man and I don't feel worthy of him.'

'Why do you think that? If it makes it easier, I've known for a while that you were hiding something from me but I believed, in time, that you'd be open with me. Is it so difficult to talk about?'

She sighed. 'It shouldn't be but it is. It's the only aspect of my life that I can't seem to put behind me completely and believe me, I've tried very hard but it's nothing that would ever affect Akina.'

'Please....let me be the judge of that. You have to tell me Mattie. If I'm to place my daughter's future welfare in your hands, I have to know, whatever it might be.'

'What did Meredith tell you?'

'Very little. She told me about Mark....that he was fond of you but that you didn't return his feelings. That was it. It's more what Meredith *didn't* say that troubles me. She clearly knew much more than she told me but I had to respect her loyalty to you. You must see that I need to know Mattie. Why don't you pour yourself a drink? It might help to loosen your tongue a little. Believe me I'm not trying to pry.'

'I think that's a good idea. Would you like one?'

'I shouldn't but I will. I'll have a small gin with a splash of lemon please.'

She returned with the drinks and sat down facing Sam. She took a sip of her drink before running her forefinger around the rim of the glass nervously as she stared ahead. 'I couldn't return Mark's feelings then because I was terrified of men,' she disclosed. 'I was sexually abused by my foster-father when I was fourteen years old and Meredith was called to represent me when I accidentally killed him. That's why she couldn't tell you. Client confidentiality it's called as you well know. It's hardly a worthy entry for a CV for child-care so I didn't tell you. That's it in a nutshell but if you like, I'll tell you the whole sordid story now. I would have told you eventually but I wanted you to get to know me before that. I'm still working on the androphobia and yes, I do love Mark but I would have been no good for him when I couldn't bring myself to be alone with him.'

Sam looked shocked. 'I'm so sorry Mattie. I'd no idea anything like that had happened to you. It must have been horrendous. Is that the reason you killed him, because he'd abused you?'

'No, it *was* an accident. He'd been abusing me for six months, so one night I decided I'd run away but he came home from the pub earlier than expected. When he tried to prevent my leaving, I cracked him across the head with my tennis racquet. He dropped dead at my feet but I was never charged. Since then, I've been unable to conquer my fear of men, that is until I came here and so when Mark began to show more than a passing interest in me, I didn't want to hurt him by giving him false hope. In my own way I wanted him too but I believed because of my past, that I could never give myself to him, physically I mean, so I gave him the cold shoulder instead and I think that's about everything.'

'And are you still afraid of men?'

'*Wary* is what I am now. I'm not afraid anymore. That's the prime reason for my moving away, from everything that served to remind me and from Mark who had learned about my past. I couldn't face him because I felt so ashamed. It was true though what I said about Seth's wedding. He *was* delaying it out of concern for me. It's been a difficult time for all of us. My brothers only found out recently.'

'You've done nothing to feel ashamed about but you should have told me Mattie. I don't want Akina to go through life being afraid of men.'

'She wouldn't Sam. I'm so much better now. Like I said, I'm not afraid anymore. I'm fine in a group of people. It's just the one-to-one situations where I'm still a little cautious. I deal with the guests here don't I? Have you seen any aspect of my behaviour that concerned you?'

'To be honest I haven't, though I have wondered why you didn't associate with men. Can I ask how you would react if Mark were to turn up here?'

'That's highly unlikely since Mark doesn't know where I am.'

'It's purely hypothetical. How would you react? Would you jump in his arms or turn him away?'

'I definitely wouldn't turn him away but I doubt I'd jump in his arms either. I'd try to get to know him first. That's what I should have done before but my dread of men opposed any romantic emotions I might have had. It's difficult to explain to someone who doesn't understand but I imagine it's the same as you, when you try to explain to others how you feel about your illness.'

'I suppose it is. So have you missed the boat with Mark? Does he have someone else lined up now?'

'I don't think so, at least not that I'm aware. He's a really nice guy. He's a widower with a young son and very dishy,' she made known with a coy smile.

'Then you should make the next move before it's too late. One more question. If things *were* to work out between you, where would that leave Akina?'

'Oh come on! She would *always* be my priority. I love her just as much as you do. I can't believe you doubt that or that you're even asking that question. Why else would I be taking on the responsibility for Akina's future?'

'I'm sorry. I'm getting the jitters now that there's a more definite time-scale and truly, I'm not in the least disturbed by what you've told me. To be wary is positive....whereas to be complacent is negative, particularly in this day and age and I've repeatedly warned Akina about talking to strangers. It's every mother's worst nightmare so I guess that makes *me* wary too,' she smiled. 'I'm pleased you confided in me. It couldn't have been easy. Have you had any contact with Mark since he learned of your past?'

'Not directly. He wanted to see me but I refused. I wasn't ready then.'

'But you're ready now?'

'Like you said Sam, it's hypothetical. I doubt I'll ever see or hear anything from Mark again. I made my position crystal clear so can we drop it please?'

'You could make a point of seeing him when you go to your brother's wedding in July.'

She made no response to Sam's reply and picked up the empty glasses. 'Come on, it's time you were in bed,' she said. 'It's been a long day.'

Meredith and Andrew made two further weekend visits over the next four weeks and on each of those occasions, there was evident deterioration in Sam's health. She was very unsteady on her feet and she had lost a noticeable amount of weight but despite that her spirit remained high.

Sam had taken Akina to the cinema shortly after receiving the test results and then they had walked in the park where she had sensitively explained she would have to leave her very soon.

She related to Meredith on her next weekend visit that Akina had taken the news well and that she had told Sam not to worry because Mattie would always take good care of her.

'She's a very sensible child for her age,' Meredith said. 'She'll go a long way in life. She's very much like Mattie, with the same drive and determination. You notice her resolve when she's playing games. She develops her strategy and she studies and reacts to situations better than the adults. I was taught by Mattie a long time ago just how strong-minded and resilient a child could be when she....'

When she paused, Sam said, 'It's alright, I know everything about her now. She told me and though I was shocked to learn of her tragic story, I realised she's stronger because of what happened. I have no doubts about her now. I watch her with Akina and I can't fault her in any way. She's the best person to take care of her and I'm hoping that someday she'll adopt her. I just wish we could think of some way of getting Mattie and Mark together to complete the perfect family unit. She's admitted to me how much she loves him. Have you ever met him?'

'I have but Mattie doesn't know. He called me a few times and I met him for lunch one day. He kept pestering me for her address but I wouldn't give it to him. I told him she needed time to come to terms with everything and that he mustn't give up hope.'

'Will he be at her brother's wedding?'

'I wouldn't have thought so. He's acquainted with Seth and he works with Stephanie, his fiancée but I doubt he'd be on the guest list.'

'The wedding would have been an ideal forum for romance to blossom. You profess to be a genius at making the unlikeliest things happen so how about you work a bit of your magic?'

'I can't achieve miracles Sam. I can hardly butt in and take over the arrangements when I'm merely a guest at the wedding myself.'

'Well if I were a guest I'd do something.'

'Yes, but you have a big gob! Just remember how you blabbed about my breast enlargement to all and sundry. I still haven't forgotten that and never will, the way Andrew keeps reaping it up!'

Sam howled with laughter. 'Do you know, if you were here permanently, I'd make a total recovery. You are such a tonic. I wish you could stay longer.'

'So do I but I'm in Court on Tuesday and I have a huge amount of preparatory work to do on Monday. Don't forget, you've got my right arm here. I really miss Mattie's help.'

'Haven't you employed someone since she left?'

Meredith groaned, 'I made the mistake of hiring a legal secretary and she's as dim as a Toc-H-Lamp. I'm not joking, she's absolutely useless but I don't have time to keep training new recruits. I seriously undervalued Mattie's ability before I lost her. She was such an asset and so dependable in every way.'

'Then sort out a wedding invitation for Mark and get them together and Mattie can move back in with you at the office. Mum and dad will want to sell up when I'm no longer here. Mum's intimated as much when we've been discussing the future. It would be ideal for Akina to be in close contact with Mattie's family. I'm sure you can come up with something if you try. Talk to Seth and Stephanie and formulate a plan. Sit Mattie and Mark together at the reception. Just don't make it look obvious.'

'*Don't make it look obvious*?' Meredith shrieked. 'You're almost dragging them down the aisle!'

'Desperate needs need desperate measures', Sam quoted. 'Don't disappoint me or I might just decide to reveal a few more of your secrets to Andrew the next time he's here.'

'Like what?'

'Like the evening of the Students' Union protest after Nelson Mandela had been on trial for treason for the best part of five years because he'd openly opposed apartheid policies. Have you forgotten that you marched across campus, wearing a homemade sandwich-board over your sexy underwear and the string snapped? That's what I was referring to when I said everyone would have known about your boob job had you had it done at University.'

'*Sam*! You wouldn't dare tell Andrew about that! Anyway, he wouldn't believe a word of it.'

'I've still got the Students' Union Magazine with the photograph splashed across the centrefold. The camera never lies and it was *extremely* explicit,' she laughed. 'Andrew would believe his own eyes.'

'You're lying....Tell me you're lying!' Meredith repeated. 'You don't really have a copy do you? No you can't have. I made a point of ripping up every copy I could lay my hands on.'

Sam stared straight at her. 'There's only one sure way to find out.'

'Alright, you win....I'll do my best. *Please*, don't show it to Andrew. I'd die.'

'Hey....hang on,' she smirked. 'Don't go stealing my thunder!'

Meredith was horrified. 'Sam! I can't believe how you can treat your condition so frivolously.'

'That's what keeps me going from day to day but you wouldn't understand. Incidentally, Akina said she'd like to go to Seth's wedding with Mattie. She hasn't been to one before. What do you think?'

'It would be a pleasant experience but how would Mattie explain her presence? She hasn't mentioned anything to Seth yet.'

'I realise that and I thought it might pave the way. It might be better to make a brief introduction first rather than spring it on her family when it's a done deal, so to speak. All she would need to say is that Akina asked to come and that Mattie welcomed the company during the long journey. She wouldn't be telling lies. It would be more a matter of her being economical with the truth. You're a solicitor. You'd know all about that!'

'I don't see any problem but they'll be away three days. Wouldn't you prefer to spend your remaining time with Akina now?'

'Certainly I would but I can't forecast how I'll be feeling then. I'm trying to be considerate by putting my daughter's wishes first.'

'Does Mattie know she wants to go with her?'

'Yes and she'd be happy to take her. How do you think her family will react when they *do* find out?'

'She only has Seth and Jack and they'll be fine if it makes Mattie happy. They'll be overjoyed.'

'Right, that's settled then and Mattie has to attend Court on Thursday with the sworn Affidavits. The new Will has been signed and witnessed, so that's more or less everything done now. I just have one final favour to ask. Would you hand me that large brown envelope please and don't start crying again. I've written everything down very clearly about my funeral. I've chosen cheerful music, not miserable hymns and I want no deviation at all from anything I've recorded. You don't need to ask anything....it's all in there,' she said, handing her back the sealed envelope. 'Please don't open it until it's time. I feel like a cup of coffee now. How about you?'

'Good idea. I'll stick the kettle on,' she answered, thankful for the opportunity to escape if only for a few minutes.

By the time she returned with the coffee, Andrew, Mattie and Akina could be heard in the driveway.

Poppy ran towards her wagging her tale excitedly.

'*Hello, have you had a nice run?*' Meredith asked Poppy in a silly high-pitched voice.

'It was lovely thank you,' Mattie answered with a straight face, causing Akina to burst out laughing.

'Andrew, do you want to play snakes and ladders with me?' she asked appealingly.

'*Let him relax for five minutes*,' Sam called from the sitting room. '*Maybe he'll feel like it later.*'

283

'I promise we'll definitely play later,' he told her. 'I'm not as young as you are and I'm a little weary after our long walk. I think Poppy would be pleased to be given a drink. I know I could manage one.'

As Akina skipped away with the dog, the others strolled into the sitting room and flopped down on the sofa. 'I'm exhausted!' Mattie exclaimed. 'What have you been doing?'

'We were reminiscing about our University days weren't we Meredith? It's mind-boggling what one remembers.'

'Isn't it!' she replied with a threatening glare.

'How do you feel about a meal at that restaurant again tonight Sam?' Andrew asked.

'Thanks but I'll give it a miss if you don't mind. You must go. I'm going to have a sleep for an hour and then I'll be awake when you get home. Was it hot at the beach?' she asked in a sleepy voice.

'It was lovely,' Mattie replied. 'The couple from room four were there with their daughter so Akina was playing with her.'

'Good,' Sam said as her eyelids started to droop.

'Come on. Let's go in the kitchen. I could murder a cup of tea,' Andrew said. 'Let Sam have a rest.'

'And we can have a game of snakes and ladders,' Akina, who had just returned, reminded him.

'We most certainly can,' he agreed.

It took a few days for Meredith to devise her plan to guarantee Mark's presence at the wedding.

Although it was a simple matter to invite him, she had to be sure he would accept. The mere fact that

Mattie would be present could provide a reason for his refusal and furthermore, how could she arrange for them to be seated side by side without making it blatantly obvious? Mattie would be on the top table and there was no justification for Mark to be seated there too unless he were to officiate in some way.

During a quiet period, she scribbled a few notes on her pad. Jack had arranged leave and would be best man for Seth, and Lucille and Sadie were to be bridesmaids, not that she would ever consider Mark as an additional bridesmaid, she chuckled to herself as she deleted those two names from her sheet, so what other role could he play?

Though Seth and Stephanie were happy for Mark to attend, they too had been unable to provide any constructive suggestion for a means of guaranteeing his presence.

Meredith put aside her paperwork and continued with her work. Maybe an idea would come to mind later, she thought.

As she was driving home from work, everything suddenly fell in place. In the absence of her father, Stephanie had asked Andrew to give her away but if Stephanie were to tell a white lie to Mark that her aged uncle wasn't fit to attend to his obligation, she might persuade Mark to take his place and it would provide cause to place him beside Mattie on the top table. Neither party would suspect anything. What a brilliant idea, she congratulated herself.

She couldn't wait to call Stephanie who thought it an excellent plan too. 'I'll talk to Mark tomorrow,' she promised. 'Are you sure Andrew won't mind?'

'Andrew will be fine about it. You attend to Mark and I'll deal with Andrew. It's all for a good cause. Just make sure Mark doesn't wriggle out of it. If he says he doesn't have a sitter for Adam, tell him to bring Adam too. I'll pay for their meals! Just make sure you get him there whatever it takes.'

'I hope he isn't on duty that weekend.'

'Listen, I don't need *you* to find excuses for him. Be ready with an answer for *anything* he says. Tell him to swap with somebody if he's supposed to be working. Convince him that there's nobody else to give you away and give me a call tomorrow.'

When she told Andrew he puckered his brow. 'I hope you've thought it all through because there's no way you'll get away with it. You're dealing with shrewd professionals who will realise immediately that it's a ploy and they'll point the finger at you.'

'So? It'll be too late then. Anyway, it's payback time for what Mattie did to us,' she smirked.

'*Payback time*? That sounds like you're unhappy with me,' he said touchily.

'Listen, the only thing I'm unhappy about is that she didn't set us up sooner.'

Andrew beamed at her. 'That was a sweet thing to say darling. I can tell you, that was one of the most embarrassing days of my whole life. You had made it so obvious that you didn't want to go out with me and we were coerced into compliance with Mattie's little scheme. You were bullied into agreement and I had to try to appear delighted. If I'm honest, I was dreading that damned house-warming party!'

'Really?' she laughed.

'Most definitely! I fancied you but I was aware I wouldn't have been given me a second look but for Mattie's intervention.'

'It was nothing personal,' she said apologetically. 'Before you arrived, Mattie was having a dig at me because I didn't have a boyfriend. I can't remember precisely what was said but it was something about her fixing me up with the next unattached guy who walked through the door and you happened to walk in a second or two later. That's the reason we were hysterical. I can understand your being embarrassed because I was too.'

'All's well that ends well,' he remarked.

'My sentiments entirely,' she affirmed. 'Let's just hope it ends well for Mattie and Mark too.'

'I'm still confused. Why can't they sort out their own love-life?'

'It's a long story and someday, I'll enlighten you. Let's just say that Mattie needs a big push. It isn't Mark's fault. He's keen enough. He's been chasing after Mattie for a while. Seriously, you don't object to stepping down at the wedding do you, assuming Mark will take your place?'

He wrapped his arms around her. 'Of course not. Besides, it'll leave me more time to spend with my favourite girl.'

'And who might that be?' she asked as she kissed his lips sensuously.

'Er....her name's Lucille. You know which girl I mean, that friend of Stephanie's.'

'*Right*!' she laughed. 'I'll be sure to remind her to save a dance for you.'

'Don't you dare! There's only one person in the whole world I want to get a grip of and that's you.'

Meredith was on tenterhooks the next day while awaiting Stephanie's call and when she phoned to confirm that Mark had agreed to give her away, she was overjoyed.

'He'll have to bring Adam with him. His parents are going to the Lake District that weekend to stay with friends.'

'Tell your mum I'll pay for the additional meals and make sure she understands that I insist. I don't expect her to pick up the tab.'

Stephanie laughed. 'She wouldn't allow that and besides, a party of four on my side can't come now. They're moving house that weekend and the caterer needed the final numbers last week. The account's already been paid so there are still two more places available if you have any more schemes that you're cooking up.'

'I haven't but Mattie mentioned that she'd like to bring a friend's young daughter. Has she mentioned her to you? She wanted company on the journey.'

'I know nothing about that but when you speak to her again, tell her to bring her. I just need her name for the seating plan. I'm getting really excited now. Seth has completely redecorated the house and it's lovely. He's moving in next week on his own and that leaves the flat empty for Jack and Mattie. He's extended the rental contract for two further weeks until Jack goes back to sea so if Mattie does bring a friend, I'll borrow the camp bed from Sally.'

'I hope it works out for Mark and Mattie.'

'You've done your best so if it doesn't, Mattie's only herself to blame.'

Sam squealed with delight when Meredith phoned to outline the plan. 'You always were a conniving so-and-so. I knew you'd come up with something.'

'You left me without choice. Haven't *you* heard the dictum, 'necessity is the mother of invention'? You blackmailed me!' she reminded her.

'So I did,' Sam acknowledged.

'I also mentioned that Mattie might bring a friend and that I'd let Steph know. Have you arrived at a decision about that?'

'Like I said, it's fine by me. Mattie's not here at the moment but I'll get her to give you a call later. I feel quite perky today, thanks for asking!'

'I haven't had chance to ask you yet! I was about to before you butted in. I'm pleased to hear that.'

'Highs and lows....that's all it is. I slept better last night and it's a lovely sunny day. Try to find time after the wedding to let me know how things went with Mattie and Mark. I'll be thinking of them and I'll keep my fingers crossed for a positive result.'

'I'll do that but I'll be talking to you again before next weekend. Give our love to Akina and tell her we're looking forward to seeing her.'

'Take care Meredith and thanks again for all your efforts.'

'*Enforced* efforts!' she replied.

# 10

It was another lovely sunny day when Mattie and Akina left for the wedding and the weather forecast for the following week was excellent too.

Sam had bought a new dress for Akina and Mattie had chosen a delightful powder-blue silk suit with white accessories.

'I'm really excited,' Akina said. 'I've never been to a wedding before. Do you think there'll be other children there?'

'Probably but you aren't allowed to charge about at the reception. Remember, you'll be dressed like a young lady so you must behave like a young lady.'

'I know. Mummy told me. Do you think you will get married someday Mattie?'

'I don't think so.'

'Good, because if you did, you wouldn't love me anymore. You'd love the man instead.'

'Darling, it doesn't work like that! I will always love you. You love your mummy don't you?'

'Of course I do! I'll love her forever....even when she's gone.'

'There you are then. You can love many people at the same time. You just love them different ways, like you love both of your grandparents. When two people marry and have children, they all love each other, like I love Seth and Jack. You'll get married and have your own family someday but that won't change the way you feel about your mummy.'

'Alright, you can get married if you want,' Akina said approvingly and Mattie laughed audibly.

As they approached the outskirts of Manchester, Mattie announced they were near to the end of their journey.

Craning her neck to peer through the window, she said, 'Are you sure? I can't see the sea.'

'I should hope not. I'm afraid we'd be lost if you could. Manchester is in the centre of the country so it's a very long way to the sea.'

'Is it too far to walk from your house?'

'It most certainly is. It's fifty miles away I'd say. It's about an hour's drive to the coast. When we go home, I'll show you on a map. A map is a drawing of the country and England is surrounded by water. It's called an island. It's so much easier to explain when I can show you a map.'

Mattie revelled in her time alone with Akina. The child was eager to learn new things and Mattie was an enthusiastic teacher. 'Remember what we talked about earlier,' she reminded her. 'For now, I'll tell people you're my friend.'

'Well I am....I'm your *very special* friend.'

'Right....here we are. This is where I used to live. Are you looking forward to meeting my family?'

'I'm looking forward to *everything*,' she replied.

Following the tearful reunion with Jack and Seth, Mattie introduced Akina to them. Politely, she held out her hand and shook theirs. 'I'm pleased to meet you,' she said with a beaming smile.

'Akina hasn't been to a wedding before,' Mattie explained.

'Neither have I,' Seth told her, 'What's more, it's *my* wedding tomorrow.'

'Oh dear! Don't you know what to do?' she asked with a frown and the others laughed.

'I hope so or I'll be in big trouble.'

'How did the stag night go?' Mattie enquired.

Jack guffawed. 'Don't waste time asking him. He can't remember. Everyone else enjoyed it though.'

Addressing Jack Akina asked, 'Are *you* married?'

'Not yet but when I find a young lady as pretty as you, I'll ask her to marry me though I might have to wait till you grow up. I doubt I'll find one like you.'

'You can't wait for *me*,' she chuckled. 'When *I'm* old enough, *you'll* be an old man.'

Seth shrieked with laughter. 'You're really losing your touch. I told you to stick tight to Lucille. Even *she* will get snapped up sooner or later.'

'Don't be cruel Seth,' Mattie said. 'Lucille means well. Are you nervous about tomorrow?'

'Absolutely scared stiff if I'm honest, so changing the subject, how have you been? You look well.'

'I am, I'm very well. Akina takes me down to the beach most days. The sea air is so invigorating.'

'What does that mean?' Akina asked.

'Yes, *I* wondered what that word meant too,' Jack remarked, winking at Akina who grinned at him.

'Refreshing, energizing....it makes me feel happy. Right Akina, shall we unpack our things? We don't want to arrive at the wedding like the poor relations tomorrow because everything is creased. Are we in your room Seth?'

'Yes and there's a camp bed for er....'

'*Akina*', she reminded him. 'It's a Japanese name. My daddy's Japanese.'

'Akina....that's a pretty name,' Seth replied with a friendly smile.

'I like your two brothers,' she told Mattie as they unpacked their bags. 'I wish I had a brother.'

'They can be extremely infuriating at times,' she explained to her.

'What does that mean?'

'It means that they get on my nerves occasionally but I love them both very much, just like I love you very much too.'


Stephanie's mother had adorned the pews and the church altar with beautiful flowers and when Mattie and Akina arrived, they sat down next to Seth and Jack who both looked very smart in their new suits.

Seth leaned forward and turned Mattie. He smiled nervously and she returned his smile.

'You look great. You'll be fine Seth,' she said.

'Half the guests haven't turned up,' he responded desolately as he cast his eyes round the church.

'Stop panicking!' she told him quietly. 'There's a crowd of people outside who are making the most of the lovely weather. Just try to relax.'

'Have you remembered the rings Jack?' he asked for the umpteenth time.

'Dash it! I knew there was something else I had to do!' he said, winking at Mattie who laughed to see Seth's horrified expression. 'They're in my pocket. Settle down for heaven's sake! You're beginning to give *me* the jitters.'

A sudden influx of guests appeared and began to take their places and Mattie glanced at her watch. 'I think the bride must have arrived,' she told Akina. 'It's almost two o'clock.'

One of the ushers walked over to the organist. He leaned over and whispered something in his ear.

He stopped playing instantly and turned the pages of his music. Seth, who was watching every move, twitched nervously.

Jack leaned towards Seth. 'Beware, the hangman cometh,' he announced as Ethel Jackson's footsteps could be heard distinctly as she walked the length of the uncarpeted aisle to take her place on the pew adjacent to Seth's. She turned to him and smiled.

After receiving his cue, the organist thundered out the seven opening chords of the widely recognised Bridal Chorus by Wagner from Lohengrin, when all the members of the congregation leapt to their feet instantly.

Seth seized the rail of the pew as if he were in the dock, prior to death sentence being pronounced and Jack was obliged to elbow and manhandle him into position as Stephanie approached.

Mattie inclined her head and smiled warmly when she drew alongside and Stephanie beamed back at her. She looked radiant and her dress was beautiful.

Seth stared ahead until Stephanie was at his side and she touched his hand gently. It was then that he turned to look at her, and when she smiled lovingly at him, Mattie could see the tension drain from his body and the marriage service commenced.

Still unaware of Mark's role before he took a step back, Mattie was astonished by his presence. When their eyes met simultaneously, he smiled pleasantly and she acknowledged his gesture with a brief but equally warm smile.

'She looks lovely,' Akina gasped. 'She's just like a fairy princess.'

Mattie was close to tears as the service continued, listening carefully to the promises each made to the other and conscious of Mark's gaze the whole time. She breathed deeply as she tried to maintain control of her inner emotions.

'Are they married yet?' Akina asked quietly.

'Almost....just a few seconds more...'

When the vicar pronounced them man and wife a short time later, Stephanie lifted her veil and smiled happily at Seth who grinned broadly.

'Now they're married,' Mattie whispered.

With a sigh of relief, Akina replied, 'That's good. I'm glad Seth got it right,' and Mattie laughed.

Outside, Mark was waiting by the door. 'It's good to see you Mattie. It's been quite a while and again you look sensational. I would say blue is definitely your colour.'

'Thank you Mark. It's good to see you too though I certainly didn't expect you to be here.'

'I was only approached at the last minute because Stephanie had nobody to give her away. Her elderly uncle who intended to officiate wasn't fit to travel.'

'That's sad. He must have been very disappointed to miss the wedding. It was fortunate that you were available at such short notice.'

'It was but I had to bring Adam. My parents have gone away for the weekend.'

'Where is he?'

He looked around the churchyard. He's over there with the usher. He kept an eye on Adam while I did my bit. It was a lovely wedding service wasn't it?'

'Yes and very emotional too. Stephanie looked so elegant. I haven't had chance to speak to her yet.'

'And who's this delightful creature?'

Before Mattie could answer, she stretched out her hand. 'I'm called Akina, I'm Mattie's special friend and I'm half-Japanese. I'm pleased to meet you.'

Mark beamed at her. 'Well I have to say you're a very gracious young lady. I'm pleased to meet you too,' he said, shaking her hand. 'How old are you?'

'I'm six. How old is your son?'

'He's seven. His name's Adam.'

'Like the first man God created! The teacher told us that at school,' she added with a cheeky grin.

He threw back his head and laughed. 'I see you're a very bright girl.'

'She's a handful,' Mattie stated but when uttering those words, she didn't anticipate the consequential embarrassment to be caused by the child's question when she asked Mark, 'Are you married?'

'No,' he said. 'I'm not married Akina.'

'That's good....neither is Mattie,' she advised him in a loud whisper.

'*Akina*!' Mattie exclaimed in total horror as Mark exploded with laughter.

Mattie's humiliation was hurriedly curtailed when she was called to the photographer. Thankfully, she made her escape as fast as her legs could carry her.

'I'll catch you later,' he called out, still laughing but she hurried away without a turn of the head.

Out of earshot, Mattie chastised her. 'Don't *ever* do anything like that again Akina. Do you hear me? That was *very* embarrassing.'

'I'm sorry,' she whimpered on the verge of tears, her bottom lip quivering.

Mattie took her in her arms. 'It's alright darling. I know you didn't realise what you were saying and I know you didn't mean to upset me. It's over now.'

'Don't you like him?'

'Yes I do like him....in fact I like him very much but you mustn't *ever* say things like that.'

Akina was confused. 'I don't understand then. If nobody tells him, how will he ever know?'

'I think maybe he knows already,' Mattie replied. 'Come on, let's have our photographs taken and we can talk to Seth and Stephanie.'

Mattie flung her arms around Seth. 'I'm so proud of you,' she said. 'So....what does it feel like to be a married man?'

He beamed broadly. 'It's feels terrific and doesn't Steph look gorgeous?'

'She does. I love her hairstyle too and it's such a beautiful dress. Her mother certainly did her proud. Where's she gone now? I wanted a word with her.'

'The photographer's whisked her away again. I'm sure she's over there, by those trees.'

'Right, I'll go and look for her. I'll see you later.'

She took Akina's hand and walked across to the two bridesmaids first. 'Hi Lucille, you look lovely. Wasn't it an emotional service? I was very close to tears when Stephanie walked into church and they couldn't have had a better day for the wedding.'

'I was just saying that to Jack. He's a smart guy when he's dressed in a suit, your Jack, not that I'm saying he's not when he's dressed er.... casual.'

Mattie laughed. 'I know exactly what you mean. I was talking to Mark who's wearing a fabulous suit. It makes such a difference.'

'Are you and Mark on or off at the moment?'

Mattie felt uncomfortable. 'For want of repeating myself Lucille, we are nothing more than friends. I don't suppose I'll see much of him today. We were merely being polite to each other,' and turning her attention to Sadie she commented, 'The flowers are beautiful. I adore freesias.'

'I do too. They're such beautiful colours....almost unreal. Have you been accosted by photographer?'

'No, we're just on our way over.'

'So, you must be Akina. I've heard all about you,' Sadie said. 'You're half-Japanese aren't you?'

Keith moved in closer and winked at her. 'Let me see,' he said, eyeing her up and down and from side to side. 'Right, I've got it. The right side is English and the left side is Japanese. Am I right?'

'No silly, it's all mixed up together,' she giggled.

'Are you sure?' he asked wide-eyed.

'Yes, quite sure,' she said and Sadie smiled.

'She's gorgeous. What I'd give to have thick hair like that. Look how the sunlight catches it and her eyes are so large and expressive. You could ask the photographer take some portrait pictures of her.'

'I might do that if he has time.'

'Trust me, he'll make the time. Photographers are an absolute nightmare at weddings.'

Mattie turned her head when Akina let go of her hand and heard her call, '*Adam*?'

The young boy turned his attention to her and she asked, 'Are you Adam?' When he nodded she said, 'I was talking to your daddy. I'm Akina.'

'What?'

'A-ki-na....it's not English.'

'Nice name....er, do you know where he is now?'

'He was by the church when I saw him.'

'Thanks,' he grinned. 'I'll see you later.'

'I hope so,' she replied.

Mattie and Akina had a few photographs taken in the gardens when the official photographs had been completed and Mark wandered across as they were about to leave. 'I'm told I have to share your taxi to the reception if that's alright by you. I arrived with Stephanie and as she's left with Seth that leaves me without transport.'

'We'd be delighted for you to share ours wouldn't we Akina?'

'Yes....so can I sit in the front please?'

Mark smiled. 'Do you have the feeling that we're being set up Mattie?'

'More so as every minute passes,' she answered perceptively and with a glint in her eye.

'Do you mind?'

'Not at all. Where's Adam?'

'He's gone with the usher and Jack in the car with Stephanie's mother. I'm starting to have my doubts about the sick uncle anecdote too but Stephanie was very convincing when she begged me to stand in. I suggest we play along for the time being and if my suspicions are true, then someone has gone to great lengths to orchestrate this reunion, not that I'd want you to think *I'm* complaining.'

'Nor am I. Come on, let's make a move or the car might leave without us.'

Akina ran off ahead towards the remaining car.

'How have you been....really?' Mark asked.

'Oh, you know....it's been a long uphill struggle but I'm getting there slowly. After the Hilda Parkes incident I had to get away from here. I felt I had to rebuild my life in new surroundings, away from the painful memories but I quickly realised that I had to deal with the past. The memories still remained and I couldn't rewrite history. A close friend taught me that I must look to the future and live each day as if it were my last....'

He walked ahead of her and opened the taxi door. Taking his place beside her, he said tenderly, 'I've missed you so much.'

Several moments elapsed before she replied, 'I've missed you too Mark.'

He wanted to hold her hand to show some gesture of his feelings for her but he was afraid to touch her and they continued their journey in silence, each in deep thought as Akina chattered incessantly to the driver.

Once in the reception hall, Mattie felt that all eyes were upon them.

Akina broke their silence by announcing she felt hungry and Mark confessed that he was too.

'We'll be sitting down for our meal soon,' Mattie said. 'You'll find some orange juice over there on that table Akina. Help yourself but be very careful please.'

'Oh yes, you must try not to spill on your lovely dress,' Mark asserted.

'May I go across and talk to Meredith? Andrew's just waved to me.'

Mattie looked across the room and acknowledged them. 'Alright, off you go but *don't* go outside this room. Promise?'

'I won't. I'll see you later.' She picked up a glass of juice and walked carefully towards Meredith.

'What a delightful child,' Mark said as he passed a glass of sherry to Mattie and took one for himself. 'I'd like to propose a toast to being set up!' He held up his glass and Mattie laughed.

'It might just be coincidence.'

'Right and pigs might fly,' he replied not without humour. 'Let's look at that seating plan. That's one tenner I'd be sure to win from Sister Flanagan.'

'What?'

'Oh nothing....I was just thinking aloud.'

They wandered across the room to scrutinise the seating plan and Mark laughed as he pointed out the names on the top table. 'There you are. What did I say? Now I know there's no sick uncle. I can assure you Mattie that I had nothing to do with any of this. Who do *you* think might be responsible?'

'Knowing my friends and family as I do, I would guess it's a syndicate. I can't be certain but I seem to recall that Andrew was going to give Stephanie away. I could be wrong but *were* that the case, then Meredith would definitely be the perpetrator.'

'I must remember to thank her! Let's circulate. I feel the back of my neck on fire from all the staring eyes.'

'You and me both,' she laughed.

Lucille bounded across and took hold of her arm. 'Come and see the cake....it's gorgeous.'

As she ushered Mattie away she said, 'Don't you just love weddings? I wonder who'll be next.'

She looked quizzically at Mattie who impassively replied, 'Probably Sadie.'

Her exuberance was instantaneously crushed as in two words, Mattie made it abundantly clear that she had no intention of divulging anything about Mark.

Mark had strolled across the room after collecting a second glass of sherry and he was talking to Seth who was relieved that the ceremony was over.

'I've never been as frightened in my life before,' he confessed. 'As soon as the organist struck up the music, I thought I were going to throw up all down my suit. Even though I knew I needed to step aside, I couldn't. My feet wouldn't move at all. It were as if they were glued to the floor and Jack were doing his best to elbow me out of the pew.'

Mark smirked. 'I know all about it. Don't forget I've been there too. I think it's fear of the mother-in-law. Nobody tells the groom anything yet we're expected to obey the rules and get everything right but it's over now Seth. I just wanted to wish you all the best for the future. Stephanie's a great girl.'

'She is and thanks for everything Mark,' he said, shaking his hand vigorously. 'Everyone appreciates what you've done today. Is Mattie around?'

'Yes she's just been accosted by Lucille but I'm quite sure she'll make her escape when she's ready. Has the photographer finished yet?'

'Gawd, I hope so. I feel like the bloody Cheshire cat. Don't they make a meal of it?' he complained.

'They certainly do and it won't be over for weeks. You'll spend ages, poring over all the photographs. You'll be asked which ones you like and Stephanie won't like any you've chosen so let me give you a tip. Let her choose and tell her you agree with her. That's the best way and also you won't get blamed for choosing the wrong ones. You'll probably never look at them again after that. I know I didn't.'

Seth laughed. 'Thanks for that Mark!'

'What are you two laughing at?' Stephanie asked as she appeared behind them and Mark nudged Seth good-humouredly.

'Did you hear that!' he smirked then whispered, 'You need permission to laugh now!'

'I've come to fetch you Seth. We've got to leave the room now,' she stated demonstratively.

'What for?'

'Because everyone will be sitting down soon and we must make our grand entrance as Mr. and Mrs. Henshaw.'

'Aw Steph! Why can't we just sit down with the other folk? I'm famished! Besides, I'll feel a right fool having to do that!'

'It's protocol Seth,' Mark informed him. 'It's the penultimate duty you have to perform, until tonight that is, so do your best to stay sober,' he added with a wink of the eye.

'Let's get it over with then,' he said as Stephanie led him away. Addressing Mark over his shoulder he grunted, 'I'd never get wed again!'

Mark grinned at Seth's facial expression and said to himself, 'I sure as hell would if she'd have me.'

As the guests started to move into position, Mark checked the seating plan to find where Adam would be sitting and noted he was on the table with Akina, close to the top table.

The children had already taken their places when he approached. 'Are you alright here?' he asked.

'We're fine,' Akina said. 'Adam is just telling me about his horse-riding lessons.'

'Alright, enjoy your meal and behave yourselves please. I'll see you both later.'

He made his way quickly to the top table and sat down next to Mattie as everyone awaited the arrival of Seth and Stephanie.

The guests arose and applauded when the newly-weds were announced and as soon as everyone was seated, the waitresses began to serve the food.

Stephanie's mother was buzzing around like a bee round a honey pot and as she hurriedly passed the front of the table, she stopped to have a quick word with Mattie. 'It's lovely to see you again and hasn't the weather been kind to us today?'

'It's a delightful day Ethel and Stephanie looks so pretty. There's obviously a great deal of effort gone into the planning of this day,' she remarked as she nudged Mark and smiled sweetly.

Stephanie was listening to the conversation when Mark asked, 'How's your brother doing?'

'My brother?' Ethel stated appearing confused. 'I don't have a....'

'*Uncle Alfred...*' Stephanie butted in. 'You know, the one who was supposed to give me away today,' she stuttered, her face scarlet with embarrassment.

'Oh right....my *brother*! Oh, he's just fine,' Ethel replied, stumbling over her words as she attempted to sound convincing.

'That's excellent news. Did he manage to make it to the wedding then?' he asked with a broad smile and Mattie burst out laughing.

'Stop it Mark. Don't embarrass Ethel any further. It's alright, nobody's blaming you. I shall deal with Stephanie later! I know who's responsible for this.'

Stephanie spluttered, 'It wasn't me, honest!'

'I know it wasn't you....it was Meredith's idea but I'll get my own back.'

Ethel smiled apologetically and hurriedly took her seat before another word was spoken.

'I'm really sorry,' Stephanie said.

'I can't think why,' Mark replied. 'We're not. As a matter of fact we're delighted aren't we Mattie?'

'Indeed we are.'

No further reference about the alleged sick uncle was made until the end of the meal when, following an amusing and anecdotal speech by the Best Man, the Master of Ceremonies invited Mark to stand up and say a few words.

He smiled cordially at Stephanie and Seth. 'I am officiating today in loco parentis. Sadly, the fathers of Stephanie and Seth have both passed away and it falls to me to say a few brief words. I will begin by

305

saying it was a privilege to be invited here today, at short notice I might add, when owing to additional misfortune, Stephanie's Uncle Alfred was not well enough to attend to give Stephanie away.'

He stared pointedly at Meredith and continued, 'I am the beneficiary of good fortune owing to Uncle Alfred's sad absence. His loss today is my gain....to be seated between two very beautiful women. What more could any man want?'

Andrew caught his eye. He grinned and winked at Mark. 'I told you that you wouldn't get away with it,' he whispered to Meredith.

Mark smiled and glanced round the room. 'I have known Seth and Stephanie for some time and I have watched their initial friendship develop into a rock-solid relationship of deep love and understanding. Their vows to each other today serve to strengthen the foundations on which their future lives will be built and the happiness they will share. I wish them both good health and good fortune. I also wish for a speedy return to good health for Uncle Alfred and finally, I would ask that you all stand with me and raise your glasses one more time please to the Bride and Groom. May you always remain just as happy as you are today. Stephanie and Seth,' he proposed, raising his glass.

'Stephanie and Seth,' everyone repeated aloud.

'That was brilliant,' Mattie said when Mark took his seat. 'Did you see Meredith? She was scarlet.'

'She was, and I bet she'll think twice before she does anything like that again. Do you reckon she'll avoid us for the rest of the evening?'

'In all probability....er hang on a minute. How do you know Meredith? You've never met her.'

'Oops, me and my big mouth! I've been well and truly caught out now. It was very observant of you to notice my faux-pas Mattie....Well done!'

'So come on then, answer the question....how do you know Meredith? Did you plan this together?'

'*No*, I swear I knew nothing about it. Alright, I'll explain how I know her. I've been pestering her for your phone number and address but she refused to tell me, so I invited her to lunch one day, hoping to work my masculine charms on her but that failed to work as well. She's a very loyal friend to you.'

'So why did she set this up today then if she's so loyal when she wouldn't accommodate you before? There's a lot more to this than meets the eye.'

'What difference does it make? Like I've already said, I'm delighted.'

'Don't get me wrong....so am I....but I know she's hiding something. I know Meredith and I intend to find out exactly what that is in my own good time.'

Mark plucked up the courage to take hold of her hand and she didn't resist. 'Do you think we could keep in touch when you go back?'

'I'd like that very much. I have a challenging time ahead of me and I'd appreciate your support. I don't want to discuss it at the moment....I can't but I will later, I promise.'

'Will you have lunch with me tomorrow?'

'I can't I'm afraid. I'd love to but I need to spend time with Jack. We get so little time together. Also, I need to leave early to get back before dark.'

'Can I have your phone number and address?'

'Er....why don't you give me *your* number and I'll call you when I can. That might be better.'

Though he found her reply to be evasive he didn't question her motives. He scribbled his number on a paper coaster and gave it to her. I'm home after six most evenings. I'd better make sure that Adam isn't misbehaving. Everybody's starting to make a move and the staff will want to clear the tables now.'

'You're right. I'd better check on Akina too.'

Mattie found her with Andrew, playing noughts and crosses and asked who was winning.

'Need you ask?' he said grumpily. 'I'm starting to develop a terrible inferiority complex.'

'Those are really big words. What do they mean?' Akina questioned.

'It means that I'm fed up of losing every time to a six-year-old child,' he explained, attempting to look disgruntled.

'Actually, I'm six and a quarter,' she told him. 'If you like, I'll let you win the next one.'

'*No!*' he shrieked. 'I'd like to win a game without your help.'

'Then you must try harder.'

The others around the table laughed heartily. 'She has an answer for everything and she's a very hard taskmaster,' one of the guests remarked to Mattie.

'You can say that again!' she said and addressing Andrew she asked, 'Where's Meredith gone?'

'Probably to dig a large hole,' he smirked. 'Don't blame me. I was dead against it from the outset and Mark's speech was spot on.'

She laughed. 'I'll go and look for her. Would you like to stay here with Andrew?' she asked Akina.

'Yes if that's alright.'

'She's keeping me company,' Andrew said. 'You have a wander round and I'll keep an eye on her.'

Mark couldn't find Adam indoors and went out to the car park where he found him with Jack, kicking a football they had found in the flower border.

'Do you fancy a game dad?' Adam asked.

'Not particularly son. I've just eaten but I'll play a little if I have to.'

'Cheers Mark! You can take over from me,' Jack said. 'I'm ready for a beer and a rest. I'm shattered. I'll see you later Adam.'

'I'm not chasing around like a clown so keep the ball low please,' Mark told him. 'Careful, there's a car pulling in. Keep to the side.'

The car pulled close to the wall and in the shadow of an overhanging sycamore tree. Mark watched as the driver wound down his window.

'*Excuse me mate but are you a guest at a wedding reception here*?' the driver shouted to him.

Mark walked to the car and saw it was a taxi as he drew close. 'Yes, are you here to collect someone?'

'No, I'm delivering a wedding present. Who's the Bride? Do you know her name?'

'Her name's Stephanie.'

The driver spoke to his passenger and said, 'Yes, that's her. Will you see she gets this mate?'

Stretching his arm through the open window, he handed a parcel to Mark and as he took hold of it, he looked past the driver towards the passenger but in the shadow of the large sycamore tree, Mark was unable to see him clearly.

The passenger mumbled something to the driver who wound up his window immediately.

'*Thanks a lot mate*,' he shouted through the glass before driving off at speed.

'That was strange,' Mark said to Adam. 'I wonder why he didn't deliver the gift in person. Come on, we'd better take it inside.'

Stephanie was sitting beside her mother when he handed her the present that was loosely and untidily wrapped in wedding paper. 'Who's that from?' she asked. 'There doesn't appear to be a card with it.'

'Maybe it's inside. I hope it's something you can put to good use,' he said. 'We received four toasters at our wedding.'

'We got three irons,' Ethel laughed. 'Have a look inside and see who it's from.'

'No, I'll wait for Seth. We're opening everything together.'

Mark returned to the car park with Adam to carry on with their game where they were joined shortly afterwards by Mattie who had ventured outside for a breath of fresh air with Akina.

When Akina ran across to join in the game, Mark was glad of the break. 'You play with Adam while I get my breath back,' he told her.

Mattie was standing by the wall with Mark when suddenly Seth stormed outside. 'I want a word with you! Who the hell do you think you are?' he yelled angrily, thrusting a package at her. 'We don't need your blood money. You can keep it, thank you very much. I'd rather work round the clock seven days a week than accept anything to do with that family.'

Mattie was bewildered. 'What is it? What are you talking about Seth?'

'Don't play the innocent with me. You know very well what it is.'

Mark intervened. 'Seth, just calm down and let's talk about this. If Mattie claims she knows nothing about it then I believe her....'

'Keep out of it Mark. It's none of your business. It's between me and Mattie and you know nothing about her. She only tells you what she wants you to know and nothing more.' Glowering at her he said, 'Did you honestly think I'd dirty my hands on that filthy money? *Well did you*?'

Stephanie had arrived during the heated exchange and she appeared as bewildered as Mattie.

Mattie looked inside the parcel and she removed a wad of money, held together by a rubber band. She looked appealingly at Mark and said, 'Please Mark, find Meredith and bring her here right away.'

As Mark hurried away, Seth continued to glare at her. 'Well, I'm still waiting for an explanation!' he said impatiently.

She looked at him anxiously. 'I can't give you an explanation Seth. It's nothing to do with me and I'll prove that when Mark finds Meredith.'

'Is there a problem here?' Meredith questioned as she approached with Mark in hot pursuit.

'It's a family matter so keep out of it!' Seth said.

*'No it's not so shut up and listen and don't dare speak to Meredith like that again,'* Mattie retorted.

'Are you a Trustee of that account Social Services funded when I was fourteen Meredith?'

'Well er....yes, that is until you're twenty-five and then it transfers to you but I don't understand....'

'Tell Seth the truth. Have I withdrawn any money from that account at any time....*ever*?'

'No, I hold the passbook and the statements come to me at the office. Nothing's been withdrawn since it was first opened.'

'*Satisfied now*?' Mattie yelled, thrusting the wad of money back in his hands.

Mark cleared his throat. 'I know it's not really my business but is that the gift I gave you earlier?'

'Yes,' Stephanie answered.

'Right, while I was playing football with Adam, a taxi arrived and stopped over there, under that tree. The driver asked the name of the Bride and when I told him, he gave me that parcel for you. There was only one passenger....a male, probably middle-aged, but with the taxi in the shade of the tree I couldn't see him clearly. He didn't acknowledge me....but he spoke to the driver, then the taxi sped off quickly. It was nothing whatsoever to do with Mattie. Are you sure there was no card or anything inside?'

'There were nothing inside or outside,' Seth said. 'We started counting the money and I were getting angry. I were already up to fifteen hundred quid and there were still a load left to count. I reckon there's about two thousand quid there and who do *we* know who'd have that kind of money to give away apart from Mattie? That's an absolute fortune to the likes of us.'

312

'Well it definitely wasn't me. That's the truth and I don't know any friends on our side of the family with that kind of money.'

Seth searched Mattie's eyes and he could see that she was speaking the truth. 'I'm sorry Mattie....I'm really sorry,' he said, appearing distraught.

'It's alright,' she said, wrapping her arms around him. 'There's no harm done and I understand why you were angry. In your shoes, I'd have been angry too but it's a mystery. Is there anybody on your side who might have delivered it Stephanie? After all, it was you the driver asked about, not Seth.'

'What about Uncle Alfred?' Mark quipped with an innocent expression, causing everyone to laugh.

'I don't have any wealthy relatives and it wasn't mum. She was as shocked as we were. Maybe it's a mistake. The taxi driver could have brought it to the wrong reception.'

'The driver asked your name,' Seth reminded her. 'How many girls called Stephanie would be getting married today?'

'I think you should bank the money and then wait to see if anyone makes contact with you,' Meredith advised them. 'Was there a name on the taxi Mark? If the driver could be identified he might be able to throw some light on the matter. Did you happen to notice what time he was here?'

'I'd say it would have been about twenty-minutes ago, about seven o'clock. I believe the name on the taxi was something like 'Speedfast'. Had I known there'd be all this kafuffle, I'd have taken down his registration number.'

'Could it have been 'Superfast'?' Meredith asked.

'That's the one...yes definitely!' Mark confirmed.

'Right, let's forget about it for now,' Seth stated. 'We'll do what Meredith says. We'll put the money in the bank and make some enquiries later. It's our wedding day and I want to enjoy it. Are you alright now Mattie?'

'Of course I am. I know that you're a proud man and I'm proud of you for that quality. Go back in to your friends now. I think everybody will be waiting for you and Stephanie to start off the dancing.'

'Oh Gawd. I'm absolutely dreading that. I've got two left feet. I think I'd rather stop out here arguing than go back in there making a fool of myself. I'm so sorry Mark. I shouldn't have talked to you like I did. I know you were only trying to help.'

'It's forgotten,' Mark said, shaking his hand. 'Go and enjoy the party and we'll join you shortly.'

Mark and Mattie stayed outdoors when the others went inside. 'Now do you see what I mean? It never ends,' she sighed. 'There's always another reminder of the past.'

It was an involuntary action as Mark wrapped his arms around her to comfort her and when she didn't resist he held on to her. 'We can't ever change the past Mattie. We can only look to the future,' he said and he brushed his lips against her forehead.

She looked up and smiled. Their faces were close together and he couldn't resist the urge to kiss her. Gently, he pressed his lips against hers and Mattie responded by closing her arms around him, where they remained, locked in each other's arms.

314

She would always remember that kiss and she lay against him for some time, her head resting on his chest and wondered what the future held in store.

'I love you,' he whispered. 'Please don't be afraid of me. I'd never do anything to hurt you.'

'I know you wouldn't. It was my fear of hurting you that kept us apart. I've been such a fool Mark.'

'That's history. What will you do now? Will you move back here?'

'I can't Mark....it's complicated but I have to stay where I am for the foreseeable future. There are one or two issues I have to deal with.'

'What kind of issues?'

'Like I said, it's complicated. Just give me a little time....please. I promise I'll explain later.'

Mark felt disconsolate but didn't wish to force her hand.

'It's getting chilly now. Shall we go back inside?' she asked.

'I think we'd better. I'll call the children.'

Mattie smiled to see Adam and Akina return hand in hand. 'Could *I* have horse-riding lessons when I get home?' Akina asked Mattie excitedly.

'We'll have to see about that. If you're out riding, who'll take Poppy out?'

'You'll have to when I can't. I wouldn't be riding *every* day. Please Mattie. Adam's told me all about it and I'd love to ride a horse. Please say yes.'

'I said we'll see so let it drop now please. We can discuss it later when we're home.'

Mark overheard the whole conversation and was shocked. Akina had addressed Mattie as if she were her mother, the decision maker, and he remembered Seth's earlier remark during the argument about the money, that she only revealed what she wanted you to know. The more that Mark learned about her, the more baffled he became. What was her connection with Akina he wondered and why had Mattie talked about home as if they lived together? Although he was puzzled, he believed it was the better option to say nothing and await her explanation.

They managed to find a table well away from the noisy music and Mark stood up to go to the bar.

'What would you like,' he asked Mattie.

'Just a soft drink please. Orange juice is fine.'

Adam tugged at his father's sleeve. 'Is it alright if we join in the dancing?'

'Yes, if you dance properly. You mustn't act the goat or be a nuisance to anyone,' he warned his son and Mattie laughed.

'I said the very same thing to Akina earlier.'

Mark forced himself to smile. 'Kids will be kids. They're so full of energy.'

'Tell me about it!'

Lucille was at the bar waiting her turn. 'You'll waiting ages,' she told Mark when he approached. 'There's only two serving and they're like a couple of snails. So, do correct me if I'm wrong but things seem to be going well between you and Mattie. Am I right?'

'You're nosy!' he said and then smiled. 'Alright, we're making progress....let's just leave it at that.'

'I must say it's not before time. So, is she moving back up here now?'

'We haven't got that far yet,' he said awkwardly. 'I'm not rushing anything. I'm just letting it take its course. It's early days.'

'Well, I could understand her running away from everything at the time that woman attacked her. It must have been horrible,' she remarked, fishing for information after her failure to procure much more from Stephanie following their brief discussion at the hospital. 'Then, I overheard Meredith talking to Steph and was surprised to learn that Mattie had no intention of coming back here when she moved in with Sam and Sam's daughter. Now there's a sweet little girl and Mattie is absolutely devoted to her but then who wouldn't be? Meredith introduced her to Sam you know and....'

As Lucille prattled on, Mark felt like he had been stabbed through the heart and *that* must have been what Seth had tried to warn him about when he said she only told you what she wanted you to know.

Furthermore, Mattie had been very evasive when he had tried to discuss the future. It was happening yet again....history repeating itself, with that bloody interfering Lucille sticking the knife in once more. Mattie wouldn't have expected him to be invited to the wedding when she was bringing Akina with her and she must have been shocked to see him there.

Mark was beginning to see the full picture. Mattie didn't even flinch when he kissed her so apparently she had overcome her fear of men when she entered into a relationship with Sam. Why on earth had he not listened to Helen McAndrew from the start and obliterated Mattie from his thoughts and why did he

317

persist in permitting her to be the cause of so much anguish he asked himself.

Lucille nudged him. 'Are you paying attention? I said you're next and don't forget, I want a dance.'

He ignored her and when the barman appeared he said, 'An orange juice and a double scotch please.' When he placed the scotch on the bar, Mark picked it up and gulped it down. 'Same again,' he grunted. 'Put another double in there.'

Mark handed Mattie her drink and he studied her as she watched the guests dancing, wondering how such a seemingly decent young woman could hurt him so much and cause him such humiliation.

He caught sight of Meredith while attempting to figure out why she had gone to such lengths to get them together at Seth's wedding when Mattie was involved with another man. Between them they had made a laughing stock of him and he was furious.

'You're quiet. Are you tired?' Mattie asked.

'I've had a busy week. Sometimes that happens.'

'Would you like to dance?'

'I'm not a dancer Mattie. I have clumsy feet.'

She persisted. 'Neither am I but I'm sure I could do as well as some of the others. Let's give it a try.'

'Alright, if you insist,' he said and he took her by the hand and led her towards the dance floor.

'Let's try a golden oldie now,' the DJ announced. 'Then the buffet will be open I've been informed.'

Mark held Mattie close as they shuffled round the dance floor to the song by the Platters, 'Only you', barely moving their feet until the music stopped. He felt very emotional and downhearted though he said nothing to make her aware of his feelings and they returned to their seats in silence at the end.

'Are you having something to eat?' Mattie asked.

'No, I'm not hungry. You get something and I'll have a look round for Adam.'

When Mattie returned, Mark still wasn't back and when Akina sat down with an enormous plateful of food, she told her that Mark would be leaving soon because he was tired.

'Who told you that?'

'Mark did. He was talking to Seth and Stephanie. He didn't want anything to eat.'

Adam joined them at their table with his supper. 'Will you be coming here again?' he asked Akina.

'I don't know. Will we Mattie?'

'I would imagine so. Would you like that?'

'Yes, I've had a lovely time and I've made a new friend too. I like Adam.'

'So do I,' Mattie said. 'Oh Mark! There you are. I thought you'd got lost.'

'I was talking to Seth. We'll be making tracks as soon as Adam's had his supper. I've already called a taxi. I'm tired and it's way past Adam's bedtime. It's been nice to see you again,' he said and Mattie detected a spurious tone in his words.

'Is something wrong Mark?'

'Not at all. Are you finished son?'

'Yes dad,' he replied.

'Right, we'll be on our way. Adam, say goodbye to Akina. It's been our pleasure to meet such a fine young lady.'

Akina beamed. 'It was nice to meet you too.'

'Enjoy the rest of the evening,' he said to Mattie. 'Take care.'

He walked away without looking back. Mattie's eyes followed him until the door closed behind him.

'He's nice. I like Mark,' Akina said. 'Do *you* like him Mattie?'

'Very much,' she sighed.

Akina related the weekend's events to Sam when they arrived home the following evening. 'It was a lovely wedding mummy. The Bride was like a fairy princess,' she told her breathlessly. 'I made a new friend too. He's called Adam. His daddy is a friend of Mattie's and he's called Mark.'

'Oh, is Mark some dark secret you've been hiding from me Mattie or would he be the same Mark you mentioned once before?' she asked inquisitively.

'I guess he must be. I only know the one.'

'Tell me more!'

'Later....not that there's much to tell. I'll just slip upstairs and put my things away. You can tell your mummy about everything that happened.'

Akina climbed up on the sofa and sat beside Sam who wrapped her arms around her. 'I missed you a lot mummy. Did you miss me?'

'You'll never know how much darling but you're here now. So, tell me all about your weekend.'

Mattie poked around in her shoulder bag, looking for the paper coaster bearing Mark's phone number. She had barely slept the previous night. Everything had been going so well earlier but there had been an atmosphere of discontent later that evening and she couldn't think of any reason why. According to her recollection, she hadn't done a thing to upset Mark so she needed to address whatever had caused him to become so distant.

When she dialled the number, she waited till his answerphone picked up her call. She listened to the recording and left a brief message. 'Hi, it's Mattie. You're obviously out so I'll try to catch you again later. We've just arrived back. I'll talk to you soon.'

Irritably, he listened to the message and promptly deleted it. Eventually, Mattie would realise he was ignoring her calls if he refused to answer the phone. She'd made a fool of him quite long enough and so had everybody else. Despite his extreme aversion to Lucille, it was she who had prevented his making a bigger fool of himself. He was very disappointed in Stephanie too. He had thought better of her and of Meredith. They had known that Mattie was living with somebody and Mattie hadn't made any attempt to be truthful with him either. She had deliberately concealed that fact when he had raised the question of their future after giving him false hope.

The phone rang again half an hour later.

'You're obviously still out. I'll call you tomorrow about seven.' the message said.

'*Don't bother!*' he shouted at the answerphone as he poured himself another drink.


Meredith had undertaken the task of determining the identity of the taxi driver who had delivered the parcel containing money to the wedding reception. At the time of her initial enquiry, she was advised it might take some time to locate the driver. Saturday was a busy night, the receptionist informed her and she would need to look at the records for calls that had been made around that time.

It was Tuesday when the receptionist returned her call. She told Meredith that the driver had collected his fare outside the betting shop in the High Street. As the call hadn't come in through the centre, there was no name or address she could give to her. The man had simply hailed a passing taxi and had asked to be taken to St. Luke's where they had waited for about twenty-minutes for everyone to come out of the church.

She said that the passenger then asked the driver to enquire where the reception was being held and he asked to be collected again from the betting shop at seven o'clock when he was taken to the reception hall. On each occasion the driver dropped him back at the betting shop and she added that the driver had described his fare as a disabled middle-aged man.

'In what way was he disabled?' Meredith asked.

'The driver thought he had a false leg. It took him some time to get into the taxi and he was pulling his leg in with his hands.'

'Which leg?'

'I don't know which leg! What difference does it make? Has he done something wrong?'

'Not at all. The Bride merely wanted to thank him for his gift. There was no card.'

'Well I wouldn't imagine the Bride having a long list of friends or relatives with only one leg, so that should narrow it down a bit,' she replied snootily.

'Of course,' Meredith responded, feeling foolish for asking such a ridiculous question. 'Thanks very much for your help. I'll pass on your information.'

Meredith called Stephanie at once and apologised for interrupting their honeymoon.

'You're interrupting nothing,' Stephanie told her. 'We're watching TV.'

'What, in the middle of the day?'

'We're having a lazy afternoon. We were both a bit tired after lunch.'

'I can imagine,' she tittered. 'I doubt you've had much sleep.'

'Shut up! Did Mattie get back alright?'

'Yes, I spoke to Sam on Sunday night and they'd been back about an hour when I called. She told me that Akina had thoroughly enjoyed herself.'

'Did Mattie say anything more about what we did to her and Mark?'

'I didn't speak to her. She'd gone up to her room. I told Sam that I'd been exposed and she laughed. I imagine I'll be speaking to Mattie soon. I was a bit disappointed when Mark left so early though.'

'Me too but he said he was very tired.'

'So, let me tell you the reason I'm disturbing you. I had a call from the taxi company earlier. Are you acquainted with a disabled male? The chap who the taxi driver took to the wedding only had one leg he thought.'

'One leg? I don't know anyone who would fit that description. It has to be a mistake.'

Meredith agreed it seemed odd but added that the driver also said that the chap had asked to be taken to St. Luke's first. 'He asked the driver to wait for twenty-minutes until you both came out and then he asked him to enquire where the reception was being held. It's very strange.'

'Creepy is the word I'd use. Did the cab company not have a name or address for the chap?'

'No, he hailed the taxi outside the betting shop on the High Street.'

'That's near the War Veterans' Social Club where I did voluntary work. That's a bit of a coincidence.'

'Was there anyone there who was disabled?'

'Don't be daft! They were all disabled or at least, most of them were.'

'This might be another daft question then but was there anyone there with only one leg?'

'I've no idea. They used to play Bingo and cards, that kind of thing, so most of the time they would be sitting down. I didn't make a point of rolling up trouser legs. I was there to hand out sandwiches and pour the tea. The veterans were there when I arrived and I used to leave when I'd finished my stint.'

'Surely they moved around. I'm not having it that they never went to the toilet. Think Stephanie. Was there someone in particular who springs to mind, I mean someone who was perhaps friendlier than the others with whom you discussed your wedding?'

'I discussed it with a few and they all knew I was getting married when I had to stop attending, in fact they had a whip round and bought us a crystal vase. Seth came with me on my last night because one of them said he'd like to meet my future husband. *My God, it was Bill*! He almost begged me to take Seth to meet him and Bill *did* walk with some difficulty. He stood up and hugged Seth and asked him to look after me. He was sobbing when he sat down and I knelt by his side until he settled down again.'

'Assuming you're right, he thought a heck of a lot about you to give you two thousand pounds. That's a fortune Stephanie.'

'I can't accept it Meredith. I'll have to return it to him. It must be his life savings and I simply cannot imagine why he would want to give it to me. I only treated him the same as the other veterans. Many of them had horrific injuries like Bill. He usually wore dark glasses as he'd lost one eye and he had terrible scarring to his face. The poor man must have really suffered. His money should go to his family, not to a total stranger. I think I'll go to the Social Club on Thursday and have a talk to him.'

'Then make sure it *is* him before you give him the money. Explain to him sensitively why you have to return his generous gift....that you couldn't possibly accept it but don't mention the amount. Try to word it so that he tells you. You *could* be mistaken about him. It could be someone else.'

'I'm not mistaken, everything fits. It couldn't be anyone else but I'll follow your advice. I feel better now I know and I'm sorry that Seth lost his temper with Mattie. I've still no idea what that was about. He won't discuss it with me and gets angry if I raise it. He says it upsets him just to think about it.'

'Then trust Seth's judgement. It's something that happened a very long time ago and it doesn't affect you. Remember that Mattie's a caring person who's had a very difficult life and Seth wants to leave the past where it should be.'

'Thanks for your help. You're always able to sort everything out. Let's hope that you've been equally successful with Mattie and Mark. That would really be the icing on the cake.'

'Wouldn't it just? I'll talk to you soon. Good luck at the Veterans' Club.'

11

Despite Mattie's repeated endeavours to speak to Mark on the phone, each proved to be unsuccessful. She began to wonder if he had been merely putting on an act of compliance to Meredith's plan to avoid embarrassment although that wouldn't explain why he had kissed her when they were alone together.

She decided to leave it for a couple of days before trying his number again.

When Meredith called Mattie on the Wednesday, they enjoyed a lengthy conversation, part of which related to the matter of the mysterious wedding gift.

'Has he been identified yet?' Mattie enquired.

'Possibly....Steph seems to think he was a veteran from the Social Club where she did voluntary work. The receptionist at the taxi firm stated the passenger was badly disabled so it fits. Steph's decided to pay him a visit tomorrow and if it *is* him, she intends to return the money. She feels that it wouldn't be right to keep it.'

'I can't think why on earth he would have wanted to give her so much. It just doesn't make any sense. Two *hundred* pounds would have been a generous amount of money but two *thousand*!'

'There's little point in speculating until we know. Maybe he has no family and felt a need to show his appreciation for her kindness towards him when he heard she was getting married. No doubt she'll find out when she goes to see him tomorrow.'

'Even so, that's one heck of a lot of gratitude and why do it anonymously?'

'I can understand the anonymity. He didn't want her to refuse. He hailed a taxi in the street to avoid detection.'

'Well, it seems very odd to me. Anyway, how are the newlyweds? I didn't like to call when they were enjoying their honeymoon.'

'They are positively glowing! They've opened all their wedding presents and they've received some lovely things. Olive gave them money, as did Sally, so they think they might have a holiday later. Sadie and Keith bought them a TV for the bedroom but I bet that hasn't been turned on yet!' she sniggered. 'Speaking of bedrooms, that reminds me....how are things between you and Mark?'

'Well you can forget about bedrooms for a start!' Mattie said forcefully. 'I believe your little plan has backfired. I've not been able to make contact with Mark since last Saturday. His phone is permanently on answerphone so he appears to be avoiding me.'

'Are you saying he hasn't returned your calls?'

'He can't....he doesn't know my number. I didn't want him calling me here. Don't get me wrong, I'm very fond of Sam but she can run off at the mouth a little. *I* wanted to tell him about Akina when I felt we had a more stable relationship. I have a delicate balancing act at the moment. I'm trying to deal with my past, work with my present and plan my future, so I need to tread very carefully. Up to now, Mark has learned everything about me from other people. Things seemed to be going well at the wedding but later on, I sensed there was something wrong when he left early. He made the excuse he was tired but I didn't believe him. He was cool and impassive and now he won't take any of my calls.'

'You don't know that for sure Mattie. Maybe he's been called away because one of his parents is sick. I'm sure there's a perfectly good explanation.'

'Well, I'll try once more tonight and then that's it. He's had a pile of messages from me now and if he doesn't pick up tonight, it's over. If you're right, he knows *your* number and he'll contact you I'm sure, so you'll be able to let me know if he does but I still don't want you to give him my number or address.'

'I promise I won't breathe a word and I'll let you know if he gets in touch. If that was a show he was putting on last Saturday, he's a damn good actor.'

'Well, he definitely had me fooled. Following the rumpus about the money, when everyone went back inside we stayed outside and then, for the first time, he kissed me so he wasn't role-playing to the crowd then. It just doesn't make any sense.'

'I'm sure everything will work out right Mattie,' she told her reassuringly though things didn't sound very promising she felt. Meredith too had witnessed a discernible coolness in Mark's behaviour when he was leaving on Saturday night but she didn't make her observations known to Mattie.

Mark's answerphone was switched on once more when Mattie called him that evening and so she left a terse message, informing him to contact Meredith if he wanted her to call him again.

Mark deleted the message and angrily banged his fist on the answerphone. He turned on his television but was unable to rid Mattie from his thoughts and the mere mention of Meredith's name continued to antagonise him for the rest of the evening.

Those feelings still hadn't dispersed the next day when he went to work and throughout the morning, his thoughts constantly returned to Mattie whom he likened to a thorn in his side.

He hurried through his morning surgery and when Jill, his secretary informed him that his final patient had cancelled his appointment, Mark looked at his watch. It wasn't yet noon and he wasn't required in theatre until two o'clock. 'I'm off out,' he informed her. 'I'll be back about one-thirty but don't panic if I'm late. I'll definitely be back by two.'

Irately, he drove at top speed to Meredith's office, screeching his car to a halt outside the building. He ran up the stairs two at a time and banged noisily on the door.

'Come in,' Meredith called and when she looked up, she was startled by his demeanour. 'Mark, what a lovely surprise,' she said. 'Please, take a seat and I'll make us some coffee.'

'Don't bother. I'm not staying long,' he answered discourteously. 'I had an hour to spare so I decided to make my point in person. Please instruct Mattie *never* to contact me again. Is that clear? That's all I came to say to you.'

'That's abundantly clear but may I ask why?' she questioned calmly, in the hope that Mark, who was obviously angry, would calm down too.

'You *may* ask why and what's more I'd be happy to *tell* you why. I *refuse* to be made a fool of by you or by anyone else. Is that understood?'

'I assume this refers to Saturday, at the wedding and I can assure you that no one was trying to make a fool of you. Mattie has very deep feelings for you Mark and it was my understanding that yours were the same for her. On reflection, maybe it was wrong of me to presume that I ought to arrange for the two of you come to your senses. Obviously, it isn't what you want and so I apologise for my interference but what I did *was* with good intent.'

'Is that right?' he said furiously. 'So if that's the case, would you mind telling me then how *Sam* fits into your scheming interfering plan?'

Meredith was astonished at the mention of Sam's name and conscious that Mattie had been adamant earlier that she hadn't to discuss Sam or Akina with Mark, she was momentarily lost for words.

'Sam?' she questioned. 'I don't know what you're talking about Mark.'

'Don't lie to me Meredith. Don't dare lie to me in addition to all else you have done to humiliate me. I know that you were the one who introduced Mattie to Sam so don't even attempt to act like the injured innocent with me. You set me up and made me look ridiculous. Was everyone else involved too? I know for a fact that Stephanie was a party to everything.'

'I'm not denying that Mark. Yes, we arranged for you to be at the wedding with Mattie because that's what everyone thought you both wanted. It was that simple. There was never any devious intent and no harm was meant as I've already told you.'

'So then I repeat, what about Sam? How does *he* fit into the equation?'

'I think you'd better sit down Mark. Now I know you've got everything wrong. Please....just give me a few minutes of your time and I guarantee that you won't be disappointed. Shouting at each other isn't going to resolve anything.'

Mark dragged out a chair, sat down and turned to face the window. 'I'm listening,' he stated coldly.

'First of all, tell me what you know about Sam.'

'I know Mattie's living with him and I think he's Akina's father. The child behaves as if Mattie's her mother, so I can't understand why, if Mattie is in a relationship with *him*, you felt a need to go to those extraordinary lengths to make a fool of *me*.'

'Mark you've got everything wrong. She intended to explain her situation later but you are right about Sam. Sam's my friend, my very dear friend whose name is *Samantha* and she's dying. She has cancer. In a few weeks' time, Sam won't be here and Akina is *her* daughter. Sam's a single parent so she's been looking for a suitable guardian for her daughter and Mattie has undertaken to accept that role. She's not in a relationship with a man. She's never even had a boyfriend. How did you get your information if you don't mind my asking?'

His head hanging in shame and humiliation, Mark almost choked on the name, '*Lucille*!'

Meredith laughed. 'I ought to have known! When will you ever learn? I heard all about the Christmas party when you got drunk because of something she told you then. Did she actually state that Sam was a male or did you simply make that assumption when you heard the name?'

332

'I don't recall. I was so astounded that I probably assumed it. My God, at this rate, we're never going to get together are we? I'm very sorry Meredith and I don't need you to make me look stupid. I am quite capable of making a fool of myself. Where Mattie's concerned, I succeed each time something different occurs. I persistently jump to the wrong conclusion and get things wrong and now I've totally wrecked anything we had, just as we were making progress.'

'Don't be hard on yourself. Have you never heard the saying about the course of true love not running smooth? You can't give up now but you'll have to act quickly. Mattie thinks you're avoiding her.'

'I know and fool that I am, I deleted her messages every time she rang me because I was so angry with her. Shall I tell you something? Normally I'm *never* bad-tempered, no matter what the provocation and I hardly ever have a drink.'

'Then I guess you're in love Mark....and love and jealousy are the two most powerful emotions.'

'What do you think I should do to make amends? I don't even know how to get in touch with her.'

Good-humouredly she taunted, 'You aren't trying to tell me you want my interference again are you?'

'Please Meredith,' he said remorsefully. 'Just one more time and I won't bother you again. I apologise profusely for misjudging you.'

'Alright then....when are you next off work?'

'Saturday and Sunday.'

'Since I've no doubt my name will be crossed off Mattie's Christmas card list when she realises what I've divulged today what else have I to lose? Here's her address. Go and find her and tell her how much you love her. That's all she wants to hear.'

'She'll be hearing much more than that.'

'What about Akina?'

Mark smiled. 'She's a bonus! Two for the price of one. I'm happy I came and I can't apologise enough for my outrageous behaviour. I thought that I'd lost Mattie forever and it was tearing me apart. Can you ever forgive me Meredith?'

'It's forgotten and I do understand how you must have felt. Good luck Mark. I hope everything works out right for you.'

He sighed. 'It has to this time. I reckon this is my last chance. I really do love her.'

'Then just make sure Mattie understands that. She was merely trying to buy time by withholding what I've revealed about Sam and Akina. Mattie's a fine young woman Mark and you shouldn't need me to tell you that. You should have trusted her.'

'Yes, you're right. Thanks again for all your help Meredith. I owe you!' he said with a warm smile.

'I'll send you my bill,' she called after him.


'Come on Steph, hurry up. I want to get this over with,' Seth said apprehensively. 'The sooner we get there, the sooner we get away. I'm at a loss to know why you had to drag me along, especially when I'm not even acquainted with what's-his-name.'

'His name's Bill and slow down will you. I'm not an Olympic heel-toe walker and I can't walk as fast as you,' she stated as he strode out briskly ahead of her. 'I need some support. That's why you're here!'

'Well I'll not be saying owt! Anyway, I wouldn't know what to say to the guy.'

'All we have to do is thank him politely and make him understand why we can't accept his gift. It was no trouble to you when you shouted and bawled at Mattie when you thought *she'd* given it to us.'

'That's different. Mattie's family.'

'Oh, so explain to me why that gives you the right to be so rude to her? *Slow down*!'

'Can't I wait outside?'

'No you can't Seth Henshaw! You'll come inside with me where you'll be polite and gracious. I need you to back me up.'

They walked up the steps alongside the disabled ramp and pushed open the door. 'If it's busy tonight we'll have to try and get Bill on one side,' she said. 'It's nothing to do with the others and I don't want any of them ear-wigging. Besides, he's bound to be offended and he might start crying again.'

As they wandered between the tables looking for him, one or two of the regulars looked up and made reference to the wedding. 'You're a very lucky lad,' one called out and Seth smiled at another who said, 'I'd have married her myself if she'd have had me.'

'You never asked me Frank,' she said with a wink of the eye and laughed. 'Have you seen Bill about?'

'Bill? *Has anyone seen Bill*?' he shouted over the noise.

'I don't think he's here Stephanie,' Bob called out to her. 'He usually sits at our table. He weren't here on Saturday either. Funny that! He's generally here as regular as clockwork, every Saturday and every

Thursday....never misses. Happen he's not well. Do you want me to give him a message if I see him?'

'No it's alright Bob. I'll call in again next week.'

'You could ask Ted in the office. He might know summat we don't.'

'I'll do that. *See you soon boys*!' she called out as she and Seth left the room.

'Hello!' Ted said with a smile as she approached. 'How did your wedding go lass? We thought about you. We all had a drink to you on Saturday night.'

'That's nice Ted. Yes, it went off very well thank you. We've just slipped in to see Bill but he doesn't appear to be here. We were wondering....'

'Bill *isn't* here,' Ted interrupted. 'What's more he won't be coming back again. He's moved away. He popped in for a minute or so on Saturday night and said he were going on Sunday. He left an envelope here for you. He acted a bit funny. He said I hadn't to mention it to anybody and I only had to give it to you if ever you came looking for him.'

Ted leaned over to retrieve the envelope from the drawer and handed it to her.

'Did he say where he was moving to?' she asked.

'No, as I recall he said nothing else. He didn't go inside to talk to the lads. Happen he were upset 'cos he were leaving. He's been a member for donkey's years. Aye I bet it'll be five years or more. I hadn't been here long when he first started coming and it's funny you know, after all them years, I never really knew anything about him. He always kept himself to himself, if you know what I mean but he were a right nice feller. Everyone got on well with Bill. He

336

might have wrote down his address in that envelope I gave you. Aye, happen that's what it is.'

When Ted's phone rang Stephanie didn't want to disturb him further. 'Thanks Ted. I'll see you soon.'

'Make sure you do. Call in anytime you want love and bring that husband of yours with you,' he said as he answered the phone.

She walked out clutching the envelope. 'What do we do now?' she asked Seth.

'I suggest we take it home and see what he's got to say for himself. It's a bit of a funny do isn't it?'

'You're right Seth....it is a bit of a funny do. It's surreal in fact.'

Stephanie ripped open the envelope and removed a single sheet of paper bearing no heading and read out the words to Seth.

'Dear Stephanie, If you're reading this letter, then you know it was me. I thought you'd likely work it out. I'm going away and I won't be coming back to Manchester and I just wanted to say a final goodbye and good luck. You must keep the money I gave to you and put it to good use. I want you to have it and enjoy it. I remember you said not very long ago that you were saving for a car so now you can buy your car and there'll still be some left for the other things you need too. I don't have any family members of my own but if I had a daughter, I would want her to be just like you, kind and considerate. Take care of Seth. He seems like a decent and caring young man. With my deepest affection and very best wishes for your future together, Bill.'

She passed the letter to Seth and sighed. 'There's no address but at least now we know for sure where the money came from. I still can't believe it.'

Seth read the letter in silence and remarked, 'You evidently made a good impression. I can't believe it either. Two thousand quid! What a great bloke.'

She started to cry and Seth took her in his arms. 'Poor Bill has no family and now he's moved away from all his friends,' she sobbed.

'It were Bill's decision. Nobody forced his hand. That's what Bill wanted,' he said compassionately. 'He were obviously a generous man who thought a great deal about you. You hear about folks like that sometimes. Shall I walk to the chippy and fetch us something nice back for our supper? Come on love, dry your eyes. Bill wouldn't want you to get upset would he? Butter some slices of bread and stick the kettle on and I'll be as quick as I can.'

She blew her nose and sat pensively when he left.

She took the letter from the envelope and read it several times with tearful eyes and then she paused and read one particular part repeatedly....'Take care of *Seth*.' A chilling and sudden rush of adrenaline pumped through her body. '*Oh Bill*!' she cried out. '*You're my dad*!'

She was crying inconsolably when Seth returned.

'Whatever's the matter Steph?' he asked earnestly. 'What's happened?'

He knelt by her side and took her in his arms. 'Is something wrong? Tell me, please.'

'You'll never believe this Seth....Bill's my dad.'

'Don't be daft. Your dad were killed in the war.'

'No, no he wasn't Seth. I know it's him. Bill's my dad and I'll prove it to you. I knew that something was niggling me about that letter and I kept reading it over and over again after you'd gone out and then all of a sudden it struck me. Look,' she said. 'Look at that capital letter 'S' He's written it twice, once for each of our names. There was a photo of my dad on the dresser and it was signed, 'love Steve' in his handwriting. That's exactly how he wrote the letter 'S', with those squiggles and that long line through it. I was forever trying to copy the way he wrote it when I was a kid. It's him I tell you. I'd recognise it anywhere. Nobody else writes it like that.'

'Alright, calm down and let's talk about it quietly. You stated your dad's name were Steve didn't you? This chap's called Bill.'

'So he changed his name. Anybody can. It's *him* Seth....I'm telling you and I have to find him.'

Seth was mystified. 'You said your mum received a telegram from the War Office at the time your dad were killed, didn't you?'

'Yes but hundreds of personnel were killed in the war. Someone must have made a mistake.'

'It were a bloody big mistake to make. Listen to me Steph....think about it for a minute. If your dad hadn't been killed, then he'd have come back home to your mum when he were discharged.'

'Maybe he didn't want to be a burden to her when he had all those appalling injuries or maybe he was shell-shocked and didn't know who he was. I don't know the reasons but I do know it's him and look at what he wrote....that if he had a daughter, he would

339

want her to be just like me. That's spoken from the heart. He *knows* I'm his daughter and that's why he gave me all his savings....as a kind of compensation payment to help relieve his guilt for abandoning me and mum perhaps. I don't know.'

'That's exactly it....you don't know and you never will. Bill's moved away now and that's the way he wants it to be and no amount of outside influence or divine intervention for that matter is ever going to bring him back unless he decides to come back and it's not our place to meddle in his life. The world is a very big place and you'd never find him. Even if what you say *were* true, he's managed to hide away for over twenty years.'

'I know but nobody was looking for him before.'

Seth was becoming exasperated. 'You're missing the point. It's Bill's life. He made his choice *then*, if you're right and he's made a further choice *now* but whether you're right or wrong, how do you imagine he'd feel were you to track him down? It's better to let go and you could never tell your mum because it would break her heart if you did.'

'Your chips are going cold,' she said impassively.

'Aye and that's what you're search would end up like....cold! You'd never find him, I tell you. It's a nice concept to think of him as your dad but leave it at that Steph. It's what he wants whoever he might be so respect his feelings, please. Remember Bill as he was, a sincere generous man and be thankful for what he's done for you.'

'For *us*!' she corrected him. 'He did it for *us* and don't you forget that Seth Henshaw.'

'I'm getting my supper. You can please yourself what you do. I'm having nothing to do with it.'

The next morning, Stephanie said she was going to her mother's house. 'I've been awake for most of the night thinking about Bill. I'm going to look for dad's photograph. I need to know for certain. One way or the other I have to know. I don't expect you to understand. Do you want to come with me?'

'No, I'll stop here and I might give them bedroom doors another coat of paint while you're out. I hope you find it's not him. I really do sweetheart.'

'I might be a while, so make yourself a sandwich if you're hungry and I'll fetch something nice back for our tea. What do you fancy tonight?'

'Come here and I'll show you,' he grinned.

'Seth Henshaw! Don't you ever think of anything else?'

He deliberated fleetingly before answering, 'No!'

Stephanie chuckled and gave him a quick peck on the lips. 'I'll see you later love.'

There was nobody in when she arrived, so she let herself in and hurried upstairs to the back bedroom, remembering that her mother kept a large cardboard box on the shelf of the airing cupboard, filled with memorabilia and relics of the past.

As she opened the box, she smiled to find her first pair of hand knitted bootees, her first bib and a tiny lock of her blonde hair wrapped in cellophane.

There were scores of photographs from babyhood to adulthood and sifting through them, she found a few of her father too but the one she so desperately sought wasn't there.

341

Only when she returned the box to the cupboard did she find it near the corner of the shelf with the frame in pieces and the glass broken. Undoubtedly her mother had accidentally dropped when dusting.

She carefully lifted it down to prevent the shards of glass from falling on the carpet and scrutinised it closely, using a fingernail to separate the miniscule fragments to reveal her father's writing as her eyes welled with tears. There was no doubt. The writing was identical. Bill was definitely her father.

How gratifying though emotional it felt to know she was right. Removing her scarf, she wrapped the photograph and placed it in her shoulder bag before making her way to Meredith's office.

Meredith was surprised to see her. 'I trust this is a social call,' she commented dryly.

'What?....Oh yes,' she laughed. 'We're still living together. I am here for advice though.'

She explained what had transpired at the Club and that she had been handed a letter written by Bill. As she passed it to Meredith, Stephanie didn't mention her suspicions.

It took a few moments for Meredith to digest the content. 'Well, that's excellent news. It resolves the issue nicely and provides some financial security. I imagine you're overjoyed with the outcome. That's a lot of money and just when you need it. Have you told Mattie yet?'

'No, I haven't told anybody,' she replied. 'Seth's aware of it because he was with me but I....' At that point she burst into tears. 'Meredith, I don't know what to do.'

'Hey, come on now. Bill obviously wanted you to have the money. His letter makes it perfectly clear so what's the problem?'

Stephanie walked round the desk and pointed to Seth's name. Look at the letter 'S'. Look at it very critically and study those scrolls and those diagonal lines. Now look at this,' she sobbed as she carefully unwrapped the photograph. 'Look at *this* letter 'S'.'

Meredith looked at the photograph and then she studied the two names on the letter before looking again at the photograph. 'They're identical. Who's Steve?'

'My dad, who's supposed to be dead!' she wept.

'Oh my God! Oh Steph, I don't know what to say to you. Bill's your dad?'

'Yes and now he's gone away and I'll never find him again. What am I going to do and what do I tell mum?'

Meredith was shocked. 'First things first....try to calm down and let's go through this again. Tell me everything you learned about your dad and how he was allegedly killed.'

She listened attentively without interruption until Steph had finished talking. 'So, your mum told you that everyone was killed in the bombing?'

'Yes, that's what she was told at the time, that all of them were blown to bits. There were no bodies.'

'Well, it's quite clear that your dad wasn't killed. It doesn't need an expert to determine that both sets of writing are written by the same hand so what we must consider is why your dad would make such a decision to stay away and how he got away with it.

Start by telling me about Bill. Describe his injuries and anything else you know about him.'

She described his gait, his facial scarring and that he had also lost an eye.

'So he must have been very badly injured when it happened. Well, the way I see it, there can only be one possible explanation, that he didn't want to be a burden on your mum but the question is how did he escape detection? I'm surmising, but let's consider this scenario. Suppose your dad had a mate with no relatives. Let him be Bill, so he was killed instantly and your dad escaped. A serviceman wears what's called a dog-tag....an identification disc around his neck. Maybe your dad discarded his identification disc or replaced it with Bill's. Determined enough, he could have dragged himself from the debris and somehow, he ended up in hospital. He could have feigned amnesia or used Bill's name....who knows? Covered in bandages, nobody would recognise him and if his regiment were due to return home shortly, he would have been repatriated, thus enabling him to continue his treatment and further his deception.'

'It sounds very far-fetched to me,' she remarked.

'It *is* far-fetched but it must have been something along those lines. You said that your mum received a telegram stating he was dead but he's alive. The point I'm trying to make is that your dad wanted it that way. How he orchestrated it will always remain a mystery.'

'Are you telling me to forget about him?'

'I'm not saying forget him....I'm saying don't try to find him and don't tell anybody else about him.

He's probably watched you grow up and I doubt his presence at the Veterans' Club was coincidental, in fact I'll lay odds he arrived on the scene soon after you'd started working there. Am I right?'

'Yes you are. I'd been working there for a couple of months I think when he turned up.'

'There you are then. He's had ample time to make himself known. Let your mum remember him as he was and don't hurt either of them by trying to bring them together. Show respect for your dad and leave well alone. He did what he believed was right. Your parents are different people now who have learned to live without each other. Deep down, maybe your dad wanted you to know but the mere fact that he's disappeared again makes it crystal clear he wanted nothing more. You have to let him go Steph.'

'That's more or less what Seth said too.'

'It's your decision and I know you'll do the right thing for both your parents but if it helps you make the right decision, remember too that your mum has been a war widow for twenty years and she'll have received a pension since your dad was presumed to be dead. You're opening a very large can of worms if you make it public knowledge that he's alive and there could be all kinds of repercussions. Your dad wanted nothing like that. He just wanted to perform an act of kindness for his daughter....anonymously. Be thankful you knew him, albeit for a short period of time and leave him in peace. That's all he wants. If he had wanted more, he would have stayed.'

Stephanie sighed. 'I knew what you'd say before I came here today and I know you're right. I don't suppose I'd ever find him if I tried and you're right when you say it would only cause heartache if mum were to find out. I'll leave things as they are but I'll never forget him. I'm pleased he met Seth and I'm happy he was there when we came out of church as man and wife. Perhaps that's why he left. Once we were married, he might have felt there was no need to keep a watchful eye on me. Thanks for listening Meredith and for helping me to do the right thing.'

Mark left for Devon with Adam early on Saturday morning after confirming the previous evening with Meredith that Mattie still remained unaware of his surprise visit. Afraid she might still be furious with him for avoiding her calls, he imagined she would be equally furious to learn that Meredith had given him her address.

Mark arrived a little after ten and shuddered like a frightened schoolboy when he rang the doorbell.

Clutching a huge bunch of flowers in one hand he straightened his hair with the other and cleared his throat as he heard footsteps approaching the door.

He was greeted by an elderly lady who gave him a beaming smile.

'Good morning,' Mark said hesitantly. 'I'm here to see Mattie....Mattie Henshaw.'

'Please come in. I'm Emily Peters. You can wait in the sitting room with Sam, my daughter. Mattie's at the bank but she shouldn't be very long. Shall I relieve you of your flowers and put them in water?'

'You're very kind. I'm Mark Wyndham and this is my son Adam. Wipe your feet,' he told his son.

'I'm pleased to meet you and I've heard all about you young man,' she smiled, patting Adam's head. 'You're Akina's friend aren't you?'

'Yes, is she here?' he questioned optimistically.

'She's at the bank with Mattie but they should be back any minute. Let me show you in and then I'll make some tea.'

Emily opened the door to the sitting room and she gestured for Mark to enter. 'Mattie has two visitors. Would you take care of them Sam till she returns?'

'Please, come in Mark,' Sam said warmly. 'And I imagine you must be Adam.'

'Are you psychic?' Mark asked, moving towards her to shake her hand. 'You knew my name.'

'Er....what was the expression Mattie used? Yes, I remember now....'Mark's very dishy',' she laughed. 'I can't argue with that. She was spot on. Now I'm embarrassing you, so I must apologise. Please have a seat and tell me what brings you to Devon.'

He had a certain fondness for Sam from the first moment they met and though she appeared close to death, he recognised a spirited sense of humour and her warm smile illuminated her pallid complexion, adding a touch of colour to her cheeks. 'Would you believe that it's Mattie who brings me to Devon?'

'I would, since you appear to be having a rough ride. Do you hope to get it together this time?'

He felt uncomfortable and shot a sideways glance at Adam. Recognising Mark's embarrassment Sam said, 'Do you like dogs Adam?' and when the boy nodded she added, 'Go to the room right at the end and you'll find Poppy. She loves children and don't

347

worry....she doesn't bite. You can play with her in there if you like until Akina comes back.'

Mark nodded his approval and he left the room.

'Sorry Mark, I should have been more considerate in Adam's presence. I hope you and Mattie manage to work things out this time. All these minor upsets must put such a strain on your relationship.'

'*Relationship*? *What relationship*?' he screeched with laughter. 'We take a step forward and at least a dozen back each time we meet but I have to say this latest misunderstanding was my entire fault.'

Propping herself on one elbow, Sam urged, 'Tell me more. I'm all ears.'

'Well, in a nutshell, when I found out about you, I thought you were a man,' he confessed.

Sam grinned widely. 'Well I've been called a fair few things in my life but that's a first....a man!'

'It was your name. A colleague at Seth's wedding said Mattie had moved in with someone called Sam and I was shattered. Until then, everything had been going swimmingly, so a day or two later I stormed into Meredith's office and accused her of setting me up at the wedding just to make me look ridiculous and it was only then that I found out your name was Samantha. I felt such an idiot to find I'd made such a simple error but by then I'd blown it with Mattie.'

'Have you resolved things with her now?'

'No, I didn't know her number and yet again, like a fool, I deleted every message she left me because I was....well er....jealous of Sam the male.'

'She'll get over it....She has a broad back. That's what I love so much about her and she has to be the most genuine and trustworthy person I know. Over the past few months she has developed a very close affinity with my daughter. Did Meredith happen to mention the plans for Akina's future?'

'She told me about both of you and I was sorry to learn you have cancer.'

'So do I take it you haven't brought me a miracle cure then?'

'I wish I had. We're making some progress with cancer treatments but there's still a long way to go. Are you receiving any medication now?'

'I just stick to palliative treatment to relieve pain. I want to keep it together for Akina as long as I can until I go into the hospice.'

'You appear to be handling it well.'

'I'm a very strong-minded woman. It isn't an act. Anyway, enough about me. My prime concern now is Akina's future. Mattie is taking over her care but you're aware of that aren't you?'

'Yes, Meredith told me and I'll say to you what I said to her, that Akina was a bonus and that I'd be getting two for the price of one.'

Sam smiled warmly. 'I like that Mark! Mattie was right about you. You *are* a nice guy and things will work out for you this time. I feel it in my soul and I know you'll be very happy. I think that's Mattie's car I can hear. I'm going to enjoy this....I just adore romantic movies!'

When Mark heard the front door close, he stood up and faced the sitting room door.

Akina dashed in first and when she saw him, she screamed, 'Mark,' and jumped into his arms.

Mark hugged her and waited for Mattie to appear, concealing feelings of trepidation and excitement.

'Hi Mattie,' he said softly when she walked in the room. 'Come here please. Put me out of my misery before I go crazy.'

With arms outstretched, she flew towards him as Sam looked on with tears streaming from her eyes at the three of them clinging to each other.

'Are you staying here with me and Mattie now?' Akina asked him.

'No darling, I must go home tomorrow but I wish I could.' He looked ruefully at Mattie. 'I can't tell you how sorry I am for my reprehensible behaviour at the wedding and for not taking any of your calls. I've been a complete idiot but I promise I've truly learned my lesson now. I'll never doubt you again. I give you my word. You have to forgive me.'

'I might but only if you tell me what I did to upset you at the wedding reception.'

'Nothing....it was just a simple misunderstanding. While I was waiting at the bar to be served, Lucille told me you were living with somebody called Sam. I think you can work out the rest.'

'Oh Mark!' she laughed. 'So that's the reason you could barely look me in the eye? Would it be right to assume you dragged the truth out of Meredith?'

'It would! I was livid with her for setting me up at the wedding *and* I had to buy a new answerphone,' he grinned. 'I'd broken the other when I thumped it with my fist following your final message because I was going crazy with jealousy. I had waited so long for you and then I learned you'd gone to live with a

350

bloke called Sam, or so I believed. I've been such a clown! I love you so much Mattie....'

'I have a confession to make,' Sam interjected. 'It was me. *I'm* the perpetrator! *I* was the one who set you up, not Meredith. It was all my idea.'

'*You?*' they said simultaneously.

'Yes, me! Mattie, you wanted Mark and I wanted a father for Akina. You'd admitted to me how you felt about him and Meredith had told me that Mark felt the same about you so I decided that the four of you would make a very happy family unit and since you couldn't seem to get your act together, I had to intervene. Don't glare at me like that. Someone had to do something!' she said. 'There's one more thing I have to do....Mark, will you take this woman to be your lawful wedded wife?'

'I will. I most definitely will if she'll have me,' he said with a broad smile as he lifted Akina down and took Mattie in his arms once more.

'And now you Mattie, will you take this man....'

Mattie didn't wait for Sam to finish. '*Oh yes!*' she cried out.

'Then you may kiss the Bride....'

'Look away,' Mark demanded before pressing his lips firmly against Mattie's.

'Mummy, he's nearly eating her,' Akina squealed with joy.

He was grinning from ear to ear as he said, 'Why don't you find Adam. He's with Poppy.'

As Akina screeched with excitement and ran off, Mark gazed intensely at Mattie. 'I love and respect you more than you'll ever know,' he whispered.

351

'Don't you just love a happy ending?' Sam sighed as she wiped her hand across her tear-stained face. So, now that we have a positive result, who'd like a drink?'

'Your mother was making some tea. Shall I see if it's ready?' Mark asked.

'I said a *drink*! I meant a *proper* drink. You know what I want Mattie.'

'Gin with a splash of lemon!'

'Alcohol Sam?' Mark said disapprovingly.

'Why, is it bad for my health?' she queried with an expression of total bewilderment. When Mattie howled with laughter, Mark was surprised at such a reaction to his concerned remark.

'Ignore us,' Mattie said. 'I used to be shocked too when I first arrived but I'm not shocked anymore. Sam explained that there's a very fine line between life and death....merely a heartbeat....a split second in time, that's all. Sam's alive now so she's living. Where's the harm in that?'

'Well er....I suppose I can't really argue with that hypothesis,' he replied awkwardly.

'Then don't. It's *my* funeral!' Sam replied glibly and she and Mattie collapsed in each others arms in hysterics while Mark observed in amazement.

Sam dried the tears of laughter from her eyes and asked, 'Where are you staying tonight Mark?'

'I'm booking in at the Lodge down the road.'

'Well I have an empty single if you'd like Adam to stay with us. Akina would love that and it would give them some time together. You could book in at the Lodge but ask for a double and take Mattie with you. For God's sake Mattie, don't look so horrified! You're going to marry the guy aren't you?'

'I'm game if you are,' he said with a broad grin.

With a taunting glint in her eye, Mattie quipped, 'I'll bet you are!'

'Is that a 'yes'?' he beamed.

'No....It's an 'I'll think about it'.'

Sam sighed. 'Thank God, progress at last! I'll tell you what Mattie....if it makes you feel any better, I can come as well and I'll show you what to do.'

Mark howled with laughter when Mattie retorted brusquely, 'I can manage quite nicely without *your* help thank you very much!'

'That was a definite '*yes*' Mark,' Sam announced gleefully. 'Pour her another drink quick, before she changes her mind.'

'I've no intention of changing my mind,' she said softly as she gazed lovingly at Mark.


'Sam is such a remarkable woman. I've never met anyone quite like her before,' Mark said later when he took Mattie to dinner. 'I can see now what you meant when you said there were things you needed to attend to here. She's going to need all your help to see her through the next few weeks.'

'She is but I've needed her help just as much. She taught me about the important things in life. I was unable to move forward until I met Sam. I couldn't have done this tonight had I not met her. I longed to do so many things but I couldn't conquer my fears until she made me realise, by her valiant example of fortitude, how I could think of living again. When you've suffered cruelty of any kind, it elevates your scepticism and fear, so it's the easier option to shut yourself away as opposed to facing your problems head on and so, after a while, you learn to accept it as your way of life....so it's a vicious circle.'

He nodded in concurrence. 'I know exactly what you mean because I felt the same before I met you. When my wife died, I firmly believed that *my* life was over too. Suddenly, at the age of twenty-seven, I was a widower with a baby to care for. I'd lost the only woman I'd ever loved and I didn't know how I could ever face life without her. We'd been in love since our teenage years and we were soul-mates.'

'Can you talk about what happened?'

'I can now but I couldn't for a while. Like you, it was so much easier to hide from the outside world. I felt guilty that I was responsible....that somehow I had contributed to her death but when I look back, I couldn't have done anything to prevent it because it all happened so unexpectedly,' he sighed.

'Not long after Adam was born, Sarah started to act strangely. She would wander into another room and sit staring into space for hours at a time and if Adam awoke for his feed, she appeared not to hear him. During her more lucid moments, she'd laugh it off and make the excuse that she'd been meditating but I could sense that there was something wrong. Post-natal depression sprang to mind and so I made arrangements for Sarah to see a colleague of mine, a psychiatrist who confirmed my suspicions.'

'He prescribed anti-depressants and shortly after, there seemed to be some improvement. Meanwhile,

I'd employed a nanny because I was concerned for Adam's safety and for about three weeks following her arrival, things seemed to be returning to normal. I'd only been back at work for a week when, out of the blue, I received a distressed telephone call from the nanny, asking me to go home right away. Sarah had gone to lie down after breakfast and the nanny couldn't awaken her. She was in a state of panic. I remember yelling at her to calm down and call for an ambulance and I rushed home immediately. The ambulance was there when I arrived and I was told that Sarah was dead. She'd taken an overdose.'

'Could it have been an accident?'

'It was a carefully premeditated act of suicide and that's what made it so hard for me to come to terms with. She had completely cleaned out the medicine cabinet and had taken all the medication she could lay her hands on but on any other day, she wouldn't have succeeded. The nanny was taking Adam to the baby clinic later that morning and Sarah knew that she'd be away for several hours, so by the time she returned and raised the alarm, it was too late. There wasn't a suicide note. There were just empty bottles strewn around the bedroom floor. It was grotesque.'

'Mark, I'm so sorry,' Mattie said as she took hold of his hand. 'And then you blamed yourself for not seeing it coming?'

He nodded. 'I used to cradle Adam and feel guilty that I'd deprived him of his mother but I swear that I'd never expected anything like that. I loved Sarah and ostensibly, she was improving. I'll never know what happened to make her take her own life.'

355

'She was out of control. I know as well as anyone how the mind overpowers reality and how wretched it can make you feel. I believed that I was somehow responsible for and deserving of all the abuse I was suffering but I suppose I was fortunate because one day, I awoke to the reality that none of it was of my making and that it shouldn't be happening to me. It was then that I brought that abuse to an end but it's taken me many more years to admit to myself that I must lay my past to rest and move on.'

'I've moved on too Mattie. It was seven years ago and though the first few years were difficult, it's all behind me now. It's hard to be a single parent and particularly so with a job like mine but I think I've done alright. Adam's a great kid and I don't dwell on the past anymore because now I have a future to look forward to with you and Akina.'

'And *you* are my future Mark, though never in my wildest dreams did I expect I would ever say that to a man following the abuse I suffered. I often think back to those times and to how the simplest act of buying a loaf of bread could change so many lives. It was November and there was a blizzard. If only mum had crossed the road to the Baker's just a few minutes earlier or later, our lives would have been so different. As she stepped out between two cars, she was hit by a bus. I don't know how it happened. Perhaps her head was down or her umbrella could have obscured her vision. Nobody could say and an accidental death verdict was recorded. The three of us were taken into care right away but unfortunately we couldn't be placed together. I learned later from

Meredith that the Social Worker had found it very difficult to place us at all so close to Christmas. My brothers were fostered together and I was taken to live with the Parkes family. They hadn't fostered a child for some years but then I didn't know that at the time. When they *had* previously fostered, they had always taken boys. Do you want me to go on?'

'I think it's important for you. It's something you need to be able to do,' he replied. 'I once said that I would be a willing listener if you wanted to talk so please continue.'

'The physical abuse began more or less from day one, mainly by Hilda Parkes. No matter how hard I tried to please her, she was never satisfied with my efforts and would use her fists at every opportunity. I recall one night when she beat me, only a couple of weeks after my arrival, I was crying in my room when Albert Parkes came in. Initially, he appeared to show concern at my suffering but I was soon to discover that it was merely a preamble to the onset of his sexual abuse which then continued for the six months I was in their care.'

Mark listened in silence as she continued.

'I was simply a victim of system failure. During my time at the foster-home I had nobody in whom I could confide so I continued to take the abuse until eventually, I began to believe that I was deserving of the oppression. It's difficult to explain but when a person makes you *think* you have no worth, you start to *believe* it and that was a sentiment, together with my fear of men that I carried within me almost to the present day. I rejected you simply because I was terrified of men and I also felt I could never be worthy of a decent man like you. I never wanted to hurt you. I moved away to protect you but it wasn't long before I realised just how much I wanted and needed you. You are a very special man Mark.'

'No Mattie. I'm just an ordinary run-of-the-mill guy with the needs, sentiments and weaknesses of any other guy,' he corrected her. 'I love you so very much but I think you know that because of the way I persistently make a fool of myself. Over the next few weeks, I'll visit you when I can and when the time comes, we'll choose a new home together for our family. We've everything in the world to look forward to now,' he said lovingly.

'Our separation won't be for much longer Mark. Recently, there's been some deterioration in Sam's health and she's very weak now. I'm trying to take comfort from the fact that we'll have the rest of our lives together when Sam's gone. I'm so happy you came today. I've felt wretched since last Saturday when I thought I'd lost you forever.'

'Me too Mattie and I can hardly wait to tell Helen McAndrew our news. She will be delighted to learn we're together at long last. I need you to be straight with me now. Are you sure about coming back with me tonight? I know you've moved forward but are you ready for this? Is it what you really want?'

'Yes Mark. It *is* what I want. I want *you*. I always did from the very first moment you looked at me in that special way at the hospital but back then I was too scared to follow my heart.'

'Was I so transparent?' he grinned.

'Blatantly obvious is the expression I'd use! You almost undressed me with your eyes and you scared me half to death because you made me experience feelings I'd never experienced before.'

'Do you remember the first time you came to my surgery to advise me of your family medical history and you wouldn't allow Sister Flanagan to leave the room?'

With vivid colour rising in her cheeks, she stated, somewhat irritably, 'I do,' and Mark laughed.

'Well, after you'd left, I had a bet with her that I could persuade you to go out with me on a date and she bet me a tenner I couldn't. I've just realised that I've won a tenner! How about that?'

'So, you're telling me you drove all this way just to win a bet?' was her slick rejoinder.

'I guess so,' he grinned.

'So tell me this....how much did she bet that you wouldn't get me in your bed tonight?'

'We wouldn't place bets on things like that! Sister Flanagan is extremely straight-laced, besides which I'm her blue-eyed boy,' he laughed.

'So I bring out the worst in you Mr. Wyndham?'

'Most definitely Miss Henshaw. You drive me to distraction. You couldn't even begin to imagine the suffering you cause me. I've spent many a restless night thinking about you....wishing you were in my bed,' he confessed. 'Particularly so the weekend we were in London together when my imagination ran riot!'

'*Mr Wyndham*!' she declared whimsically. 'I do believe I'm coming over all faint.'

'Then allow me escort you to your boudoir so you may lie down,' he teased.

She smiled at him and replied softly, 'I love you so much Mark....'


Mark unlocked the door and Mattie went in ahead of him as he paused to turn on the light.

After placing her jacket and overnight bag on the chair, she walked around the pleasant and spacious room. She proceeded to the bathroom and washed her hands in the white porcelain basin. Everything was spotlessly clean and the tablet of soap smelled of lavender.

When Mattie returned to the bedroom, Mark was sitting on the edge of the bed, his head held low.

Clasping her arms around his neck and kissing the top of his head, she asked softly, 'What's wrong?'

'I don't know. I suppose I'm feeling nervous,' he confessed with a cautious smile. 'It's been many a year since....well I think you know what I mean and I wasn't expecting this when I arrived today.'

Mark clasped his arms around her, regarding her with questioning eyes. 'I need to be sure it's what you want.'

'It must be what we both want, not just what Sam wants for us....that's not why we're here.'

She slipped off her shoes and stretched out on the bed. 'Come over here next to me please. I want to hold you. I've dreamed of that for so long Mark.'

He moved alongside her and held her close to his body. 'You feel warm and you smell nice,' he said. 'I could stay like this forever. I adore you Mattie.'

He kissed her lips gently once then again but that time with passion and Mattie returned his passion. Then, when he released her he smiled at her and his smile suddenly broke into uncontrollable laughter.

'*I don't believe this*!' she exclaimed. '*What now*?'

'Forgive me,' he spluttered apologetically. 'I was just thinking. I felt exactly like this when I took my driving test. I'm embarrassed to admit I'm a bag of bloody nerves. Promise you won't tell Sam?'

'What do you take me for Mark? I don't tell Sam *everything*. So, enlighten me, when you took your driving test, did you finally calm down?' she asked light-heartedly.

Confidently he replied, 'Oh yes, after about five minutes I was alright.'

'That's encouraging to know. I'm sure I can wait for five minutes,' she commented dryly. 'After all, I've waited for twenty-four years to make love to a man so what's five minutes? More importantly, did you pass your driving test?'

He laughed aloud. 'No, I failed miserably. I made an absolute cock-up of my first test. Half the time I was in the wrong gear. The car kept jerking up and down, I repeatedly stalled the engine and then, wait for this....I was driving my own car and I ran out of petrol!' he howled. 'There I was, stuck right in the middle of the road and the examiner had to get out and help me push the car towards the kerb. Luckily I had a can of petrol in the boot or he'd have had to walk all the way back to the test centre.'

Mattie was aching with laughter. 'I can't believe he failed you just because of *that*. What a nerve!'

'I passed easily the next time though,' he declared triumphantly, attempting to redeem himself. 'I was *very* good the second time.'

'In that case, I'll look forward to the second time for us,' she said dryly. 'I have to admit that *my* test wasn't a bed of roses either. You know what I was like then so I'd requested a female examiner only to discover when I arrived at the test centre, that she'd gone home sick so I was faced with the dilemma of opting for a male or waiting for another date. After much deliberation I chose the male which was more fearful than the actual test but after a rickety start I passed, which clearly demonstrates that women are *much* better drivers than men!'

'Er, I don't quite grasp the logic of that argument but if that's the case, perhaps you should take over now,' he said softly.

'No, I think I'd feel much happier with you at the wheel. Like I said, I can wrestle with my hormones for another five minutes until you to settle down.'

Mark smiled and looked deeply into her eyes and she recognised the meaningful and penetrating look of passion she had seen so many times before.

'You don't have to wait a moment longer. You're so beautiful,' he whispered tenderly, his eyes ablaze with desire. He ran his fingers through her hair and kissed her with passion.

At that moment in time, Mattie's past was finally laid to rest as she gave herself to Mark and returned his love.

12

Over the next two weeks, Sam's health began to show visible signs of deterioration. Mattie remained at her side and stayed in contact with Meredith who fought off a burning desire to visit her friend, after being informed that Sam didn't wish to see anyone.

Sam barely had strength to derive any satisfaction from her daughter's presence and had specifically requested there be no more visitors before she was nearing the end of her life.

Tearfully, Mattie made the final arrangements for Sam's admission to the hospice, when she required the care she and Emily could no longer provide.

'I'm ready to say goodbye to everyone now,' Sam told her when they were ready to leave.

Mattie held her hand. 'I'll let Meredith know and Mark would like to be here too if that's alright.'

'Yes, I'd like that. I've enjoyed his company over the past weeks. My one regret is that I won't make it to your wedding. Be good to each other Mattie.'

'We will. We've crossed our final hurdle now.'

'And I'm to cross mine very soon. I'm sliding the slippery slope now and there's no way back but I'm ready now so please don't be gloomy. I've done all the things I wanted to do.'

Mattie smiled compassionately and stroked Sam's hand. 'We've decided we'll spend our honeymoon in Florida with the children. That way, we can take them to Disneyland.'

Sam smiled. 'I knew you wouldn't let me down. I am so indebted to you for your companionship.'

'I won't let you down about Japan either. I have money put aside that I intend to use for that purpose when Akina's of an age to understand the culture. My brother never stops talking about the Far East.'

Sam was exhausted when the ambulance stopped outside the hospice. 'Come back later with Akina,' she said almost inaudibly. 'I need to rest now.'

Two carers came out to assist her as Mattie left to walk the short distance back home.

Emily was pacing the floor restlessly when Mattie returned. 'How was Sam when you left?' she asked.

'She was exhausted. I didn't go in with her but I promised to go back later with Akina.'

'Her dad and I will leave it for now. We'll see her when she's settled in but promise me you'll let me know before it's too....'

'Of course I will,' she interrupted. 'I'm going to call Meredith right away. Sam wants her family and friends around her now.'

Meredith was distraught and wept bitterly when made aware that the end was drawing very close. 'I have been dreading this day,' she sobbed.

'Sam's in a wonderful place Meredith. She'll be made comfortable and the carers are such amazing people. How soon can you come down?'

'Do you think I ought to leave right away?'

Mattie cleared her throat and choked back tears of sorrow before answering. 'Yes, I do. The Minister's coming to see her this afternoon. I'm going to call Mark now. I hope he can take a couple of days off. I need him more than ever at the moment.'

'We'll be there for you, Meredith assured her.'

Mark promised to do his utmost to rearrange his rota. 'Don't worry, I'll be able to work something out. Just try to be supportive for Sam. That's what she needs right now and I'll see you soon.'

'You can stay here with me so come to the house. If I'm not here, I'll be at the hospice up the road.'

Meredith and Andrew arrived early in the evening after Mattie had returned with Akina and following a tearful reunion they enjoyed a quiet drink together and discussed the good times before leaving to visit Sam, whose condition had continued to deteriorate. Emily and Norman accompanied them with Akina.

Sam smiled weakly at Meredith and managed to exchange one or two few brief words with her.

Akina sat beside Sam stroking her hand. 'Will the angels come for you soon now mummy?'

'Very soon darling but don't worry,' she replied softly. 'Mattie and Mark will take care of you.'

'And Adam too,' she reminded her.

'Adam too,' she whispered with a strained smile. 'Where's Mark?'

'He's on his way Sam,' Mattie said.

Sam's eyelids slowly drooped and she drifted into oblivion as Emily and Norman looked on silently at their dearly-loved daughter who began to slip away peacefully over the next few hours.

When Mark arrived, he took his place quietly by Mattie's side and held her hand in his.

Everyone's eyes were upon Sam as her breathing became more laboured.

Emily gazed at Mark with desperation in her eyes and he nodded sensitively to advise her it was time.

Choking back her tears, she spoke tenderly to her granddaughter. 'I think it's time to say goodbye to your mummy now darling.'

Akina leaned over and placed her small hand on Sam's. Affectionately she whispered, 'I have to say goodbye to you now mummy. I love you very much and I'll never forget you.'

When she kissed her cheek, Sam half-opened her eyes and attempted to smile.

'I'm going to miss you so much Sam,' Emily said quietly as she stroked Sam's hair and slowly she led Akina away, turning once as she reached the door to take a final look at her daughter, while the others looked on tearfully.

Meredith buried her head in Andrew's chest and sobbed audibly.

Mark moved nearer to Sam and took hold of her hand. 'It's alright Sam....It's alright to let go now,' he said gently. 'All your friends are here with you.'

As Sam expelled her final breath, he checked her pulse for some moments before announcing quietly, 'Sam's gone. Would you inform somebody please Andrew?' Respectfully and in a broken voice Mark added, 'I feel proud to have known you Sam,' and he closed her eyes as Mattie clung to him tearfully.

'I'll go and talk to Akina and Emily,' she said.

Meredith stood up. 'I'll come with you.'

When Norman, Andrew and Mark followed on a few moments later, they found them in each other's arms as they wept openly.

'I'm glad you arrived in time Mark,' Mattie said on their way home. 'How long can you stay?'

'For as long as you need me. I've taken ten days' leave.'

'I'm very grateful Mark but what about Adam?'

'He's staying with my parents. He'll be fine there. It's Akina we need to keep a watchful eye on now.'

'My other concern is for Emily and Norman. In a week or two, when I leave with Akina, they'll have lost everybody they love. I mentioned to them that they might like to consider moving up to the north to be closer to Akina. When it's appropriate, try to work your charm on them Mark. I'm certain they're waiting for your approval and that they are holding back because they don't want us to believe they'd be interfering.'

'Don't worry. I'll make sure they understand that we need them. Leave it to me.'

Meredith gathered everyone together back at the house. 'I haven't looked at this,' she said, making reference to the envelope that Sam had given her on an earlier visit. 'It's Sam's funeral arrangements.'

Andrew poured everyone a drink.

'Knowing Sam, I've no doubt that the instructions will prove contentious but she insisted that it has to be a happy occasion with no morbid hymns and that there must be no deviation from her directives.'

She started to relate what Sam had written. 'She wants a black Gospel choir to sing 'Joyful joyful,' as she is brought into church and there's a number here I need to call to arrange it. According to this, she's already spoken to someone about it. She goes on to say that anyone who wants to say a few words may do so but it must be kept brief and not be over-

367

sentimental. She wants flowers from her family and friends who were with her at the end and donations to Cancer Research from anyone else would be very much appreciated by the organisation. There's also a note to remind everyone that she adores lilies.'

'They're my favourites too,' Mattie remarked.

'Sam's already spoken to Reverend Watson about the cremation service and it must be Akina's choice where to scatter her ashes. For her music at the end she has chosen something that she holds very dear to her heart and that always made her feel protected whenever she felt threatened....Hang on while I turn over.'

'I don't think I've heard that one,' Emily laughed and the others joined in the laughter.

Mattie was suddenly reminded of her time at the Parkes' house and the words she always chanted to herself when *she* felt threatened. Not surprisingly, her heart raced when Meredith turned over the page and announced, ''All things bright and beautiful....' There's reference to the catering arrangements and that's everything apart from a note that's addressed to me saying she'll make everyone laugh after she's gone. I haven't a clue what Sam had in mind when she wrote that.'

Meredith checked the pages once again but could find nothing pertaining to that final remark.

'There's a small envelope you removed from the large one,' Andrew pointed out.

Meredith picked it up and silently read the words that Sam had written across the flap. 'Go on, open it Meredith, I dare you!'

With quivering fingers, she opened the envelope and removed a familiar and well-handled Students' Union Magazine from nineteen-sixty-one. Crimson with shame, she turned to the centrefold. 'Oh God! Oh my God, I don't believe this!' she cried out and burst into laughter, simultaneously shedding tears of joy and sorrow as she recalled happier days with Sam when they had been young and carefree.

'What is it?' Andrew queried eagerly. 'Share the joke Meredith. Let's all join in the fun!'

Meredith turned towards Mattie and Mark. 'I was blackmailed by Sam into setting you up at Steph's wedding because of this. She threatened to show it to Andrew if I didn't agree to her demands.'

'There you are Mark. What did I tell you?' Mattie said. 'I knew there was good reason for Meredith's involvement at the wedding. So come on then, what is it?'

'Yes, what is it?' Andrew repeated.

'See for yourself and pass it round everyone. It's Sam having the last laugh, like she said she would.'

As they each studied the photograph and caption while listening to Meredith's apologetic revelations about the madness of their youth, everyone laughed heartily.

Mark stood up and cleared his throat. 'May I have everyone's attention please? I would like you all to raise your glasses to Sam, a truly amazing woman of great warmth, humour, strength and courage who touched the lives of so many and who will never be forgotten,' he said holding his glass high.

'To Sam,' everyone responded respectfully.

A peaceful calm descended on those present and they gazed sorrowfully at Akina, fast asleep in her grandmother's arms.

Mark slipped his arm around Mattie's waist. 'Are you alright darling?' he asked sensitively.

She smiled lovingly at him and replied, 'Yes I am now, thanks to Sam's help. I have a new family and for the first time since I was fourteen years old, I'm experiencing a sense of belonging. Apart from the sadness of this day, I have never felt happier in my life.'

| Branch | Date |
|--------|------|
| TS | 9/9 |
| | |
| | |
| | |
| | |